THE ATHENA FILE

JENNIFER HAYNIE

For the veterans who served in Iraq and Afghanistan
and have been forever changed. Thank you.

"For I know the plans I have for you," declares the LORD, "plans to prosper you and not to harm you, plans to give you a hope and a future. Then you will call on me and come and pray to me, and I will listen to you. You will seek me and find me when you seek me with all your heart."

—Jeremiah 29:11-13

Camp Romeo, Ghazni Province, Afghanistan

April 2009

"Captain Ward-Bocelli, I need you to come with me."

Abigail jumped at Major Ray Watson's baritone voice that pierced the silence of the small room she called an office. She whipped around. "Sir?"

Their host at Camp Romeo had already turned away.

"What did I just see?" Bryson Bishop, her sergeant, stared after him. "I don't get it. What is it?"

Her gaze flew to the e-mail message that had landed in her in-box seconds earlier. The subject line told her enough.

Extension of Assignment to Camp Romeo.

"Trouble." She slapped shut the lid of her Panasonic Toughbook, grabbed her patrol cap, and stuffed it on her head as she bolted into the hall. She ran to catch up to the major. "Sir, you want to tell me what's happening?"

"Bad stuff." He pushed through the door.

Abigail grabbed it to keep it from hitting in her face. "As in?"

"An SF team got hit at a village fifty klicks from here." He clipped his words as he strode toward the eastern end of the camp.

Even at her five-foot, ten-inch height, Abigail hustled to keep up. "Casualties?"

"Ten. Plus who knows how many locals. A real massacre." The major swore. "And it sounds like you drew the short straw to figure out what went down."

Her mind flashed to the orders she'd received but not had a chance to read. "Sir?"

"I got word from your CO. Looks like you'll be our guest for at least a few more days."

Oh, great. Just what she needed. Camp suspicion still hit high on the wariness scale after she and Bryson had investigated a soldier who'd gunned down an unsuspecting local. Being a part of the Army's Criminal Investigation Command, better known as CID, tended to engender distrust among the rest of the Army. She ground her teeth. "We'll do what we can, sir. Where was the SF team based?"

"Kandahar." He bit off that word. His pace kicked up dust on the dirt road.

Jonathan.

Her brother's name slid unbidden through her mind. As a Green Beret, he'd been in-country for almost a year, but he hadn't ever shared where. But he wasn't anywhere near here. Was he?

They slowed as they approached the eastern end of the camp with its airstrip for transporting supplies, personnel, and prisoners.

Next to the scarred concrete stood a series of tents. The combat support hospital. Crucial to any location near an active theater of operations.

Abigail almost laughed at that. Where in Afghanistan *wasn't* a field of operations?

She jumped as the doors to the nearest tent banged open. Two nurses sprinted down the walkway to the edge of the strip with a gurney between them.

Even now, the deep thump of rotor blades throbbed a bass rhythm. She peered through the midday glare that her sunglasses barely shielded. To the east, four shapes materialized in the washed-out blue. They rapidly grew. Two Black Hawk Medevac helicopters and two Apache attack helicopters. The Apaches peeled off, most likely headed back to the scene of the attack.

The two Black Hawks landed. Abigail winced as their rotor wash sent dust and sand whirling into the air.

The nurses darted forward and ducked under the still-spinning blades as the side door to the nearest Black Hawk slid open. The engine cut off. A crewman hopped onto the tarmac, holding an IV bag over his head. He bent low and shouted something to the nurses.

Someone else leapt from the bay.

He looked familiar.

Careful to avoid the blades, Abigail drew closer.

Dirt streaked the newcomer's face. So did something else. Blood? He wore his beard long, almost to the point of shaggy, most likely as a way to gain rapport with the locals. He held the hand of the man on the gurney and bent close over him as he said something.

Abigail gaped at the blood-soaked bandage wrapped around the victim's left leg. Another bandage encircled his neck. *God, please…*

The nurse said something to the injured soldier's buddy. Gently, she pried his hand away. She and her colleague hustled toward the CSH with the gurney rattling between them.

His friend hung his head and swept his hands through disheveled sandy blond hair.

That one gesture connected it for her.

Jonathan.

Her brother stood before her.

She opened her mouth to shout to him, but it remained locked in her throat.

Jonathan! Her cry echoed in her soul. Heart racing, she tried again. "Jonathan!"

She rushed toward him.

His head snapped up. His eyes, a clear green now reddened by dust and emotion, widened. "Abigail?"

She ran to him and threw her arms around him. He clung to her as he shook from head to toe.

"What…what are you doing here?" he finally gasped.

"An investigation. Your friend." She stared in the direction of the CSH.

"David."

She whipped around. "David Shepherd?"

He looked away.

Now that the helicopter blades had stilled, the sound of quiet weeping reached her.

A young woman crouched in the open doorway. She wore a torn uniform of some sort that was streaked in gray and mottled brown. Her headscarf had slipped down enough to reveal a streak of raven black. She hugged herself and rocked back and forth as if catatonic.

Jonathan extended his hands and said something in Pashto. Whatever platitudes he murmured seemed to work because she finally uncoiled from her crouch and allowed him to help her from the chopper. The mewling continued.

Abigail's heart pounded. "What's going on?"

"This is Nabeelah," her brother said. He refused to relinquish his grip on the girl. "She needs to get checked out."

"So do you."

Someone nudged Abigail aside. "I'm Major Ray Watson." The major forced himself into their small group. "If you'll come with me, I'll get you to the hospital. Captain Ward-Bocelli, it seems as if you two know each other."

"He's my brother, Sergeant First Class Jonathan Ward." A lump in her throat overtook her.

"Then I suggest you join us." Without another word, the major turned on his heel and gestured for Jonathan and Nabeelah to head toward the CSH.

Abigail remained rooted to her little spot of tarmac, gaping at them as they walked away.

"Abigail?" Bryson's voice reached her as if from a distance. "Wait, is that why we got orders extending our stay here?"

"Yep." She took a deep breath to steady herself. "Sounds like the boys at the Pentagon want to know exactly what happened."

Camp Romeo, Ghazni Province, Afghanistan

Abigail hunched over the desk in the closet-sized office that was now her home away from home for another few days. Nothing broke the stillness. No chatter. No laughter. No nothing. She flipped the pages of her tablet as she reviewed the notes she'd made while debriefing Nabeelah Khan. In the silence, the noise sounded like she wadded up a ton of newspaper.

The young woman had crossed the fine line between deeply grieving and inconsolable. Throughout their two hours together, she'd barely been able to string together a sentence of somewhat comprehensible English before lapsing into weeping again. Well, who wouldn't be that way after losing all of her family, including her beloved father? Not to mention friends and comrades. And seeing David Shepherd injured so badly? He remained in surgery as the doctors struggled not only to save his leg but also his life.

She closed the notepad with a snap. Abigail rested her elbows on the desk and scrubbed her face with her hands. Her stomach rumbled. She hadn't eaten anything in close to eight hours.

"I heard that." Bryson's voice reached her.

She cocked an eyebrow as he settled at the desk across from her. He set a candy bar and a can of Coke on the blotter in front of her. "I know this isn't good for you, but it's the best I could come up with."

"Are you finished with Jonathan?"

"Yeah." His chair squeaked as he leaned back. He swung his feet onto his desk and popped a can of Dr. Pepper. "I'm surprised they're letting you on the case since you're his sister."

"That's why you debriefed him. I just happened to be in the neighborhood."

He shook his head. "I've never seen anything like this."

She frowned. "What do you mean?"

"It's almost like, at least from what Jonathan said, the hit was well planned. Maybe someone supplied them with insider information."

"How could they?"

He shrugged. "It's just a theory of mine. I think we should run it down."

"We might get our chance."

"I'm not following."

She opened her laptop, typed in her password, and turned it around. "We've been ordered to head to the village to check it out. Under heavy escort, of course."

"They'd better," Bryson muttered. He took off his glasses and cleaned them with a rag he pulled from his pocket.

"Then at first light day after tomorrow, we're to head back to Germany." She rubbed her eyes.

"Go and see your brother." Bryson's soft advice reached her. "And tell him his buddy's through surgery and stabilized."

She opened her eyes a crack. "You went by the CSH?"

"Yep. They'd just wheeled him into recovery. The doc said they'll fly him via medevac chopper to Bagram, where they'll transfer him to a flight to Ramstein."

"What were his injuries?"

"A nick to the neck which was nothing. The bullet that got him in the left leg broke his femur."

She flinched.

"But they're optimistic that they were able to do enough of a repair here to save it. So how about you run along and pass that to your brother? He's in the guest quarters next to my room. I'll bring us all some food later."

"I'll do that. Thanks, Bryson." She jumped up and pushed through the door into the night. The cold bit through her ACUs, but she didn't care. It wasn't too far of a walk to the heavy canvas tent that made up the guest quarters of the small camp. She stepped through the main door. A central hall ran down the middle, dividing the eight rooms and two bathrooms neatly in half. Cheap wood formed the walls. She shivered in the chill.

She paused at Nabeelah's room and opened the door a crack. A closed-loop heater in the corner popped a little but had warmed the room so that Nabeelah wouldn't wake up freezing. The young woman finally slept, her hair fanning onto the pillow in raven waves. Then Abigail heard her cries. The tragedy stalked her even in the depths of medicated unconsciousness.

Why her? Why David and Jonathan? Why did they have to lose so many close friends at once?

She let the door softly close and found her brother's room. She tapped on the door. "Jonathan?"

No answer.

She pushed it open.

A soft glow filled the room from the lamp that sat on a footlocker someone had pushed against the wall in a poor attempt at a dresser. Folded ACUs sat on top along with a toiletries kit. His heater had worked its magic, and she shucked her ACU jacket.

To her right, Jonathan hunched on the edge of his rack. His elbows rested on his knees, and he hung his head as he stared at the plywood floor. Fresh fatigue pants and a T-shirt probably offered him a modicum of comfort. He'd shaved, and a shower had removed the soot, dirt, and blood from earlier that day.

"Jonathan."

This time, he turned his face toward her. The deep sadness emanating from his green eyes bludgeoned her soul.

He returned his gaze to the floor. His hands shook as if he'd downed too many energy drinks.

Abigail stepped all the way into the room and shut the door behind her to avoid releasing any more heat. Words held no currency during times like this, so she eased onto the bed beside him.

"Is David through surgery?" His voice rasped.

"Bryson said he's out and stable enough that they'll transfer him to Lundstahl in the morning. We can go see him later if you like."

He nodded. "And Nabeelah?"

She sighed. "I finished debriefing her about an hour ago. She's beyond distraught."

"We...we didn't stand a chance." His hands clenched into fists.

She scooted closer to him so their shoulders touched.

"There were too many of them. They came so fast, and—"

"I'm here." She rubbed his arm.

The trembling now emanated across his body. "They got Mackie first. A head shot. He was dead when he hit the ground."

Her throat tightened.

"Then the grenade took down Captain and Oso. Oso, he was gone instantly. Captain took it in the stomach. I tried to save him, Abigail. I tried. But I...I couldn't." A tear slipped down his cheek.

She gathered him in her arms and held on tightly.

With a low cry, he wept.

Camp Romeo, Ghazni Province

The sound of pounding reached Abigail where she lay on her rack. Her heater had switched off, and cold now pressed close to her face. She grunted and buried further under the rough wool blanket.

"Abigail!" The man's voice grew in volume.

She stirred. "Huh?"

"Wake up!"

She bolted upright. "Jonathan?"

Had David died?

She yanked on her jacket and combat boots, then nearly ripped the flimsy door off its hinges. "What's going on?"

Her brother stood there, his hair mussed, his eyes wide. "Nabeelah's gone."

She tried to make sense of what he'd told her. "What?"

"She's gone." He grabbed her hand and nearly dragged her across the hall where the young woman had stayed. He slammed open the door.

Abigail gasped. "She's not in the latrine, is she?"

"No, I checked. There's no way she could have left on her own, right?"

"No. There's just one way in and out." She glanced around the Spartan room. "Wait! Her things aren't here."

"What things?" Jonathan pushed past her and paced around the small space.

"Some of the nurses who were her size donated some clothing to her. And a headscarf. And toiletries. None of that's here. This smells of something." Abigail dashed down the hall, throwing her hair into a hasty ponytail as she ran. Forget the patrol cap. This wasn't a formal visit to their host.

With Jonathan at her heels, she burst into predawn darkness dimly lit by a streetlight over the exercise yard. Only a few soldiers on night duty stirred.

She found Major Watson coming out of the mess hall with a steaming mug of something in his hand. "Sir, a word with you, if you would."

He stopped as if busted for being somewhere he shouldn't have been. Slowly, he turned. "Captain Ward-Bocelli, isn't it a bit early to be up?"

"Not when someone's missing." Jonathan didn't bother to salute as he glared at the major.

"I'm not following."

Abigail inserted herself between her brother and their host. "Nabeelah Khan is missing. You want to tell me what you know?"

"That would be nothing. Now if you'll excuse me, I've got to brief the men who will be taking you to the village." He began walking toward the command center.

"Major Watson, I think you forgot one thing," Abigail called. "I'm in charge of investigating what happened in that village fifty klicks east of here. An eyewitness I interviewed has gone missing."

He stopped.

She squared her shoulders and narrowed her eyes. "From what I remember about Camp Romeo and what you showed me, there's only one way in and out of here. Meaning you can't say that she just happened to walk away because I'm not going to believe you on that. Someone in this camp took her away. Now I want to know where they took her."

He glowered at her. "I can't tell you."

"I think you're forgetting my occupation. CID, remember? You lie to me, you lose your career. Come clean with me now or at a court-martial later. Your choice."

Major Watson's gaze shifted from her to Jonathan. "Both of you, this way." He walked them toward the command tent and to his office. Once

Jonathan had shut the door behind them, the major eased onto a chair that groaned in protest. "They showed up an hour ago."

"Who is 'they'?" Abigail remained standing.

"I don't know."

Jonathan folded his arms across his chest. "Bull."

"Seriously, I don't."

"Were they in uniform?"

"No. Civvies. They flashed paperwork stating that they were authorized to remove Ms. Khan from our custody."

"And you believed them?" she asked.

"Yes, because that authority came from way beyond my pay grade."

"Like how far?"

"I can't say."

"What do you mean, you can't say? I say you're lying, and if you are, I'll—" Jonathan clinched his fists and took a menacing step forward.

"Jonathan, no." Abigail grabbed his arm. His biceps flexed under her grip as she pulled him away. "It's not worth it." She turned to the major. "And you have no idea of where they were taking her?"

"None." Major Watson held up his hands. "None at all. Believe me that if I could have kept her here, I would have."

Jonathan slammed out of the office.

Abigail studied the major for a moment. He maintained a steady gaze. Sweat had broken out on his brow despite the chill in the room. No matter how much she wanted to say he'd lied, she couldn't. "Though I hate to say it, I think you're telling the truth. But if I find out you've lied to me, you can kiss the rest of your time in the Army goodbye. Got it?"

The major pressed his lips into a grim line and gave her a slight nod.

"Thanks for your help. Either Bryson or I will be by to take an official statement after we get back." She pulled open the door and headed out.

Where could Jonathan have gone? It wasn't that Camp Romeo was small, but with a contingent of five hundred troops around, there weren't a lot of hiding places. A scene from the day before flashed across her mind, and she turned her steps toward the air strip.

Cloaked in his jacket, her brother huddled on a crate next to the small hangar. To the east, beyond the concrete wall and barbed wire, the sun struggled over the jagged mountains in a sickly yellow haze.

Abigail approached and eased onto the rough wood beside him.

"She's gone." His head drooped. "What if they turned her out because they suspected her to be a traitor? She'd never survive in the village. Not by herself."

"I'm headed there today. I'll—"

"No!" He grabbed her arm with crushing force.

"Ow!" She pried his fingers loose.

"It's not safe, they'll—"

"We'll be escorted, okay? I'll look." She sighed. "I'll try to find out who took her. Still, there's only one thing we can do."

"What?"

She faced the sunrise. "Pray."

1

Ghazni Province, Afghanistan

March 2016

Christine Parker cinched the four-point harness tighter around her. She focused on Jonathan Ward, her boyfriend and COO of SecureLink's Ghazni compound. He stood at the rear of the convoy's lead vehicle, a four-door Jeep Wrangler with a 50-cal machine gun mounted on the back. Chip Johnson, the protective detail supervisor, kept his helmet tucked under one arm as he chatted with him. Jonathan clapped him on the shoulder and strode toward the armored school bus that would ferry their clients, sixteen doctors and nurses, to a remote village high in the mountains.

Please look at me. Christine's stomach knotted on itself as she recalled the spat that had replaced what should have been a clandestine bit of romancing.

Curse the no-fraternization policy that prevented them from being open about their relationship.

He gave the driver and bus guard a mock salute and headed in her direction.

His clear green eyes met hers. The corners of his mouth quirked up in the slightest of smiles. Someone called something, and he turned.

Some of her worries eased.

But not all.

Once more, she tightened her harness.

"Any tighter, and you will not be able to breathe."

At the teasing statement in accented English, she glanced up. Ali al-Saad, an Iraqi gunner who qualified for the sunniest disposition of the group today, grinned. The straps of his helmet dangled along the sides of his face.

"And any looser for you, and your helmet will fall off."

He laughed and secured the Kevlar. "Not anymore." He patted her on the shoulder and climbed into his position behind the 50-cal machine gun. The bullet belt rattled as he made one final check of his weapon.

Eddie Horton climbed into the driver's seat. "Looks like we're ready to go. You locked and loaded, Parker?"

Ahead of them, the big engine of the school bus groaned to life.

Jonathan approached. "You guys set?"

"As much as we'll ever be." At least her voice didn't shake.

"Head on a swivel, y'all. Godspeed." His focused on Christine. "I'll see you tonight." He mouthed "I love you."

She released her breath. "See you soon." She shoved her wraparound sunglasses onto her face before he noticed the tears filling her eyes.

He slapped the front fender of the four-door Jeep Wrangler. "Move out. Chip'll call us when y'all get there."

The lead Wrangler—which held Chip, a driver, and a gunner—led the way through the massive iron gate. The school bus followed, then their Wrangler. Christine gripped her rifle to keep it from bouncing around.

Once they cleared the gate, they picked up speed as they rolled along the asphalt road toward the Kabul-to-Kandahar highway. Eddie handled the vehicle as if they headed to the grocery store rather than the heart of Taliban country.

A stream of cars and trucks became visible as they neared the highway. They pulled up parallel to one another. Christine glanced at the school bus. Gregory Jordan, the guard, stood on the steps. He flashed her a thumbs-up sign.

When Eddie caught a break in traffic, he pulled onto the road first to allow the other vehicles safe entry. Once everyone had come up to speed, Christine's thoughts turned inward and spun as fast as the wheels of their Jeep. Automatically, her mind ticked to a little over twelve hours before when Chip had sent her to Jonathan's office to summon him for the security team's final briefing. He hadn't wasted words or even a kiss before he'd asked his question.

"What's going on?" he'd demanded.

And what had she done? Ducked the question. Sidestepped his followup. Tried to pick a fight. And all because she couldn't figure out why she couldn't tell him about the secret that now burdened her.

I'm scared, she mentally told him now, as a truck piled high with tires blew past them. *I'm scared of what I found. I couldn't tell you last night because I hadn't found all of the evidence until after everyone went to bed.*

"You're mighty quiet." Eddie raised his voice to be heard over the wind rushing through their open-air Jeep.

"A lot on my mind." Christine rubbed the forestock of her rifle.

"Try me."

She studied him. "The doctor is in?"

The black man laughed. "Something like that. Try me."

Christine sighed. *You've talked to Eddie before about past relationship stuff. He's talked to you about stuff in his marriage. You two have a friendship. So trust him, why don't you?* "Have you ever been in a situation that you know you have to share something with someone, but you're too scared to?"

"Why would I be scared?"

"Because you thought you weren't ready at the time. And now, you realize you should have."

"Girl, you are so not making sense. Try again."

"Last night, I was pretty sure something was going on, but I wasn't one hundred percent sure. Then the person who has the authority to do something about it—who is also someone I really care about—started demanding answers. I couldn't tell him because I wasn't certain."

"Let me guess. Ward's the guy you really care about."

The flush heated her cheeks faster than the sun as it rose past the mountains. "Uh, yeah. How did you know?"

"You and I work together. Now the wife would say I'm not the most clued-in guy, but I can tell you're troubled."

That got a wry laugh out of her.

He sobered. "That being said, if it's serious and involves something at the compound, you need to tell Ward regardless of any reservations you have. That good enough for you?"

A smile finally broke through her tension. "Yeah. Thanks."

"That's why I'm your driver today. Yes, ma'am. That's why." Eddie chuckled.

The hum of the tires dropped as the convoy slowed. They turned from the smooth asphalt onto a rutted macadam surface.

"Okay, guys, look sharp." Chip's voice crackled over their comms units. "We're half an hour out. Eyes out for tangos."

Christine's grip tightened on her rifle. Her free hand crept to the emergency release button for her four-point harness. Like she had each mission, she rehearsed the sequence Chip had pounded in their heads. *Release, rifle, roll.* She scanned the mountainside of scrub, rocks, and other features rushing past as they wound their way higher and farther from the supposed safety of the highway. She glanced at the digital clock on the dash. Ten minutes in. Twenty to go until they reached the village.

An explosion kicked a dust cloud from the sides of the mountain.

Christine jumped.

The bus screeched to a halt, and Eddie barely avoided rear-ending it.

"Chip, what's going on?" Eddie shouted into the comm.

"IED! Red alert." Chip's voice remained even and steady, despite the impending ambush. "Base, this is Convoy Two. Ambush. We caught an IED in the—" His calm words shattered on a scream. A loud rifle report rocketed through the narrow valley.

Christine slammed her hand onto the emergency release. The straps popped free, and she rolled from the Jeep with her rifle in hand. As she hit the ground, Gregory tumbled to the road. He didn't try to stop his fall.

He was dead.

Sniper.

Another bullet slammed Ali in the chest. He collapsed backward.

She rolled underneath the Wrangler and stayed on her stomach.

A woman screamed.

"Don't!" Christine shouted, but the dust choked her words so they came out as a whisper.

One of their clients fell to the ground. Then another. The sniper went to work in earnest.

Christine shifted her gaze toward the left-hand side.

Taliban poured over the lip of the road.

She shuddered as their war cries filled the air along with the popping of small arms fire. She couldn't breathe, couldn't move. Her hands felt clammy as they clasped her rifle.

A pair of booted feet crunched dirt mere inches away. A pistol shot echoed above her.

Eddie crashed to the ground. His sightless eyes stared at her. Blood oozed from the hole in his forehead.

"No!" She scrambled forward and drew a bead on the killer. One shot finished him just as surely as he'd taken the life of her friend.

Her cry drew the attention of the others.

She couldn't even count their number. She rolled to her feet and fired blindly as she dashed across the road. Two more dropped.

Her gun jammed.

She tossed it aside as the slope steepened. She began sliding on the loose gravel and rock surface.

An explosion rocketed through the air.

She skidded as she turned. Her hands touched earth.

Black smoke billowed into the air, carrying with it the screams of their clients. People she was commissioned to protect. She clutched at the rocks around her. "Oh, God! No!"

Robed jihadis jerked toward her voice. With high-pitched war cries they charged her location, the ends of their turbans fluttering behind them.

Her heart lodged in her throat. She couldn't outrun them.

Not now.

She yanked her pistol from its holster and fired three shots, dropping three.

She turned and ran as fast as she could.

Her quads burned. Her sides heaved. She scrambled against gravity as it tugged her closer to the stream bed at the bottom of the slope.

If she could reach just the stream bed, she could outrun them.

But why weren't they firing at her?

Her ankle twisted, shooting hot pain up her leg.

She pitched forward, losing her pistol, and skidded down the uneven slope on her belly. Her momentum drove her straight toward a massive rock. She thrust out her hands but still smashed her head against the unforgiving boulder. Blackness oozed through her senses. She tried to shake it away and raise herself from the gravel.

A knee slammed into her back.

Her breath whooshed from her lungs. She sucked in another.

Rough hands pawed at her, and her attacker yanked her knife from its sheath. It clinked onto the ground, oh, so close, yet too far away to do her any good.

He flipped her.

She pushed herself to her elbows. Five gathered around. She could still get away. She could fight them.

Then the small crowd of Taliban parted to reveal an older man. Henna streaked his long beard. His eyes had that flat, dull look she'd come to associate with evil.

Chills wracked her.

He dropped onto her, pinning her hips to the ground.

He slapped her, and she yelped. His hands fumbled with her helmet strap. It rolled off her head, and he reached behind her.

"Stop!" She flailed beneath him and struck out with her fists, her only weapons at that point.

Two of his men pinned her wrists to the ground. The man grabbed her hair and yanked it from its bun. He jabbered in Pashto too quick for her unseasoned ear to understand.

He fingered her hair as he smoothed it out. A smirk curled his lips, and he directed a question toward a comrade. He cackled when he received an affirmative answer.

She strained against the hands constraining her. "Get your filthy paws off me."

The leader spat in her face.

"Let me go! Help!" she shouted uselessly.

He hit her again, this time so hard that she saw stars. His image split into two before merging.

Then he spoke in slow, clear Pashto.

Thanks to Jonathan's careful tutoring over the past eighteen months, she knew exactly what he said.

"She's the one."

She thrashed as he reached into the folds of his robe and drew a knife with a blade as long as her forearm. He raised it.

"No, please, don't." She yanked at her wrists. Nothing.

The leader closed his eyes. He began chanting in Pashto like he was in a trance. His grip tightened around the handle.

In a flash, he brought it down, straight into her throat just above her armored vest.

Pain arced through her, and the scream that escaped her wasn't her own.

She couldn't breathe. Blood filled her mouth. She tried to cough. *I'm dying.* The thought raced through her mind. *God, no. I'm dying. Please. Please! I...*

"Jon...Jonathan." Her back spasmed in agony. Hot tears filled her eyes as blood spilled from her mouth. Her heart thudded in her ears, slowing with each weakened pump. Blue sky turned to gray, then nothing.

2

Ghazni Province, Afghanistan

Smoke belched into the deep blue sky. It billowed in thick black clouds like from a dragon that had finished a hearty meal. The sharp edge of the curve kept its source out of sight.

Jonathan's heart hammered against his ribcage as the SecureLink Humvee jerked to a stop at the old armored personnel carrier blocking the two-lane road. Two soldiers from the Afghan army stood in front of it.

"Jonathan Ward." Captain Sayad Rasheed's voice reached him from the right.

His head snapped toward the sound.

Sayad didn't wear his usual welcoming smile.

Today was not a time for the usual greetings.

Jonathan adjusted the bulletproof vest he wore and stuffed his Kevlar helmet onto his head. His Pashto words almost tumbled over one another. "What's the status?"

"We have the scene secured at both ends of the road. Come with me. You and your men."

Jonathan gestured toward the two vehicles that had pulled up behind his. Nine guys piled onto the hot pavement. "Any initial assessments?"

"Not good, my friend."

Christine.

Her name hit him square in the heart. Jonathan started toward the source of the smoke, but Sayad caught his arm, forcing him to slow.

He shook his head. "Jonathan, no running ahead. Please."

Jonathan had to settle for a brisk walk as they rounded the bend.

"Oh, my…" The words died from his throat.

Three motionless vehicles stood before him. The armored school bus in the middle, which had held their clients, blazed as the fire fed on the interior and diesel with an insatiable appetite. And the rear vehicle? Punctured with bullet holes. A body lay beside it.

Detached professional interest gave way to raw, personal fear. "Christine!"

Breaking Sayad's grip, he rushed toward the front passenger seat of the Wrangler.

She wasn't there.

"Christine!" He whirled on Sayad. "Is she with your men?"

"No. When the distress call came across the radio, we were only five minutes north of here. They were gone by the time we arrived."

Five minutes.

Three hundred seconds.

An eternity in hard combat.

"Sir!" Roy Wildman's Aussie accent sounded behind him.

Jonathan whipped around. "What is it?"

"I think I know what happened." Roy stood nearby.

Jonathan glanced at the Afghan army captain. "Sayad, can your men keep the perimeter secure for a bit?"

"As long as you need. Though I recommend leaving by sunset at the latest. Ghazni is not secure at night."

Jonathan nodded. He pulled out a small digital recorder and and made a terse, introductory statement into it as he joined the Aussie. "What do you have?"

Roy shook his head. "Bad stuff. They picked the perfect spot for an ambush. Twenty minutes north of the highway. Winding mountain road." He broke off and gestured toward the front of the convoy, his mouth set in a grim line. "Come with me."

Jonathan followed him to the front of the lead Wrangler.

Roy pointed to the crater under the front wheels of the Jeep. "This started it. IED. Whether or not they set it off too early or right on time, we don't know. The blast took out the axle. I think they were lying in wait either just below the lip of the slope or around the curve. They also had a sniper up top." He jerked his head upslope, which was on the convoy's right side.

Jonathan nodded. The outcropping of rock up there would have provided a perfect sniper's hide. "Could be."

"Judging by where the blood and guts are, the sniper got Jimmy." Roy nodded at the gunner, who slumped over the 50-caliber machine gun. Blood and gore spattered the interior of the left side of the vehicle. "Had to be armor-piercing since the bullet penetrated his lid."

They paced around the Jeep to the right-hand side. "Chip tried to get out. Didn't get far." He nodded toward the passenger's side.

Chip's body lay collapsed against the wheel with blood running from underneath his helmet.

"Sniper got him too."

Jonathan grimaced when he saw the protective detail supervisor. "He's the one who called it in. He said they were ambushed. Then came a scream. Then... nothing." He lowered his head and muttered a cuss word under his breath.

Roy took his arm and walked him to the other side. He pointed to where the driver crumpled over the steering wheel. Scarlet soaked the man's front from the bullet hole in his face. "Jericho didn't even get to undo his harness, which is why I think they were right below the lip of the slope. That shot came from almost point-blank range."

A headache kicked up behind Jonathan's eyes. "The bus..."

"That gets even better." The Aussie jerked his chin toward the armored bus, one in a fleet of ten that they used when transporting clients. They crossed between the vehicles to the right side.

A body lay crumpled at the foot of the steps. "Gregory got popped by the sniper when he got off. Double tapped in the chest. Mickey? Well, they got him with a head shot to the face through the driver's window. Close range. Most likely a pistol."

"They tried to get out." Jonathan stared at where the three bodies of their clients piled up on the steps.

"Three of 'em did through the front. The sniper got them." Roy grimaced. "Close as we can figure, someone tossed a grenade through the driver's side window. Scored too, since only four made it out the back."

"Lord, help us all." Jonathan's stomach twisted on his breakfast of eggs and bacon. "So what the grenade didn't get, the fire did."

"Pretty much." Roy marched to the back, where the emergency door to the bus hung open.

Two women lay on the ground, clinging to one another in death with a path of bullet holes across their chests. Their head scarves had fallen off. Beyond, the bodies of two doctors sprawled, the bullet holes in their backs screaming how they'd died.

A puff of wind whispered along the mountainside and caressed Jonathan's hot cheeks. It kicked up the smell of burning plastic and diesel fuel—and something else. He moaned as his stomach heaved. With hands braced against his knees and his head hung, he said, "Get someone to put out that fire."

"Roger that."

Jonathan barely heard his order. Finally, he lifted his face. "The sniper got them."

"Pretty much. He had himself a field day. Including Ali." Roy moved to the last Wrangler and the body of the driver sprawled on the ground. "And Eddie."

Jonathan couldn't help it. He swore under his breath, then nearly choked as he inhaled. "Christine…"

"She's not here."

His head snapped around. "What?"

"She's nowhere around here." Roy escorted him to the other side and pointed to the front passenger's seat.

The uncertainty in those gray eyes of hers as she'd gazed at him before the convoy had left this morning gnawed at his gut. Tension from the night before had riddled her body. As he'd mouthed his affection to her, he'd silently promised to make it up to her when she returned. "What do you think happened? Do you think she escaped?"

"Could be." Roy nodded. "I think she got away. Or got captured trying to escape."

"Why do you say that?"

"She's not here, and this guy is dead." Roy nudged the body of a Taliban fighter with his foot.

Jonathan's heart did an awkward thump. "Sayad said she wasn't with his men. Could she have gotten away?"

Roy didn't answer.

Suddenly feeling faint, Jonathan clapped his hand over his mouth as his breakfast tried to come back up. Hope battled against panic. Could she have really slipped from the Taliban's grasp? They needed to find her. Now. Because if she'd escaped, the Taliban would be hot on her trail. He lowered the hand which held the recorder. "We've got to do something. She could be in danger, and—"

Roy reached up and hit a button on it, making it pause. He crowded close to Jonathan and in a low voice asked, "Are you romantically involved with her?"

What could he say? No? Not when his reaction screamed otherwise. "We are."

"I suggest you tamp that down. We've all got work to do that needs a clear head, especially if we're to have a shred of hope of finding her."

Jonathan took a deep breath. "You're right."

A ghost of a smile flitted across Roy's lips. He reached up and restarted the recording. "Let's see what the rest of the group found."

They walked around the rear of the Jeep.

Two of the men doused the flaming bus with fire extinguishers until the spray silenced the crackling beast. The remaining six huddled at the edge of the crumbling macadam. Bryson Bishop, the man responsible for maintaining law and order at the compound, didn't. He braced his hands on his knees and threw up. His groan reached Jonathan. The other five fixated on the wreck, knuckles white where they gripped their rifles. A few had fingers lightly resting on triggers.

Jonathan doubted the safety switches were on.

They wanted a fight, a chance to avenge the deaths of comrades, friends, and roommates.

Roy was right. Investigating the crime scene and finding Christine were the top priorities. Panicking over her whereabouts wouldn't do anyone any good. Not when he needed to take charge and talk some of his men down.

"Guys, I know we've all lost comrades, friends, and roommates." Jonathan cleared his throat as Sayad joined them. He fixed his eyes on Bryson, whose roommate was among the dead. "But one of us is still out there. We think Christine either escaped or was taken by the Taliban. Roy, you and Sayad take Marco, Bruno, and Cal and fan out. My gut's saying they probably escaped along the creek bed." He nodded toward the toe of the slope. "Be back by 1600 hours."

"Roger that." Roy took Sayad's arm, and the small group stepped onto hard dirt.

"Bryson, stay here and help me investigate the scene. Work with Kimbo, Craig, and Mark to get a total body count once the bus cools enough." He focused on Bryson. "Are you okay?"

"I will be." His reply came out more as a croak. "Certain smells make my stomach turn."

"You spent how many years working with Abigail as a CID investigator and have seen how many bodies in various stages of decomposition?"

"Too many." His attempt at a smile twisted into a grimace. "Go ahead. Laugh. She certainly did."

"Not now." Jonathan peered at the wrecked vehicles. White dust coated the bus, and it feebly put out faint contrails of smoke. "Look. I know Eddie was your best buddy and roommate, but I need you to focus. The Afghans have secured the scene. Take pictures of everything here because once we leave, we're gone. I'll ensure that Sayad and his men get the bodies to us for positive ID and notification of next of kin. Before we go, we're going to torch our vehicles so the Taliban can't use them. While you do that, I'll check out that sniper's hide."

A terse nod answered him.

Jonathan began his climb, scrabbling with both his feet and hands to keep his balance. Halfway up, several rocks broke loose, and he slid downward. His fingers clawed the hard soil as he eased to a stop. Once more, he picked his way upward until, at last, he arrived at the outcropping he'd seen earlier and rested his feet on a small ledge. It was maybe two yards wide, barely enough for a pile of rocks and someone to remain concealed.

He peered over the rocks. A mat lay on the ground, as did a canteen, and several small objects scattered across the mat. He sucked in a breath and released on it a growl as he recognized the pieces to a Mark 300 rifle, the same brand used by SecureLink. It lay partially disassembled with one of the pieces being a scope.

But why would the sniper have left it behind?

He snatched the small UHF radio from its clip at his waist. "Bryson, get up here."

"Where's here?" Bryson's reply crackled.

Jonathan rose and waved.

The small figure at the edge of the burned bus began its climb.

Jonathan surveyed the rugged terrain as he said into the recorder, "The road curves well to the right in a blind curve. To the left too. Excellent fields of fire from the sniper's nest approximately two hundred fifty yards upslope of the ambush site." He paused as he noticed Roy and the small group that walked along the stream bed. "A dry stream bed is located at the bottom of the slope, which would be a perfect way for egress by the ambushers…"

Five minutes would have been all it took. Twenty-three dead. Maybe twenty-four. Chip's frantic radio call echoed in his mind. He had burst into the Skype session Boss Man had been holding with the transition team. The news had sent the compound into Red Alert.

Bryson finally reached him, and he extended a hand to help him onto the narrow shelf. "What's up?"

"Check it out."

"What?" Bryson's voice faded. "Is that what I think it is?"

"Looks like one of our weapons, doesn't it? Or at least pieces of it."

"Yeah."

"Bag and tag these, okay? And see what you can find out."

"Will do." Bryson knelt and placed a placard with a number beside the rifle before making a notation on his clipboard. He took a picture.

Jonathan's radio squawked, drawing him out of his contemplation. "Ward, Wildman here. We found something."

His heart hammered. "Christine?"

"You need to get down here. Now."

His gaze flew to the stream bed. From his angle, he couldn't see his crew. "Bryson, finish up here. Then follow me. Roy found something."

He didn't wait for his friend's reply. His heart hammered as his momentum nearly knocked him off his feet. He skidded downward, his feet and hands fighting for purchase. When he hit the road, he tumbled forward, skinning his palms. He swore beneath his breath and staggered to his feet as he crossed behind the last Wrangler.

For the first time, he noticed the robed bodies of two more Taliban near the far edge of the road. He raised his radio to his lips. "Where are you?"

"Ten o'clock from your position." Roy's reply came through sharp and clipped.

Jonathan scanned the ground to his left. A rifle caught his eye. One of theirs. Maybe Christine's? Scuff marks told him all he needed to know. He wove his way among boulders until a small cluster of men came into view. His hands began shaking as he forced himself to slow to a walk. "Roy?"

"We found her."

Sayad looked away.

"Oh, no…" He locked his knees to keep his legs from buckling. He clamped his jaw tight against the bile flooding his throat as he studied the still form of the woman he loved.

Christine lay on her back, the handle of a knife protruding from the hollow of her throat just above the armored vest she wore. Blood, quickly going from red to brown, coated both sides of her neck. Her gray eyes were open, and the breeze blew wisps of dark brown hair across her face.

He clenched his fists. God help him, he'd find whoever did this—and they wouldn't have a prayer against his fury.

16

Ghazni Province, Afghanistan

"I want your butt here tomorrow at 0700 hours, you understand me?" The CEO's words blistered the raw wounds in Jonathan's soul.

Jonathan glared at Harry Bossman, better known as Boss Man at the compound. His headache, which had started as they'd returned from the convoy, amped up. As COO, Jonathan was just one level below, but he didn't feel like playing the subordinate right now.

The former Marine colonel matched his gaze with a flinty blue one of his own.

"Sir," Jonathan measured his words carefully, "Bryson is finishing his investigation. I've also lined up a time to talk with Jeb, and—"

"You are to stay out of it." Boss Man pointed his pen at him. "You took yourself out of the equation the moment you admitted romantic involvement with Parker. You understand?"

"Sir, I haven't I—"

"Enough! I don't want to hear it." Boss Man jumped to his feet. With both hands braced on his desk, he leaned forward. "Let me get one thing straight. You clearly violated SecureLink's policy of no fraternization with those in your *chain of command*."

Jonathan's fists tightened at the insinuation. As if he, a retired, highly decorated Green Beret sergeant, had no clue of what that meant.

"And because of that, you are too personally involved in the investigation. Stay out of it and let Bishop handle it. You hear me? Your job is to brief me. That's it. No more."

Jonathan glared at him. To argue any further wouldn't have gotten him anywhere. "All right."

"What'd you say?"

What was he? Some sort of green private fresh out of boot camp or something? "Yes, *sir*."

"Dismissed. I'll see you in the morning." Boss Man muttered under his breath and turned toward the coffeemaker sitting on his credenza.

Jonathan marched into the hall and slammed the door behind him harder than he intended. For a few moments, he leaned against the cinder block wall and willed himself to calm down. He glanced at his hands. They shook, from shock, anger, agony, or all of that, he didn't know. He flexed his fingers and pushed away from the wall.

Like an ant drawn to sugar, he headed toward the building that housed the brig and offices for Bryson and Jeb, the Chief Weapons Officer. Lights blazed from the building in the fading dusk, meaning that Bryson, the head lawman, was hard at work processing all that he'd learned.

"Jonathan, hey." Bryson blinked from behind his glasses.

"Anything yet?"

"Not yet." He remained guarded, and Jonathan wondered if Boss Man had already gotten to him. "Look. I know you want to know, but officially, you're not part of this investigation."

Check the box for Boss Man having already paid Bryson a visit.

Jonathan swallowed hard. "I know. I could ask. Just…let me know what I'm supposed to pass on to Boss Man." He stood there for a few seconds as he struggled for something to say. "I, um, well, I'll see you later." He turned to go.

"Jonathan," Bryson called in a low voice.

Slowly, he swiveled so he faced him.

"Close the door."

"Okay." Jonathan shut the door and leaned against it with his arms folded across his chest. "What's going on?"

Bryson shuffled through some photographs. "I've found some stuff that concerns me."

"What about this whole situation doesn't?"

"True. That rifle up in the sniper's hide? It's one of ours."

Jonathan blinked. "Come again?"

"I'm convinced it's one of ours."

"Wait. You think there's guns being run through this compound?"

"I'm not sure. I'm going to talk to Jeb later. I've also got a call in to the sales department at Mark Rifles." He hesitated. His gaze flicked to Jonathan, then away.

"There's something else." Jonathan nodded toward the pile of photographs on the black surface of the lab table. "What is it?"

"I…" He winced and bit his lip.

"C'mon, Bryson. It's written all over your face."

He removed his glasses and polished them with a microfiber cloth. "I…I'm wondering if the hit on the convoy might have been a cover-up for murder."

"You lost me." Jonathan pulled over a lab chair and nearly fell onto it.

"I think the Taliban were after Christine."

Jonathan's breath hitched. Coldness swept over him. "How…how do you know that?"

"Think about the crime scene. What do you remember?" Bryson gathered the photos into a neat stack.

"There were multiple women on that trip."

"Oh, I know. But only one on the protective detail."

"They couldn't have known that." Jonathan rubbed his temples in a futile attempt to ease the headache. "At least not by looking at them. When we all got gunned up, you couldn't tell Christine apart from the shorter guys."

"True." Bryson swept his hands through his hair. "What else do you remember?"

"I don't know." He shot up from the chair. "Look. I'm tired of playing games, okay?"

"Sorry." Bryson sighed. "Okay. Everyone died from gunshot wounds, either from the sniper or from the guys that were hiding below. Christine must have realized how outnumbered they were and how many had already died, so she ran. I get that. And she took down five of them in the process. But why didn't they just shoot her?"

"She wore armor like all of us do."

"But they could have hit a leg to bring her down. They didn't. Doc didn't see any bullet holes in her. Only the knife wound and assorted cuts and scrapes indicative of falling while she ran."

"I get that. But that still doesn't lend itself to murder."

"I know. I know." Bryson paused as if carefully considering his words. He shuffled his photographs and handed one to Jonathan.

He lowered himself back on the chair and flinched. Christine stared sightlessly at him from the photo. Her dark brown hair spread around her face with that one lock the breeze had blown across her cheek. Already, the lifeblood draining from her body had added a deathly pallor to her face. The image seared his mind and would most likely haunt him for days.

"Why undo her hair?" Bryson's question came from a great distance. "She always put it in a bun or braid when going out. Did she have it that way today?"

Jonathan nodded. She'd worn it in a bun when he gave the final briefing to their clients. "She did."

"It's almost like they needed positive identification."

"But for what?"

"Maybe she knew about the gunrunning."

Last night—was it really just twenty-four hours ago?—he'd queried Christine and gotten rebuffed. She'd been scared. Maybe Bryson was right. "We need to figure that—"

"First off, there's no 'we' involved. You need to stay free and clear of it, okay? I'll brief you when I'm done."

"But—"

"Seriously." Bryson shot him a direct stare. "Besides all I have are theories and circumstantial evidence. Nothing even close to good enough to take to Boss Man, understand?" He took the photo and returned it to the pile. "I've got to talk with Jeb and do some more investigating."

"I want to see everything."

"I know. I'll brief you, but seriously, let me do the investigating."

"I will." Jonathan slowly climbed to his feet. "Bryson, thanks. That's a lot of good work in a short amount of time."

"I'm sorry. I knew something was going on between you and Parker."

"Were we that obvious?"

A small smile broke through his somberness. "Only to those who know you well. I'll swing by when I'm done and fully brief you."

Jonathan nodded. He could do nothing but wait now. He pushed through the door and stepped onto the road. The back gate sat to his left. Ahead of him, lights still glowed in the administration building. He was sure

Boss Man burned up the satellite link between the compound and Se-cureLink's home office in the Tidewater area.

Jonathan strode toward the residential side of the compound. To his left, the SecureLink helicopter sat silent on its pad. Thanks to the Red Alert, staff walked to and from the dorms with rifles slung across their shoulders and cloaked in combat vests and Kevlar helmets. Normally, a low rumble of male voices filled the air as his staff began switching from afternoon to evening. Not tonight. Now, no one made a peep. He came upon the guest house where their clients stayed before shipping out to various points across eastern Afghanistan. The sound of crying reached him. He couldn't blame them, not when they were heading into the danger zone. Well, no convoys would go out until he and his men delivered the bodies to the nearby airfield to be shipped to the next of kin for burial.

The image of that photo assaulted him. A lump rose to his throat, followed by a bit a nausea as the headache throbbed. He needed to purge the sight from his mind, to seek solace.

His sister Abigail's name slid unbidden into his mind. She didn't even know what had happened.

He quickened his steps to his dorm across from the women's building and took the stairs two at a time to his room on the right end of the second floor.

He shucked his combat gear and dove toward his desk and the one picture of Christine that always filled his heart with love. They'd gone to her parents' fiftieth wedding anniversary celebration. He'd worn a suit and tie, and she, a deep blue dress. Her hair spilled across her shoulders in dark brown waves. The sparkle in her eyes said it all. That night, they'd talked about marriage and her decision to resign from SecureLink. Their lives had held such promise. But now…

He gently ran his thumb across her image, feeling each shard of his broken heart slash at his insides. When he could no longer stand it, he clutched the cold frame against his chest, threw his head back, and released a savage wail from deep within his gut. "Oh, God!"

His shoulders shook as he wept until he felt dry. Dry and empty and numb.

He glanced dully at his cell phone on the desk. He needed to call his sister. Now. Before he lost his sanity.

3

She had him. Abigail felt it deep within her bones as she crouched in the muddy barnyard and leaned against the rough wood of a dilapidated outbuilding. Water from the drizzle dripped from the eaves until it ran down her face in big rivulets. The wet had seeped into her jacket, chilling her. She didn't care. They'd trapped their suspect, and the only way out was through the door they now guarded.

Abigail pulled away slightly. The Sig Sauer P228 felt comfortable in her hand, almost like an old friend. *Come to mama, you little worm.* Her lips curled. She glanced at her sergeant, who stood ready across from her with her own weapon in hand.

Marti grinned. "Got 'em," she mouthed.

Abigail pounded on the door. "U.S. Army! We have you surrounded."

It burst open, knocking Abigail off her feet. With a splash, she landed on her rear in the mud puddle she'd worked so hard to avoid.

A loud buzz filled the air, and The Worm, as she'd started calling their suspect, flew past them on a comically small moped.

Marti tried to give chase, but she slipped in the mud and sprawled onto her front.

Abigail scrambled to her feet and dashed after him.

The Worm kicked up more mud in her face as he zipped into the pasture toward the far end. He didn't get far. Most likely having not anticipated the wet grass, he went into a skid as he tipped the moped in a turn. He tumbled from the motorbike and rolled a few times.

Abigail thundered after him, her arms and legs knifing through the air as if she ran a sprint race. Marti followed.

The Worm approached the electrified boundary fence. Rather than slow, he picked up speed and dove onto his stomach. As if on a slip'n slide, he skittered underneath. He rolled to his feet as if he did that every day.

Abigail lunged and slid as if she were beating the throw to home plate. The wire passed overhead so close that the hum of the current whispered in her ear. She staggered to her feet.

Marti yelped. She hadn't been so lucky.

Abigail gained ground. Another barn came into view. *You're not getting away from me. Now way, no how.* She increased her pace. Her lungs burned. So did her quads.

The Worm climbed the pipe-rail fence and leaped off of it. Only this time, when he rose, he fell and got a face full of mud. Or something else.

She spied the pigs and flinched. They grunted and scurried to the other side of the pen. She took a running leap and scaled the fence. Using the top rail as a springboard, she thrust herself toward The Worm as he struggled to his feet. She hit him, once more sending him face first into stink that confirmed her worst fears.

Oh, great. Reyes, her cohort stationed with CID at Fort Stewart, owed her big time for this.

"Let me go!" The Worm shouted. "You're roughing up a suspect."

"No, you're helping me with that."

He kicked her, striking her on the back.

"Knock it off before I get real mad and shove your face in the mud." She grabbed his wrists and reached for her cuffs. "Reginald Osborn, you're under arrest for—"

"Just what in the name of Jim Beam is going on here?"

She froze at the question delivered in the deep drawl of a native Georgian.

A farmer, dressed in soiled overalls and an equally dirty undershirt, glared at her. So did the double eyes of the shotgun he held in his hand. She knew he wouldn't hesitate to use it.

Keeping her knee in The Worm's back, she located her cred pack covered in goop. She leveraged it open. "I'm sorry, sir. Major Abigail Ward, Army Criminal Investigation Command."

"Reggie, that you, boy?" The farmer's eyes narrowed. "Just what kind of trouble have you gotten yourself into this time?"

"The legal kind. Sir, I'm really sorry for upsetting your pigs." Abigail's own country drawl, a product of her fine Southern upbringing in Raleigh, reappeared. She hitched the cuffs around The Worm's wrists and hauled him to his feet, then marched him toward the edge of the pen. "If you would please open the gate, sir, I would appreciate it."

The farmer complied. "Yes, ma'am. You didn't hurt them none. Reggie, does your mama know you're here?'

"No, sir." The Worm's eyes widened in his muddy face. "Please don't tell her. She'd like to kill me for what I done."

"That is?"

"Rape," Abigail simply replied.

"Did I hear you right, ma'am?"

"Yes, sir, you did."

"Reggie Osborn, your mama is going to beat you up one side and down the other. You should be ashamed of yourself."

Her sides heaving, Marti joined them. "Sorry about that. The wire got me."

The Worm started laughing.

The farmer popped him across the head. "Fool boy. And when your daddy hears, you gonna be in a heap of trouble, son."

"Maybe time in the brig is better than with your family." Abigail shoved the stinking specimen of mud and poop toward her comrade. "Sergeant, read him his rights and walk him to the car. I'll be along in a moment."

"Ma'am, do you need a statement from me?" the farmer asked.

"No, sir. I do thank you kindly for not putting buckshot in me."

The farmer laughed. "You're all right, Major Ward. You and your friend. Have a good day."

Despite the mud, chill, and stink, she strutted toward the road with her head held high, though she denied herself a victory dance. She'd helped out a friend and added another takedown to her record. Of course, Olivero Reyes really owed her now. She'd figure out what he'd have to do for her. Maybe head to the Caribbean to bring home that suspect who'd stolen some classified information. No, that'd seem like too much of a vacation. A trip to the Midwest in January might be good. She'd have to drum up a reason for it.

She came to the road. Half a mile down between the two farms sat the black Suburban they'd taken for that day's junket. Ahead of her, Marti was hauling The Worm through the unrelenting drizzle at a quick clip.

The cell phone at her waist began barking, the ringtone that meant her brother called. Usually, they talked on Sundays regardless of where she was in the world. Why was he calling now? She cleaned it off before bringing it to her ear. "Jonathan, hey."

"Hey, girl. How's it going?"

"Oh, I'm covered in mud and pig poop."

"Huh?"

She grinned. "I just made an arrest for a friend. Reyes was going to do it, but he came down with a stomach bug and was so sick that he couldn't make it out of bed. I was down here on business and offered to make the bust for him because tips on suspects have a short shelf life."

He didn't laugh at her humor.

Abigail stopped and stared at the Suburban ahead of her. "What's going on?"

Nothing.

"Jonathan? Are you there?"

"Yeah." That one word came out low and raspy.

"What's going on? You sound like something's wrong."

"Christine's dead."

The news sucker-punched her in the gut. "What?"

"She's dead, Abigail."

"Oh, no…" She turned away from the road and sank into a crouch on rubbery legs. "What happened?"

"The convoy got ambushed. Twenty-four dead. The Taliban got them."

Her eyes filled. Images of the day when Jonathan's Special Forces team, the Mighty Men, had gotten ambushed seven years before flashed across her mind. "Oh, wow."

"There's more. Bryson suspects it was a targeted murder with the ambush used as cover."

"Targeting who?"

"Christine."

Abigail tried to shake the fog from her head. Nothing he said registered. "I don't—"

"Don't you see it?" Anger pushed his words.

She rubbed her forehead. "How can I? I'm not there."

"Sorry." He blew out a sigh. "I'm…angry."

"I know." A lump filled her throat. "Why does Bryson say that?"

"Theories he has. That's it for now."

She pressed a muck-crusted fist to her mouth and closed her eyes as they filled. "Are you safe?"

"Yeah. Bryson's investigating since Christine and I were seeing each other."

Jonathan had mentioned the no-fraternization policy and how it had torn at him.

"Let him keep investigating."

"I know. He'll share when he's done so I can brief Boss Man."

"Watch your step, okay? If what you say is true, then you've got some bad characters there."

"Don't I know it." A long pause ensued, and only the hiss of the international line told her he was still there. "We were only sixteen days away from coming home. I…I was going to propose to her over Mother's Day weekend."

A tear trickled down Abigail's cheek. She closed her eyes. "I'm sorry. I wish there was something I could do."

"Pray for me?"

"Always. I love you."

"I love you too," he whispered. "I—I've got to go. Bad headache."

"Bye." Dead air filled her ear. Abigail remained in her crouch with her head in her hands.

"Abigail?" Marti had edged the Suburban closer to her on the road and now leaned against its fender. The Worm glowered at her from the backseat. "Are you okay?"

"No. Jonathan called." She got to her feet. "His girlfriend died in a convoy hit in Ghazni."

"Oh, no. Abigail, I'm sorry."

"He thinks it was murder," she added before she could stop herself.

"Is he safe?"

"He says he is." Abigail stared toward the east, longing to see beyond two continents and ten hours to where her grieving brother had most likely holed up in his room. "I'm not so sure. And that's what worries me the most."

4

Burning Tree, Utah

David Shepherd's eyes snapped open precisely five minutes before six. Totally unwilling to face the late March chilliness of his bachelor apartment, he didn't move. Then his left quad twitched as if chastising him for such silliness. He rubbed his hand down the long scar that ran almost from hip to knee. Arching his back, he stretched and flexed his muscles before settling into warm stillness again.

Ranger whined. The two-year-old shepherd mix raised his head and gazed at him as if imploring him to get up.

Finally, the alarm buzzed to announce the new day. David cut it off and sat up. Really, he didn't want to throw the covers aside. The heater hadn't fazed the chill yet. With a deep breath, he thumped across the bedroom and down the short hallway to the kitchen, with only a quick stop to turn on the shower. He ran water into the teakettle and set it on the burner to heat. Ranger pawed at the sliding glass door, and he let him outside.

David's shower took a total of five minutes. He emerged just as the kettle whistled its own version of a morning greeting. With a towel around his waist, he returned to the kitchen, dropped a peppermint tea bag into the mug, and added hot water.

With the hot drink further awakening him, he dressed in a pair of jeans, a T-shirt, and a fleece. He combed the gunk Kyra had given him to tame his curls into his hair. It fell past his shoulder blades, and he chuckled as he recalled for the umpteenth time how his hair was now longer than his sister's.

He continued working on his tea as he wandered into the living area and eased onto his recliner. With his right hand, he picked up the foam ball that was the size of a tennis ball and began his daily regimen of physical therapy. Squeeze. Release. Squeeze. Release. Now, his grip had strengthened to where he could ride his bike without assistance from the gripper one of his buddies had devised for him to use. During his most recent session a couple of weeks before, his physical therapist had praised him for the progress he'd made. She'd said he'd come a long way. He agreed. Almost three years ago, he'd been unable to hold a pencil, let alone write with it. All thanks to the knife wound that had damaged several nerves.

As he set his tea aside, footsteps pattered up the outside stairway that led to his deck. Little Bit shoved the sliding glass door open and burst inside. She threw her arms around him. "Uncle David! I'm hungry."

He laughed as he pulled her onto his lap with his left arm. "You're hungry, huh? What for?"

"French toast."

"And where would that be?"

"The diner."

"Which one?" He grinned, enjoying his game.

"Uncle David!"

He laughed and inhaled that little girl scent of Dove and flowers. "Why don't we go see if we can remedy that?" He set her down, rose, and rinsed his tea mug before placing it in the drainer.

"What's remedy?" Little Bit's black curls, so much like his own, bobbed in two pigtails as she climbed onto one of the bar chairs.

"We'll fix that." He eyed her Tasmanian Devil sweatshirt, a hand-me-down, and her jeans. "Where's your jacket, young lady?"

"Don't need it," she answered, sounding like her older brothers.

He fought his smile. "We'll see about that. Let's go."

They descended the steps and strolled down the concrete driveway. Across the two-lane highway at the end of the drive, the red rock mesas of central Utah spread before him in the growing dawn. Blue sky rapidly began lightening. It was shaping up to be another glorious early spring day. David silently began counting down. *Three… Two… One…*

"Catherine Martin, you get back here right now and put your jacket on!" Kyra's voice rocketed across the yard.

He turned to see his sister charging down the front steps with a denim jacket in her hands. His chuckle escaped him before he realized it. "She told me she didn't need one."

"Beware of the fibs of small children." Kyra shook her head. "Catherine, you know better."

"Here, Little Bit, put this on." David held the little jacket with a picture of *Frozen's* Elsa embroidered onto the back. "Sorry, Kyra, I should have made her get her jacket."

She shrugged. "This isn't the first time. I swear she's impervious to cold. Well, you two have a good time. Catherine, I'll pick you up at ten, okay?"

"I love you, Mommy." Little Bit threw her arms around her mother.

Kyra hugged her tightly. "Love you back. Be gone with you two."

With Little Bit's small hand engulfed in his, David led her down the front walk. They turned right and strolled along the sidewalk toward the small town of Burning Tree. Beneath the bridge they crossed, the river turned and snaked north of town as it burbled between the pale green cottonwoods that contrasted with the red rock. They paused at one of two stoplights where the road into the town turned.

The whole time, Little Bit chattered like a magpie about what she wanted to do on her last day of spring break. Catch bugs and snakes with Uncle David and help him repair pipes in her granddaddy's hotel. Then go that afternoon and see *Zootopia* with her best friend, Megan, and Kyra. Then come back and have a sleepover with Megan. David smiled. Tough chick meets Disney.

They arrived at the diner. David slowed, and he opened the big silver door with his left hand. Little Bit tugged against his right one. Fortunately, his grip held. "Just a second, Little Bit."

"But I'm hungry!"

"So am I." In one rapid glance, he assessed the room like he'd done when busting down doors in the sandbox. About a dozen people sat in the booths, most on the left, a few on the right. Four sat at the counter. No one showed weapons. He relaxed, and Little Bit charged toward the counter and clambered onto one of the glittery blue vinyl stools. "Can we sit here, Uncle David?"

"Sure." He inhaled and savored the sharp scent of bacon frying in the back and the banter between the waitresses and cook. Metal clinked on metal. Nearby, a waitress popped some gum as she flipped through her order pad. He noted the guy two stools down and grinned. "Mitch Patterson. What's up?"

Mitch, dressed in a brown deliveryman's uniform, put down his fork. "Shepherd, I didn't expect to see you here. I thought you always had your chow at home."

"Not when it's spring break and I get time with my favorite niece."

"I'm your only niece!" Little Bit piped up.

"Therefore, you're my favorite." He laid a menu in front of her. "How about you, Patterson?"

"I started my day early this morning. Spring break too, ya know? I want to take my boys fishing before it gets dark, which means finishing my rounds early. Thought I'd get some chow from my favorite waitress."

"You're too funny, Mitch." The waitress, her dark hair pinned up in a pile on her head, approached and pulled out a pen. "Good morning, you two." She smiled at Little Bit. "What can I get you to drink?"

"I want French toast!"

"To drink?" David tweaked her nose.

She scowled. "To eat. And orange juice to drink, please."

David ordered the breakfast combo special of two scrambled eggs, bacon, and hash browns with a cup of peppermint tea and juice as well. Once she'd entered their order, the waitress brought Little Bit a place mat for coloring and some crayons.

On the wall above the drink machines and shelving that held glasses, two televisions featured CNN and Fox News. He focused on the one with

CNN. A blond anchorwoman stood next to a counter and held a sheaf of papers. The graphic beside her emblazoned itself in his mind.

Convoy hit in Afghanistan. 24 Dead.

His blood froze. He studied the closed caption scrolling across the screen. The white letters on a backdrop of black told it all. A private security contractor named SecureLink had been escorting sixteen doctors and nurses to a remote village to provide medical care. The Taliban ambushed them, killing all of the medical staff plus eight SecureLink personnel.

The waitress slid a steaming mug of hot tea in front of him, and he jerked his attention from the screen.

David glanced down and in a shuddering gasp released the breath he hadn't realized he'd been holding.

"Tough news, isn't it?" Mitch remarked from where he'd been shoveling his own meal of eggs into his mouth.

"Yeah." David glanced at Little Bit, who was involved in giving the rabbit in the *Zootopia* drawing orange and purple ears. "Brings back a lot of memories."

"You served in Afghanistan, right?"

"Yep. You?"

"Iraq, then Afghanistan. Where were you based?"

"SF out of Kandahar." The Incident that had changed his life had occurred in the Ghazni Province, the same place where the SecureLink convoy had met its most unfortunate fate.

"Kandahar? Me too. When did you leave?"

"Not soon enough," David muttered. Laughter from the Mighty Men echoed in his mind when they'd played a game of cards near a flickering fire in the village where they'd embedded.

"Sorry. Just asking a question. I got out in 2007 after Kandahar. I was with the MPs there. Man, talk about a tough job. I was always scared I wouldn't spot an ANA guy who'd turned traitor. And the clashes with the locals when one of our guys went bonkers? Man, did I hate them." Mitch shrugged and raised his hand for the check. "Well, gotta head on out. Good to see you, Shepherd. Let's ride sometime soon."

"Will do. Hey, sorry if I was brusque. That brings back too many memories," David added. He extended his hand.

Mitch shook it. "No problem."

At least now, David's grip didn't feel like a fish handshake. "Later."

Mitch left, and David checked on Little Bit. She'd created not a red fox but one that was green with orange spots. Oh, the imagination of his niece. He tried to focus on her drawing but found it futile. As if under the spell of CNN, his attention returned to the television. Now, it showed images of the three burned vehicles in the box on the left side of the screen. All were blackened, most likely destroyed by the SecureLink personnel so the Taliban couldn't pilfer them. That did nothing to disguise puncture marks he knew to be bullet holes. Twenty-four people dead in less than five minutes.

He braced his elbows on the counter and rested his forehead on his hands. *God, no...* More images came, these of Captain as his commanding officer had burst into the mess tent at their base in the village. "Shepherd, get the crew together. Now. We've got company coming."

David took a deep breath, held it, and released it. The memories faded.

He glanced at the images on the right-hand side of the screen. A press conference from 0900 hours local time was being replayed. Two people sat at the table with several others in a row behind them. One he didn't recognize, but the other?

"No way!" The words escaped his lips before he realized it.

Jonathan Ward, his former best friend, stared at the tabletop. He didn't say a word but let the man beside him do all of the talking.

David flinched.

"Let's do it, bro." Jonathan's drawl from eighteen years before echoed in his ears. "You and me. *Sola gratia*, right? 'Cause we're brothers-in-arms. Brothers-in-Christ."

David stared at the tattoo he'd gotten on his forearm. Rather than the Latin, he'd had By Grace Alone etched in black. Now, a scar cut through the middle, effectively severing the ink. Kind of like his friendship with Jonathan. Torn. Never to be mended.

"You okay, David?" the waitress asked.

Suddenly, he noticed how his hands gripped the ceramic of the mug. The liquid in it quivered because his whole body trembled. He met her gaze. "Uh, yeah. Do you, um, mind changing it from CNN?"

"Oh, sure. Sorry 'bout that." She picked up a remote and changed it to the Cartoon Network.

David flexed his fingers. The tremors had ceased. If only he could erase those images from his brain that quickly.

Burning Tree, Utah

"Hand me that jar, would you?" David asked as he focused on the scorpion he'd found hiding out in one of the bungalows at his parents' resort. The small beast clung to the headboard of the king-sized bed. The guest, a businesswoman who'd proclaimed she'd needed a vacation, had come out of her bathroom to find it crawling on the dark wood. Now, she huddled in the corner, her blond hair in wet strands, the terrycloth robe tightly wrapped around her.

Little Bit, his willing assistant, handed him a glass mason jar they'd brought with them. "Can I do that, Uncle David?"

"Nope. This guy's a big one, and he's not in a good mood. But watch this." David unscrewed the lid, then shoved aside a plump pillow. Placing one knee on the mattress, he held the jar beneath the scorpion. With a quick brush of the lid, he knocked the eight-legged critter inside and slapped the lid onto it before the scorpion had a chance to figure out what had happened.

The woman whimpered from her corner. "I hate those things."

"All done. Call the front desk if anything else happens." David tightened the lid back on the jar. "Little Bit, hold on to this until we get outside. We'll release it down by the river."

"Can I?" she asked, her dark eyes, so like his, big.

"Of course." With a hand on her shoulder, he guided her to the door, then turned to their guest. "Have a good day, ma'am."

They stepped into the bright morning light. The warm rays relaxed his muscles. Could all days be like this? When he did work around the resort and got to hang out with his niece?

They strolled along the winding path of tiny pebbles that led toward the river. Little Bit scampered ahead with her prize. Once the path swept to within ten feet of the water, she slowed and squatted at the edge. "Are you sure we can't keep him?"

"Your mama wouldn't let you. Besides, scorpions are dangerous."

"Why didn't you kill him?"

"Because they're just as much God's creatures as we are."

"But you kill cockroaches."

He bit back his sigh at this child philosopher. "It's a long story. Release him. But be careful. Hold out the jar and tip it up. Let him fall to the ground."

She obeyed, and the arachnid plopped onto the hard-packed earth before scuttling under a rock. "Cool. Are you sure I can't have one?"

"Isn't Lilly enough?" Only two weeks ago, the Martin clan had brought home the Australian Shepherd puppy. "C'mon. Your mama's probably wondering where we are."

He found Kyra chatting with the attendant at the hotel's front desk. Ranger lounged on the braided rug in front of the massive fireplace where low flames crackled. "Ranger didn't want to be alone?"

"He missed his daddy." Kyra giggled. She led him away from Little Bit, who'd fallen to her knees beside the dog.

"What's up?" David frowned.

"I saw what happened this morning."

He knew what she talked about. His breath caught as he tried for innocent. "Saw what?"

"About the hit on the convoy. And Jonathan. I feel so bad for him." She sighed.

"Ghazni's not for sissies. He knew what he was getting into."

"David!" She grabbed his arm and escorted him onto the wide stone terrace that overlooked the river. Thanks to the chill, no one lounged on the rockers or the Adirondack chairs around the fire pit. No one took pictures of the river with the red rock looming beyond it. "That's not nice. Especially when his fiancée was one of the dead."

"I don't follow."

"Christine Parker was on the security detail. She died along with everyone else."

He shrugged.

Her eyes narrowed. "What is it with you and him?"

"Nothing. I've got nothing to say about him. Or to him," he added as a barb. "After what happened six years ago, why should I?"

"Because maybe he's your best friend despite everything? Because he saved your life almost seven years ago?"

"Enough with the guilt already." He spiked the jar against the stone floor like a football. It shattered into a hundred satisfying pieces. The lid sat on the glass. He stared at it a moment, then glared at Kyra. "He wasn't there when I needed him. Why should I care?"

Kyra, bless her, didn't jump, didn't cower from his show of temper. She closed her eyes for a long second and slowly released a sigh. "You know, sometimes you frustrate me so much. Why can't you get over yourself and that stinking pride of yours and reach out to a friend who's hurting? I'm sure his sister could give you his contact information."

"Not interested."

"I know." She fell silent as if struggling not to fan the flames of his angst. "Well, I've got to get going. See you tonight? We're making home-made pizza."

David merely grunted his reply. He turned his gaze toward the mess he'd made. The jar lay in a glittering disarray. Kind of like the remains of the contentment he'd felt.

Little Bit ran onto the terrace and threw her arms around him. "Bye, Uncle David. I'll see you tonight."

He held on until she squirmed free.

He watched her run to Kyra and take her hand.

Kyra was right. Jonathan was hurting. One look at the television this morning had shown how the hit on the convoy had aged him. Losing his fiancée had completed the damage. Maybe he should try to find Abigail and get his contact information.

No. Some things were best left untouched and in the past. As he went to get a broom to sweep up the mess he'd made, he tried to convince himself of that.

Problem was, he didn't get too far on the convincing part.

5

Ghazni Province, Afghanistan

Nicole Chardet gripped the window frame as she stared into the night. From the nearby gym, metal clanked on metal as some of the guys lifted to relieve their grief. In the rec hall next to the gym, no one laughed at the muffled dialogue of a comedy. How could they after the memorial service that morning? And especially not before a convoy carrying the bodies of twenty-four people would head to the airport in less than twelve hours.

Behind her, the refrigerator door sucked open. Roy cleared his throat. "I lost two friends yesterday. And a good supervisor."

With both hands braced on the fridge, he stared at the assortment of beer bottles, soda, and bottled water she'd stored inside.

How many times had he brought this up? Any more times, and she'd lose it and scream at him. She slammed the window. "You knew it had to be done."

"With so many lives lost?"

"I can't believe I'm hearing this." She snatched a wineglass from a cabinet and slapped the door closed. "If I remember correctly, Roy Wildman, you concocted this plan. You said it had to happen to make it look like an ambush by the Taliban. And since you helped Chip put together the personnel roster for yesterday's convoy, you could have left the names of your pals off."

"You really think that? They'd been off duty for nearly a week and were due to rotate back on. Just how could I leave them off without raising their suspicions and that of Chip's?" Roy grabbed a beer and kicked the door closed. With a bottle opener, he snagged the top. The lid spun into the air and landed on the floor against the cabinet with a metallic clink. He tossed the opener into a drawer. "We could have done this differently."

"How?" She smashed the glass onto the counter. It cracked, and she swept it onto the floor where the tile completed the destruction. "Tell me how."

Roy whirled on her. He opened his mouth, but no sound came out.

Nicole gave him a knowing smile and lifted her chin. "That's what I thought. Parker knew about our operations. She had to go, but there was no way to do it quietly. Bishop's a good investigator. If it hadn't been by ambush, we'd be walking out of here in handcuffs."

Roy's shoulders sagged.

Chalk one up for her.

He retreated to the couch in the living area and sprawled onto the cushions as he lifted the bottle to his lips. It shook slightly.

Leaving the broken glass, Nicole sidled over to him. She eased down beside him and ran her fingers down his arm. Muscles rippled lightly at her touch. She rested her head against his shoulder and took his hand. "We had no other way. Since Parker and Ward were apparently an item, it was only a matter of time before she squealed on us."

"Do you think she did?"

"We're still walking free, aren't we?"

"I'm still not—"

"Roy, enough." She went back to the kitchen and yanked open the door to the pantry. "I'm tired of discussing this. We had a plan. It worked." She snatched the broom and slammed the door. "End of story."

She began sweeping the pieces of the wineglass into a sparkling pile. One skittered across the floor.

"You're right." Gentle hands took the broom from her. "Here. Let me do that."

She hitched herself onto the counter, lit a cigarette, and took a drag. She blew out a steady stream. Her taut shoulders relaxed as the nicotine hit her bloodstream. She sighed, let her head hang forward, and softly groaned as tense muscles began releasing. "But you're right to be worried. I overheard Boss Man giving orders to Ward. He's to let Bishop investigate and isn't supposed to be involved save for passing along information."

"You told me." Roy stooped and swept the pile into a dustpan.

"After the press conference, they were talking. Bishop found a rifle. Or at least pieces of one."

That earned a glance. "What?"

"A rifle." She inhaled and let the cigarette dangle from her fingers. "It was one of those we sold to the Taliban a few years ago. What were they thinking?"

"They did what we asked."

"Oh?" She hopped off the counter and paced. "They could have taken the rifle with them when it jammed instead of leaving it." She jabbed her cigarette into a saucer and muttered, "I thought Taliban weren't supposed to panic."

Roy emptied the dustpan and returned everything to the pantry. He reached up and ran some of her hair through his fingers as his smile revealed the dimple she'd come to love over the years of their courtship. "Baby, look. They had five minutes to do the job."

"How do you know that?"

"Because Captain Rasheed told Ward they were only five minutes away when the distress call went out. There were no survivors, including my friends. Ward thinks it was an equal opportunity killing."

"Then why did he bring up the rifle?"

"Because Mark Rifles makes a ton of them and we happen to be one of their clients. All Ward has is one rifle with no serial number." He disappeared into his thoughts. "And a whole bunch of dead people who won't squeal."

Nicole scowled. If he mentioned them one more time, she'd—

He focused on her. "From what I could see, even if Parker tried to escape, it still looks like a simple ambush."

"Fancy how you found out she was Ward's girlfriend. Imagine that." For the first time, a smile tipped her lips. Some of the worry lifted. Cause for celebration. She opened the wine fridge and chose one from among the labels.

"Oh, I've got something for you."

"What?" She glanced up as she pulled a wine opener from a drawer.

He grinned and held up a small package. "This came in today's mail run courtesy of El Lobo."

Her pulse raced as she snatched it from him. "This is what we've been waiting for. Perfect timing." Using the end of the wine opener, she ripped open the flap. She tipped it, and a small silver jump drive fell into her hand. "Close the blinds and go get my computer. Hurry!"

She opened the bottle and poured the red wine into a fresh glass.

Roy returned with her laptop.

Her fingers quivered from excitement as she typed in her login password. When the home screen popped up, she slid the drive into a USB port and caught her breath. "Bingo."

Roy peered over her shoulder. "What is that?"

"Something that's going to earn us an extra bonus from our other boss." She scanned the files and clicked on them. "But why Shamal Khan wanted these, I have no idea." She clicked on a file. "That's weird."

"What?"

"This. A file called Athena." She tried to open it. A password and a Top Secret declaration popped up. "I hope Shamal has the password—unless he put it in the package."

"He'd just unprotect it rather than do that." Roy leaned closer. The cologne he wore tickled her nose. "Athena. You know what that is? Or who?"

She shrugged. "Nope. It's classified so we certainly can't find out. How about go and stick this with the guns? We'll get it to Shamal Khan when we make the trade in a couple of weeks."

As he left the room with the drive in his hand, she took a gulp of wine. A puffball of warmth spread in her stomach. She smirked. The two million in bonus money to pass along information would go far in setting her up for retirement.

"Done." Roy's deep voice reached her. "And I've got a present for you."

"Huh?" Her thoughts returned to the present.

He held a small box in front of him.

"What is it?"

"Open it."

She lifted the lid. Her cheeks warmed as she noticed the midnight blue satin and lace of a negligee. Then she saw a jump drive on top. "What's this?"

"While you went to work after the memorial service, I took the liberty of going through Christine's things. I found this stuffed in the toe of one of her shoes. It's got everything she wrote up on us. And I mean everything. The last update was yesterday morning before she left on the convoy."

"So she was definitely getting ready to squeal on us."

"Most likely when they returned. Only they never did." He picked it up and let it dangle from its lanyard for a moment. Then he dropped it on the floor. Without hesitation, he raised his foot and brought it down hard on the fragile plastic and circuitry. The drive shattered beneath the hard sole of his boot. "Now no one will ever know. I'll throw these out in garbage cans all over the compound. Case closed, eh?"

He stepped close and draped the negligee across her shoulders. "I think we need to celebrate." He raised his beer bottle in a mock toast. "To our next deal with the Taliban."

She clinked her wine glass against the bottle, then leaned forward and kissed him.

As he nuzzled her neck, her thoughts began shifting.

She smiled. "To our next deal."

6

Ghazni Province

Jonathan gripped the rail of the Juliet balcony of his room and leaned against it. The razors of the concertina wire topping the perimeter wire glinted in the late afternoon light. He stared at the distant mountains shimmering in the heat as the sun fell toward the western horizon. He barely noticed it, hardly felt the hot breeze of the fading day caressing his face. Instead, images from earlier flashed through his mind.

The words of his speech to the remaining members of the protective detail who would escort the convoy rang in his ears. Every one of the men who had traveled to the convoy two days before had volunteered, including Cal and Roy. Four escort vehicles and four trucks bearing the caskets had rumbled through the gates, saluted by the staff remaining behind. Along with five others, Jonathan himself had carried Christine's casket aboard, gritting his teeth to stave off the grief. Since her funeral would be long over by the time he arrived home, it was his last chance to have one last, private moment with her. Only Jeb's hand on his shoulder had saved him from completely crumbling.

Now, pain distracted him. The tendons in his hands bulged from his too-tight grip on the rail. He pushed away and willed his mind to focus on other, more pleasant things—like what Bryson had told him and what he'd witnessed at the memorial service the day before.

45

The image burned itself into his mind as surely as if he'd pressed a brand in his side. Nicole, Roy, Cal Bacon, and Frisco Montoya had sat together. The look on their faces? Utter boredom as if Boss Man had made them go to a library lecture rather than a memorial to lives given in service. Then Nicole's lips had twitched in a sneer.

What was he missing?

He turned away from the window and approached the desk and work-table that formed an L across the half wall separating the living area from the sleeping area and the inner wall. Photographs plus printouts of Bryson's notes and his own handwritten ones lay scattered across the top. That mess of paper told a story he didn't want to contemplate.

The gun he'd found? Bryson confirmed that it had misfired. It had no serial number, but it contained a key piece of evidence, a small imprint of the SecureLink logo and shipment number in the metal.

Bryson dug some more and located altered orders and shipping manifests. Not by their Chief Weapons Officer because Jeb was a terrible liar and didn't count any of the Gang of Four, as Jonathan had taken to calling Nicole, Roy, Cal, and Frisco, as friends. Bryson had officially cleared the CWO.

And what about the potential of the convoy hit being a cover for murder? Jonathan shuffled through the pictures to reveal the gruesome ones of the bodies, including Christine. All had died of gunshots but her. Her killer had taken the time to remove her helmet and then loosen her hair. Bryson had theorized that she'd been singled out. Again, Jonathan recalled his argument with her the night before the hit, then the trembling smile on her lips as the convoy had left on that fateful trip.

In his mind, it all made sense. Problem was, they had only circumstantial evidence, not solid proof.

I've got to find the guns.

He began gathering the pictures into a neat stack. Where would they hide the arms? The warehouses where they kept the weapons would be out since Jeb kept things under lock and key. The auto garage had no hiding places. The same with the gym. What about the rec hall and mess hall? Too many people were in and out of all rooms, including the basements where the HVAC units were kept. The three dormitories where the guys stayed? Too busy as well, as was the guest house where clients bunked.

Jonathan stilled. The women's building. A tiny smile even formed on his lips. Designed to house any single women at the compound, the building had eight bedrooms, four upstairs and four downstairs along with a large living area and kitchen. Like the other buildings, the basement had lockers for long-term storage and for any valuables. Since Christine and Nicole had been the only two occupants, they'd stored everything in the spare bedrooms and didn't use the basement.

This was the only plausible explanation. He locked the envelope in the safe underneath the table. He had only one option. Go and check it out.

He logged into the server and located Nicole's calendar. She was in a Skype session with Boss Man as well as the new CEO and CFO, who would arrive in a little under two weeks. It wouldn't end until eight, meaning he had plenty of time to search.

He opened the lower drawer of his desk and pulled out a pair of nitrile gloves that he normally used for spot cleaning. After stowing the pair in his jacket, he stepped onto the walkway. He jumped when Jeb opened his door.

His neighbor grinned. "Headed to supper?"

"Uh…" Jonathan scrambled for an answer. "Actually, I was headed over to do some work." He offered a weak smile. "Got behind, you know."

"C'mon and grab some grub with us." Jeb nodded as several others began heading down the stairs. "I'm sure you need the company. It'll take your mind off things."

"I know, but I really need to get some work done." His stomach betrayed him by rumbling loudly.

"You sure?"

"Uh, yeah." His stomach growled again.

Jeb grinned at the obvious rebellion. "How 'bout I get some chow to go for you and bring it back here? Say, I'll be back in an hour? Growing boys need to eat, after all."

Jonathan chuckled, but it sounded weak to his ears. "Sure. If I'm not here, just stash it in my refrigerator."

"Will do. Have fun working." He turned away. "Hey, wait for me!"

Jonathan remained rooted to the step and watched as the small group headed across the street and between the women's building and guest house. To create the illusion of heading to work, he followed but turned right onto the street leading toward the administration building. When he'd passed the guest house, he ducked between that and the small building where Boss Man lived with his wife, who was his administrative assistant and human resources guru. He peeked into the alley. According to the rumble of voices, everyone had gathered for the evening meal.

At a crouch, he scurried along the dirt path to the women's building. He stepped onto the back porch and tried the knob. Good. Like everyone else, himself included, Nicole didn't bother to lock up. He opened the door and called, "Hello. Anyone home?"

No one answered.

He slipped inside and stole down the central hall toward the front. As he opened the basement door, the phone clipped to his belt rang.

He snatched the phone and brought it to his ear. "Bryson, what is it?"

"Good news." Excitement hummed in his investigator's voice. "I checked the vehicle logs. We have a pattern. When we had weapons shipments, of course Jeb always went. But Roy, Cal, or Frisco always went too."

"Interesting." Jonathan's gaze shifted from the front to back door. "I'm in the women's building. I think Roy's stashing the guns in the basement here because no one ever goes down there."

"I'll be right over—"

"No, no. I've got this."

"Didn't Boss Man tell you to let me do the investigating?"

"He did, but I'm already here. I've got this. Send me that info."

"All right." He sounded dubious.

"Let me do this, okay?"

"Keep me posted."

"Will do." Jonathan silenced his phone and continued down the stairs.

He pulled the cord on the overhead light. A dim glow emanated from the bare bulb.

On one side of the basement, the air blower loomed like a prehistoric monster. It kicked on and filled the air with its loud hum. If Nicole happened to show up, he wouldn't hear her until it was too late.

He scanned the remainder of the basement. There they were. Small sections surrounded by chicken wire signaled the eight long-term storage areas. Inside each were large footlockers with latches on them for the storage of any valuables. None had locks on them. A good layer of dust covered all of them as if no one had bothered opening them in ages.

He poked around the remainder of the basement. Nothing. Nothing near the HVAC unit. Nothing behind the pallets leaning against the wall. He slammed his fist into one of the pallets. They had to be here! He glanced at his watch.

He had half an hour before the Skype session ended.

"Think, think, think!"

As if released from a spell, a conversation he'd had once with Christine about her housemate flitted into his mind.

"Nicole's not the happiest person in the world," she'd said. "Matter of fact, she made it clear that she has domain over the bedrooms on the first floor."

Could she have hidden the guns there? No, that would have been too dangerous.

Something didn't jive.

He peered again at the footlockers.

"Afghanistan is known for many things, and one of them is being dusty," he liked to tell new recruits during their orientation session "The joke at the compound is that if you stay still for more than three minutes, you'll have to dust yourself off."

Even in a basement, a good layer could accumulate in the span of a month or so. He rose, approached the first one, and touched the lid.

The dust didn't move.

"That's strange." He got the same result on some other lids. Why?

He pulled out his key chain. Using the tiny Mag lite on the chain, he shone it along the top. A sheen appeared, almost like someone had layered something clear on top and let the dust accumulate in it. Repeating the process would yield a perfectly disguised lid someone could open and close at will.

He began raising the lids of each unit. Underneath the third one, the dark metal of a gun barrel gleamed in the dim light.

"Pay dirt."

He shoved the lid all the way up and snapped a picture with his phone, then pulled on the gloves and reached into the bin.

By the time he finished, he'd pulled out fifty rifles from five bins, plenty to make an exchange worthwhile. He took his time and snapped pictures of the stack. He focused on the company logo along with the numbers 12 and 13 at the other end of the barrel. He had no doubt that the number he pulled, when added to the numbers Jeb logged in, would make up the total orders Nicole filed.

He glanced at his watch. 7:00. He had what he needed with plenty of time to spare.

He leaned over to replace the first rifle. As he set it inside, his fingers brushed something. He gathered it in his hand. A jump drive? What was on it? And why was it so important that Roy concealed it with the rifles?

Jonathan bit the inside of his cheek. If he hustled, he could head to his room, review the drive, and return it before Nicole finished with her Skype session. First, replacing the rifles took precedence.

As he lowered the last lid, a door shut upstairs. A female voice laughed at something a man said.

Nicole. Roy was with her. The Skype session must have finished early.

Sweat broke out on Jonathan's palms. He reached up and pulled the cord, sending the room into darkness, and pressed himself against the stairs.

"Let me get my jacket. Then we can go shoot some pool."

She crossed above Jonathan, her footfalls knocking loose some dust that sifted onto his head. Her steps echoed through the thin wood of the basement door as she headed toward her room.

He couldn't make a run for it—not with the open floor plan of the downstairs. He had to wait. Getting caught would not be good, not good at all. Nicole was smart, and it wouldn't take her long to figure out what he'd discovered. Scarcely breathing, he remained still. Seconds ticked by.

More footsteps overhead. "I'm ready to go."

"You are *hot*." Roy chuckled deep in his throat. "Tonight, baby, you're mine."

"Ooh, I like the sound of that." She giggled. A door shut.

Jonathan waited another precious few minutes. He crept to the top of the stairs and listened. Nothing. Darkness now filled the house. He stole toward the back porch. Keeping in the shadows, he darted to his room.

After closing the the blinds, he settled behind his laptop and inserted the drive into a USB port.

"Yo, you're back." Jeb's voice sent adrenaline rocketing through his system. He jumped and slammed the lid of the laptop shut. His friend had arrived without his even noticing.

"Hey, sorry. I didn't mean to scare you, man. You must have been concentrating."

"Something like that." Jonathan tried to smile as he took the Styrofoam container.

Jeb pulled a bottle from his jacket. "Thought you'd like a beer, too. Fresh from the fridge, so it's not too warm."

"Thanks. I appreciate it."

"Take it easy. See ya tomorrow?"

"You bet." The smile felt like it'd fall off his face. Once Jeb had gone, he popped the top on the Corona and settled at his desk. He opened the directory for the jump drive. It held three icons, two folders and one file. He began clicking on files in the folders called Ops and AARs. "What on earth?"

The folders held all of the operational plans and after-action reports of the missions run by the Mighty Men during their time in Afghanistan. He rubbed his chin. Why would they have these? And why would they need them? He drew a blank and turned his attention to the file entitled Athena. It was a PDF. Huh? He clicked on it. The words *Top Secret Need to Know Only* popped up in bold red letters in a box, as did the space for a password. He'd seen no such thing on any of the other files.

He took a sip of beer. Nothing made sense anymore. Why would a jump drive show up with guns being run by Roy and his crew? Why did it have ops plans and AARs associated with the Mighty Men when those quickly became irrelevant? And just what did the Athena file contain that required a password?

Regardless, he didn't have time to ponder it. He had to return that drive before Nicole and Roy finished playing pool. Jonathan opened his safe and retrieved the jump drive holding Bryson's notes from his investigation. He copied the AARs and ops plans onto them. He highlighted the Athena file to copy it. The computer beeped.

File cannot be copied.

Jonathan rose and paced the living area. He sorted through what he had and added this new bit of information. Twenty-four people dead, including Christine after the Taliban had singled her out. Guns being skimmed and run through the compound to the Taliban by Roy and company. Four people, including Roy and Nicole, who could have cared less about the memorial service. A jump drive full of operational information related to the Mighty Men and a mysterious file called Athena.

Christine had died a cruel and senseless death. All because Roy and Nicole wanted to earn some extra cash and betray them at the same time. He slammed his fist into the closet door.

He had to keep that drive.

Boss Man's words from the butt-chewing the two days before rang in his ears. "You are too personally involved in the investigation. Stay out of it and let Bishop handle it. You hear me?"

Not this time. Jonathan's fingers tightened around the bottle. His gaze slid to that picture of Christine and him together. Even then, he could still smell the lilac perfume she'd worn.

He hurled the bottle at the cinder block wall next to the television. It shattered, raining pieces of clear glass onto the floor and leaving a trail of golden liquid running down the cream paint.

This time, I'm helping.

He'd make sure they paid for her death.

No matter what.

7

Ghazni Province, Afghanistan

Still tingling with afterglow, Nicole strolled into the cool foyer of the administrative building and up the stairs to the second floor. Most of it had something to do with the rather pleasant night spent with Roy. The other part? That came with knowing that within a couple of weeks, she'd be one very rich woman.

Across from the stairs lay the break area. Someone had already started the coffee, so she located her mug in the dishwasher and leaned against the wall to wait for it to finish perking.

"Staring at it won't make it perk any faster," a male voice commented.

Ward. He stood in the doorway with his own mug in hand.

She appraised him with a sharp glance. Lines between his eyes and on his brow had aged him. Could it be he had some gray appearing in his mussed blond hair?. But his eyes were what disturbed her. Red tinged the green. And that look when he met her gaze? Molten anger.

She took an automatic step back. "And top of the morning to you."

He shrugged and broke his gaze.

Had she imagined that anger?

The coffeemaker coughed out the last few drops.

He picked up the carafe. "Coffee?"

"Uh, thanks." She forced a smile to her face. Once he poured hers, she took her time with the cream and sugar and watched him out of the corner of her eye.

He wordlessly filled his own mug and stepped into the hall. A door slammed a moment later.

For sure, he was angry.

How much did he know? How could he know anything? She knew from the conversation she'd overheard between him and Boss Man a couple of days before that all they'd found was rifle that had misfired.

She shrugged and continued to her office. Several papers rested in the box outside her door. She snagged those and stepped inside. Once logged into the system, she sorted through the order requests. She had one for the mess hall. Boy, did the guys here know how to eat. Another one had come from the HVAC guys requesting parts in preparation for the harsh summer looming in a few weeks. She also noted the stack of invoices Ward had developed for all of the protective details they'd run in March. The one from three days before was obviously absent. He must have come in early to work that morning. At least now she had everything she needed for the quarterly report.

As she began generating orders to their vendors, voices distracted her. Not from the hall but echoing through the vent between her office and Boss Man's.

Ward was there. His voice rose and fell like it drifted on an ocean current. "Case…breakthrough…guns."

She stopped typing, closed the door, and shut the blinds over the floor-to-ceiling window beside the door. Like she had so many times before, she knelt at the vent and listened.

Ward was speaking. "We've found enough evidence to clearly show that Roy Wildman, Cal Bacon, Frisco Montoya, and Nicole Chardet are running guns through this compound."

"What kind of evidence?"

"Altered orders. Jeb always gives Nicole his orders. Then when she places the order with Mark Rifles, she changes it to be more than that but still below the number that would trigger it having to go through the home office. The shipments come in early evening. Roy, Cal, or Frisco always goes with the truck to pick them up."

"I'm not sure when they'd have opportunity to take out the guns." Someone, most likely Boss Man, drummed their fingers on a desk.

"That's the beauty of it. They get in so late that Jeb doesn't pop the crate until the next day. That's plenty of time for them to take out the difference."

"If he keeps them under lock and key, how do they get in?"

"Keys are easy to copy. All Nicole has to do is to swap out an order forged in Jeb's handwriting to match the altered order she sends to Mark Rifles and their resulting invoice. And since it doesn't go through the home office, no one is the wiser for it." She could almost feel Ward's satisfaction.

Nicole gripped her knees and bent so her ear was closer to the vent.

Something tapped on a desk, most likely a pencil. She silently rooted for Boss Man to dismiss the whole thing as a figment of Ward's imagination. Finally, the CEO spoke. "You have pictures?"

"I do."

A computer chimed.

Boss Man muttered a curse word. "Where did you take these?"

"In her cellar. There's fifty rifles in all. And you can see our logo stamped on the muzzle along with the shipment number. When I added that number to those on original orders that Jeb turned in, they equaled what she ordered. My theory is that they get a little each time to avoid suspicion. Then when they have enough, they do a trade."

"I—I don't believe this."

"Sir, it's more than that," Ward said.

"Then what? What else did you find?" Boss Man sounded like someone who'd already received too much bad news.

"It's not what. It's motive."

"Spit it out."

"I think the ambush was a way to cover the fact that Christine had found out about the gunrunning."

"What? Come again?"

A chair creaked, and Nicole envisioned Ward leaning forward as he tried to convince the CEO that he had a case. "Maybe she went down to the basement. Found the guns. She confronted Roy about them, and he knew he had to get rid of her. So he paid off his client, and they murdered her along with twenty-three other individuals. Only they got greedy and singled her out by murdering her in a different manner because she was stabbed when the rest were shot. At some point, they pulled off her helmet and undid her hair. Maybe to confirm who she was? We don't know. Maybe Roy fingered her as a target, but we can't be sure. I do think she knew something."

"You have proof of that?"

Ward sighed. "No, sir. Not right now. Only the fact that the night before the convoy, I could tell she wanted to talk to me about something. Then she backed off."

"I see." Though he didn't sound convinced. "Your pics seem to show that you might be right. Who do you think is the ringleader?"

"Probably Roy. Or Nicole."

"Chardet? You're crazy."

"Am I? She's capable."

Heat rose in Nicole's chest at the words.

Boss Man shot out a breath. "She was vetted just as much as you and I were. You understand?"

"I know."

"What's Bishop's opinion on this?"

Jonathan cleared his throat. "He agrees."

A chair creaked. "Did he do the work?"

"Most of it. I wanted to search for the guns myself."

"I still think your personal involvement with Parker is impeding your judgment."

The conversation bounced back and forth, and it sounded as if Ward had begun convincing Boss Man at least to search the basement.

Nicole's hands balled into fists. Panic turned the coffee she'd drunk acidic. She tried to straighten, but the blood had drained from her lower legs. She wound up in a sitting position against the wall beside the vent. Her breath came in small, whispered gasps.

She had to call Roy.

Now.

Grasping the edge of her desk, she hauled herself to her feet. If Boss Man saw the guns in the basement, the four of them would leave the compound in cuffs. Ward would be glad to be the one to slap them on her wrists.

She snatched her cell phone from her desk and dialed Roy's number. "Answer me. Now!"

He did on the third ring. "Hey, baby."

Metal clanged, and several guys laughed in the background. He had to be at the gym pumping iron since he didn't have a meeting until that afternoon.

"Are you alone?"

"With Cal."

"Listen to me. I only have time to say this once."

"What's wrong?"

She outlined what she'd overheard through the vent. "He's on to us. You've got to get those rifles gone. Understand? If he finds them…"

She cringed at the potential ramifications.

"We're going over there now. Where should I stash them?"

"I don't care. Anywhere. Just not in the cellar. Ward will be so focused there that he won't think to look somewhere else."

"I've got the perfect place."

"I don't care. Just go." She blew out an impatient breath and tossed her phone onto the desk. She collapsed onto her chair and picked up her coffee mug. The dark liquid trembled.

She'd know very soon about how successful they were.

Ghazni Province, Afghanistan

"I've laid out everything I've got." Jonathan swallowed hard. He'd done it. He'd found the evidence needed to send Roy, Nicole, and the others out of the compound in cuffs. Satisfaction flowed through him like endorphins after a hard workout.

Boss Man speared him with his intense blue gaze. "You're sure about this."

"Positive."

"All right." He continued flipping the wooden pencil through his fingers, just as he had the entire time Jonathan had spoken. "And you're sure Wildman is the ringleader?"

"Either him or Nicole. You know they're a couple. The weapons are in the cellar of the women's building. She drew up the orders. She has the ability and means to fake a manifest or to give Roy the access. She also has the ability to swap out files as needed."

The pencil in Boss Man's fingers snapped, and he tossed the pieces into the trash. "I hear you. Anything else?"

The jump drive. He had yet to say anything about it. As if warning him to keep silent, a cold feeling washed over him. He shook his head.

"Why don't you and I have a chat with Chardet and check out the cellar?" Boss Man rose and stepped into the hall to her closed door. He tapped on it. At her muffled reply, he opened it. "Chardet, you have a moment?"

"Uh, sure." She cocked a perfectly coiffed eyebrow and hit a key on her computer. "What's up?"

"Ward here has some serious concerns."

"Oh?" She studied him with narrowed eyes as she pushed back from her desk. She ran her hands down her black hair, which she'd pulled into a ponytail. "Why do I think these 'serious concerns' involve me?"

"They do." Boss Man cleared his throat. He spread his legs and crossed his arms. "You see, he thinks you and Roy are running some guns through this compound."

Nicole's gaze hardened as she focused on Jonathan. "Really? You think I'd do that." Her question came out more as a statement.

"Is it true?" Boss Man demanded.

Jonathan fought the urge to roll his eyes. His CEO seemed more interested in saving his legacy than anything else.

"I find the accusation ridiculous and groundless, as if, thanks to his Christian convictions, he has to crucify someone, even an innocent person."

She studied him. "I think *Jonathan* is angry and upset that his girlfriend was one of the ones killed. I think his grief is impeding his judgment."

"Leave Christian out of this," he snarled. "This is the result of detective work, not some crusade of mine."

"Where's your evidence?"

"We have enough to take a look at the cellar in your building," Boss Man told her. "Now."

She glared at them for a moment longer. Then she sighed as if they were asking her to walk to Kabul in one day. She snatched her sunglasses from the blotter and headed toward the door. "You're wasting your time."

"I'm not so sure about that." Jonathan followed her.

"Whatever," she muttered.

She led the way downstairs and into a bright morning already heating up as the sun began its scorching march across the sky. Within seconds they arrived at the Women's Building and stepped into the relative coolness of the foyer. "Go ahead. Search the cellar all you want."

She opened the door and gave a mock bow.

Jonathan led the way downstairs. He cut on the light.

"By the way, did you have a search warrant to come down here?" Acid laced her question.

"Don't need one," Jonathan told her. "Afghan soil, you see."

"Yeah, right." She snorted.

He marched over to the storage unit where he'd found the guns and flipped up the lid.

Nothing but blackness.

"Wrong unit, Ward?" Nicole's voice taunted him.

He slammed the lid on the next unit, then dove to another. Empty.

"They were here. I swear they were all here. I saw them with my own eyes!"

Boss Man's face had turned bright red. Tendons bulged at his neck, and a vein pulsed at his temple under his gray buzz cut.

"Chardet, please forgive the inconvenience. You may return to work. Ward, to my office."

Jonathan kept his focus on Nicole.

Boss Man turned and stomped up the stairs.

Before Jonathan could move, Nicole shoved him into the wall. She crammed against him so close that coffee intermingling with stale smoke on her breath filled his nostrils. Her manicured nails dug like claws into his arms.

He winced, sure that dents would remain in his arm like tattoos.

"It's nice to know you think so highly of me as to falsely accuse me of running guns and murdering your girlfriend. Maybe next time, you'll pick your battles more wisely." She released him. "Now get out of *my* house."

"You can't hide the truth, Nicole. No matter what, you can't, even if you think you have." With that parting taunt, Jonathan stomped upward and into the hot morning toward the administrative.

Boss Man waited for him.

When he arrived, the CEO slammed his door so hard that a commendation from Marine Corps fell from the wall, shattering on the floor. Expletives whistled past like shells going downrange.

"I've had it with you, Ward. Understand?"

"Yes, sir. But I saw—"

"I don't care what you saw."

"The pictures—"

"Didn't you hear me? I. Don't. Care. How do I know you didn't fabricate them? It's clear to me that your connection to Parker clouded your judgment. You went on a witch hunt. You desperately wanted someone to take the fall, and Chardet made an easy target."

"Sir, if I may, you wanted us to work fast. Bryson and I did—"

"Shut up, Ward. Just *shut up*. Who searched for the guns?"

"I did," he muttered.

"When I specifically told you to let Bishop do the work to avoid precisely *this*." Boss Man leaned with both of his hands on the desk and glared at him. "You are done. Finished. You hear me? This case is closed since it's clear that you disobeyed a direct order and are biased."

"Bryson can finish this."

"No, Bishop is done too. You got that? You're to hand over all evidence to me. All electronic files are to be put on a DVD, removed from the server, and handed off to me. You understand? Hard copies will come to me. The same for him. I want everything."

"Sir—"

"You're done here at the compound. And I mean done. Off all work. Matter of fact, you're confined to the compound. Any sign of you leaving, and I'll have Bishop toss your butt into the brig. I don't care if you two are good friends. You can stew in your own juices until you leave. And when we get back to Chesapeake, I personally am going to file a complaint with Wyatt Edwards. He'll have your head for this."

"But sir—"

More expletives flew in his direction. Boss Man pointed at the door. "Get out and stay out. I don't want to see your butt in this building again until the handover meeting with the new team."

Jonathan stared at him for one last, long moment.

The CEO didn't break his gaze.

As if at a formal changing of the guard, he did a crisp about face and crossed to the door in one long stride. His head spun as he stumbled to his room. He collapsed onto the couch.

He'd been discredited. Somehow, Nicole had found out about his search and had gotten someone—most likely Roy and his cronies—to move the guns. He thought about asking Boss Man to search the remainder of the Women's Building, but he knew where that would lead.

Precisely nowhere.

"God, I was so sure," he murmured into the stillness. "Where did I go wrong?"

He lowered his head and rubbed the back of his neck as his thoughts turned to almost seven years ago to the day in 2009 when the Mighty Men had been hit. He'd wondered the same thing then as he'd sat on his bunk that night and relived the horror of watching his ten closest friends die.

He leaned over and picked up a picture from the half wall that separated the sitting area from the sleeping area. It was of the Mighty Men, taken sometime in Afghanistan shortly before what he called his Hell Year began. Twelve men crouched in a semicircle. All held rifles and wore confident smiles. They knew they were cool.

Only he and David survived that fateful day.

Here he was again, having lost something significant—his credibility.

Unless...

Nicole's taunt echoed in his mind. "It's nice, Ward, to know you think so highly of me as to falsely accuse me of running guns and murdering your girlfriend."

His lips turned upward the tiniest bit.

She had tipped her hand.

Somehow, she'd learned that he'd suspected the ambush was a case of murder, something he'd revealed only to Boss Man.

The second thing?

He still had an ace up his sleeve.

The jump drive.

His smile dimmed. Was Boss Man friend or foe? Was he in with Nicole? He was pretty certain he wasn't and was only a man concerned about a tarnished spot on his record that Jonathan's discovery had threatened to dirty even further.

He needed more evidence to convince the CEO.

Something to show that Nicole was the gunrunner.

And a murderer.

The problem was, he had no way to get it now.

8

"I don't trust myself anymore." Abigail moved her rum and Coke in little circles on the dark wood of the bar. Free friend therapy. That's what she called it. A chance to catch up with her best friend in college while having drinks at her favorite pub near her apartment. The raucous blues music wafting over the speakers fit her mood perfectly.

Gabrielle Stanton cocked her head as she studied her. "Why do you say that?"

"Do you know how many dates I've been on since Nick and I split?"

Her friend shrugged.

"Two." Abigail held up two fingers. "That's it."

"Have you talked to him at all?"

"Nick? No way! Uh-uh. The last time we saw each other was January 2010 when he stormed out of the courtroom after our divorce proceedings. He'd moved down to North Carolina and started with the Raleigh Police Department shortly before that. Good thing Raleigh's a big town." She sighed. "But seriously, it's like ever since then, I haven't trusted my judgment."

Over the speakers, the saxophone wailed as if to agree with her. Lost love. She wanted to jump onto the small stage where bands sometimes played and sing her own version of the blues.

"I think you're being too hard on yourself." Gabrielle took a sip of her martini and set it on the bar. "Look. I think you learned something from your time with him."

"Yeah, like how to pick cheaters."

"Abigail."

"Sorry. I know better than to lump all members of the male species into one category. It's not that I don't trust them. It's just that..." She threw her hands into the air. "I don't know."

"Sometimes, you've simply got to take the chance. Like with that guy over there." Gabrielle nodded in the direction of the pool table. "Every opportunity he's had, he's been looking this way, and I promise it's not me he's interested in."

Abigail glanced toward the pool tables, where several guys, Marines it seemed from their haircuts, drank and knocked balls around the table.

An especially tall specimen of male, with blond hair and muscular build lined up a shot and took it. Once he finished, he turned his attention toward the bar. He winked.

Her cheeks warmed. "You sure he's not looking at you?"

"Hah, I rather doubt it." Gabrielle grinned. Then she sobered as she refocused her attention on Abigail. "Okay. Here's a quick story. Shane and I got married twelve years ago, right?"

"Yeah. I was maid of honor, remember?"

"Oh, I do. Talk about a fun weekend." They giggled, and she continued, "I knew I wanted children, but I doubted my abilities, especially since I'd been an only child and had never babysat in my life. I procrastinated for years. Shane, bless him, didn't push me. Finally, he asked me what I was so scared of. I told him exactly what you said earlier. I didn't trust myself to be a good mom. That's when he said something that stuck to me. Essentially, taking a big step like that takes faith. And faith is trust in action. You're trusting that God will guide you."

"But my heart is so deceptive."

"That's why you stay close to God." Her phone rang, and she glanced at it. "Speak of the munchkins, that's Shane. Let me say goodnight to the

64

boys. Then we can plan the rest of our weekend. And maybe your man will come over and chat while I'm gone."

"He's not my man...yet," Abigail added when she realized how Captain Hunk had noted her friend's departure. She imagined the little report going on in his brain.

Scout to base. The target is now alone.

She fought a giggle, especially when the corner of his mouth lifted in a smile.

Her phone chirped, signaling a text from her brother. After a week of silence, he'd finally written. Her brain made the calculation. He'd written at five in the morning his time.

"Pray for me," his message said.

She paused. What a strange and not-so-strange request, all at the same time. "You know I do," she typed. "And what are you doing up so early?"

A few seconds passed before her phone beeped. 'Seriously. Things have gotten bad. The convoy was a cover for Christine's murder. I've been discredited."

She caught her breath as she digested the message. She tapped out her reply. "I don't understand."

Almost a minute passed, and she imagined him feverishly beating out a response on his phone. "I found guns. So gunrunning. They got wise to me and hid them, which discredited me. Now I'm confined to the compound. Boss Man crushed the investigation."

Abigail's thumbs raced across the screen.

Another message from Jonathan popped up before she could finish. "I found a jump drive with the guns. It had a file called Athena on it that seems to be a Top Secret Need to Know file. It couldn't be copied, so I had to keep the drive."

Her heart began hammering. "Are you safe?"

The reply was slow in coming, almost as if he doubted the words he typed. "I believe so. But pray for me."

"I will," she murmured. She typed out, "I love you," then placed the phone with its blackened screen on the bar. She pressed her fingers to her mouth. *Jonathan, please, please stay safe. I wish there was a way I could help, I mean more than praying.*

"You got another Dark Dog IPA?" a deep voice asked.

She jumped.

Captain Hunk leaned against the bar and signaled the bartender.

Abigail ripped her mind back to the present. Oh, yeah. Blue eyes, just like she'd imagined. Her nose twitched at the smell of his cologne. Had she started salivating?

Down, girl.

He smiled at her. "Sorry. I didn't mean to startle you."

"No, no. Just...texting with my brother." A flush started low in her neck.

"You come here a lot?"

Oh, boy. This was not the conversation she wanted to have, not after Jonathan's news. She forced a smile to her face.

"She does," Gabrielle said as she joined them. She stuck out her hand. "Gabrielle Stanton. Visiting Abigail here for a girls' weekend away before my husband and kids get here to look for housing. He's transferring to Quantico with the Marines."

Captain Hunk handed over his credit card to the bartender, then gave her his full attention. "Rick Hamrick. So Abigail, do you have a last name?"

"Uh, yeah." Boy, could she sound any dumber? "It's Ward."

"Well, Abigail Ward," Rick took the receipt and scribbled his signature, chatting while he wrote, "if you're going to stick around, would you and Gabrielle like to join my buddy and me for a couple of games of pool?"

"Yes," Gabrielle answered before Abigail could open her mouth.

Abigail shot her a dirty look.

"We'll be done with our present game in about fifteen." His gaze never leaving Abigail, he smiled again before swaggering to his table with beer in hand.

"Way to let me talk." Abigail scowled.

"Sorry. I just couldn't pass up that opportunity for you." Gabrielle leaned closer. "What's going on? You look like you wanted to run screaming out the door."

"Jonathan texted." In terse words, she rehashed the conversation.

"Oh, wow. I'm sorry." Gabrielle shook her head. "I overstepped, and I apologize. Look. If you want to sneak out, I'm sure we can. It's not like we're obligated to pool, especially since I stink at pool."

"No, I'm fine." She sighed and ordered another rum and Coke. "What I'm worried about is how Jonathan came into the possession of a Top Secret file."

"Do you think that they'd figure he stole it?"

"It's possible. But there's only one way for that file to be stolen from government servers because there's so many tripwires and firewalls in place. That's to have TSNTK clearance. He certainly wouldn't have that. Nor would any of the gunrunners, most likely, since they're all civilians. And from what he's said in the past, no one there is a computer geek."

"So someone in the Armed Forces."

"Or at least with the needed clearance." Suddenly, she realized the enormity of what she now knew. "I need to tell Sal."

"Who?"

"Salvador Torres. He's my CO here at CID. I'm just…I don't want to get Jonathan in trouble."

"I'd say that either way, your brother's in trouble."

"I know." Abigail rubbed her forehead to erase the frown lines. "I know."

Quantico, Virginia

Monday morning, Abigail slouched at her desk at CID headquarters and scrolled through the news websites. Even after a week and a half, any mention of the hit on the convoy in Afghanistan had faded in the minds of the general public in favor of news about the Kardashians and the ongoing presidential primaries. Of course, the rest of the world wasn't as intimately familiar with the incident as she was.

And what could she do about it? Absolutely nothing right now. Jonathan was coming home in a week, and when she headed to Raleigh on leave to see him, they'd sort it out.

In an effort to dispel her worries, she released a sigh and inhaled the steam from the fresh brew of Kona coffee she'd prepared a few minutes after her arrival. Gabrielle's words to her before she'd left for work that morning made her smile. "Take each day on faith. If Rick calls you like he promised, great. If not, that's okay too."

"'Tis true, my friend," Abigail now murmured. Maybe she'd have some news when she met Gabrielle and her family for lunch before they began their house hunt.

She took a sip of coffee as and turned her thoughts once more to her brother's predicament. By pilfering a Top Secret file called Athena, he'd put himself square in the middle of a heap of trouble from both the right and the wrong sides of the law.

She had to tell Sal.

Leaving her phone on her desk, she rose and headed toward his office. No Sal. She checked her watch. Seeing that it was almost 0745 hours, he was probably preparing for the weekly briefing.

Bingo.

She found her CO standing behind the podium of a small auditorium that could hold fifty people. Lieutenant Colonel Salvador Torres frowned as he stared at the laptop and then at the large monitor on the wall. He grunted as he hit several buttons.

Abigail cleared her throat. "Sir."

His dark eyes shot up and met hers. "Abigail, good morning. What do you know about AV equipment?"

"I wasn't the class pet in elementary school, so not much."

He cocked an eyebrow. "Oh?"

"The class pets got to be the AV kids." She stepped around and surveyed the laptop. Its screen glowed with a PowerPoint presentation while the monitor remained blank.

He laughed. "This has greatly perplexed me." He hit another key, one which made the presentation go live on the monitor but blacked out the computer's screen. He sighed and rubbed his hands through his short, dark hair, mussing it in the process. "I'm sorry. You seem like you have something on your mind."

"I do. Something came up." She glanced at the open door. Since it was only 0745 hours, no one had arrived yet. "You know about what happened with the convoy in Ghazni week before last?"

"You said it was your brother's company that got hit."

"It was." She leaned against the table where he'd placed each person's file of assignments for that week. "Bryson Bishop now works at that compound, and he's the one who investigated. Apparently, he's come to the conclusion that the hit was a cover for the murder of Jonathan's girlfriend."

"Bryson Bishop." His focus not leaving the laptop's screen, he rubbed his chin. "Why do I know that name?"

"He was my sergeant here until early 2012 when he mustered out. I recommended to Jonathan that he hire him as the head of security for the compound. I'm sure he's run a good investigation about the hit because he always did here."

"That's interesting." He hit a few more keys. He muttered under his breath.

"Sir, it's more than that." She fought the temptation to shut the laptop's lid to make him pay attention. "Jonathan did find guns. He also found a jump drive with the guns. A file on it, called Athena, had a TSNTK clearance. Do we know anything about that?"

That got his attention. "Athena, you say?"

"Uh, yeah." Something uncurled within her, something she could only term as unease. Why? Was it because Sal had gone from completely distracted to focused within the span of a second? "He said it couldn't be copied, so he had to take it."

"Your brother has the file?"

She could have sworn his voice rose with the question. "Yes. But he got discredited by the gunrunners. I—I didn't know if it was something I could help—"

"It is CID's case, and you're to leave it alone."

"But, sir, I'm available, and—"

Sal slammed the lid. "Didn't you hear me? I've already assigned this to the Computer Crimes Unit. They'll handle it."

"I can—"

"Don't you have enough work to do already?" Anger hardened his voice. "From what I remember, I've yet to see your AAR from Georgia. Plus a few others. And you have leave in a week."

"I know, but from what it sounds like, this is important. What's it about?"

"Abigail!" He advanced on her. "Listen to me. I said that the case has been assigned. To someone else, that is. I appreciate the information, but I want you to stand down. You understand?" His fine, very lightly accented English ripped into her like bullets. "You are to let CCU handle it. I don't even want you asking Al, Mark, or anyone else about it. If I hear you have, I will consider that in direct disobedience to my order, and I don't think you want that in your file, now do you?"

She shrank away. No, she didn't, not after almost losing her career once. "Uh, no sir. I, um, I'd, well, I'd better go and get my notepad."

"That you should." He returned to the podium and muttered something as he raised the lid.

She stepped to the door.

"And, Abigail."

She turned.

Sal stared at her, his eyes an obsidian color that did nothing to obscure the power radiating from them. "I'm glad we have an understanding."

A chill washed over her, and she shivered slightly as she retreated to her office. Had she fallen down a rabbit hole or something? Normally, nothing rattled Sal, but a few minutes ago, he'd essentially threatened her. Why? Who knew? Rather than contemplate the reason for her CO's anger, she reached for her phone and smiled at a text from Rick.

"Good morning, beautiful. You want to go for a run together after work?"

Her mood lifted a little as she remembered the way he'd flirted with her. Thing was, she'd responded and had even given him her phone number. She tapped out her response. "Absolutely. Let's talk this afternoon."

Her phone began ringing.

Gabrielle.

"Abigail, hey," her friend gushed when she answered. "Shane called. They'll be picking me up at eleven, and we'll meet you at 11:30 for lunch. How does that sound?"

"Um, fine. I'm...already ready for lunch."

"You are—wait. Are you okay?"

She stared at her doorway. A couple of coworkers strolled down the hallway, chatting on their way to the briefing. "I'm...not sure. I think my commanding officer just shut me down. Big time."

9

Burning Tree, Utah

David lay under the massive sink next to the dishwasher at Kyra Lane Cafe and Restaurant, the restaurant Kyra owned with her business partner, Lisa Lane. He'd run the new water line from the valve to the faucet, and now all he needed to do was to connect it. Problem was, the nut was located in an area where he couldn't use his left hand. And thanks to his broad shoulders in a tight space, he had no room to maneuver his entire right arm, only his wrist.

He worked the wrench. Hopefully it would be tight enough now.

He pulled back, reached over, and twisted the valve.

Water squirted from the connection.

He grumbled irritably and jammed the valve closed.

"Are you okay?" Kyra's voice floated to him from somewhere above.

"I didn't get it tight enough." He snatched up the wrench, settled it around the nut, and twisted the blasted thing with a strength reinforced with his frustration. After all this time, his grip was still weak and grew weaker with every failed attempt to tighten the nut.

He might as well have greased the metal handle with lard. The wrench slipped and belted him across the neck right at the scar from the bullet nick...

The Incident, as he called it. Seven years ago. The day when ten of his closest friends had died. His adopted little sister and her family as well. Tomorrow marked that awful day.

Kyra tapped him on the leg. "Let me try."

"I can—"

"Seriously. I'm smaller than you. Let me try."

At least she hadn't pointed out that her grip at that moment was probably three times stronger than his. With a grunt of acknowledgment, he squirmed from underneath the sink and pushed himself upright.

Kyra, still dressed as a manager in dark slacks and silky blue top, knelt beside him.

"You'll mess up your outfit."

"That's what washing machines are for. Where's the wrench?"

Almost reluctantly, he handed it to her. At five-three, she was a much better candidate than he to be under the sink. As she worked, he mopped his face with a towel and tossed it aside.

"Okay. I think I got it. The valve's on, and no water's leaking."

"That's a good sign. Let me try the faucet now." He raised his right arm and grasped the lip of the sink. His useless hand simply slid off the metal. This time, he kept the foul word inside his head as he used his left hand. No problem there except that his left leg barked at him a little.

Curse The Incident.

He offered a hand to Kyra, and she rose as if climbing under sinks were an everyday occurrence for her.

She stared at the piles of dirty dishes and the empty shelves where they should have gone. According to her report when she'd called him up frantic at 8:30, the fitting between the faucet and waterline had broken on one of the busiest, most crucial nights of the year since the restaurant hosted a rehearsal dinner as well as regular customers. The guy doing the dish washing only had time to shut the water off to avoid flooding the kitchen. David had offered to fix it for her, and after ensuring that the neighbors would watch his nephews and niece, he'd stopped at the hotel to gather his supplies before heading to the restaurant. In the meantime, business had continued, and fortunately, the dishes had lasted until every last item had been used.

His sister rubbed her eyes. "I guess I need to do these."

"Can't your staff help?"

"I'd have to pay them overtime, and honestly, we can't afford that right now. And with that bridesmaids breakfast and the wedding being a Friday event..." She hung her head.

"Let me help, then."

"But the kids—"

"Rod and Daisy are watching them. I'll rinse. You fill the racks."

A weary smile crossed her face. "Thanks."

For the first few rounds, they worked in comfortable silence. At least on the outside. Inside, David's gut churned like the dishwasher's motor. He couldn't seem to stop the thoughts about The Incident now pouring through his head. What had happened to that contentment from a couple of weeks ago when he'd spent the morning with Little Bit?

Bingo.

Ever since then, since Kyra had suggested that he contact Jonathan and offer his condolences, David had lost his peace. Her suggestion stalked him. He'd fled from it by working longer hours than needed or working out harder than he normally did. When he fell into bed each night, exhaustion had stunned him into a dreamless sleep.

"Did you ever try to call Abigail Ward?" Kyra asked.

Oh, great. Did she have to bring that up? Again? "Uh, no. I wouldn't know where to start, you know?"

"The Army. They have a personnel office. It's easy."

"So says you."

She filled a couple of trays of glasses and slid them into the dishwasher. She shut the door and started it. "I know it's easy because I took the liberty of calling them and getting her number. I've got it at the house."

David's mouth worked, but no sound came out. Finally, he found his voice. "You went behind my back?"

"I wouldn't say that." She turned to the two racks of plates and began drying and stacking them. "I knew you wouldn't, so I did. And it's not like I called her."

"I don't appreciate that."

She shrugged. "Maybe not, but I still think you need to call her to get Jonathan's—"

"I don't *need* to do anything. Especially anything like that." He picked up a plate. Carefully, completely opposite of what he wanted to do, he dried it and set it on the counter.

"Like I said two weeks ago, Jonathan's your best friend. And he saved your life."

The image of briefly coming to in a sea of pain flashed before his eyes. That bright light from an operating room lamp seared his soul like it had his vision seven years before. He flinched.

Kyra had her back to him as she set the plates on a shelf, so she didn't notice.

"I don't care."

The dishwasher beeped, and she turned toward it. "What?"

"I said I don't care. He doesn't need my sympathy, and I'm not going to give it."

"David, honestly, I think—"

"You know what?" He threw down his towel. "I'm done here. It's been a long day, and I need to crash."

Her gaze shot to the four twelve-high piles of plates, scads of dirty silverware, and remaining glasses. "But, I need—"

"I don't care. I'm sick of discussing this. And since you seem intent on doing so, I'm out of here. Good night." With that, he stomped from the restaurant.

His anger kept him warm only for the first twenty feet as he strode along the path winding behind his parents' resort. As he passed between the river and the terrace, the memories of that day two weeks before sank into his soul. The sound of the mason jar shattering echoed in his ears. A chill of guilt swept over him. He should have stayed.

No, then Kyra would have pummeled him again and again about how he should call Jonathan. He shoved away the thought and followed the path as it turned toward the highway. Within minutes he opened the gate to the backyard.

Ranger whined as he joined his master.

"Hey, boy." David knelt and worked his fingers through the dog's thick fur.

Ranger rewarded him by swiping his tongue across his cheek.

"C'mon. Let's head upstairs." He headed up the steps to his apartment. Already, he dreamed of crashing on his rack and catching a solid night's worth of Zs, just like he'd done the past several nights.

Not this time.

Eleven came. Then midnight. Guilt surged as he listened carefully through his open windows for signs that Kyra had returned. He should have stayed and helped. He settled for staring at the ceiling as he studiously worked to keep his mind blank.

Shortly before one, the front door opened and closed. Below, Kyra greeted Rod. Then the door shut again, and silence reigned. Or did he did he hear the smallest sound of a sniffle?

David turned onto his stomach and clamped the pillow over his head. *Kyra, I'm sorry.* He had to make it up to her, but he didn't see a way to do so. He'd work on it. Later.

10

Burning Tree, Utah

David awoke before dawn with a headache. Rather than follow his normal morning routine, he popped a couple of aspirin to ward it off. He pulled on a pair of cycling pants and a shirt with a fleece over it. With his hair pulled back at the nape of his neck and his shoes in his hands, he crept down the stairs. Once in the silent kitchen, he filled his backpack with water bottles for him and Ranger, lunch for him, and dog treats for Ranger. He needed to get away and think on his day of mourning The Incident.

He tiptoed outside and to the shed where he kept his mountain bike. With his helmet on and Ranger beside him, he walked it down the driveway. Only the sound of his cycling shoes scraping against the concrete reached him.

With Ranger trotting beside him, he glided into town and to the restaurant. He slid his key from the back pocket of his shirt and let himself inside, where he flipped on the light. And stared. Kyra had done more than finish the dishes. Now, snowy white tablecloths adorned twelve tables. The nice china they'd washed the night before gleamed creamy white with deep red and gold rims. Freshly washed silverware sparkled, and goblets waited to be filled. Stunned, he wandered into the kitchen. Not a dirty dish remained anywhere. She'd even taken out the garbage.

Man, he felt like a Class-A jerk. What was he—a two-year-old? No, even toddlers behave better than he had last night. He owed Kyra a super-sized apology.

Retreat to his sacred spot had turned into a fantastic idea, especially as his internal darkness pressed closer. After locking the door, he rode toward the highway heading south of town. Only a few lights glowed in some homes, and the outlines of the buildings came clear as the day began getting dressed in the gentle pinks, oranges, and yellows of dawn.

The chilly air raised goose bumps along his arms as he turned south onto State Road 15, which led toward ranch land full of soaring mesas and buttes. As soon as the lights from Burning Tree faded behind him, he turned onto a secondary road that meandered westward and paralleled the river when it once more crossed the highway.

He pedaled faster around the twists and curves, trying to drive away the memories that pursued him.

It didn't work.

They stung him like a swarm of Africanized honeybees.

"Who the hell do you think you are, Sergeant Shepherd?" Those words came from Tina, the Mighty Men's comms specialist Jessie's widow, at the PX that hot July day when he'd shopped for some chow and run into her.

"I don't remember anything," he'd told Abigail Ward-Bocelli and Bryson Bishop as he recovered at Lundstahl shortly after the Incident. *"Seriously. It's like I have no coherent thought after Captain called me to get the guys together."*

He shoved those thoughts from his mind and focused on making the turn onto the dirt road that led to the top of the mesa. For the next ten minutes, sucking precious air into his lungs and feeling his quads, glutes, and hamstrings burn took his mind off the day.

Once he leveled off, he pushed harder and harder against the pedals. His muscles trembled. His chest heaved. Thankfully, he'd been smart and used the gripper for his right hand. Ranger loped beside him, a faithful dog steadily keeping up with his master. David reached the barbed wire marking the border of his parents' land and gingerly passed over the cattle guard. He turned off the road and bumped over packed desert soil along a hiking path. Finally, it came into view.

The burning tree. The very one that had given the town its name.

He slowed to a stop several feet away and gazed at the massive hulk of blackened wood near the edge of the mesa. It stood over fifty feet tall, which had made it a prime target for a lightning strike. The hit had happened over a hundred years before, when his great-great grandfather arrived. According to legend, the tree had survived and gone on living until a few years ago.

Until the day of The Incident.

At least that's what Kyra told him because their father had gone there to weep shortly after he received news of The Incident.

Legs shaking from exhaustion, David released his right hand from the gripper, climbed from the bike, and laid it on the ground.

Beside him, Ranger whined.

"Sorry, boy." David eased the pack from his back and pulled out a collapsible bowl and a bottle. He poured some water. "Here you go."

As Ranger lapped it up with eager slurps, David remained in his crouch and stared at the tree. Not a green leaf grew on the charred branches.

A faint breeze washed over him. He swallowed hard as the memories crowded around him like evil ghosts. This time, his defenses had crumbled, and the darkness closed around him. He closed his eyes and bit down hard on his lip.

Captain's command to gather the Mighty Men echoed in his ears.

Mackie's laugh turned into his typical snort as they shared drinks one weekend night at Fort Bragg. The rest of the Mighty Men guffawed.

Then came a memory of passing around cigars when Oso, the Mighty Men's other ordnance sergeant, had announced the birth of his first child.

"Why, God? Why? Why?" He groaned and sank to his knees. The burning tree blurred through his tears.

David had awakened from the surgery in Germany to feel his father's hand in his.

The Mighty Men's CO, Captain, smiled as he shared a picture of his wife shortly after he'd taken command of the Mighty Men. "I know SF is a tough mistress, but I also know that marrying the right woman allows me not to worry about things at home."

David grimaced as his harsh words to Kyra the night before slammed into him. He hugged himself, willing the agony to lessen.

It didn't.

"You're weak." Tina's harsh words echoed in his mind. "You're no leader. You caused Jessie to die. You failed him and everyone on that mission."

"I didn't, God. I didn't. No!"

Ranger, who lounged in the shadow of a scrubby pinion pine, raised his head.

"What else could you have done?" Captain's widow had asked. Sadness tinged her smile as she stared at her now-empty house. "David, don't blame yourself. Please. And don't worry about me. Or any of us. God has us in the palm of His hand. It's hard to believe, but this did not surprise Him." She'd moved away the next day to be closer to her parents.

He rocked back and forth as his chest heaved. Tears streamed down his face. "Where were you, God? Where were you when that happened? We wanted to honor You! We had a job to do. We thought You were with us. But You weren't."

The accusation rang in the still air.

Only the crows cackled at his angst.

He collapsed onto the ground and clawed the hard soil. A sob escaped him.

"God was there, bro," Jonathan had said six months after The Incident on the one night they'd been brave enough to talk about it. "If not, no way would we have survived."

Now David cried into his hands. "Were You really there? I can't believe that."

He lay there for a few more minutes, his breathing shallow. He clung to the hard earth as if trying to survive a firefight. He forced his eyes open enough to stare at his right forearm. Those tattered words rippled as he clenched and unclenched his fists.

"You've been silent in my life for too long." His allegation against God came out as a growl in the still desert air. "How do You expect me to be in that pew with Kyra and the kids? How can I? You deserted me. Deserted us."

There. He'd said it. He'd laid out his reasoning for not going to church in seven years. Wasn't that enough?

David lay prostrate until a whine reached him. Ranger licked his cheek. That brought him back to reality. As he took a deep, wavering breath, he sat up, and the agony receded a little. "Thanks, boy. You saved me."

Ranger sat on his haunches and scooted so close to his master that his entire side touched him.

David put his arm around him.

Gradually, his pulse calmed. The agony burning in his soul receded. He dragged his backpack over and pulled out his lunch. As he ate, he surveyed the tree.

Still as dead as his comrades seven years in the grave.

He gazed down at his left leg. The cycling shorts ended a little above his knee. He ran his finger down the Lycra, tracing the crease left by the efforts of the combat surgeons to save his leg. The scar was a doozy.

Little Bit had seen it once. Rather than crying in terror, her mouth formed an "O." And her look? Utter fascination. David had grinned, tweaked her nose, and told her she'd make a great nurse one day.

"I'd like you to come to church with us," Kyra had said shortly after his return to Burning Tree.

His reaction? He'd told her to butt out. She had, but only after a few more attempts to roust him out of his apartment on Sunday mornings. His parents had tried the same thing but to no avail.

How could he step forward and embrace God and Jesus when so much had happened? Not when he'd lost ten of his closest friends. Brothers-in-arms. That was what they'd been. The best team ever.

The Mighty Men.

He'd needed to numb the pain, the feelings of failure. Both had led to his descent into addiction and subsequent homelessness that had lasted for nearly two years and left him with a lifelong reminder. If Kyra hadn't found him, he'd be dead by now.

He needed to apologize to her. And soon. The bridesmaid breakfast would be over. And by the time he arrived in town, so would lunchtime. He could have some of her iced tea that had a reputation all across central Utah. Maybe they could even sit on the patio in the shade and talk it out.

And as long as God stayed in His corner, David would stay in his.

11

Burning Tree, Utah

That night, a cool breeze blew through the open windows on the lower level of the Martin house. The lonely howl of a coyote floated on the evening air. Another answered from nearby.

David headed down the hall to make sure his nephews had turned out their lights as he'd requested.

Success. Both boys slept soundly.

He next checked on Little Bit. The child, born weeks after The Incident, remained snuggled underneath the quilt, her dark curls spilling across the pillow, the stuffed cat she'd had since she was a baby clutched in her arms.

He bent and smoothed the quilt around her before kissing her hair, then returned to the hall. A glow from the end distracted him. In her haste to change before heading for the restaurant to fill in for an ailing Lisa, Kyra must have left a lamp on. He stepped inside. Like the rest of the house, her room was neat. Her Keds sat in the open door of the closet. She'd draped the Capri pants and blouse she'd worn that day over the back of the chair at her dressing table, meaning she fully intended to wear them the next day.

The only thing out of place on the dresser and nightstands was the picture of Michael, her husband. It lay face-down on the bed as if she'd been gazing at it. He checked the garbage can beside the dresser. Several wadded up tissues with makeup on them littered the bottom. He finally connected the date to the significant event in her life.

Seven years ago today, the very same day as The Incident, Michael had died in a climbing accident in the Wasatch Mountains. Two highway patrolmen had paid Kyra a visit early the next morning.

"Where have you been?" Kyra's cry flew to him as quickly as her body had earlier that afternoon. "I've been worried *sick* about you!"

"I went cycling," David's smile faded as her heart hammered against him.

"You never bothered to tell me you were going somewhere. Do you know how much I freaked when I couldn't find you or Ranger? I thought you'd gone off and gotten hurt or something. Or—"

His sister pulled back and clamped her hand over her mouth.

The sheen of moisture across her eyes confused him.

"I biked to the burning tree like I always do on the anniversary."

"And you never told me." She jabbed her hands onto her hips as she glared at him. "You could have been killed, and I wouldn't have known where you were. Gee, thanks for scaring me to death!"

Now her tears and sharp questions made sense.

How could he have forgotten?

"I'm sorry," he murmured. "I was so wrapped up in remembering The Incident that I forgot how your suffering began seven years ago as well."

He vowed to make things right with her—about everything, not just his cluelessness from that day. Hopefully, the way he'd cleaned the house and washed the dogs would be a good start on his apology.

With Lilly the puppy toddling after him, he fixed himself a cup of peppermint tea and wandered onto the front porch. He took a deep breath, held it, and released it. Another anniversary had passed, and he'd survived. With a sigh, he eased onto one of the rockers.

Heels tapped on the sidewalk. A moment later, Kyra climbed the wooden steps and opened the gate that kept Lilly and Ranger from running into the road. She stood there, a weary figure in a black sheath, her short, dark curls still pinned back with a rhinestone clip. She eased from her heels and knelt to scratch the puppy on her head. "I'm beat."

"Want to join me?"

"You know? I think I will. Let me get comfortable." The door banged softly shut as she stepped inside.

A truck rumbled past on the two-lane highway in front of their house. Then came a car, followed by a silence only found in the desert. From somewhere in the distance across the river, another coyote howled.

"Much better." Kyra joined him, and a deep sigh escaped her lips as she sank onto the porch swing perpendicular to the rocker. She wore a pair of sweats and a sweatshirt to ward off the chill. "I'm totally wiped out. Did the kids go down okay?"

"Yeah. We washed not one dog but two."

"I'll bet Ranger liked that." A smile tipped her lips upwards.

"He only thinks he doesn't like being clean." David rocked back and forth.

She set her mug on a side table and picked up Lilly to nuzzle her fur.

Time to apologize. He couldn't procrastinate any longer. He took a deep breath. "Hey, Kyra?"

She glanced at him. "What's up?"

"I have an apology—no, apologies—to make. I'm sorry about last night. I was…"

"A jerk?"

He grinned in spite of himself. "Well, I was going to use a little less nice of a word, but that will suffice. I shouldn't have stuck you with the dishes, but I did. And I'm sorry that I didn't tell you where I was going today and that I forgot that today also marks the day that Michael died."

"Forgiven. I…I guess I'm used to this moodiness of yours that sometimes overtakes you. Just not its harshness. That surprised me."

"I know. And I'm sorry."

She held up her hand. "No need to keep apologizing."

He shifted onto the swing and wrapped his arm around her shoulders. They stayed that way for a few minutes, and the only sound was her sniffles punctuated by the occasional passing car.

He stroked Lilly's head. "Does it get better? I mean, missing him?"

His sister stayed silent for a moment. "Maybe a little each year. Having to take care of the kids forced me to keep busy. I only cried when I was by myself. I still miss him fiercely, but I guess I've gotten used to it by now enough that I don't feel as lonely." She sipped her tea. "Why do you ask?"

He rose and leaned against the post to stare at the stars. "I was curious."

"How about you?"

"I miss them. Along with Jonathan, they were my best friends. We had something I'll never have again." He turned his back to the post and faced her. "I cried today. Makes me think something's wrong with me."

"Why? Because you're a guy?" She shook her head. "It's okay to cry. You care about people in a big way, and it's one of your finest traits. It's good to care enough to cry."

"Is it?" He turned and resumed his contemplation of the night sky.

"Of course. Like you said, it's something you lost, something you know you'll never get back."

He shook his head.

"David, it's okay." The chains on the swing creaked as she pushed it back and forth.

The sound comforted him, reminding him of more innocent times when they spent warm summer nights on the porch at his parents' house.

"About…well, about calling Abigail to get Jonathan's info. I just…I just can't. And I don't know why. It's like too much time has passed. I wouldn't know what to say."

The tiniest of sighs reached him, but Kyra didn't push.

Without her prodding him, he found it easier to avoid any thoughts of what contacting Jonathan might mean. Reconciliation. Something he wasn't willing to contemplate.

"Besides, I'm happy here." He folded his arms across his chest. "Why would I want to change that?"

She didn't say anything. The growl of a passing truck filled the void. "I know you're happy here. You're a different man than you were when you returned three years ago. You've recovered. Wouldn't you agree?"

He nodded.

"But there are times, like tonight, like yesterday, when I sense something inside of you, deep inside. Something like restlessness. You're made for more."

He began shaking his head.

"Just listen. Please," she added as if she realized she might have been too hard on him. "You loved the Army. You had leadership there. Camaraderie. A purpose that was a higher calling. Friends who were tight with you."

David closed his eyes as the pain from The Incident and ensuing events that led into his descent into addiction and homelessness flared near the box where he'd stuffed his memories. "And look where it got me."

She ignored his deflection. "Burning Tree has been good for you to recover. Still, I think you're wanting more but are afraid to face it. It's like a vibe I'm picking up in you. You want back into that role where you fight for the innocent and protect those who are helpless."

"Are you trying to turn me out?"

"What? David, no!" She set Lilly down, rose, and wrapped her arms around her brother. She was so petite that her head rested on his chest. "I'm not saying that at all. I only want you to understand that you shouldn't feel bound here. Maybe it's time to explore your options, to talk with Jonathan and see how he wound up in his current job. He might have some wisdom."

A flash of anger burned its way through him. Despite everything that had happened, no way would he call Jonathan, not after his friend had abandoned him during his time of greatest need. "Sorry, but I'm not interested. Burning Tree is where I need to be right now. You and the kids need me."

Kyra pulled back. For a moment, she gazed at him, her dark eyes liquid in the moonlight that sprinkled silver on her short curls. Then she shook her head, a wisp of a smile crossing her lips. "I appreciate your kindness, but the kids and I were doing fine before you joined us."

She turned and picked up Lilly. With her free hand, she opened the screened door. "All I ask is that you think about what I said."

The door banged softly shut behind her.

He faced the night sky again. Faintly, as if his CO's spirit surrounded him, he heard Captain's voice encouraging his men to see that their mission was greater than simply the objective for that day. Then came distant cheering from Oso and Ray, almost like they urged him onward to consider his sister's words.

David returned to the rocking chair and tried to purge Captain's challenge and Kyra's words from his mind.

He couldn't.

His sister was wrong. He wasn't made for more than where he was now. That much, he knew. And nothing would change that. Not now. Not ever.

12

Ghazni Province, Afghanistan

Pariah. An outcast. Any person or animal that is generally despised or avoided. Those definitions from the dictionary popped into Jonathan's mind as he stared at his half-eaten meal of rice and roast beef. It sat on the coffee table alongside the bottle of beer he'd gotten at the cantina. For what seemed to be the umpteenth time, he dined with only the satellite television as his company.

Now he knew how a pariah felt. Alone. Rejected by the pack, thanks to his missteps. Eating by himself in the Mess Hall while others accused him with their stares had become too much. Not that it mattered. He still heard the whispers, even when going about his new daily routine of gym workouts and gazing at the four walls of his room.

"Did you hear Jonathan was going to arrest Nicole for treason?"

"Who's next? Jeb for being Chief Weapons Officer?"

"What would happen if he found out I *'borrowed'* a pen from the office?"

Suddenly, his meal tasted like desert dirt. He tossed the plastic fork into the Styrofoam container and closed it. Monday couldn't come soon enough.

His laptop, which sat open on his desk, chimed with an e-mail from the new COO. Jonathan needed to compile all of the standard operating procedures under his purview into a binder to leave in his old office. Good. At least he had something to keep him busy. And now, he had permission to go to the administration building. No way could Boss Man stop him since he wasn't CEO of the compound anymore. Happy to be on the move, Jonathan laced on his hiking boots and shrugged into his leather jacket to ward off the chilly night air.

Once he arrived at the administration building, he opened the door to his office and flipped on the light. He'd cleaned it out that morning after the initial meetings with the new management team. The only things remaining were his computer and the files he'd be leaving behind. As he worked, he picked up a scent that was out of place in the sterile office with painted concrete walls and tile floors. He sniffed like a dog going after a steak.

Pungent. Spicy, almost.

He strained to recognize it. Then it hit him.

Cloves.

I must be imagining things. He shook his head and got back to work printing the SOPs and filing them in a large binder. When he finally called it a night at 10:50, he drifted into the hall. Thanks to the transition, no one else milled around, and his footsteps echoed on the bare walls.

Once outside, he paused. A Toby Keith song boomed across the bare stretch of land that served as a sorry excuse for a front lawn. Since no convoys would go out the next day, a party had started in the cantina attached to the Rec Hall and sounded like it was going full blast.

Yearning for company, Jonathan wandered in that direction. The music shifted to Bon Jovi's "Dead or Alive." A bottle broke, and people laughed. The longing turned into an almost physical ache. As he drew closer, he noticed two people standing on the porch and smoking as they talked. One of the grunts on the protective detail and Frisco, the former Spanish army mechanic who ran with Nicole, Roy, and Cal.

The tip of Frisco's cigarette glowed as he inhaled. When Jonathan was within ten feet, he blew a stream of smoke in his direction.

Jonathan stopped.

Frisco glared at him. "Who said you're welcome here?"

Jonathan changed his plans and his direction as the smoke wafted over him. His nose twitched. Cloves.

Weird. Of course, everything was weird right now.

He should've expected a barb from Frisco, from anyone at the cantina. That's what happened to pariahs. He returned to his room and shucked his jacket. From the interior pocket, his phone chirped. Probably Abigail had texted again. He pulled out his phone and toggled it on. The message came from a blocked number.

"You are in danger. They will kill you tomorrow night."

Jonathan frowned. Dismissing it as a crank text from someone at the compound, he tossed the phone onto his desk. Someone wanted to torment him further by sending him crank texts. Chalk one more up to being a sudden outcast.

He shivered at the chilliness in the room. Why had he left the French doors open? After closing them, he turned up the heat and flipped the switch for the ceiling fan. The blades stirred the air.

That clove smell hit him again. Frisco had been in his room.

The phone chirped again.

This time, he lunged for it and snatched it up. Same unidentified number.

"You must get to safe haven before they kill you."

What? He tapped out a reply. "Whoever this is, if this is some sort of joke, it isn't funny."

Nothing.

Though warm air now poured from the vents, he shivered. Death lurked nearby. As a highly decorated retired Special Forces operator, who had survived a war and three very hazardous tours of duty, Jonathan didn't scare easily. That changed with the message.

Someone tapped on his door.

Heart hammering, he whirled toward it.

"Jonathan?" The voice was soft as if not to call attention to itself. "It me. Bryson."

Relief swept over him. He flung open the door.

Bryson stood there, cloaked in a leather jacket and toboggan with a backpack over his shoulders. Behind his glasses, his eyes blinked owl-like in the brightness of the room. He ducked inside. "Shut the door."

Jonathan did. "What's going on?"

"Trouble." Bryson dropped both jacket and backpack onto the couch, then dug around in one of the backpack's pockets. "Nicole and her crew have designs on you, and they aren't pretty."

He held up a jump drive and nodded toward Jonathan's laptop. "May I?"

Jonathan nodded.

"After Nicole discredited you, I planted bugs in her room and the downstairs of the Women's Building. Not admissible, I know, but it's going to save your life."

"I don't understand."

"Take a listen." Bryson hit a button.

Nicole's angry voice spilled from the speakers. "What do you mean, you can't find the drive? I told you to put it with the guns."

"I did." Tension clipped Roy's words. "I did exactly what you said. But I didn't notice it when I was moving them."

"And you didn't tell me?"

"I figured you had it."

Nicole cussed. "He took it."

"Who?"

"That rat Ward took it. We need to get it back."

"But how?"

"Frisco's staying behind. I'll have him search for it while we're gone. It shouldn't be so hard since Ward has to at least go out to eat." Another cuss word exploded from her. "We're screwed if he can't find it."

"Are we?"

"What do you think? Of course!"

"I'm not so sure. Think about it." Roy reasoned with her. "He can't copy the file. All he can do is go to Boss Man with it. Then it'd be him looking like he stole a classified document."

"But we can't pin it on him without tipping our hand." Her voice sounded strained. "There's another problem. Ward's sister is Army CID. Chances are good he'll hand over the drive and tell her everything. We've got to find it."

"That, and something else."

"What?"

The next sound was a *schnick,* from the action of a pistol being pulled back. Roy chuckled. "Ward must die."

Bryson hit a key, and the audio fell silent.

Jonathan's stomach began turning on his meal. "Oh, man, oh, man, oh, man. This is not good. So that's why you sent me those texts."

"What texts?" Bryson cast him a glance as he clicked some more files.

"These." Jonathan showed him the messages.

"I didn't send those. I don't have an unidentified number, and even if I did, I couldn't because I was out of range."

"Then who did? And where were you?"

"To the first, I don't know. To the second, I followed Nicole, Roy, and Cal as they made the trade tonight. Look." Bryson hit a button.

Jonathan's heart pounded as he watched the video his friend had recorded. The trio made the trade, but it was clear that their client had expected the drive and given them an ultimatum. Provide the drive, or they would suffer. The video vindicated him, but Nicole and Roy were willing to kill to silence him. "Bryson, this is…this is what we need. I'll go to Boss Man—"

"No. He may not have had a hand in it, but he's too worried about preserving his own legacy to do anything with it." He swiveled in his chair. "And there's more."

"How much more could there be?"

"Someone else was there. I didn't see them, not at first. But they knocked a small rock loose, which almost got both of us busted. So someone else was watching."

"Do you know who?"

"Hey, I was so busy saving my own hide that I didn't see them." Bryson turned to the computer. A few more clicks transferred the file and another one onto the laptop. "You're leaving soon. I've copied everything onto your computer. Get it to Abigail. That drive with the Athena file makes it fall squarely into her territory. She'll know what to do." He rose and pulled on his jacket.

"Yeah." Jonathan swallowed hard. Then he gripped his friend in a tight hug with three slaps on the back. "Thanks, Bryson. You've been a good friend and great to work with."

"Same to you." Bryson took off his glasses off and rubbed his eyes. "Dang dust. Be safe, okay?"

"Will do." Jonathan watched his friend go. When he shut the door, he locked it for the first time in four years. He watched the video for a few more minutes. He had enough evidence to put at least Roy and Nicole behind bars. The thing was, he had to live long enough to hand it to Abigail.

"Think!" he muttered. He grabbed a water bottle from his mini-fridge and uncapped it.

He needed to go to ground, to let things cool down before heading to Raleigh. But where? Slowly, an idea gelled. Two calls changed his final flight destination from Raleigh to Atlanta. Another yielded a rental car he'd take to the beach house he'd purchased in January. No one, save for his Realtor and the lawyer who had done the closing, knew about it. There, he'd lay low for a bit.

Only one phone call left to complete his change in plans. But he'd wait until he was safely out of the compound. Then he'd call his sister.

He spent the rest of his time showering and packing the remainder of his belongings that he hadn't already shipped to the States three weeks before. By the time he slid his laptop into his backpack and zipped it shut, his final sunrise at the Ghazni compound had begun.

He shoved aside the blinds one last time, then dialed a number on his cell phone to set his plan into motion. When a man answered, he stated, "Sayad, my friend. It's Jonathan. Something has come up, and I need your help."

13

Ghazni Province, Afghanistan

A flame flared in the darkness of the living area of the women's building. The tip of a cigarette glowed red. Then came a female sigh along with a stream of smoke. Nicole's lips curled in a smile as she stared at Ward's darkened room through the window. Most likely, he'd sacked out in his rack for his penultimate night at the compound, completely oblivious that these next few minutes would be his last.

Footsteps echoed on the tile, and Roy rested his hands on her shoulders. "Are you ready to go?"

"Let's do it." She crossed the room and stubbed out her cigarette in the kitchen sink. "You have what we need?"

"Right here." He held up a capped needle and syringe. "Potassium straight from the pharmacy."

"We need to make sure we don't leave any marks of struggle on him." She shrugged into her black hoodie.

Frisco stirred near the back door. "Cal and I will take care of him." He held up a small box. "And in case the fool locked his door, I've got picks."

"Good thinking." Nicole switched off the back porch light. "Let's go."

They filed into the darkness, their feet barely making a sound as they flitted between the guest house and the women's building. Thanks to the new CEO calling a pre-dawn meeting the next day, silence reigned save for a few snores coming through the open windows of some of the dorm rooms.

They stole up the stairs to the second floor of Ward's dorm.

Nicole located his room on the end. Frisco took the lead, and she stepped back to allow Cal to pass.

Frisco put his hand on the knob. Slowly, he turned it. He glanced at Cal, his fingers silently counting down. The two men exploded into the room.

Nicole darted forward with Roy right behind her.

Cal's soft cuss word confirmed what she saw in the flashlight's bright beam.

A bare bed and no Ward.

"What the…" Roy bumped into her.

Nicole flipped on the light and flinched in its glare.

The gray and white mattress lay across the metal frame. That was it. No luggage on the floor, ready to be packed. Nothing on the top of the dresser and desk save for a keyring containing Ward's office and room key. No nothing. She ripped open the closets. Empty. Same thing for the bathroom.

Ward had tricked them.

She picked up the keys and hurled them against the outer wall. They tumbled to the floor in a jingle of metal on tile. "Back to the house."

This time, they returned through the front door. Nicole slammed it and cursed a blue streak. She kicked the foyer table, sending it crashing over. Ripping off her hoodie, she stomped into her study and threw it onto the floor.

"Could he be hiding somewhere at the compound? Maybe in someone else's room?" Cal's voice reached her.

"No one would cover for him except for maybe Bishop." Roy's logic did nothing to comfort her.

Cal murmured something.

Ignoring him, Nicole logged into her e-mail. She had only two messages, one from Air Express with the flight manifest for later that morning, the other from Air Express with the flight manifest for Monday. Both had arrived only an hour before. She opened the one for Monday.

No Jonathan Ward listed.

She pulled up the manifest for today, Sunday. There was his name, meaning he would be long gone in three hours.

Cold anger swooshed through her. A growl started in her throat.

Gentle hands rubbed her shoulders and kneaded away the tension. She leaned back in her chair as a headache began pounding behind her eyes. "We're screwed."

Roy didn't say anything. His fingers massaged her tense muscles.

"We've got to stop him from boarding that flight."

"How?" Roy asked.

"Just…stop him."

"We don't know where he is." His truth infuriated her.

"He's got to be somewhere nearby. We can tear this compound—"

He swung her around in her chair so she faced him, then knelt and took her hands. "We can't do that because if we did, we'd tip our hands and go out of here in handcuffs."

"Maybe he's with Captain Rasheed and his men—"

"What do you want to do? Go in there with guns blazing? We can't create an international incident over this."

"Then we're history." She hung her head.

He lifted her chin before reaching up and running some of her hair through his fingers. "No, we're not. C'mon. Cal has an idea."

"Cal?"

"Yeah. You're going to love this." He tugged her to her feet. With her hand in his, he led her into the kitchen where their two henchmen leaned against the counter. "Cal, tell her what you told me."

He smirked. "I got me a friend from the Army who lives in Raleigh. Better yet, he works with the Raleigh Police Department. I might could call him and tell him we need him to let us know when Ward shows up at his house. But it'll cost us."

"Start with five grand," Nicole said without a thought. "If he gets greedy, we go to ten. Give him a call. Now."

She paced and smoked another cigarette as Cal made contact. The conversation didn't last long, but it seemed to swing into the affirmative. Ten grand sealed it. Good. Now they'd be able to find Ward and get their drive back. What a way to spend her vacation. At least she'd stay at the home office, but Roy would return to the compound with Cal and Frisco. And if they didn't get that drive back? Shamal Khan, their very angry client, would overrun the compound.

Cal handed over the phone to Roy, who talked with their contact for a few more minutes before signing off. "It's a deal. His codename is Darius, and he said he'll keep tabs on Ward's house. Apparently, Ward has the RPD check on it while he's away, so it's easy enough to find out."

"Then it's settled." She finally smiled. At least now, they had a plan. "Guys, we'll see you tomorrow. We'll plan more when we get Stateside." Her smile faded. If they didn't get that drive back, they'd all be hung.

Despite the early hour, Roy popped open a beer and flopped onto the couch. "Baby, come here."

"Roy…" She remained where she was with her arms wrapped around her middle. Ward's disappearance, the missing drive, the danger they were in—she felt like everything was spinning out of control.

"Come here. Let's chill down a little before going to bed. It's not like we have to be at that meeting in the morning. We can sleep in if we like." He patted the cushion beside him.

With a sigh, Nicole curled up against him. "This is freaking me out."

"You know it'll be okay. We've played our hand well."

"Not with Ward."

"Yeah, he's a weasel, all right. We'll bide our time by going to Chesapeake and making our plans. Then when Darius calls, we get our butts down to Raleigh. We grab Ward and the drive."

"And leave his body for his sister to find." Sweet irony.

"I want you to relax, okay? As of now, we're on vacation for six weeks." He rubbed her back in slow, steady circles that made her mind start to roam. He nuzzled her cheek. "No more worries."

Nicole accepted his kiss. "Okay. No more worries."

If only she could convince herself of that.

14

"You, Abigail Ward, are a wonderful cook."

Abigail smiled over the rim of her wine glass at Rick, who leaned back in his chair, patted his washboard-tight stomach, and smiled back at her. "I'm glad you liked it. That chicken dish is one of my favorite recipes."

"Where did you learn to cook like that?"

"Mom taught me." She rose and carried her plate to the kitchen. Funny how he didn't follow. Well, maybe he didn't feel quite comfortable with doing that since it was his first visit to her apartment. "Why don't you head on outside? I'll throw these into the dishwasher."

"You want some more wine?" He nodded toward the bottle of chardonnay sitting in the granite wine holder she'd bought years before.

Maybe that would help take the edge off the thought that things about Rick, in the very short week she'd known him, weren't adding up so that one plus one equaled two. As she started the water in the sink, she watched him through lowered lashes. He filled his glass almost full. Hers too. Again, not a good sign.

Without another word, he stepped onto the large balcony of her apartment that had sweeping views of Quantico Creek gliding by her complex.

It only took her a few minutes to rinse the dishes and stash them in the dishwasher for running later. Just as she reached for her glass, her cell rang.

101

Jonathan. Her heart hammered, and she grabbed it from the basket on the bar before it had a chance to ring again. "Jonathan!"

"Hey, sis." Weariness lowered his voice, or was it something else? In her mind, she did a quick calculation of the time. Eight o'clock in the evening on Saturday meant six in the morning on Sunday for him. Had he slept at all?

"What's going on?"

"I wanted to call you and let you know that there's been a change in plans."

"What? I'm officially on leave now." Her gaze shot to Rick. He leaned against the railing as he sipped his wine. Already, the glass was half empty.

"I know, and I'm sorry. Is there any way you could change that?"

Abigail wanted to run her head into the nearest brick wall until the feeling of frustration went away. "Yeah, but it's going to be, well, awkward." She didn't want to divulge Sal's reaction to her news about the Athena file. "But it can be done. Why the change?"

"Because someone's planning to kill me."

Knees shaking from the news, Abigail eased onto a bar chair. "Where…are you?"

"I'm with Sayad and his crew." Jonathan murmured something to someone on the other end, and she wondered where he stayed. "I changed my flights, and I'm leaving in a little bit. Sayad smuggled me out yesterday afternoon, so I'm safe. No way would Nicole and company try to create an international incident by attacking an Afghan army post."

"One can hope."

He laughed, but it held no humor. "You're right on that. Anyway, I'm going to ground for a couple of weeks, which is why I need you to change your leave. Can you do that for me?"

She closed her eyes and tried to imagine the fear consuming him. Such images weren't good for her peace of mind, so she shut them down. "Um, uh, yeah, I can. Where will you stay?"

"Someplace safe. That's all I can tell you. I'll call you when I'm headed to town. It shouldn't be more than two weeks. See you then?"

"You bet. I love you."

"Love you too, sis."

She laid her phone on the bar, then raised her gaze and found Rick standing in the doorway. A look had gathered in his eyes, almost as if he were annoyed that she'd spent less than five minutes on the phone with the one guy who meant the most to her in the world.

Then his ruggedly handsome features smoothed. "I was wondering about you."

"Sorry. That was my brother. He's going through a bad period of work." *If you can call it that.*

"On a Saturday night?"

"He's overseas, so it's Sunday for him. And when he's there, he works seven days a week." Not wanting to divulge anything else to him, she picked up her wine and joined him. Her broomstick skirt swished around her ankles.

"You two must be close."

"We are. After Mom and Dad died, he's all I have left. He means the world to me."

"That's nice. Hey, how'd you come by these digs?"

That's all you can say? She tried to shrug away her discomfort. "I got in at a good rent when they were opening the complex. Then, when I passed the five-year mark, they locked my rate. I love it here, especially this patio." She wandered toward the corner where she could catch the best breeze coming off the creek and rested her hip against the rail. Would Sayad really protect her brother? Where would he go to ground? Would Nicole and her gang follow him?

"Hey, earth to Abigail." Rick's gentle teasing pulled her to the present. "You look a million miles away."

"I'm sorry." She took a sip of wine and resisted the urge to gulp it down to gloss over the wrinkles she'd seen appearing in their fledging relationship. "I'm worried about Jonathan."

Rick stepped closer and curled a lock of her hair around his fingers. "Why's that?"

"He's in a...touchy situation." As if running for his life could be considered touchy. No, more like deadly. "He asked that I delay my leave for two weeks."

"He's good. He can take care of himself. Not to mention, that leaves you with more time for me."

I did not hear what I thought I just heard. Did I? She wanted to pull back, but he slid his free hand around her waist and pressed closer. Curse the scent of his cologne. Her nose fairly quivered, and that, coupled with the wine, caused any rational objections she had to recede into some little corner of her mind. "He'll be fine. It's just my duty as his sister to worry at least a little." Or a lot.

"Then let me wipe that worry away." With that, Rick tipped her chin and kissed her.

It was as if every nerve stood on end with color bursting all around her. When she finally pulled back, her heart hammered. "Oh, wow."

He chuckled and led her to the couch where they watched the sun set.

He knew how to push her buttons as he stroked her arm and kept her close. Still, she wasn't buying it. Finally, after a half an hour, she rose and stretched. "Hey, today's workout wiped me out, and I'm dropping fast. I also need to be up early for church. You mind calling it a night?"

The annoyance in those blue eyes of his told her that yes, he did mind. Then he smiled. "Sure. I'll call you later."

Please don't. She wanted to shout that, but her southern manners locked her jaw shut. Grrr! She wished she'd had the fortitude right then and there to say no way, no how was this going to work out. Now she'd merely delayed the inevitable talk.

Once he'd gone, she locked the deadbolt and wandered onto the porch. His cologne lingered, but at that point, it made her slightly queasy. She stared over the creek. To the northwest, lightning flashed. The first thunderstorm of the season headed in her direction. Her mind churned much like the waves the breeze now kicked up along the surface of the creek. Rick. Jonathan. Sal. Why had the men in her life suddenly created chaos for her?

She knew what she had to do with Rick. Tell him she was done. After all, all of the signs emanating from him pointed to a very possessive man as an admirer at best or an abuser at worse.

And Sal? She floundered a bit as she tried to figure out how to explain to him why she'd delayed her leave at the last minute. Something had come up at work for her brother. That as all she would say. Could say.

As for Jonathan, they needed to have a talk. A long one.

15

Raleigh, North Carolina

Two weeks later, Jonathan turned his rental car into the Dogwood Hills neighborhood along the edge of Raleigh's downtown. When he came within view of his property, he eased to the side of the street and stared at the corner lot with the gray house and white trim where he'd grown up and now lived. He leaned his head against the seat and closed his eyes.

"I'm not sure I'm ready for this," he muttered. He'd been talking aloud to God a lot lately. Christine too, which made him question his sanity. His touched the jump drive hanging on a lanyard under his shirt. He'd stashed an identical copy along with the pilfered drive in his safe at the beach.

He reached for the Bojangles cup of sweet tea in the cup holder but hesitated. "Are You with me? Will You see this to the end with me?"

Through the open windows, the pleasant scents of azaleas, gardenias, and other blooming plants tickled his nose. He inhaled deeply, and the tension of the past several weeks began melting away. Peace crept over him, if only for the briefest of seconds. That was enough.

He knew.

God walked with him.

He put the car in gear and drove the last block to the house. After he pulled into the driveway and parked in the carport beside his Jeep Grand

Cherokee, he stared at the back door that led to the kitchen. His worry returned like a panther jumping out of hiding. Maybe this hadn't been such a good idea. For a moment, fear rooted him to the spot. He shook his head.

I'm being paranoid.

Finally, he climbed from the car and began a walk-around of the house by strolling down the sidewalk and checking the side. Nothing looked disturbed. He turned the corner and investigated the front. Same result there. Someone, most likely his neighbor, had placed pots of petunias in a lively purple and white on his front steps.

"Why Jonathan Ward, what a surprise," an older female voice with a Carolina lilt exclaimed.

Dottie Parker, his next-neighbor, stood at the low picket fence in front of her house, two more pots of petunias in her arms. She opened the gate and hurried through it.

He stepped forward and hugged her, flowers and all. "Hey! It's good to be back."

"Did you just get home?"

"Yes." The less she knew, the better. He glanced up and offered a smile as a marked Raleigh Police Department cruiser rumbled past. "Thanks for looking after the place. Looks like Raleigh's finest did the same."

"They were by here every night. I had some leftover petunias, so I thought I'd share. It makes people think someone's here all of the time." She winked. "Harold will be so glad you're home. He's been wanting to play chess with you."

"I'll have to take him up on that." He glanced up and down the street. "Everything else was good here?"

"It was."

"And no one's been around the house in the past couple of weeks?"

"Not a soul. Is something wrong?"

"No," he lied. "Sometimes it's hard coming off a hazardous duty station."

"I'm sure." She patted his arm. "I heard about Christine. Abigail called us. Please know I'm sorry. I'm sure you miss her terribly."

He nodded because right then, the massive lump in his throat blocked any words.

"Well, let me get these flowers on your steps." She set her pots down.

"Is Harold around?"

"He's at his drawing class right now."

"Do you think he could give me a lift from the airport this afternoon so I can return the rental car?"

She knelt and fluffed the blooms. "I imagine he could."

"And how about if you two come over for supper tonight?"

"Why, you shouldn't have to cook on your first day back."

Finally, he poked a real smile through his shroud of grief and paranoia. "I know, but I've been on the road so much that I'm ready for some home-cooked food. Not to mention, there's a grill out back with my name on it. And I'm sure Harold will want to play chess."

"If you put it that way…" She smiled. "Then we'll be over at six. I'll be sure to bring my knitting so you two can play to your heart's content."

"I'll see y'all then." He watched as she headed to her porch. Once he returned to the carport, he unlocked the kitchen door for the first time in over three months. After shutting it behind him, he snagged a butcher knife from the magnetic strip over the counter next to the refrigerator. With it held at ready by his side, he made his way through the small kitchen, past the dining room, and into the living room. Only the curtains swayed slightly in the air conditioning. His moccasins whispered across the floor as he stepped into hallway and cleared the master bedroom, the downstairs guest bedroom, and the bathroom on the first floor.

Nothing.

Carefully placing his feet to avoid the places on the steps that creaked, he made his way upstairs. His fingers tightened around the knife as he peered into the front guest room. Empty, as was the second bathroom. His study at the back of the house remained undisturbed as well.

The tension in Jonathan's shoulders eased. He dug a small safe key out of his desk drawer and opened the closet that contained a file cabinet and a safe. After inserting the key, he punched the numbers, which were identical to the safe he had at the beach. The door popped open.

He traded the knife for a Beretta, which he stuffed with its holster into his belt at the small of his back. Then he lifted the second lanyard from his neck and slid the small drive into the safe until he could share it with Abigail.

By tomorrow evening, he'd have a concrete course of action. Finally, something positive was about to happen.

He closed the safe and dropped the key into his shirt pocket.

After reconnecting the rental car's GPS to the battery, he hauled his duffels inside and dumped them in his bedroom. Home. He could breathe again. Nothing compared to this wonderful sense of belonging.

Now in bare feet, he wandered into the living room. He'd lived in the house his parents had willed to Abigail and him ever since they'd died in an auto accident six years before. For a bit, Abigail had lived there too as she recovered from her own set of troubles. While they lived together, she'd helped him decorate, from repainting and making other cosmetic changes to the rooms to helping him put his own unique stamp on the place. Part of that consisted of filling the bookshelves and glass-fronted cabinets with pictures and books.

He perused all of the frames as if seeing them for the first time. Several were of friends and family from over the years. One portrayed the day when he'd graduated with a degree in business nine years before. Mom beamed at him from the picture, so proud that her son had finally received his bachelor's degree. Dad, ever the professor, did as well. Another picture held his mentor, Judge MacKenzie. Without his wise guidance, Jonathan would have ended up in jail.

He came to a photo of Abigail and him. In this one, he saluted her when she received her gold second lieutenant's bars on commissioning day, right before she graduated from college. For him, it'd been a happy day to see his little sister follow him into the Army, even if she'd outranked him at the tender age of twenty-two.

Next to the one of him with his sister sat one of Christine and him. The rose arbor at the back of his yard framed them. Her smile was wide, teasing. She never did things halfway, including her smiles. He picked up another photo of them, this one taken by a retired couple when they'd been hiking in the Rocky Mountains near her Colorado hometown.

"I miss you, Christine. I guess part of me always will." He brushed his fingertips across her image, then replaced it on the shelf.

To his right was a shot taken in 2007, shortly after the Mighty Men had come together. They crowded around a long picnic table with frothy mugs of beer held high. The picture had been taken in Mexico. They'd conducted joint training with Mexico's *Federales*. Once it wrapped, they'd hit one of the local bars with their local brothers-in-arms until the manager finally ordered them out. Good times.

In the last picture on the shelf, he and David Shepherd stood at the top of a mountain. Which one, he didn't remember. Both had their right legs propped up on rocks, their right arms cocked in a bodybuilder pose. The grins on their faces indicated how proud they'd been that day. The faint lines of a tattoo peeked from Jonathan's arm.

His right forearm bore a tattoo revealed by the rolled-up sleeve of his sailcloth shirt.

Sola gratia.

By grace alone.

Having gotten it at eighteen right after he'd finished basic training, it symbolized the most important thing to him.

A peace that defied his current situation blanketed him. "You're with me, God. I can feel it now. Thank You."

Time to hide the key. But where? He picked up the picture of David and him and popped off the backing. It took some doing, but once he'd stowed the key behind the picture, he replaced the backing so that it stayed secure with the help of a little Scotch tape.

What had happened to his best friend? He'd lost touch with him when his Master's Degree and his first year at SecureLink had consumed him. Five years ago, David had left him a message for him to call when he could, a message blurred by alcohol or something. He'd returned the call the next day, only to receive a message that David's phone had been disconnected.

Maybe once he got things sorted out, he'd call Kyra, David's sister, to get his contact information. Reconnecting with his best friend would help push him past the gash created in his soul by Christine's death.

Quantico, Virginia

I'm on vacation. I'm on vacation. Those words hummed through Abigail's mind as she turned off the engine of her navy blue Honda Accord and climbed from behind the wheel. She grabbed her bags from her Wal-Mart trip on the way home. Thanks to her brother's call before noon, she'd bolted to Sal's office and announced her intent to take leave for two and a half weeks. At least by this time, his sense of humor had returned. He'd laughed as he handed her the paperwork to sign and told her that her leave began at 1600 hours. Now, she actually did a small skip in her step as she headed toward the stairs leading to her third-floor apartment.

"I saw that." A teasing male voice drifted her way.

She froze, and her cheeks heated as she noted Lance Murphy, one of her across-the-way neighbors, climbing from an old gray Mercedes that looked like the sides would fall off. He still wore his Marine ACUs, meaning he'd just arrived home from work. "Uh, hi."

"Someone's happy tonight," he added as he let her precede him upstairs.

"I'm on vacation as of" —she checked her watch— "an hour and a half ago."

"Are you cooking tonight?" He gave her puppy dog eyes that usually meant she'd wind up cooking for more than just herself, which was always fine, since it meant she wouldn't eat alone.

"Not tonight. I don't have a drop of food in the house since I'm leaving town tomorrow. I'm sorry," she added when his puppy dog eyes turned into a hangdog look.

He heaved a great sigh. "I guess Ames will cook, then. It'll be spaghetti out of a jar for sure."

"Why don't the three of us go out? You know, so I can start vacation off the right way."

The Marine captain visibly brightened, and a grin crossed his dark features. "Then no spaghetti out of a jar. Sounds like a plan to me. Ames is home already. Want to meet downstairs in fifteen?"

"Works for me." She tossed him a mock salute, then unlocked her apartment.

She changed into jeans and a blouse and was just about to tug on one of her favorite cowboy boots when her cell phone rang.

Rick. Again. All because she'd avoided having The Breakup Talk. Instead, she'd put him off with excuses about being busy at work—which was true since she'd been following up on several cases that had loose ends. Why could she be direct with suspects but not with a suitor? Curse her Southern roots. She yanked on her boots and let the call roll to voicemail.

With a windbreaker in hand to ward off the chill later in the evening, she joined her neighbors at the base of the steps. Lance led the way to his Mercedes.

"You ever going to sell this?" she asked as she slid into the front seat.

"Nope. Not when my girl enjoys riding in it." He chuckled as he started the old car. It hacked as he backed up.

"Your girl needs to have better taste in cars," Ames Forsyth said from the backseat.

"No, my girl has perfectly good taste in cars. Where to? The pub?"

"Of course."

On the short ride to the restaurant where she'd met Rick, she settled for listening to the banter between the two roommates. At the pub, cars packed the parking lot. "For a Tuesday night, it seems kind of crowded."

"My bet is that they have the deck open, and after a week of rain, people want to be outside." Ames hopped from the car and led the way inside. When they ran smack into a wall of people at the hostess's podium, he nodded. "Yep. Count my suspicions as correct. You guys go get some drinks and maybe grab a pool table."

"Just make sure we're outside," Abigail replied. "C'mon, Lance. A rum and Coke awaits me. I'll grab you a beer if you tell me what you want."

He gave his order and wandered in the direction of the pool tables.

Once she had their drinks in hand, she joined him as he racked the balls. He handed her a cue stick. "You get opening shot, lady."

"Why, thank you, kind sir," she drawled in her finest Southern accent. He laughed.

She leaned over and placed the cue stick on the bridge formed by her finger and thumb. She lined up her shot before letting the stick fly. Perfect hit. The balls scattered across the green felt, and a stripe and two solids dropped into different pockets.

"Phewee. Good shot, Abigail." Lance chuckled. "I take it you want solids?"

"Of course." She winked in his direction. She located her next shot and began lining up. As she did so, the hair on the back of her neck stood on end. She tried to ignore it, but the feeling intensified. She took the shot, missing by a wide margin.

Lance circled the table and eyed the new setup.

Abigail stepped back and picked up her drink.

Just as she lifted it to her lips, Rick whipped her around and pushed her against the wall. The rum and Coke crashed to the floor.

Uh, oh. Her delay had landed her in trouble.

"Uh, hi." She tried a weak smile.

Jealous anger sparked from his blue eyes, and the way his jaw flexed told her he meant business. "What do you think you're doing?"

"I'm not sure I follow."

"Who do you think you are? You go behind my back and go out with that—" He let loose with a racial epithet hurled in Lance's direction.

Lance glared at him. "What did you call me?"

"Excuse me, but we're not exclusive." Abigail shook loose. Or tried to. He had too tight of a grip on her arm. "We aren't even dating."

"Says who? You?" He called her a foul name.

Lance tossed his cue onto the table. "Let her go!"

"And you stay out of it." Rick held out a hand before getting right in her face, smothering her with his alcohol breath. "You and me, we're going to go and have a little talk."

"Let me go, and do it now," she stated in a low, calm voice. Her heart rate sped up as adrenaline pumped into her system.

"Not on your life."

Lance grabbed him. "I said, let her—"

Rick repeated his racial slur as he shoved him, sending him crashing to the floor.

Murmurs rose as a crowd formed.

"Hey!" Ames's voice barely penetrated the buzzing that suddenly filled Abigail's head.

She flipped into automatic pilot. Before she realized it, she'd kicked Rick's feet out from under him. As he crashed to the floor, all six feet, two inches and two hundred pounds of him, she yanked his arm behind his back and twisted it until he yelped. She dug her knee into his shoulders.

"Let me go!" He called her another name as he squirmed.

"You listen to me and listen to me good. You are coming very close to assaulting a Federal law enforcement officer. You understand, you drunk idiot? I have every right to arrest you here and now." Her voice boomed in the silence of the stunned crowd gathered around them. "You have one chance and one chance only to leave here peacefully. You blow that, and you walk out of here in cuffs. Not a good solution for a Marine Corps officer."

Keeping his arm twisted behind him, she hauled him to his feet and frog-marched him toward the door. She released the pressure.

Rick whirled, swinging a wide right hook toward her face.

This time, other patrons—a whole host of other Marines now angry at their brother for besmirching their rep—tackled him.

"You Army hag!" he shouted.

Her cheeks flamed. "Boys, he's all yours."

Several men dragged a still-shouting Rick outside.

Abigail fumed as she returned to the pool table. All she wanted was a peaceful evening with her friends.

Lance stood by the table, his eyes downcast. She touched him on the arm. "You okay?"

"I should be asking you that."

"No biggie. I'm sorry, guys. That was a guy who thought he could be my very possessive, apparently abusive boyfriend." She shuddered. "C'mon. Let's play."

At least after that, the evening immensely improved. The manager came and offered them a primo table overlooking the water as well as another rum and Coke for her, this one on the house. Lance gradually recovered, and they wound up having a good conversation about race relations. Once they arrived back at the apartment, she gave each guy a quick hug with promises of seeing them in a few weeks.

She needed to talk with someone—or multiple someones. She carried a steaming mug of tea and her cell phone to the sofa on the patio, her new favorite spot now that warm weather had arrived.

Gabrielle answered on the first ring. "Okay, girl, what's wrong? You never call me this late unless something's going on."

Abigail sighed so deeply that her friend chuckled. "Sorry. I know it's late, and the kids are probably in bed and—"

"It's no problem. Is it Rick?"

"Was Rick." She rubbed her eyes and recapped the evening.

"Oh, wow. I'm sorry. I guess I had such high hopes."

"Yeah, me too." Why couldn't she have something go right when it came to guys? She always attracted the worst of the worst, kind of like flies that always invaded picnics. "You know something, I think I'm done."

"Done, as in…"

"Done with the dating thing. I just don't think I have the best judgment."

"No, I think you have perfect judgment. I mean, you knew Rick wasn't right, that there was something wrong with him. So you ended it, thankfully before he succeeded in hitting you."

"That will never happen."

"Good thing."

"Maybe saying I'm done isn't the best thing to say. Maybe it's just that…I'm not going to push it. I mean, I have a life now. I'm happy with it. Let's leave it at that."

"Maybe that's where God wants you to be. And that's okay."

Abigail considered her words for a few moments. "Yeah, but the prospect of not having someone to share that life with is daunting. But, you're right. Free friend therapy works again."

Gabrielle laughed. They chatted for a few more minutes before she insisted that she absolutely had to get to bed.

Abigail wrapped her arms around her knees. More than ever, she wanted someone with whom she could share her life, but she also wouldn't risk her own self-esteem to find that someone. She had too many good things going on to worry about having a man in her life. Then why did she feel so empty?

Raleigh, North Carolina

Jonathan slowly became aware of the muted bong of the clock on the fireplace mantel. He opened his eyes a crack. Just like he'd thought. After talking with Abigail for a bit as he nursed his beer, he'd dozed in his recliner. In front of him, the low buzz of a baseball game emanated from the television.

That was a good sign. He was home. Completely relaxed. Safe, too. If Nicole and her gang hadn't shown up at the house yet, most likely they wouldn't. They probably figured he'd gone into hiding. Maybe hiding in plain sight was best at that point.

He rose, yawned, and wandered to the kitchen to toss the empty bottle into the recycling bin. A groan escaped him when he noticed the forgotten garbage bag containing the salmon scraps from his meal with Dottie and Harold. It sat near the door, looking as if it were a pet waiting patiently for its owner to let it out.

Practicality fought with exhaustion. He was wiped out and bleary from sleep, so bed seemed like the best option. But if he left it where it sat, his whole kitchen would reek of spoiled fish. Not the best thing for Abigail to smell upon her arrival home. Jonathan sighed. Sighing, he stashed the gun at the small of his back, picked up the bag, and undid the locks on the back door. He stepped into the carport toward the garbage cans standing near the corner of the house.

Darkness blanketed the area instead of the light he'd turned on earlier that evening.

The hair on the back of his neck stood on end.

He whirled and thrust the bag upward. It connected with something, and garbage rained down on him.

He kicked out.

Someone grunted.

He reached for his gun.

Pain exploded in his head. Stars sparked in his vision. Another blow between his shoulder blades made him stagger. His forehead slammed into the bumper of the Grand Cherokee. He crumpled to the hard concrete as the gun fell from his hand.

Someone grabbed him and dragged him into the kitchen and down the hall to the living room.

A door slammed. Wood scraped on wood.

"Tie him up." Nicole's voice.

He was shoved onto the stiff wooden frame of a dining room chair. Cord bit into his wrists and chest.

He forced his eyes open. For a moment, pairs of blurry figures stood in front of him. His vision cleared, and the double images merged into one.

"Surprised to see us?" Nicole's sarcasm echoed off the ten-foot ceiling.

He squirmed against his bonds.

Roy folded his arms across his chest and glared at him. "You screwed us over, you know that?"

"Where's my drive?" Nicole demanded.

"What drive?"

Roy cuffed him across the head. "The lady asked you a question, Ward."

"I don't have it."

She cussed. "Boys, search the place."

Frisco and Cal, who stood near the opening between the living room and hallway, fanned out.

Nicole leaned down so her slate blue gaze bore into him. "Do you know how much trouble you've caused us? Do you? You were smart when you slipped out of the country on us like that. By the time we got to Munich, you were long gone. But you didn't count on us having assets already in place, did you?"

Across the room, Roy shoved all of the pictures onto the floor with two sweeps of his arms. The frames crashed, some breaking apart. Glass crunched as he stepped on others. In the dining room, china shattered.

Jonathan flinched.

His canned goods clunked to the floor in the kitchen.

Nicole's voice drilled him again. "You want us to tear up this place completely? Tell me where the drive is."

"I don't have it."

"You lie!" Nicole popped him across the face. She stepped away a couple of paces, then whirled and pointed a finger at him. "You *will* tell me where that drive is."

He clenched his jaw shut.

In the kitchen, silverware clattered to the floor, followed by pots and pans. Crumpling noises from the hall told him they'd gone to work on the bedroom.

"You have a safe in here?" Roy yanked open the glass-fronted doors. He pulled all of the books onto the floor. "Maybe upstairs? Cal, Frisco—"

His phone chimed. He turned away and answered in a low voice. The call lasted less than thirty seconds. "Baby, that was Darius. Sounds like someone called the cops on us."

Nicole shifted her gaze for a moment before refocusing on her captive. "You're coming with us." She pulled out a Taser and fingered it as a smile danced across her lips. "And to make sure you come quietly…"

She jabbed it into his side.

His body went rigid. Every muscle caught in a cramp. When she finally released the voltage, he sagged against his bonds. Before he had a chance to recover, two of Nicole's men cut the cords and yanked him up by the shoulders.

He'd erred, this time perhaps fatally so.

16

The sound of meowing awakened Abigail. She opened her eyes a crack. With wakefulness came a stiff neck. Oh, great. She must have fallen asleep after talking to Jonathan. In front of her, the television glowed with *The Tonight Show*. Beside her, Oscar, her tabby, purred from his crouch on the sofa's arm. Sylvester, her black and white cat, had curled up on the back.

The meowing ringtone continued its incessant plea.

Finally, she reached for her phone. "Major Ward."

"Abigail?"

"Nick?"

"Yeah, it's me."

She pushed herself upright and scrubbed her face with her free hand. Why was her ex-husband calling her at such a late hour on a weeknight? "Is work at the RPD that slow? Because if you're calling to chat, it's a bit late, and I need to get to bed."

"This isn't a social call, all right?" His New Jersey accent flared with irritation. "I'm calling about Jonathan. Seems there was a kidnapping at his house tonight."

Coldness struck her, like he'd dumped a bucket of ice water on her body and soul. "What happened?"

"The long and the short of it is that someone heard a shout and called the cops." He paused, his breath whispering, most likely with the inhalation of cigarette smoke. "You need to get down here, the sooner the better."

"I'm on my way." She hung up and shot to her feet so fast that Oscar jumped off the sofa. Sylvester ran under the dining room table. It took her ten minutes to pack enough clothing to last for several days, then another fifteen to collect her gear bag from her office before she hit the road for Raleigh. Almost four hours of hard driving brought her to the Dogwood Hills neighborhood.

She saw the blue lights first. They strobed the spring foliage of the trees with flashes of sapphire. Yellow crime scene tape festooned the perimeter of the property, and a few bystanders milled beyond them. Lights glowed from several of the homes while news crews from the local stations stood sentry at various points.

Abigail parked a block away. She pulled booties and a pair of gloves from her gear bag. As if she belonged at the scene, she slipped under the tape.

A sharp female voice reached her. "Ma'am, you're not allowed in here."

A uniformed cop stood there, her eyes alert, her hand resting on the butt of her gun.

"I'm looking for Detective Nick Bocelli."

"And you are?"

"Major Abigail Ward. Army CID." She flashed her cred pack.

The cop cocked an eyebrow as if doubting her.

"Abigail." Nick called to her.

She whipped around. Her cheeks flushed at the sight of her ex-husband. She glanced away.

"Thanks, Carla. I've got this." He glanced toward where the press had gathered. A couple of reporters turned curious glances her way. "Looks like you might get company later."

"I'm just the sister."

"Yeah, yeah. C'mon. Let's talk over here." He took her arm and walked her toward the house.

They paused near where the forensics team had set up portable Klieg lights. Their bright glare lit the mess of garbage between the door and Jonathan's Grand Cherokee. A forensics tech knelt near the front of the SUV and placed a placard on the concrete.

Abigail pulled her booties and gloves from her purse. "I'm ready to go in. I even—"

"You're staying here."

"What? Nick, I—I don't understand. It's not like I haven't seen a crime scene before." She strained to peer through the kitchen windows.

"But that of your brother? Nope. Sorry. No can do."

"But—"

"You're the sister, remember?"

"Nick!" She put her hands on her hips.

He sighed and leaned toward her. His nearness meant his aftershave hit her nostrils, conjuring up memories she didn't need right then. "Look. I know you're CID. You don't think I remember that? But you are family. How about if you head to my cruiser?" He nodded in the direction of the unmarked Dodge Charger sitting behind the crime scene tape. "Let me finish up, and I'll fully brief you."

She scowled at him. "Oh, come on. Really?"

One of the techs glanced at them.

"Don't be difficult on this." Nick hooked her arm through his and led her toward his cruiser. He paused. "Please."

She glared at him for a long moment. Finally, she huffed out a sigh. "Fine. Have it your way. But I want a full debrief of everything you know."

"Wilco on that. I'm going to post a uniform here to keep the reporters away."

"Yo, Nick!" A detective with a baby face stood on the back steps and waved to him. "We need you, buddy."

"I'll be back." He turned on his heel and strode toward the carport.

She slid into the car and slouched against the seat, which was a bit cramped thanks to the laptop on its rack beside her. It cast a cold glow through the car. The radio crackled softly as the police and fire department responded to other calls around the city.

Maybe the crime had been something random, like a robbery gone bad. No, she'd be a fool for assuming that. Whatever trouble had started at the compound in Afghanistan had followed Jonathan to Raleigh. She stared out the window.

Carla took up residence at the front fender of the vehicle.

Abigail's gaze shot to Nick, where he stood next to the Grand Cherokee and conversed with the baby-faced detective. The two turned and stepped inside the house.

Abigail knew Nick would start asking her questions that would be typical of an investigation.

She thought about her conversation with Jonathan a few hours before. His main request? Keep mum until they could talk.

How much would she say to Nick? Enough to satisfy him but not too much.

Only a few people remained outside, mostly reporters hoping for a morsel. Maybe a few of the neighbors too. Dottie and Harold stood at the gate. Harold had his arm around his wife, who rested her head against his shoulder.

A movement caught Abigail's attention. She straightened as she stared hard at a woman dressed in leggings, a tunic top, and low-heeled boots with her dark hair clipped at the nape of her neck. She focused on the crime scene as if she wanted to soak in every detail. A reporter, maybe? They made eye contact.

Abigail's breath caught in her throat. She knew the woman. But from where?

The woman tensed, potential energy ready to strike.

Abigail opened her door to approach her.

The woman shifted away and melted into the shadows.

Why had she fled? Was she involved in the kidnapping? Or had she been a simple bystander embarrassed by her voyeuristic actions?

Abigail winced as a headache kicked up between her eyes. She had to put her theories to rest since she had only one blip of data and nothing else.

She yawned like Sylvester waking up from a nap. Five in the morning according to the dashboard clock. Close to her normal awakening time. Two hours of sleep would not sustain her. She pinched the bridge of her nose as the pain worsened. The low crackle of the radio acted like a lullaby. With her head resting against the doorpost, she closed her eyes. Within seconds, she dozed.

The sound of a car door opening and closing brought her back to full awareness. Nick had slid into the driver's seat.

Now, dawn tinged the area with enough light to make out the outline of nearby homes.

"Sorry if I woke you." He pulled out his notepad and flipped to a page of his scribbles.

"It's been a long couple of weeks."

"We're just about finished at the house."

"What did you find?"

"We think things started in the driveway. Looks like someone loosened the bulb and ambushed him. He couldn't get to his gun. He's got a permit for that, right?"

"Concealed carry."

"Good enough. Does he make a habit of carrying it around with him?"

Abigail shook her head. "No. I assume he had good reason."

"They probably took him inside. We found a dining room chair in the living room and some sort of cord we think is clothesline because the line in the shed had a chunk cut out of it. They probably interrogated him."

"Why do you say that?"

"Blood on the floor. We don't think he gave them what they wanted because the downstairs is a total wreck."

Abigail swallowed hard. Maybe it had been a good idea to wait outside. "Not the upstairs?"

"We think they got wind of the cops being on their way and took Jonathan with them for further interrogation."

Abigail lowered her head.

He massaged her neck muscles, tense from the news. "Abigail, I'm sorry."

"Nick, stop." She took a deep, shuddering breath.

He removed his hand. "Sorry. I have a few questions for you, if you don't mind."

"Fire away."

"Did you know Jonathan had a safe upstairs in his study?"

Abigail nodded. "Yeah. He keeps his gun in there."

"Anything else?"

Abigail thought through what she knew about the safe. "His financial stuff since he travels a lot. Maybe some keepsakes? Honestly, I don't know."

"Any knowledge about where he'd keep a key? There wasn't anything in his desk."

She shook her head.

"Did he give you an additional key and the combination?"

"It's not with me."

He sighed. "Okay. The techs said they'll release the crime scene after we get the safe drilled."

She nodded. A lump filled her throat. She closed her eyes. "What else did you find?"

"Sam talked with a Dottie and Harold Parker, Jonathan's neighbors. They said he pulled up in a rental car a little after ten yesterday morning. Dottie found that kind of surprising since normally, he'd catch a taxi from the airport. Did he tell you where he was coming from?"

"No."

"Sam's running down the rental car info. Jonathan and Dottie talked. She said he asked a lot of questions about whether someone had been by the house. Besides RPD, that is. Does that strike you as odd?"

She shrugged.

"He invited them to supper, and they grilled salmon. Then he and Harold played chess. They left around 9:30 or so, and she remembered Jonathan turning on the back porch light for them. Around 11:00, she couldn't sleep, so she decided to sit on their deck for a bit. She thought she heard a noise and scuffling. Jonathan's screened-in porch blocks her view of the carport, but she thought she might have seen some characters. She did hear a door slam. When she heard things breaking, she got scared and called us. She stood at the fence and reported a group of people leaving in a hurry, tires screeching, and an engine racing as they drove off. She couldn't get a description of the vehicle because she didn't have good line of sight."

"I assume the people who broke in took Jonathan with them."

"That's what we think. This wasn't a simple robbery,"

"Agreed." She rotated her head, wincing at her muscles tightened again from the long drive and stress.

He drummed out a staccato rhythm with his left hand. "What does your brother do?"

"He works for a company called SecureLink. They're out of the Tidewater area and do private security contracts in hot spots all over the world. He was coming off a contract in the Ghazni Province of Afghanistan."

"What did he do for them?"

"Chief Operations Officer for the compound. He oversaw the day-to-day operations, which included the protective details for convoys."

Abigail's cheeks heated as she realized she'd inadvertently supplied him with a clue. *No, no, no. You know better.*

"Convoys…convoys…" He rested his head against the seat and closed his eyes. The drumming stopped. "In late March, it was his company that had a convoy hit."

She had no way around the truth. "Yeah."

"Interesting."

She felt his gaze burning into her. Careful to keep her expression neutral, she focused on where her hands twisted on her lap.

"When was the last time you saw him?"

"The first part of January or so. I was down on leave, and I went out with him and Christine—" She crashed to a halt as she realized her next blunder. What was it with her tonight? She knew better than to spill everything to Nick. Maybe it was her exhaustion. Or the intoxicating aroma of his cologne.

Suddenly, the interior of the Charger seemed too hot, even with the open windows letting in a faint dawn breeze. She wanted out of the car and away from Nick since he knew how to pick her apart better than anyone else thanks to being married to her for two years.

He leaned toward her. "Who's Christine?"

"His girlfriend."

"And she lives, where?"

Abigail flushed as her nose quivered. "She doesn't."

"Doesn't what?"

Could she just shut her mouth? It had to be his nearness that made her confess. "She, uh, isn't alive anymore. She died in the ambush."

Nick pulled back and began tapping the steering wheel again. "Wait a minute. She died in the convoy? How?"

"She was a member of the protective detail."

"Interesting." He paused long enough to jot down a few notes. "When did you last talk to Jonathan?"

"Last night."

"Do you know why he would have driven up in a rental car when the airport is only about half an hour from here?"

"No." She clenched her teeth. The less said right then, the better since detectives latched onto loquaciousness like a dog going after a hamburger.

"So nothing indicated he was worried?"

She shook her head. Under no circumstances would she reveal anything else she knew about the goings on at the compound that had sent her brother on the run.

Nick leaned against his door and assessed her. His gaze held hers, those dark eyes she'd so loved liquid in the dim light.

Her heart hammered. He'd worn her down before with that look.

With a sigh, he snapped his notepad closed. "We've got to give Sam and the evidence techs time to finish up. I took the liberty of making some hotel reservations for you."

"You didn't—"

"I know we may not be married anymore, but at least let me take care of you, okay?"

Old anger from her last memories of him flared. "I can take care of myself."

"I know you can. Look." He heaved a great sigh. "Can't you at least let me try and make amends by being nice to you?"

"Nick…"

"Please." He reached out and took her hand.

The heat shot to her cheeks.

"Please," he repeated softly. "Just this once."

Finally, she nodded but jerked her hand away as if setting boundaries.

"Then it's settled. They'll keep your location confidential."

"Will you keep me updated?"

"Of course." He smiled.

She narrowed her eyes. "What do you want from me?"

The smile dimmed a little. "I show a bit of kindness to you, and you assume I have an underlying motive?"

Abigail hung her head. That had been a low blow, and she knew it. "I'm sorry. I'm—I'm really tired."

"Then go check in and get some sleep. I'll call you later today. Let me walk you to your car." Nick climbed out and opened her door.

In silence, she walked with him. Now that she'd sampled his cologne, she wanted to follow him around like a lost puppy. *Girl, you're wandering into dangerous territory.*

He stopped at her car. "Be gone with you. I'll talk to you later."

She climbed inside and started the engine. Checking into the hotel took longer than the drive.

Jonathan was in deep trouble and was now in the hands of the kidnappers. Knowing her brother, he'd probably written down everything related to Christine's murder. Most likely, that information resided in the safe, meaning that it'd be in the hands of the police if they drilled it. While she would ingratiate herself to Nick, she couldn't trust him to share anything he found.

She walked a tightrope, one where a fall either way would spell trouble.

With any luck, she'd not fall off and straight into Nick's arms.

Or into the clutches of the kidnappers.

Regardless, she had to take matters into her own hands.

17

Raleigh, North Carolina

Wednesday evening, Abigail sat at the local Starbucks and sipped a steaming brew of Kona coffee as she mentally churned through everything she knew. Most likely, the gunrunners were the ones who'd kidnapped her brother because they hadn't found what they'd wanted. Something related to the gunrunning resided in Jonathan's safe. What remained unclear. And Nick hadn't called her, at least not yet. Then there was the matter of the woman who'd shown more than a passing interest in the crime scene.

Abigail rubbed her temples. *Think. Think. Think. Why does she look so familiar?*

Nothing came to mind.

"I thought I'd find you here." A growly tenor and cigarette breath wafted her way.

Abigail glanced up.

With forearms on the wrought iron fence, Nick leaned next to her table. He glowered at her.

She tried a smile. "Uh, hi."

"You stay right there, you understand?" He jabbed a finger at her table. "We need to talk."

Her eyes narrowed, and she drawled, "Okay."

A few minutes later, Nick joined her on the patio. The chair across from her scraped as he yanked it out, turned it around, and straddled it.

"Just how did you find me?"

Nick grinned, but in no way did it hold any humor. He held up his cell phone. "GPS location."

"You've been *tracking* me? What the…why? Why are you treating me like I'm trying to flee a crime scene?"

"I like to know the location of my vic's family, and I don't think you're telling me the whole story."

"And why is that?"

"Sam found out some info on the rental car and your brother's travels. Jonathan flew out a day earlier than planned from Ghazni. Then he changed the last leg of his travel to fly not from Munich to Raleigh-Durham but from Munich to Atlanta, where he rented a car. There's a two-week gap on the GPS files because he probably disconnected it. Do you have any idea of where he might have been during those two weeks?"

"None."

"You're sure?"

"Yeah, I am."

He stared her down as he lit a cigarette and took a drag. "Did he talk to you before he left Afghanistan? Did he tell you about how he'd been discredited?"

"I talked with him right before the convoy got hit."

"And not since then until yesterday?"

She sighed as she lifted her coffee to her lips. At least her hands didn't shake. "He was busy, as I'm sure you could imagine. All I did was text him to check on him since I knew what had happened."

Nick tapped some ashes into his coffee cup lid. He didn't say anything as he perused her with his dark eyes.

Not one to be intimidated, she maintained her steady gaze.

He looked down and moved his cup around in tiny circles. "You want to tell me why you held out on me?"

"About what?"

"About a call he made to you two weeks ago the morning before he left Afghanistan?"

"Wait." She held up a finger. "You pulled his cell records? Geez, Nick, whose side are you on?"

"Yours, all right?"

"Then why do I feel you're portraying him like a criminal?"

Nick sighed. He stubbed his cigarette into the lid. "Sorry. All I'm doing is trying to get to the bottom of things. This may surprise you, but I care about your brother. And you."

"Then stop treating me like I planned his kidnapping."

"You're right. Sorry."

Yeah, whatever. He wasn't a bit sorry, and she knew it.

"For your information, we didn't talk about much." Abigail hesitated as she scooted past any thought of the Athena file. "He said to delay my leave for two weeks, which I did. All I know was that he was very tired and sad. He hardly said anything about what happened."

Okay, so she fuzzed the truth a little. She had to until she could get to the bottom of things.

"He changed his airline tickets, rented a car, and disabled the GPS until he arrived in Raleigh, and he did all of that because he was tired and sad?"

She clamped her jaw shut to avoid mouthing off at him.

Nick took her hand and rubbed his thumb in circles across the top. "Look. I want to help here, but I'm sensing that you're being less than forthcoming with me, like you know more than you want to tell me. Why, I'm not sure."

Her pulse quickened. Here it came again, that impact his touch had on her. "You know what I know."

"You're sure?"

"Nick!" Abigail jerked her hand from his grasp.

His cell phone began chiming. He grimaced as he checked Caller ID. "Sorry. I've got to take this."

She folded her arms across her chest. As he spoke in hushed tones, she stared at the passerby on the sidewalk.

A woman strolled toward her, one dressed in jeans, low-heeled boots and a top with a windbreaker over it. Even though dusk approached, she wore sunglasses. Her head turned. Almost imperceptibly, she hesitated before turning her face away and hurrying past.

The run-in rattled Abigail. She'd definitely seen her someplace, and she struggled to figure out where.

Nick lowered his phone and rose. "Someone knocked over a convenience store in southeast Raleigh. I've got to get going."

"Before you go, when do you plan on drilling the safe?"

"Tomorrow morning at eight sharp."

"Will you let me know what you find?"

"Why should I when you've been less than forthcoming?" His smile turned derisive. "You're just the sister, right?"

With that, he strode from the patio.

The jerk.

He'd cut her completely out of the investigation.

That meant she had to put her own plan into action.

The sooner, the better.

Raleigh, North Carolina

An hour later, Abigail walked toward the house she and Jonathan shared. A marked police cruiser sat on the curb by the sidewalk leading to the front door.

"You scumbag." She muttered more unpleasant words about Nick under her breath.

He must have suspected she might try to pull something like she'd planned.

She shifted from Plan A, waltzing up to the house and letting herself inside, to Plan B, sneaking in the back door. She zipped up the black hoodie she'd pulled on, retrieved from a pocket a small radio she'd brought, and ran an earbud to her right ear. A few seconds of fiddling with the tuner brought the police band into fine tune before she dropped it into a pocket. She placed a ball cap over her head and lifted the hood so it covered both her cap and ponytail. With gloves on her hands, she cut east one street and approached the driveway side of the house.

She paused and listened. Everything remained still. A car drove by, and she ducked behind Jonathan's SUV. Mindful of the cop sitting not a hundred feet away, she crept to the kitchen door. After disarming the alarm, she wasted no time in slipping inside and pulling a penlight from her backpack. Its red glow picked up cans, pots, and pans everywhere.

Anger churned her stomach. Skirting the rice and flour on the floor, she crept into the short hallway. Shattered china and crystal glittered red in her light. Whoever did this would pay, not just for kidnapping her brother but for destroying family keepsakes. But she couldn't let that stop her. She continued into the living room.

Here, numbered placards littered the floor where the forensics techs had taken notes and pictures. She noted the dining room chair Nick had described as well as cord on the floor. Spatters, black in the red light, showed near the chair.

Oh, Jonathan, what did they do to you?

She crept toward the stairs. Almost halfway up, one creaked. In the silence it sounded like nails across a chalkboard.

She flinched and paused.

Nothing stirred, and she continued, this time taking more care in where she stepped.

One check of the desk drawer in the study confirmed what Nick had told her.

The keys to the safe weren't in their normal spot.

She searched the study and the bathroom. Nothing. The same with the room where she stayed when she visited. She crouched on the landing at the top of the stairs. What she'd found confirmed her theory. Whatever was in the safe held such importance that Jonathan had hidden the key. But where?

Their house contained so many hiding places that the thought almost overwhelmed her. She needed a course of action. Fast. She straightened and tiptoed down the stairs. Even though it was a mess, the living room contained the fewest amounts of hiding places. She glanced at her watch.

A quarter to eleven.

She had until dawn to get her work done, and at the rate she was going, it could take all night.

Starting with the pictures first seemed to make more sense than the books because it'd be more difficult to hide a key in a picture frame. Several were cracked. Others lay on the floor with broken frames. Add one more reason why the kidnappers would pay for what they did. They'd violated her brother's sanctuary.

Her gaze landed on the one of Jonathan and her from her commissioning ceremony.

"I'm coming, Jonathan," she whispered. "I'll find you. I promise."

Each time she picked up an intact frame, she carefully examined the back before replacing it the way she'd found it. Finally, she came to one of Jonathan and his best friend, David Shepherd. Were the situation not so dire, she would have laughed at the way they imitated Mr. Universe. For a moment, she cradled it in her hands.

The back seemed to bulge. She clamped the penlight between her teeth and carefully checked the back of the picture. The tape told her what she needed to know. She undid the fasteners. The cardboard popped off and fell to the floor.

A key that looked like it would fit in a safe tinkled onto the hardwood.

"Bingo." She slid it into an interior pocket of the backpack and studied the picture. Why had Jonathan chosen that particular picture? There had to be a reason. She stashed it in the pack as well on the hopes that the place was such a mess that Nick wouldn't notice her pilfering.

She started up the stairs to open the safe but stopped. The combination resided in the gun safe of her Quantico apartment.

What could she do now? One glance at her watch told her that she had no chance of driving to her apartment, retrieving the combination, and returning to Raleigh before dawn stole her cover.

Oh, great. She'd run out of options before she even started. Tears filled her eyes, and she remained where she was as she struggled to keep them from falling. *God, You couldn't have led me this far and dropped me. What do I do?*

She surveyed the living room. Could Jonathan have written down the combination and hidden it somewhere? It was possible, but the number of places where he could have hidden a slip of paper skyrocketed. She simply didn't have the time to go through the entire house.

She glimpsed the family Bible face down on the floor. Mama and Daddy would put her on their laps and read from it. It had been in their family for at least three generations, and both she and Jonathan intended to make it a fourth. Somehow.

She knelt, cradled it on her legs, and smoothed down pages bent from the assault. She flipped to the eighth chapter of Romans. Over the years, she'd drawn strength from the words there, as had Jonathan. They'd had many discussions about that particular chapter. She read the words of encouragement and hope.

Wait. Something wasn't right here. She fanned through the rest of the Bible.

Since it was the family Bible, Mama and Daddy had kept it clean and free of any pen marks, instead preferring to mark up their personal copies. Yet in chapter 8, someone had underlined three verses, 18, 23, and 26.

She frowned and sat back on her heals. Why were those underlined? Jonathan used his own Bible. He always kept it on the kitchen table during his morning times with God.

She read through the verses. Paul's words echoed in her soul, and they must have resonated with Jonathan as well for him to underline them in a family keepsake.

A memory teased the edges of her mind like she was in a darkened room searching for a light switch.

Then it came to her.

One day over the holidays, she'd been chatting with Jonathan about something while they shared hot chocolate in his study. He'd just finished balancing his checkbook. Then he opened his desk drawer, pulled out the safe key, and inserted it into the safe in the closet. Preferring to enjoy the taste of the hot chocolate and the Christmas music coming from the computer's speakers, Abigail had remained where she was. Six beeps echoed in her memory, followed by the click of the door.

"That's it!" She didn't care if she spoke those words aloud. Using a pen she'd stashed in her pack, she scribbled the verse numbers on her hand.

She was about to jump to her feet when a shadow blocked out the porch light.

Adrenaline rocketed through her body. She cut off her penlight.

A uniformed patrolman approached the front door and rattled the knob.

She scurried behind Jonathan's recliner and huddled in the shadows.

The bright beam of a flashlight cut through the glass.

She drew her knees to her chest and hugged the Bible tightly to her. Her breath came in short pants.

The beam moved closer. It brightened the chair, then moved past it.

She closed her eyes as it stopped and arced toward her again.

She didn't move.

The flashlight clicked off, returning the room to darkness.

She remained where she was as the cop moved down the porch steps, then eased around the recliner and huddled against it. The beam flashed through the windows beside the fireplace. A few minutes later, the back doorknob rattled. She remained frozen as she carefully listened to the police band. None of the chatter indicated the cop had found her.

Several minutes passed. Finally, she rose and crept up the stairs to the study as fast as she dared. With her penlight once more glowing red, she opened the closet door and crouched in front of the safe.

With the key in the lock, she peered at her hand and silently recited the verses, ordering them in her head like she thought Jonathan might. *And not only the creation, but we ourselves, who have the firstfruits of the Spirit, groan inwardly as we wait eagerly for adoption as sons, the redemption of our bodies.* Verse 23.

Likewise the Spirit helps us in our weakness. For we do not know what to pray for as we ought, but the Spirit himself intercedes for us with groanings too deep for words. Verse 26.

For I consider that the sufferings of this present time are not worth comparing with the glory that is to be revealed to us. Verse 18.

The lock clicked, and she turned the handle. The door popped open slightly.

I'm in!

For the first time, she allowed herself a smile as she surveyed its contents. Most of it seemed to be files laid flat. Two objects resting on top beckoned to her.

A jump drive and another safe key

She slid both into an inner pocket of her backpack.

She picked up the files and fanned through them.

She couldn't take them, especially since Nick would have the safe drilled within hours.

Who cared? She could photograph them.

She turned the blinds of the windows overlooking the backyard so they would hide any incidental light. Then she put the small desk lamp on the floor and turned it to shine on the stack. Since the file was thick, she didn't waste any time. With her camera in hand, a rhythm developed.

Click. Turn. Click. Turn.

Three beeps sounded on the alarm pad in the study.

Oh, no! She drew in a sharp breath, shoved the files into the safe, and cut off the light. Darkness enveloped her, leaving her night vision temporarily useless.

"Thanks for calling. Now what did you see?" A voice reached her from the foyer.

Nick.

She grimaced and scowled.

"I thought I saw a red glow from inside," another man stated, most likely the uniformed cop.

"Red glow?"

"Yeah."

"Where?" Intensity filled Nick's voice.

"Inside. Downstairs in the living room. That's why I called you since you said you wanted to be notified on the down-low of anything amiss."

"You did the right thing. Stay here, and I'll check." The door shut.

Abigail rose and replaced the lamp on the desk. She stepped closer to the door for a better listen.

"It doesn't look like anything has been disturbed," Nick said, this time sounding like he stood near the hall leading to the kitchen. "Did you see anything upstairs?"

"I didn't come in and check."

Abigail's pulse began thudding in her ears as her mind raced in all directions. Automatically, she withdrew.

Her elbow bumped into something.

She whirled.

Almost in slow motion, a plastic margarita glass full of coins that Jonathan kept on the corner of his desk wobbled.

She grabbed at it. Her fingers brushed smooth plastic, sending it over the edge.

About five dollars' worth of pennies crashed onto the hardwood floor and rolled all over the place.

Footsteps thundered across the floor below and echoed on the stairs.

Abigail rushed to the door and slammed it. She pressed the lock just as something big crashed into the wood. It shuddered.

Nick.

"Abigail, I know you're in there!"

She cringed and pressed into it as he slammed his shoulder against it.

The door bounced again, threatening to give way. She glanced down.

A wedge.

Without hesitation, she shoved it under the door with her foot.

Grabbing her backpack and swinging it across her shoulders, she bolted across the room and slipped on the pennies. She caught herself on the desk and staggered to the window behind it. She yanked up the blinds.

The door threatened to give way.

"Abigail!" Nick's bellowed.

She threw open the window and climbed onto the credenza.

Frames and a plant toppled over.

With a loud crack, the door gave way.

Abigail hurled herself through the window and bolted toward the edge of the screened-in porch's roof. Without hesitation, she leapt into the air.

Her heart plummeted as time hung suspended almost like she did. She hit the soft lawn and rolled to dissipate some of her energy.

She didn't look back as she fled into a neighbor's yard. Darting into the neighborhood bordering Dogwood Hills, she took several deep breaths and walked a couple of blocks south.

As she cut west toward downtown, her breath eased.

She'd made it.

Then she sucked it back in.

Had she?

Time would tell.

18

No lamps glowed in the hotel room. Only a pale, sickly fluorescent glow peeked from the cracked bathroom door. An ice bucket sat on the dresser with a companion cup of water on the nightstand. Dressed in her nightshirt, Abigail hunched on the mattress of the king-sized bed. The file of Bryson's notes from the investigation of the attack on the convoy, courtesy of the drive she'd pilfered from the safe, glowed in a cold light from the laptop's screen.

She stared at the contents. Her former sergeant's notes filled the screen and contained almost a blow-by-blow description of how things had gone down the day the Taliban hit the convoy. An IED marooned the lead Jeep. Under fire, Chip Johnson had radioed for help. Five minutes later, all were dead, sixteen clients and eight security personnel. The photographs of the dead bodies didn't move her. After all, she'd seen her share of crime scene photos on the past.

Then she came to the description of what Bryson thought had happened to Christine. She'd fought, taking out one Taliban at the Jeep. She tried to escape. The result? Five more Taliban dead. Somehow, they'd caught up to her. Then they'd brutally ended her life in a completely different manner. Rather than death by gunshot, someone had sent a knife into the hollow of her throat. Cause of death? The blade had pierced her carotid artery, and she'd bled out. Poor Jonathan must've been dying inside, knowing Christine had been singled out like that.

The gunrunners had used the hit on the convoy and the murders of twenty-three others to eliminate the one person who could have stopped them. She read the end of the notes Jonathan had made that had drawn those conclusions with her jaw clenched.

She watched the video Bryson had taken of the gun trade between Nicole, Roy, and Cal with a man whose name she knew all too well. Shamal Khan, a poppy grower and a known leader of the Taliban. Also the man responsible for the annihilation of the Mighty Men, a fact Jonathan hadn't missed.

Problem was, it didn't seem like things had all gone as planned. Shamal Khan had wanted the Athena file, something now in her brother's possession. Why remained a mystery, one she had to figure out because it somehow stretched further into her brother's past than his last few days at the compound. And because she, Abigail, didn't have the file in her hands, she still had no jurisdiction.

She remained only the sister.

Her lip curled at the way Nick had needled her with that.

She closed the video and the Word file and opened up the directory on the jump drive again. She began reading through the Mighty Men's operational plans and after-action reports, including her own investigation of the battle that had wiped out everyone but David and Jonathan.

As she perused them again, her phone began ringing.

She checked Caller ID.

Nick. For the third time.

Like the other calls, she let this one roll to voicemail. During her foray to the house, she'd left her phone in the hotel room on the pretext that she'd been sleeping. It was best to continue the charade.

She scanned the op plans and reports a third time. A theme emerged. She pulled out a notepad and jotted down her thoughts. The Mighty Men had taken up residence at a village in the Ghazni Province in eastern Afghanistan. They'd been tasked to develop a relationship with the local chieftain and train the village men to fight the Taliban. They'd succeeded beyond their wildest dreams. Then the chieftain's daughter, home on leave from university, joined the local militia with her father's blessing and even trained alongside her twin brother to the point where she went out with the Mighty Men on direct action missions to assist with gathering intelligence from the local women. From what Abigail could tell, David and Jonathan had taken the lead in training her, especially David. He'd seen potential in her and had recommended that she come to the States for more specialized training.

"Wait, something's not right," she muttered and tore through the reports again. Heavy black lines marred every page.

Abigail opened the file containing her own investigation years before. The same result. No name for the young woman. She searched for the photo she'd taken of her. Gone. Her report told of the carnage the young woman had witnessed, of how the Mighty Men had fought side by side with the local militia, only to be slowly picked off.

She closed her eyes and shivered. She'd mentioned that Shamal Khan had most likely received intelligence from an inside source. Who, she'd never discovered, and in the overload of work she'd had, she never had the chance to pursue it.

Something else teased her memory. She hopped up and paced as she swept her hands through her disheveled hair. "Think, think, think! You're missing something, Abigail."

It teased the edges of her consciousness. She closed her eyes as she stretched her mind back to that fateful day. Then it hit her. The woman she'd seen twice the day before was the very same woman who had been with Jonathan. She had to be the chieftain's daughter. What was her name? She couldn't remember. But she'd written a profile about her based upon her interviews with her, David, and Jonathan. She logged into the server at her workplace and searched for the file. "I don't believe it!"

She couldn't find it, not where she'd filed it on the server, and not in the back files. Someone had totally removed it from the system. It was as if the woman had never existed.

A loud knock on the door exploded through the room.

Abigail jumped. She shut the laptop and shoved it under the covers along with the notepad, then fluffed the pillows and blankets to make it look like she'd slept.

"Abigail!" Nick's voice and more pounding gave her an indication of his mood.

One hundred percent foul.

"Nick?" Abigail tried to sound bleary. She rubbed her eyes to make them red as if he'd disturbed her slumber.

She undid the chain lock and the deadbolt.

Despite his height being almost equal to hers, Nick loomed over her. Dark stubble coated his jaw, and his shirttails hung out while his tie remained loosely looped around his neck.

"What are you doing here?" she asked.

He shoved her aside and stomped into the room. "Where were you at eleven tonight?"

"What?"

"You heard me." He forced her up against a wall as the door thumped closed behind him.

"I was sleeping."

"Then why didn't you answer my calls?"

"Because I muted the phone." She slipped away from him and picked up her phone. "You called?"

"Like three times."

She muted her phone while pretending to thumb through her calls menu. Just in time because it lit up once more with his call. "What...You don't trust me?"

"Nope."

"Why is that?"

"Because someone broke into your brother's house tonight. No, they waltzed inside like they had the key and the fob to the alarm. And you, as co-owner, have both." He ripped open the dresser drawers and shoved her clothing around. "Where's the hoodie?"

"What hoodie?"

"The one you were wearing."

"I don't have one." She'd tossed the hoodie into a dumpster somewhere near Fayetteville Street.

"Ah. Backpack." He knelt beside the dresser and yanked open the zipper. He pawed through it before turning it upside down. A book, a couple of magazines, and her small travel Bible tumbled to the floor, all items she'd replaced upon her return.

The drive resided with the computer under the covers. Paranoia had gotten the best of her, and she'd taped the safe key to the underside of the nightstand drawer. "Do you mind? C'mon, Nick! Because I have a key, I would have shown up and asked for entry, don't you think?"

"Nope. You were there. I know it."

"No, I was here. Someone else was there." Her pulse pounded. She had to distract him, to dissuade him away from his theory. She gently tugged him away. "I promise I was here. I'm exhausted." She softened her tone as he faced her. "I came back here after I had coffee and chilled for a bit with some ice and water before trying to grab some rack time."

"The hotel reported a key entry at 11:45."

"That was me getting the ice because I couldn't sleep." She conveniently left out the fact that she hadn't let the door close when she'd slipped into the hall.

The tautness in his shoulders finally relaxed. "Okay, okay. I guess I've got no choice on the matter."

He ran his hands through his dark hair, mussing it like she remembered from their marriage. She'd always teased him and woven her fingers through those locks. A hated blush began. She could only hope he didn't see it in the dim light emanating from the bathroom. She leaned against the wall and studied his face. "Are you sure that's all? You seem really stressed."

He sighed. "Sorry. It's been a bad night made worse, and it's not even half over. And I hate myself for reacting so badly when I know you're stressed as well."

She shrugged.

He finally undid his tie all the way. "I've also wanted to…well, to…"

"What?"

He stepped close to her. "I've missed you."

Surprise stole her voice.

He placed a hand on either side of her head and leaned toward her so she fell into his sphere of influence. "I know we parted on bad terms, and I know that it was pretty much all my fault. We had something good, don't you agree?"

No, we didn't. We were not a match at all, she wanted to tell him. The words remained stuck in her throat as his cologne brought her under his spell again. It was as if its musky scent had paralyzed her muscles.

He skimmed her cheek with his thumb. "You seem surprised."

"I'm…I'm…floored, to be honest," she finally said. Goosebumps popped up along her arms.

"I've learned a lot since then." His fingers skittered down her arm.

So have I, like to stay away. Again, his touch stole her voice.

"Like how to treat the woman I care about." He nuzzled her hair back as he closed the gap between them.

"Nick." She choked out his name.

"Let me take care of you tonight." He murmured the same words that had landed them in bed together in the first place. His lips brushed her neck. Then he cupped her face in his hands and kissed her.

His touch weakened her resolve.

"You could use the company tonight, and quite frankly, I could too," he whispered. His arms tightened around her, and one hand drifted toward the hem of her nightshirt.

"Nick, I—"

His phone began chiming.

He pulled back, muttering something about calls coming in at the wrong time.

Face flushed, pulse pounding in her ears, Abigail retreated to the other side of the room.

"Abigail."

She cocked her head.

"Some kid got shot, and I've got to go. Think about what I said, all right?"

"Which part?"

He grinned. "All of it."

With that, he stepped through the door.

That was close. Too close. She collapsed onto the bed and took several deep breaths to calm herself and reintroduce common sense into her brain. Only a few more minutes with him would have spelled disaster.

Once her pulse had returned to normal, she pulled out the laptop and scanned her notes Finally, she reached a conclusion. Well, two. First, in attacking the village over seven years before, Shamal Khan had intended for none of the Mighty Men to survive. Second, the chieftain's daughter shouldn't have survived either. This stretched beyond the simple need of the Taliban leader to exact revenge on his family for being cast out. She needed answers. Obviously, Jonathan couldn't give her any. But David?

It took her only minutes to find his sister's phone number in the Veteran's Administration records. He had none listed. Grabbing her cell, she punched in the digits.

Although it was past eleven in Burning Tree, Utah, the woman who answered sounded wide awake. "Hello?"

"Is Kyra Martin there?"

"Speaking."

"This is Abigail Ward, Jonathan's sister. Is David around?"

"He is. What's going on?"

"Jonathan's been kidnapped. I think it involves the Mighty Men and what happened in Afghanistan. David was there, and he might be able to help."

Kyra's reply came instantly. "Let me get him. He's upstairs, so hold on."

Abigail waited. Footsteps receded, and a door closed. A few moments later, the steps grew louder. The phone clattered.

Kyra sighed. "I'm sorry, Abigail, but David doesn't want to speak with you."

"What? My brother's life is at stake!"

"I know. I told him that." Kyra drew in a sharp breath. "He said he doesn't want to have anything to do with you. I'm sorry, but I have to abide by his wishes."

"I—I understand." Tears stung Abigail's eyes.

"I'll keep trying because I know what it feels like to almost lose a brother."

"Thanks." She carefully laid the phone on the nightstand and scowled. So David didn't want to have anything to do with her. Period. Obviously, something had happened between Jonathan and him. She didn't care. David Shepherd was critical to this puzzle.

She pulled up the airline schedules and checked flights to Utah. There were plenty of seats on the 6:35 a.m. flight to Salt Lake City. Her fingers flew across the keyboard.

If David didn't want to have anything to do with her, she'd go to him. Then he'd have to listen.

19

Burning Tree, Utah

Oil-changing day had arrived at the Martin residence. David had already completed the job on Dad's pickup, Mom's Subaru Outback, and Kyra's Subaru Forester. All that remained was his Wrangler. He popped the hood, slid onto a backboard, and rolled underneath the vehicle.

He used his left hand to loosen the plug. Only a few weeks ago, he could say he derived great contentment in being a help and support to his family. Today, he couldn't. Thanks to Kyra's challenge a couple of weeks before, he couldn't.

Oh, he'd tried to convince himself he was fine. He liked being a surrogate dad to his nephews and niece and a good brother to his widowed sister.

But still...

He grunted as he came to his feet. Who was he fooling? When he paused long enough to consider her words, he realized how he felt. In some respects, he sat on the sidelines of life, happy to be a spectator to the issues everyone else faced. Hadn't he had enough issues of his own already? Or was there more out there for him to do?

He wiped the plug with a rag before placing it on a clean cloth on the fender. As he shifted to the front and checked the radiator and other fluids, the sweat ran down his bare back in rivulets. The heat built up under his hair banded at the nape of his neck. He mopped his face with a bandanna before tying it around his head.

"David Shepherd?"

He paused at the pleasantly husky female voice behind him.

A woman stood amidst the dancing shadows created by the camouflage netting above his work area between the carport and the shed. Her stance, with feet planted shoulder-width apart, and rigidly held shoulders, told him she was in the military, was totally confident in herself, or both.

He leaned against the front fender and wiped his dirty hands on a rag. "That's me. And who are you?"

"Major Abigail Ward. Jonathan's sister." She offered both a smile and her hand.

"David, Abigail Ward's on the phone," Kyra had told him the night before when he'd hung out on his deck. "Jonathan's been kidnapped, and she wants to talk with you."

"I don't want to talk with any member of the Ward clan." He'd leaned forward with his elbows on his knees.

"David—"

"No, Kyra. That's final." He rose and stomped into the living room.

Now David remained where he was. "You came an awful long way for nothing."

She finally lowered her hand. "Did I? You tell me. I'm sure Kyra told you that Jonathan's been kidnapped."

"She did." To hide the heat rising in his cheeks, he returned to his work. He stepped to the left front fender, uncapped a bottle of wiper fluid, and poured it into the tank. "I'm sorry to hear that. Let the cops handle it." He capped the tank and returned to the front.

"This is bigger than a simple kidnapping. Much bigger." She shifted so she stood near his left shoulder and leaned one shapely, jeans-clad hip against the right front fender.

The flush rose higher as he focused on her face. The resemblance between brother and sister was strong, from the square jaw to the sandy blond hair. He twisted the lid onto the bottle.

"I don't follow," he lied.

"I don't expect you to, at least not yet. Jonathan's girlfriend, Christine, was murdered in a hit on a convoy in Ghazni Province. The investigation revealed a gunrunning ring. He found a jump drive with the operational plans and after-action reports of all of the Mighty Men's missions in Afghanistan."

So what? Why should he care? He tossed the bottle onto the table and grabbed a wire brush, then attacked the battery terminals with more force than necessary to scrape away the acid buildup. "You know those are meaningless after a few years."

"I agree. The thing is, when viewed together, a theme emerges."

He threw the brush on the table and used a rag to wipe some spilled fluid. "And what would that be?"

"The Mighty Men were responsible for training the local villagers to be a militia to fight the Taliban. You succeeded."

"So give us a medal," he grumbled. He grabbed a wrench and began undoing the bolts holding air filter intake assembly. He reached inside and undid the casing clips.

She put her hand on his arm. Pleasant tingling rippled upward. He stopped sliding the old filter from the case and gaped at her. He knew what she'd discovered. He didn't want to talk about it. Not now. And certainly not to her.

"You also trained the chieftain's daughter. She went with your team on direct-action missions and served as your translator and bridge to the local women. Matter of fact, you recommended that she come to the States for additional training."

He flinched and shook off her hand, then ripped open the box holding the new filter. He shoved it into place. What did she know? A bunch of nothing about their time over there, not the unofficial stuff. Like the satisfaction he'd derived in training Nabeelah Khan, who'd come to admire him and Jonathan, almost like they were big brothers to her. "Yeah, so what? It didn't matter in the end. She died. They all died save for Jonathan and me."

"The Mighty Men, her family, and the village, yes. Not her. She's alive. Very much so."

She lied. She had to! Nabeelah was gone, collateral damage in a battle that had stolen life as he'd known it. He braced his hands on the Jeep and hung his head. "You don't know anything."

Abigail rested her lower back against the front. "I know more than you think."

Over the smell of sweat and auto fluids, he noticed a soothing scent. Gardenia, maybe? He shifted away and grabbed the wrench to undo the oil filter. He shoved her aside and wrapped the loop around the cylinder. With his left hand, he turned it until it loosened. "I don't see how."

"Please look at me." Her unruffled voice came from his right side.

He didn't want to. Really, he didn't. Against his will, he did.

She examined him with hazel eyes rimmed in green. Wisps of hair not held back by the sunglasses on her head teased her cheeks.

A flush started again, and it had nothing to do with the heat.

She broke eye contact and toyed with the plug where it sat on the fender. "I was at the base when the medevac chopper arrived. Because I was there with my sergeant, we were tasked with investigating everything that happened. Though I didn't know it was you at the time, I saw them offload you. Then Jonathan climbed out with the daughter. She was gone the next day. I don't know what happened to her."

"They probably sent her back to die in her village, or what was left of it." He stepped around her and set the old filter full of oil on the table. He jabbed the wrench at her. "Now don't you see why I say she's dead? She would have never survived on her own out there."

And that's the cold, hard truth, Abigail Ward. He ripped open the new package and added a bit of oil. He over-filled it, and a little spilled down the sides as he shifted it to fit it against the engine. Crap. His fingers slipped.

Abigail laid her hand on his forearm. Again, that tingling feeling shot up his spine. "David, please. Just listen. She's not dead. That much, I can promise."

He closed his eyes and wagged his head.

"I promise she's not. I can do that because I've seen her twice since Jonathan got kidnapped."

David glared at her and shook her off. "You're lying."

"I'm not lying. Why would I do that?" The tiniest hint of exasperation pushed at her words. "At first I didn't recognize her, but then when I saw the reports, I remembered that day seven years ago. She may have aged, but I'm pretty sure she's the same person."

David dumped in the first quart of oil.

"I think what happened seven years ago in Afghanistan is linked to the gunrunning ring, which is linked to Jonathan's kidnapping."

"That's a stretch." He added the second quart.

"Not when the guns went to Shamal Khan."

Years before, the village chieftain had told him, "My brother, Shamal, is not to be trusted. He chose to align himself with the Taliban, and we cast him out of the clan."

David shook his head to dispel the memory and grabbed the third quart of oil with his right hand. His grip weakened, betraying him. To avoid dropping the bottle, he added it so quickly that he nearly overflowed the funnel. Could she be right? Could Nabeelah be alive? And what did that have to do with Jonathan getting himself kidnapped? And why should he care after his best friend's betrayal years before?

Abigail's husky voice brought him back to the present. "I think the Mighty Men were targeted, maybe the chieftain's daughter. Why, I'm not sure. And I still don't know her name."

He remained silent.

"That's why I called you. I'm pretty sure you and Jonathan—as well as the daughter—were intended to die in that ambush. Only the team coming in to replace you at the end of your deployment had already arrived at base. Their quick reaction saved the three of you. But it's more than that."

David grabbed the fourth quart of oil and tried to undo the cap with his right hand. His grip failed, but that didn't stop him. His fingers barely closed around the cap. "How can there be? We were hit. Only Jonathan and I survived, apparently along with the chieftain's daughter."

"When I investigated the incident—what?"

He glared at her as she used the term he did. "I call it The Incident."

"Okay," she drawled. She pried the bottle from his fingers, uncapped it, and tipped it into the funnel. "When I investigated, I thought things went off too well. They knew your vulnerabilities, how you'd hardened your location. They knew you were isolated, and they sent an overwhelming force against you. In other words, they had inside help. From whom, I'm not sure."

His heart went cold. "You're saying someone in The Mighty Men betrayed us?"

"I didn't say that, I—"

"Get out."

She backed up a step. "David—"

"Get out of here and go home, Major Ward. How *dare* you accuse the dead like that."

"I didn't—"

"Go!"

She didn't wilt, didn't flee. She held her ground. In a voice low with anger and hurt, she said, "I don't know who, all right? What I do know is that right now, my brother stands a very good chance of dying. Also, there's a woman out there who may be in danger—and you, too." She straightened. "All right, if you insist, I'll leave. But I'd hate for you to live the rest of your life knowing that you might have been able to help me save them and set things right."

Trembling started deep within him. So Jonathan was in danger. So what? He, David, had been in trouble six years before, and what had happened? His best friend had abandoned him, left him to a fate that could have killed him and did scar him for life, both on the outside and the inside. But still... Abigail had traveled a very long distance to talk to him personally when he'd blown her off on the the phone. Didn't that count for something? No. She'd insinuated a betrayal deeper than he could imagine. She didn't deserve his help, and he wouldn't leave the comfort of Burning Tree to help someone who hadn't lifted a finger years before.

He shrugged as if he didn't care.

"Oh, and by the way, Master Sergeant Shepherd, you forgot to put the plug in."

She turned and stormed toward the house.

"Huh?" He glanced up. Sure enough, the plug sat on its rag where he'd placed it, and a gallon of oil had run into and out of the engine. He stared after her, his gaze drawn to the grace and strength of her stride.

She slammed the back door behind her.

Grumbling, he grabbed another case of oil. Using his knife, he slit the tape. The blade slipped and opened up a cut along his hand. "Ouch!"

A line of red formed and ran down his tan skin in a bead. He closed his eyes. An image from The Incident flashed before him. Blood everywhere. He shuddered. He found a Band-Aid and stuck it over the cut. He'd clean it after he finished.

After inserting the plug, he glanced toward the back of the house. Kyra stood on the patio, her hands on her hips. She supervised Lilly the puppy but glared his way.

He'd hear about this later.

Burning Tree, Utah

An hour later, David brooded in cargo shorts and a ratty T-shirt on the couch with several items scattered before him on the coffee table of his bachelor apartment. He alternated between staring at the photographs and citation ribbons and the tattered scar on his right forearm.

Heels tapped on the steps leading to the deck.

"What did you say to her?" Kyra, clothed in a deep scarlet dress, stood in the doorway.

He glanced at her, then back at the last items remaining from his former life before he'd been cast onto the streets.

"Whatever you said, she came back into the house looking like she was about to cry. When I asked her what happened, she only stated she was going to take a nap."

His head snapped up. "She's staying with us? Can't she stay at the hotel?"

"Not when it's booked up for the night, and certainly not when she's the sister of your best friend."

"He's not my—"

"Can it for a bit. Please." She shook her head and came all the way inside. "She asked for your help, and you must have turned her down."

"Why should I help her?" He picked up a photograph of Jonathan and him. He tried to remember where they'd raised frothy mugs of beer. It could have been anywhere. "She's Army. CID nonetheless. She doesn't need my help."

"Then why would she essentially spend a day of travel coming all the way out here?"

"Well, if I was rude, I'm sorry. And regarding what she said, MYOB."

Kyra turned away with her shoulders slumped and arms folded across her chest. She sighed. "This reminds me of when you first came off the streets and returned to Burning Tree. Of how you didn't want to open up, didn't want to trust. And that hurt."

What could he say to say to that? With his index finger, he pushed around the citation ribbons he'd received over his Army career. For bravery, for valor. Once upon a time, he'd believed in all of those things. And what had happened? He picked up a picture of the Mighty Men. All dead save for him and Jonathan. And Nabeelah. No, Abigail lied.

Kyra smoothed her dress as she seated herself beside him. For a moment, she didn't speak. Then she drew in a breath. "I still remember that last phone call I made to you in 2011. Foul didn't begin to describe your mood."

"It was the alcohol and painkillers talking."

"I know. I let you be for a bit. And then when I called a month later, your phone had been disconnected. I figured you didn't want to have anything to do with us." She picked at some imaginary lint on the fabric of the dress. "But I was still concerned. I knew something wasn't right. Mom, Dad, and I talked about it, and we decided to let you be in the hopes you'd make contact. You don't know how hard it was."

He gazed at his Purple Heart and Silver Star.

"Finally, I couldn't stand it any longer and in 2013, I started hunting for you. It took some doing. The apartment complex was helpful, the storage place not so much. I didn't have a way to find you."

"Why are you talking about all of this?"

"I truly feared for your life, but I had no idea where you were. For all I knew, you could have been…" She took his hand and continued, "When you got knifed, the hospital got enough from you to contact the VA, who finally got around to calling me since I was next of kin. By the time I got to Raleigh, you'd already checked out of the hospital and vanished. I worried that I'd not find you alive but you as an unclaimed body in a morgue. I can understand what Abigail's feeling. She's scared. She loves her brother, and she doesn't want to lose him. But it's worse for her. She doesn't have any other family. She's alone in this." She released his hands and picked up a picture of Jonathan and him at a party they'd had at their apartment. A small smile crossed her lips. "This is Jonathan?"

"Yeah." He rested his elbows on his knees. He'd forgotten that Abigail and Jonathan were all that remained of the Ward clan. Maybe he'd been too hard on Abigail. No, he'd suffered thanks to her brother.

"I can see the resemblance between him and Abigail." She set it on the table. Softly, she continued, "Look. I'm not asking that you go with her. That's between God and you and her. All I'm asking is that you hear her out. Don't think of her right now as a major in the Army. Think of her as a sister who's terrified of losing her brother. I've made reservations for you and her at the restaurant at six. She'll be waiting for you downstairs. I'll even let this one be on the house."

"But I've got to watch the kids—"

She raised her hand to stop his protest. "Taken care of. I took them to Daisy's and Rod's for supper, and they'll keep them until I get home."

He shook his head. "I don't want to rehash the past, to feel that kind of pain again. And I'm not sure I can help her anyway. Not when—"

He stopped. How could he say that he felt like a total failure for losing his friends?

Kyra took his hand. "God will provide you with the tools that you need, with the courage as well. You know He will." She nodded toward the citations and awards. "You've got twenty years of proof right there. And you know what? I think God has brought you to this moment for a reason."

His gaze landed on the picture of the Mighty Men. From its stillness, they beckoned him.

Continue the mission. Be a warrior. Save those in danger.

"Okay. We'll be there at six."

She leaned forward and kissed him on the cheek. "That's all I ask. I'll see you tonight."

She rose. With one last smile, she stepped through the door. As her heels clicked on the stairs, he resumed his contemplation of the pictures. He came to one of three people. Jonathan, David, and a girl. Her headscarf couldn't hide the sparkle of her eyes or the grin a mile wide. She'd been in her element that day.

Now Abigail swore she lived.

He doubted it.

With one sweep of his hand, he pushed the ribbons and pictures into the bandanna that had held them during his homelessness. He thumped into his bedroom and yanked open the closet door. In the back corner of the closet was the crate he'd used during his homeless stint. In the crate was the backpack that had held every material thing he'd owned when he'd lived on the streets. He dumped the bandanna into it and shut the door.

Then, he stepped onto the balcony overlooking the highway. Below, Kyra strolled toward the restaurant.

He turned away.

He'd honor her request, but that was it.

20

Burning Tree, Utah

Abigail dropped her fleece onto the couch as her phone began ringing. Nick. For a fourth time since she'd left Raleigh. Six o'clock had arrived, and David had yet to make an appearance. Right then, she should have been driving to Salt Lake City, not waiting on a man who obviously wanted nothing to do with her.

Except that Kyra had gotten involved.

"I made you two reservations at six," his sister had told Abigail an hour earlier while she'd huddled on her bed in the guest room. Lilly had found her and slept beside her. "The kids are taken care of. Maybe he'll be more willing to hear you out now."

I doubt that, Abigail almost blurted, but Kyra had faith in her brother. Apparently a whole lot more than he had in himself.

The sound of footsteps on the porch made her cease her pacing. David must have gone around front for some reason. She flung the door open.

A man in a brown uniform stood on the porch, his finger extended to the doorbell. He jumped. "Whoa! I didn't expect anyone to be here."

"I'm sorry about startling you." Abigail offered what she hoped was her best disarming smile. "Do I need to sign for this?"

"Nope. But I was hoping that Shepherd was around."

"David?"

"You two know each other? I thought you might be Kyra's friend."

"Yeah, we just—"

"Patterson, hey." David's voice boomed into the kitchen. He dropped his jacket onto the couch and joined them. "I see you and Abigail have met."

"Not officially. Mitch Patterson." The deliveryman extended his hand.

"Abigail Ward." She shook it. "And I take it that you two know each other."

"We bike together. And Burning Tree is on my usual route. Hey, speaking of which, here's a package for Kyra." Mitch extended a cardboard box. "And I also wanted to see if you'd be up for fishing sometime soon. I mean, after company leaves." He turned to Abigail. "How do you know this big lug?"

She managed a smile as if she and David were best buddies. "He and my brother, Jonathan, are best friends." *Try and deny that, David Shepherd.*

"Cool. Well, I'm off. Got to get down to Cedar City. Later." Mitch bumped fists with his buddy before trotting down the front walk and to his truck.

"It's a small world," Abigail muttered before she realized it.

"Out here, you'd better believe it." David picked up his jacket. "You ready to go?"

"We're going to walk?"

"It's not like Burning Tree's a metropolis. We'll be there in less than five minutes."

She followed him outside. Once on the sidewalk, they crossed the river and turned right into the town proper. "I can't believe how small Burning Tree is."

"Two thousand people. Back when I was growing up here, it was half that size. Too small for me at the time, but now, I like it."

How can you like being in a town this small? She bit back her question because it'd come out as patronizing. They made a right turn toward the river and passed the hotel and resort his parents owned. An adobe structure boasted the words *Kyra Lane Cafe and Restaurant* stenciled in gold cursive on a navy background. "This is the place? But I thought Kyra's last name was Martin."

"It is. Her partner is Lisa Lane, so they combined the two. It had always been Kyra's dream to start the restaurant when the kids were older. After Michael died, she sold the house in Park City and used the proceeds from that and the life insurance money to build a house here and open the restaurant with Lisa. They just passed their sixth anniversary."

So now he was Mr. Chatterbox. Like maybe Kyra had busted his chops for acting like a jerk.

"Your sister is amazing."

"Don't I know it." He opened the entry door for her.

The hostess greeted him by name and led them to the patio through the interior filled with glass-topped tables, glass walls, bolts of tulle draped over the exposed rafters, and glimmering candles. Strings of lights hanging from an overarching pergola twinkled overhead. The same types of tables were outside. Each held a lit candle and a rose. All in all, a truly romantic atmosphere.

Except that she wasn't there for romance—at least not that night and not with him. But he was built, all right. The David Shepherd she'd seen this afternoon, all dirty and sweaty, showed off toned muscles on his shirtless torso. Great abs. Solid pecs. He was definitely built.

Stop it, she told herself. No point in getting attracted to someone who hated her.

He pulled out a chair across from her. "Anything's good, but save room for the chocolate silk pie. Her chef makes the best I've ever had."

Abigail seated herself and glanced at him. "Is that your gold standard?"

"Something like that."

The entrees listed on the menu, from the fillet mignon to the bison to the wild trout, made her mouth water. Her stomach even rumbled.

She flicked a glance at David. "How long have you and Mitch known each other?"

"About two years or so." A smile played about his lips, as if *he'd* been the one watching *her.*

"I would have thought from Army days."

"Why do you say that?"

"He has that watchful look that never goes away."

He shrugged. "Yeah, he was an MP. I thought that invoking Jonathan's name would make him realize you and I were just friends."

"Invoking. You make it sound like Jonathan's some sort of evil spirit."

"Sorry, wrong choice of words, I guess." He glanced up as the waitress approached.

With a bright smile, she announced the specials for the night.

Abigail ignored her as she sat there and fumed. He wasn't remotely sorry. She ordered a Merlot, and David stayed with the water the waitress had brought. Finally, she could stand it no longer and leaned forward. "What is it between you two?"

David's expression hardened. "Do you know what it's like to be brought so low, so far down that you have no options left?"

"Actually, yes, I do."

"Then you'll understand. In 2011, if your brother had answered when I called him, we might not be sitting here today."

Her breath caught. What, exactly what had happened to him? Between him and Jonathan? She didn't dare ask. Not when she needed his help. "If whatever happened to you stemmed out of his abrupt retirement and return to Raleigh, I'm sorry. You can blame me if you want."

"I'm not following."

"He retired because of me." She focused on the menu.

He raised an eyebrow. "Why is that?"

"Why should I be so forthcoming when you're certainly not?" With a sigh, she snapped her menu closed. After forcing a smile to her face for the waitress's benefit, she ordered the bison. Once they'd placed their orders, she leaned forward. "Look. Can we let bygones be bygones about what happened this afternoon?"

He leaned back, his left elbow on the arm of the chair, his chin resting in his hand, and studied her with an intense gaze.

She'd been a fool for even coming out here.

She busied herself with tasting her wine. Most excellent. Maybe burying her head in the whole bottle would make her forget her foolishness for even thinking David Shepherd cared about her brother.

"Her name is Nabeelah. Nabeelah Khan. Niece of Shamal Khan."

She straightened. "What?"

"Her name is—"

"No, no. I got that part. She's the niece of Shamal Khan?"

"How much do you know about him?"

"Not much." Abigail tried to recall what she'd read. "He's a poppy farmer of large proportions. Like whole villages and their crops are under his control."

"There were three brothers in the Khan clan, who ruled the village where we were camped. Nabeelah's father was the oldest son and therefore chieftain. Shamal was the middle son. The youngest acted as the chief law officer. When Kabul fell to the Taliban, they kept their heads down. They had to. The chieftain and his youngest brother taught their daughters quietly since they couldn't attend school. Shamal hated that, but he had no say."

"The middle brother. Too old for the attention like the youngest and too young for the responsibility required of the oldest." Memories bubbled to the surface, those of when she'd met Nabeelah. The girl had sobbed so hard at first that she couldn't speak until Jonathan calmed her down.

"When we took down the Taliban in 2001, the clan made it clear that the village would side with us, save for Shamal. He picked the Taliban, and the clan disowned him. He was dead to them. When we arrived in 2008, we became, by extension, part of the village."

She digested that one in silence. Her mind darted back to her interview with the frightened, traumatized girl who'd been with Jonathan. "The Taliban were intent on annihilating anyone who'd had a hand in disowning Shamal."

"I don't know. You tell me." He glanced up and thanked the waitress, who had arrived with the tray of their steaming entrees. He dug into his. "Tell me something."

"What's that?" Abigail sampled the mashed potatoes. She sighed in delight. "These are delicious."

"How did you get that drive? Or how did Jonathan get it?"

"The gunrunners apparently had it, and he found it when he went searching for the guns. You know he works for SecureLink in Ghazni Province, right?"

"I saw the press conference after the convoy was hit. But we haven't spoken in close to six years."

Abigail let that one slide. "He was COO over there. My former sergeant worked for him, and through his investigation, both he and Jonathan concluded the hit was a cover for Christine's murder."

She pressed ahead before she lost him. "The investigation broke open a gunrunning ring with weapons going to Shamal Khan. All I know is that Jonathan found the drive. He slipped out a day early and told me to hang tight for a couple of weeks before joining him in Raleigh. The night he arrived home, he was kidnapped. He'd hidden something in his safe and then stashed the key."

"This drive you keep talking about?"

"No. I found another safe key and a drive with his notes and the operational files."

"Wait. You said you found it. How did you?"

That hated blush returned. "I, um, had to break into the house we share to get to it."

"Why?"

"Because the cops haven't exactly been forthcoming." She stuffed a bite of bison into her mouth to avoid blurting out that her ex-husband was the detective on the case.

David remained silent. As she ate, his appraising gaze unnerved her. It was almost like he could see into her soul or something. "You, Abigail Ward, are a piece of work."

"I'll take that as a compliment." Bold, even for her.

They fell silent as they finished their entrees. When the waitress cleared their dishes, David leaned forward. "So why me? Why ask me to help you when you have all of CID at your disposal?"

"Because this is not officially my case. It's personal right now. And when detectives work a case, they work it in pairs. Not just to have each other's backs but to bounce ideas off each other. Right now, I'm flying solo on this and really need someone who's smart and capable. Look." Abigail blotted her lips and set her napkin on her lap. "Jonathan always spoke so highly of you. You two hung tight together. You survived. Now, I want to get Nabeelah to safety. I want to find Jonathan, and I want to know why he was kidnapped and if all three of you are targeted. What better a person than someone who fought side by side with him?"

He glowered at her over his water glass.

She was losing him. "David, please. I need you to have my back on this. Honestly, I've got no one else—"

"I'm not your man."

"Please." Desperation began seeping through the cracks of her composure. How could she make him understand? "You're a hero. A survivor. You fought one of the toughest battles ever and survived."

"That man ceased to exist the moment I woke up in Germany seven years ago."

"But I need you as my wingman to be my eyes and ears and to—"

"No, you don't. You need another detective, not me. What about that police detective working the case?"

No way, no how. Uh-uh. She'd never work with Nick. Ever. "They've cut me out of the investigation."

"I'm sorry, Abigail, but I'm not your guy for this. I don't have the brains or brawn you need."

She'd lost him. So much for all of her time, money, and effort spent. What had it come to? Nothing. She wanted to lie on the floor and cry as she flailed in frustration. "Then I'm really out of options." She jumped up. "I'm sorry. I need to be alone."

To avoid melting down like a toddler in public and being put in time out, she rushed outside.

Burning Tree, Utah

Mitch Patterson dropped his last package off at Burning Tree's only bar and grill before pausing at the western end of town to gas up his truck. As diesel ran into the tank, he stared east as if he could see the Martin house. Someone had shown up out of the blue, and that didn't bode well for him.

It wouldn't matter that it had absolutely nothing to do with his relationship with Shepherd. He'd get dragged into it anyway. He had to make a call. Now.

He returned the nozzle to the tank before climbing behind the wheel and starting the engine. He drove his delivery truck onto the highway and headed east, passing the Martin house. He glanced at the windows. Dark, just as he expected. By now, Shepherd had gone to supper with his girl. Beyond the town limits, Mitch parked on the side of the road and dialed a number on his cell phone.

"What is it?" El Lobo's voice, laced with the faintest of accents, came across clearly as if he were right beside him.

"We have a problem," Mitch said. His gaze shifted down the highway toward town a mile away.

"That would be?"

"David Shepherd had a visitor today. A woman by the name of Abigail Ward."

"Interesting."

"She said she's the sister of Shepherd's best friend." Mitch hopped from the truck and paced to the edge of the asphalt. When the silence grew from seconds to a minute, he rushed on, "Honestly, that's the only thing that's happened this year. I don't think it's important, but you told me if any-thing—"

"You let me decide what is important." After a few seconds of nothing but air, El Lobo added, "I need you to do something for me. No, two things."

Mitch sagged against the side of the truck. "What would those be?"

"First, if you see any other strangers in town, and I mean *any*, I want you to report to me. I'll figure out whether they are of consequence." His handler exhaled hard, probably blowing out the cigar smoke Mitch remembered so well from his days in Kandahar. "The second is that I want you to warn David Shepherd."

"What?"

"You see, I have come to the conclusion that others in my pay have made a foolish error in kidnapping Abigail Ward's brother. You are to warn the two of them to back off, to stay away from anything related to the kidnapping."

"But if I warn him, then I reveal myself."

"Are you so dense?" The question came across as a growl. "Warn him covertly, of course. How you choose to do so is up to you."

Mitch flinched at the idea of what he insinuated. "Burning Tree's a small town. I can't just waltz up to the front walk. People talk around here."

"You will do what needs to be done. Remember that the money I'm paying you is going for a good cause, is it not? If you don't do my bidding, your lovely little girl won't get any more cancer treatments, right?"

He had to bring that up.

Mitch closed his eyes and scrubbed a hand across his face. He always held little Vespa in his arms during her chemo treatments. It was too much for a five-year-old to bear sometimes. "Okay. I'll do something."

"Report to me when you're done." A click sounded.

Mitch slid the phone into his pocket. What could he do? He hadn't been lying to El Lobo. People talked in town. They'd let David or Kyra know if they saw something suspicious. Maybe waltzing up the front walk was exactly the right thing to do. His mind churned as he pulled onto the road and reversed course.

A minute later when he arrived at the house, he had his story in place. He'd mistakenly handed off the wrong package earlier that evening and had come to exchange it. And he'd leave a note for Kyra that he'd been in their house to do the exchange.

With another box in hand to confirm his cover, he climbed the steps and rang the doorbell. Ranger barked, but no one came to the door. Carefully, he turned the knob. Like all Burning Tree residents, Kyra didn't bother to lock her door, so it opened on soundless hinges. "Ranger, hey, buddy."

Mitch loved on the dog for a few minutes. Lilly whined from her crate in the kitchen, and he let her lick his fingers before returning to the living room. He'd deal with Abigail first, then with Shepherd, all without putting a scare into everyone else.

With one last look around, he headed to the guest room and went to work.

21

Burning Tree, Utah

The waitress returned, holding two desserts for a table occupied by one. She watched Abigail hurry out. "Is she coming back?"

David offered his best smile. "I'd better get those to go."

Across the way, Kyra put her hands on her hips and glared at him. She only shook her head and turned to talk to a customer.

He shrugged.

Abigail had been foolish to think he'd be able to help her. How could he after all that had happened?

"You failed him and everyone on that mission." Those words from Jessie's grieving widow echoed in his ears.

He closed his eyes and rubbed his temples.

Seven years ago, he'd sat with Captain, Jonathan, and the chieftain in the chieftain's home as they sipped strong cups of overly sweetened hot tea. David spoke in halting Pashto. "Sir, your daughter has gifts that very few men have, even fewer women. I'd like her to come to the States for training. With your permission and blessing, of course."

The chieftain, a man of few words, cradled his cup. For the longest time, only the fire hissed from the family hearth. Slowly, the old man nodded. He smiled, revealing both missing teeth and his pride in his daughter. "It is so. You have both my blessing and my permission."

"David."

He jumped. The waitress must have called his name more than once. She extended a clear box holding two slices of chocolate silk pie.

"Thanks."

Once she left, he dropped a ten on the table to cover the tip and rose. Only then did he see Abigail's fleece. He grabbed it and headed into the deepening dusk.

Outside, Abigail leaned against a post of the restaurant's porch. She had her arms folded across her chest. Her head drooped, and her dark blond hair cascaded alongside her face and framed it in waves of a rich wheat color. For a moment, he drank in her profile. Yes, she and Jonathan definitely favored each other. Though some light remained, she shivered in the increasing chill.

He cleared his throat. "You forgot something." He held up her fleece before offering his jacket. "Here. You'll be warmer."

"Thanks." She shrugged into it and started to step off the porch into the parking lot.

He took her arm. "Let's go this way. It's a prettier walk." When she resisted, he gently tugged her onto the path leading along the river and behind the hotel. "Besides, we haven't finished talking."

"I have. It's clear you have no desire to help."

"I don't think I said that."

"Whatever."

He stopped where the path ran parallel to the river, then leaned against the rough wood of the railing separating the walkway from the riverbank. "Mom and Dad got into the hotel business about ten years ago, which includes the bungalows behind us. He always wanted to make the riverfront an attractive place for townspeople and guests alike. Building this fence was one of the first projects I did for him when I returned three years ago."

Abigail ran her fingers along the top rail. For the longest time, only the water burbling along some nearby rocks filled the air. Finally, she speared him with her gaze. "I take it you were homeless."

He started. "How did you know?"

"I pulled your history and noticed a gap in the VA records. And the way you talk as if you're the worst failure in the world." She shifted away a few feet and glanced at him. "Why do you think that?"

"Because I was homeless. I mean, who lets himself get into a situation like that?"

"It happens to the best of people."

"Says the woman who has it all."

She glared at him. "You don't know a thing about me, David Shepherd, so don't you dare say something like that." She turned back toward the house.

"Abigail, wait."

If anything, she quickened her pace as they passed through the remainder of the resort. The path moved away from the river to meet the sidewalk along the road. She turned left toward the house and almost bolted to the porch steps.

"Abigail, please."

She faced him. Since dark now enveloped the area, the porch light cast her face in shadows. She yanked open the screened door. "Sorry, but until you look back over your life and realize what a lie you've believed, we have no business together."

"Can you at least hear me out?"

"Why should I?" She turned the front door knob.

"Because I have more to say. And besides." He held up the pie. "We haven't had dessert, and you promised you'd try it."

She rolled her eyes, but she didn't slam the door in his face. "Okay. Fine."

"There's a fire pit in the backyard. If you get it going, I'll meet you out there."

She muttered something under her breath and let Lilly out of her crate. Both dogs headed outside with her.

David paused at the sink and ran some water into Kyra's electric teakettle. He found some peppermint tea in a decorative clay pot on the counter. As the water began heating, he gazed out the window above the sink.

Abigail had lit the fire. In its glow, she tossed a ball for Ranger, who ran out, grabbed it, and brought it back. He charged after another throw. Lilly squealed as she nearly got run over by her larger companion. Abigail picked her up and cradled her. She settled onto one of the wooden Adirondack chairs. Did she even realize how her face transformed when cuddling the puppy?

He leaned against the counter and closed his eyes.

On a chilly August afternoon in 2008, Nabeelah lay prone with an M-4 in her hands. She had glanced over her shoulder. "How did I do, Sergeant David?"

David had peered through the scope. "You're so close. Here." He adjusted her hands and the way she held the gun. "Try that."

She fired.

David did another check. Perfect. "You hit it square on, little sister."

She grinned. "It is good?"

"Very. Now you must repeat over and over for it to be natural."

"You're our Athena," Jonathan said from where he crouched nearby.

Nabeelah turned to him. "I am what?"

"Do tell, professor's son." David grinned at his best friend.

"Athena was a Greek goddess. Goddess of wisdom. Goddess of courage. She'd only fight fiercely when defending her homeland." Jonathan's gaze switched to their protégé. "Just like you, Nabeelah."

"She's what we need," he had told his commanding officer months later, shortly before they spoke with the chieftain. It was now March of 2009, and the Mighty Men were due to return to the States in eight weeks. "She knows how to get the information we need from the women quickly but gently. She's got the endurance, and she's got the gift of independent thinking needed for units like ours. I think with further training, she can be a very valuable asset to SF here in Afghanistan."

The lieutenant colonel studied him before shuffling the papers on his desk. "How long has she been attached to your team?"

"Seven months," Captain answered, standing at parade rest beside David.

"I can see a distinct increase in direct action successes. More insurgents caught. No casualties, hardly any injuries. All of these, I've reported to my superiors, and they said to keep doing whatever we're doing to maintain our successes." Their CO tapped a pen against the paper. "You say it's because of her?"

"Yes, sir," David replied.

"And you had a hand in training her?"

"He did most of it. Sergeant Shepherd taught her well," Captain said. "All he had to do was tell her once, and she did it. Heck, she's a better study than some of our guys."

The lieutenant colonel studied them for a long minute. "I'll have to get buy-in from my superiors, but I think they'll be interested. If they say yes, you'll plan out a suitable curriculum for her?"

David fought against a grin of success. "Yes, sir, I will."

"Then it's settled. I'll get back to you soon."

Captain and David returned to the village. Within a week, they had their answer from the CO. "Extract her when your team moves back here to return to the States. I'm leaving you in charge of this, Shepherd. You do a good job of this, and maybe we can parlay this into a bigger training."

The teakettle's whistling brought him back from the memory. After pouring water into the mugs, he dished out the chocolate pie. He joined Abigail and set both mugs and plates on the stone edge of the fire pit. "Have some. I hope you like peppermint tea."

"I do." She sampled her pie. "This is definitely yummy."

"I told you it would be." He fell silent. How much could he help her understand? How much should he tell her? Finally, he dove in. "I realize, as I look back on my life, how I had it pretty easy in the Army, all the way up until I returned to Womack at Bragg in May 2009. I got out of the hospital in June. Sure, I'd been in a war and had already done two hazardous tours of duty in Iraq after that. I'd never gotten hurt, even though I lost buddies and had others who'd gotten injured. After that, things got really hard. Jonathan and I were trying to put together another team, and it wasn't working. The captain was a yes-man who only wanted a promotion. The rest of the guys were whiners to the nth degree. And though I most likely didn't need the painkillers by the end of 2009, I kept taking them as a way of coping. Booze helped too. Then Jonathan retired."

"Are you blaming my brother for what happened to you?" She leaned forward and studied him with narrowed eyes.

At that point, the best answer was a non-answer, so he continued, "Things crumbled after that. Shortly after he retired, I heard about a program offering early retirement to personnel who'd put in their twenty and had done at least three tours of duty in the sandbox. I jumped on it and moved to Raleigh. I had a hard time, a really hard time, adjusting to civilian life. I couldn't find a job until I got offered one to be the assistant manager of a drugstore. And by that point, I was so deep into painkillers and alcohol that I couldn't keep it."

Silverware scraped on pottery as Abigail finished the last of her pie. She set the plate on the edge of the fire pit and sat back with her mug cradled in her hands. "Why are you telling me this?"

She baited him. He knew she did, but he couldn't help but answer. "I'm telling you this because if I've been such a failure at life, I'm not capable of helping you."

"I think you're lying."

He scowled at her. "I'm not lying to you. All of that happened."

"Oh, I know it did," she said. "That's not what I'm talking about."

"Then what exactly am I a liar about, Major Ward?"

"How long were you in the Army?"

His back stiffened. "I don't like being interrogated."

"How long were you in the Army?"

"Twenty years. The same as your brother."

"When did things get bad?"

"The last year or so."

"And how long were you in the civilian world before you became homeless?"

"Less than a year."

She remained silent as if to let him come to his own conclusions. Finally, she asked, "When looking back on your life, starting in 1990 and running until 2011, what do you see?"

He bolted to his feet. "You have no right to ask me that. How dare you come in here with your insinuations?"

"I'm insinuating nothing because I know better." She approached him, stopping within inches of him as she stared into his eyes. Her gardenia scent wafted to his nose. "If you were a true failure, you would have felt no reason to justify it. Yet you expended a lot of breath explaining why you think you are one."

Her words stung him deep in his soul. "I don't have to hear this. Good night, Abigail Ward. Have a safe trip home. And good luck on finding your brother."

He stomped up the steps to his apartment. Once inside, he slammed the door and headed toward the bedroom.

She's right, you know. The thought stopped him in his tracks. *There's something more happening here, and you need to figure it out.* He returned to the door, and opened it a crack, then slipped onto the deck and peered at the fire pit.

Abigail had resumed her seat and now had her head in her hands. Did she cry? No, it seemed as if Major Abigail Ward cried for no one.

Ranger came up beside the chair and pawed her leg. She reached out and scratched his head before rising and gathering their plates and mugs.

Even his dog had betrayed him.

Huffing out a breath, he headed to the bathroom and flipped on the light. And came face to face with a message scrawled across the mirror.

Stay away from this.

The dark red lipstick resembled the color that had graced Abigail's lips—the woman who, right this moment, stole his dog's affections and his sister's sympathies.

He needed to put a stop to this. He strode into the bedroom and toward the door but stopped.

Someone had jabbed his hunting knife into the dresser top. He took a step closer. The intruder had speared the picture of Jonathan, Nabeelah, and him. The tip went straight through Nabeelah's face.

This wouldn't have been Abigail's doing. Besides, when would she have had the time?

She was alone downstairs. Was she in danger?

He thumped through his apartment and onto the deck, almost colliding with her and sending her head over heels back down the stairs.

She threw a hand up to stop him. "Whoa!"

Off balance, he caught her around the waist with his right arm and grabbed the railing with his left hand to keep both of them from tumbling to the concrete below. His right-handed grip began around her waist weakened, and he tightened his hold until he felt her heart hammering against his chest. "Are you okay?"

"Y—yeah. I—I can't breathe."

"Sorry." David eased his hold.

She extracted herself and stepped onto solid ground. "Someone's been here. They left a message on my mirror."

She led the way inside to the guest room and waved him toward the note on her mirror.

Leave here and don't come back.

That same deep red of Abigail's lipstick.

"You got one?" Her question broke into his thoughts.

He jerked his chin in a nod. "Somewhat similar."

"Show me." She led the way upstairs and read the note left for him. "This has to be related to Jonathan's kidnapping."

"There might be more."

"What do you mean?"

"In here." He led her into his bedroom.

She frowned at the knife and picture. "I think someone's trying to warn us." She ran downstairs and to the guest room with him hard at her heels. After taking a picture of the writing on her mirror, she pawed through her backpack. "My laptop is still here. So's the drive, but who knows if anything was copied?"

She yanked open the dresser drawers and began throwing things into her suitcase.

"What are you doing?"

"I'm headed out. We seem to be at an impasse, and since there are no flights out until Saturday, I'm driving back."

"That's like a day and a half drive if you don't sleep."

"So? I'll get there at the same time as if I flew."

"Abigail, wait." He stepped between her and the bed where she'd tossed her suitcase. "I didn't say no."

"But it's clear you're not interested."

"Give me some more time to think about it."

She glowered at him. "I. Am. Out. Of. Time."

"Just until nine tomorrow morning. Please."

She blew out a sigh and shook her head. "Okay, fine. I may be a fool, but if I don't see you here and ready to go at nine tomorrow morning, I'm leaving. Got it?"

"Oh, yeah, I do." His gaze slid to the mirror. "I guess we should call the cops."

"They'd say it was a lost cause since y'all don't bother to lock your doors." He opened his mouth to protest, but she held up her hand. "Seriously, we might as well just wipe them off the mirrors and not worry Kyra." She slid from his jacket and shoved it into his arms. "And here. I almost forgot. Nine tomorrow. I want your answer. Having none, I'll make flight reservations for one."

She'd dismissed him. With jacket in hand, he returned to his bedroom upstairs. He jerked the knife out of the picture of Jonathan, Nabeelah, and him and eased onto the bed to stare at it.

Not helping Abigail might be deadlier than any risk he took with her.

22

Burning Tree, Utah

David arose before dawn the next morning and pulled on Lycra cycling pants and a bright blue cycling shirt with the scenery around Moab stitched in hues of red, orange, and yellow. He gathered his hair in a band and tied a bandanna on his head in a do-rag. Once he softly called to Ranger, he tiptoed downstairs and prepared his pack with enough fluid for both man and dog.

After adding the collapsible water bowl, dog treats, and some protein bars, he pulled a sheet of paper from the pad beside the phone. He hesitated, then scrawled a short message to Abigail assuring her he'd be back by nine, that he'd return with his yes or no in hand.

Everyone slept, even Little Bit. He opened the door to Abigail's room. She lay curled on her side with the blanket pushed down to her waist as if she'd tossed and turned for a long time before falling into slumber. His gaze drifted from her cheek to the curve of her figure as it narrowed to her waist before widening to her hips. How easy it would be to dip his fingers into the silky tresses of her hair.

He didn't dare.

He dropped the note on her nightstand. Once outside, he pushed his mountain bike down the driveway. The chilly air on the ride down the highway whispered along his skin and raised goosebumps. Or was it from seeing Abigail asleep?

He arrived at the mesa and made the turn onto the dirt road. The whole ride up, his mind hummed like the wheels along the pavement. Her solid frame in his arms when he'd almost bowled her over intermingled with her gardenia scent.

As the sun began lifting over the horizon, he found it easier to put her out of his mind, if only for a bit. He arrived at his destination and laid his bike on its side, then shucked his shirt and placed it on a nearby boulder to dry. Beside him, Ranger whined.

"Time for some water, eh?" He poured some into the bowl. As he crouched to ensure that his dog drank, he gazed at the hulk of wood black against sky the color of a robin's egg. As the sun rose higher, the sky color deepened to a rich blue. He left Ranger to his water and approached the tree until he reached up and put his hand on the charred bark.

"God, You know this is my most sacred spot. You remember how I always came here when I had a decision to make? Like joining the Army and before we shipped out to Afghanistan?"

He closed his eyes and kept his hand on the tree. "The tree was alive then. Dad said it died the same day Michael died. The day of The Incident." He raised his gaze to the sky.

A hawk shrieked in the distance.

Other than that, silence reigned.

"I think you're lying." Abigail's accusation from the night before flew into his mind.

"I'm not," he whispered as he hung his head.

"When looking back on your life, starting in 1990 and running until 2011, what do you see?" Again, her question challenged him. It was clear she had faith in him.

So did his sister. "You've got twenty years of proof right there. And you know what? I think God has brought you to this moment for a reason."

Then why didn't he?

Over seven years ago, when they were in the village, he and Jonathan shared a campfire.

"You know something, bro," Jonathan had said. "I've been doing some thinking."

"About?"

"You've heard that saying that God gives only as much as we can bear?"

"Yeah."

"I think God gives us more than we can bear because that's when we learn to throw our trust fully into His hands. What do you think?"

Back then, he'd agreed. But now?

"Abigail's so capable. She can do this on her own. But Nabeelah…" He turned his eyes heavenward to talk to the Lord. "I worry about her. I—I don't know if I have the strength now. I'm… I'm a broken-down, washed-up vet, one who likes it where he is and is terrified to leave Burning Tree."

He turned and walked away a few feet. The hawk's cry came to him from overhead, and he watched as the bird turned lazy circles as it rode a thermal high into the sky. "I guess we're not on speaking terms, God. Kyra says it's me and not You. What do You want from me?"

He knew the question was a loaded one.

To voice it meant he'd opened himself up to God, who could ask more than he was willing to give. Until then, it'd been so easy to exist in the small, protected world of Burning Tree with his sister, parents, and a few friends being the ones he trusted. He knew what God would ask of him. He would ask him to open himself up again, to rely on the One who he thought had abandoned him.

I'm not sure I can do that.

It dawned on him with clarity.

He knew.

No one had spoken audibly to him.

He simply knew.

He had to go with Abigail.

"God, I'm not so sure about this. I'm honestly not sure I'm able, or if I'm even willing."

Trust.

That word that came to his mind unbidden.

"Trust? That's hard to come by. Except when it comes to my family."

Trust. Gentle, but insistent. *Trust Me.*

"I'm not sure I can do that." The potential costs of trying to find and save Jonathan and Nabeelah made him nauseous.

"I'm afraid. I am. The last time I did that, I nearly died. Lost my purpose. Wound up on the streets." He drew in a deep, shuddering breath.

I am with you always, to the end of the age.

Those words rang in his soul like a gentle, persistent bell.

Suddenly, something filled his being, something like certainty.

God would be with him.

"You'll walk with us? Guide us? Keep us safe?"

Ranger growled, distracting him. The mesa rose up in a series of small terraces until it flattened out again. Along the way, boulders littered the red rock. Ranger faced those rocks. A breeze puffed downward, which meant that his dog had picked up a scent.

Another low rumble came from his dog. The fur along his back rose, and his tail stood at attention.

"Ranger, what is it?"

Ranger growled again. His lips curled to reveal his fangs.

David scanned the rocks. "Ranger…"

A rock tinkled downward.

Ranger started barking.

Heedless that he wore his cycling shoes, David started up the steep path.

A figure bolted from hiding, one dressed in a fleece, pants, and hiking boots. Long, dark hair fanned out behind her. David blinked. "Hey, you!"

She didn't slow. She cast a long look over her shoulder as she darted away on a trail that led downward to his level yet several feet away.

That face. Years ago a headscarf had covered her hair, but he'd never forgotten her heart-shaped face. His mind struggled to send the frantic message to his lips. His voice finally worked. "Nabeelah!"

She ignored him.

Heedless of the slick soles of the cycling shoes he wore, David charged after her.

Nabeelah vaulted a large rock.

David did too. He skidded but continued his pursuit.

She dashed along the hiking trail that ran by the burning tree and dropped off to begin a rapid descent from the mesa to the valley below. She hopped from rock to rock like a mountain goat before hitting dirt and darting around a corner out of sight.

He did the same. As he landed on the trail, his feet slid from underneath him. He fell hard on his hip and skidded toward the edge of the path and a precipitous drop that would spell his death if he went over. He clawed at the ground with his right hand and caught a rock, then thrust his leg out and slid to a stop.

He didn't dare roll on his back. If he did, he'd plunge over the edge. *Hold. Please hold,* he silently begged his right hand as he pulled. He eased onto his stomach. Only then did he risk a look. Yep, he'd come close today. He sagged to the ground and remained that way for a few minutes before crawling away from the edge.

"Not smart, Shepherd," he muttered quietly as he used a nearby boulder to haul himself to his feet. He rubbed his hip and rotated it. That helped. He'd have a bruise but thankfully nothing more.

Ranger peered at him from the top of the trail.

Carefully, David navigated upward to level ground. He scratched his dog on the head. "Next time, your master will try to exercise a little more in the brain department. C'mon. Let's go home."

He headed toward the dirt road and began the descent downward. He'd seen Nabeelah for his own eyes. Had she been the one to leave the messages? Most likely. *Why* remained a mystery. And was she friend or foe? He couldn't answer that either.

Maybe Abigail was right. Nabeelah was in danger, and she'd warned them with the messages. Should he try and find her in Burning Tree? Or find the source of the danger?

Any hesitation in going with Abigail disappeared in the face of his questions.

But before he did so, he had one more stop to make.

Once he arrived at the town limits, he crossed the highway and pulled up to the bike rack in front of the rotating red and white barber's pole. He made his request to the barber, who shook his head in disbelief. "You're sure about this, Shepherd?"

"I am," David replied through the hammering of his heart.

Half an hour later, the barber turned David around in the chair so he could look at himself in the mirror. For the first time in five years, the man gaping at him had short hair and a very closely trimmed beard like he'd kept it during his time in Afghanistan.

Part of him trembled as he stared at himself. He rubbed his jaw.

David, the warrior, had returned.

The reluctant warrior.

Burning Tree, Utah

Abigail glanced at the clock on the microwave above the stove. Nine in the morning on the dot. Where was he? David's note, which she'd found when she'd awakened at seven, had promised he'd be back by then.

"At least he left a note this time," Kyra had told her as she'd headed out the door with the kids. She'd grabbed Abigail in a quick, tight hug. "Thanks for coming out here. I'll be praying for both of you."

The printer that had been spitting out image after image from her foray into Jonathan's safe finished its whirring. Abigail picked up the stack, clipped it together, and slid it into a folder. That went into her backpack. It sat beside her suitcase, which she'd packed within minutes of getting ready for the day. She shot another glance at her watch. Time to make her flight reservations for the next day. She was done. Finished. She couldn't count on David for help, so she'd manage on her own as best she could.

As she turned away, she thought she saw a flash of color through the window above the bench at the kitchen table. Hard shoes clonked against concrete. A moment later, a large man sauntered through the door like he owned the place.

The electric current of adrenaline shot through her. She backed toward the kitchen. "Who are you? No one invited you here."

She dove toward the counter and snatched a knife from the butcher block.

"Whoa! Abigail, it's me. David."

She stared at the short, dark hair covered by a ratty bandanna and face with a short beard that hugged his jawline. And then there was the cycling get-up. Uh-huh. He was built, all right.

Good grief, she'd almost slashed the very man who lived here.

As the adrenaline drained away, she laid the knife on the counter. "I—I'm sorry. I—I didn't recognize you."

"That's okay." He stooped to pick up Lilly, who'd run to greet him. "At least Lilly knows who I am." He chuckled and speared Abigail with his gaze as the puppy licked his arms. "Give me an hour. Then we can hit the road and make it to Salt Lake by supper."

Surprise had stolen her voice, so she only nodded.

He stepped through the door and called to Ranger. Their steps echoed. Above her, a floorboard creaked. Then toward the front of the house came the sound of two shoes hitting the floor. A shower started.

Her cell phone chimed. Nick. Again. For the sixth time since the night before.

Like the five before, she let it roll to voicemail and settled for playing with Lilly.

Finally, David joined her, this time dressed in a pair of cargo shorts, a T-shirt, and Tevas. His dark curls, now so short they almost clung to his head, glistened in the clear light of the kitchen. A large backpack rested across his shoulders. He reached into the fruit bowl and grabbed an orange. "You ready?"

"As ready as I'll ever be. Let's get those flight reservations made before we head out." Within ten minutes, she grabbed her bags and carried them to the car. Once they began winding their way eastward as they followed the river through the red rock, she nodded toward the backpack she'd placed on the floor of the backseat. "Grab the folder that's in there and look at the financial info I printed."

"Financial info?"

"I knew the cops were going to drill the safe, so I had to take pictures of all of Jonathan's bank and credit card statements. Kyra was kind enough to let me use her printer."

David set the folder on his lap and spread a paper towel over it. He began peeling his orange. Its tropical aroma filled the car and mingled with the scent of whatever he'd used on his hair. Sexy. Abigail inhaled deeply.

Stop it! she ordered herself. *Wrong time. Wrong place. Wrong guy. Definitely wrong guy.*

"I saw her," David said as red rock gave way to grayish brown desert that reminded her of the middle of nowhere in Iraq or Afghanistan.

"Saw who?"

"Nabeelah." He dropped the orange pieces of peel into a grocery bag.

Abigail stared at him.

"Eyes on the road," he warned her. "Especially out here."

"Sorry." She refocused. "You saw her?"

"When I went to the burning tree."

"What's that?"

He separated the orange wedges. "It's on my parents' ranch land and is what gave the town its name. I was out there thinking. And…praying, I guess."

"She was there?" Her heart rejoiced at the news.

"Ranger started growling. He'd picked up a scent. I went to investigate, and she bolted."

"Do you think she left the messages?"

"Likely so, yeah."

She cast another look at him. "What made you cut your hair and trim your beard?"

"You were right."

"What?"

"You were right last night when you accused me of lying. It got me to thinking. I need to have faith, to trust God. This is my way of showing that trust."

"Why did you keep your long hair and a thicker beard until this morning?"

"To remind me of what it was like to be homeless."

Abigail drawled, "Okay."

He blew out an impatient sigh. "I lived on the streets for over two years. I couldn't stay sober long enough to get a job, so I had no choice. At least I had to give up painkillers because I couldn't afford them. My hair and beard grew out and got ratty. My clothes were turning to rags. If I was lucky, I'd bring in thirty dollars in a day. Sometimes I got gift cards to a fast food joint. Other times, people would throw things at me. I got hit in the back by a glass bottle once."

How awful for him. "Did—"

He rushed on as if caught up in his memories. "I always worried that people were going to take what little I had left. They tried. Boy, did they try." He held up his right arm to reveal a tattoo on his forearm, one bisected by a long scar. "I got this when someone attempted to rob me while I slept. They knifed me. Cut some nerves. I lost use of my hand and still don't have a great grip at times. Do you know what it's like not to hear someone call your name for over two years?"

"I—"

"It's the worst thing in the world. They called me Big Guy at the camp. At least until…until Kyra showed up at the interchange where I was panhandling. Hearing her call my name was the sweetest thing in the world. She got me back to the hotel where she was staying. I got cleaned up. I was emaciated, had dropped fifty or so pounds. She got me set up with the VA, got me some counseling, a dentist, a doctor, and good therapy for my hand. More than that, she got the creditors off my back enough that I could have some semblance of a normal life. If it hadn't been for her…"

"She's—"

"You insinuated yesterday that I blamed Jonathan for being homeless. Yeah, I do. If he'd let me bunk with him. If he'd answered the phone when I called—"

"Now you wait a minute, David Shepherd." Like a match to kerosene, hot anger flashed through her. "Don't you *dare* try to blame him for your problems. You don't know what was going on with him. With us. You may not remember The Incident, but I can promise you he did and still does. *Every second of it.* And losing Mom and Dad, and then—"

She broke off and fumed.

"And then what?"

"I'm not talking about it with you." She clamped her jaw shut.

"I'm sorry." His words were soft, placating.

"No, you're not."

"I am."

"Whatever." If she hadn't needed her wingman and if her rental car had an ejection button, she would have pressed it at that moment. "Just…look through those records."

He sighed. "What do you want me to look for?"

"Anything abnormal. He keeps three years' worth of bank statements. The charge card statements only go back a year." Abigail started a Johnny Cash album as they turned onto I-70 and headed east toward Green River. By the time she turned northward on US 191, Johnny had been switched for Josh Turner.

"I found something." David's voice rose above the song.

"What?"

"Late November of last year, he got a rather large deposit. Then, a week later, a cashier's check was cut for that same amount."

She darted a glimpse at him. "What?"

"A cashier's check."

She picked up her phone from the center console. "Can you call the bank's number? I've got it set up on Bluetooth and can take it from there."

David dialed.

When the operator came onto the line, Abigail said, "This is Major Abigail Ward. I'm the sister of Jonathan Ward and have power of attorney to take care of his finances when he's out of the country. He's on travel now, and I need to check on a transaction he made in December."

"One moment." Muzak filtered over the speakers.

David grinned. "Not as stimulating as Josh Turner."

She scowled. She wasn't going to talk to him unless she had to. The phone rang through to another person, this one a guy. After she repeated her request, he asked, "The name of your favorite pet?"

"Sylvester."

"Your father's middle name?"

"Mitchell."

The man's voice filled the car. "I see that Mr. Ward did list you as his representative in his absence. When did the transaction in question occur?"

"The second of December in the amount of three thousand dollars. A cashier's check. I need to know who that was made out to."

"Wilson and Sculley attorneys at law, out of Wilmington, North Carolina."

How odd. "Thank you. I appreciate it."

"Is there anything else?"

"Uh, no." Abigail hit a button, and the music returned. "David, could you—"

"Doing so right now." He held up the phone. "Wilson and Sculley is a law firm out of Wilmington. They handle the legal aspects of real estate transactions all up and down southern shores of North Carolina."

"Call them."

"Wilco." The phone rang across the stereo.

"Wilson and Sculley, how may I help you?" the pert female voice on the other end asked.

Abigail said, "I'd like to speak with whomever dealt with a real estate transaction for Jonathan Ward."

"And you are?"

"Major Abigail Ward, U.S. Army. I'm his sister and have power of attorney when he's out of the country for work."

"One moment." A click and more Muzak told her she'd been put on hold.

"Stretching the truth a bit, aren't we?" David murmured.

She ignored him.

"Rupert Sculley."

"Mr. Sculley, this is Abigail Ward." She repeated her story and added, "Jonathan is my brother, and I had a question about a transaction he did. I assume you handled the closing for him?"

"I did indeed. Quite a nice gentleman, and he said he had a sister who was his proxy when he was out of the country. I'm happy to help."

"Can you tell me what he bought?"

"At the end of December, he closed on a house down in Holden Beach. I could e-mail the information to you if you wish."

"Please. I'd appreciate it."

"You're welcome. If you have any additional questions, please call me."

The phone pinged a few minutes later.

"Check that," Abigail ordered.

"Yes, ma'am." David mock-saluted and pulled up the message. "It's got some attachments."

"What are they?"

"Looks like some papers, maybe a contract. Then also one that looks like a real estate listing for..." He thumbed the phone. "Sunset Place. That must be the house he bought."

Their childhood beach house. How many years had they spent at least a week there? Many with the fond memories to go with it. Why hadn't he told he he was even contemplating such a thing?

"Abigail?" He reached out and touched her shoulder.

She brushed away his hand. "That...that's the place where we always went to the beach while growing up. Boy, that's a surprise."

"You didn't know about it?"

"Can't say I did." Her mind spun nearly as fast as the tires. It wasn't that her brother had lied to her. He'd held out. But why?

David flipped through the credit card statements. "This is interesting."

"What's that?"

"I'm looking at his credit card bill for transactions made in late December. The statement date is for the fourth of January."

"He must have paid it right before he headed back to Ghazni."

"Maybe. It's for a purchase made at Office Depot for almost five hundred dollars, made on the second of January."

"He'd have no reason to purchase that much in office supplies, mean-ing…" this would explain everything, "meaning he purchased a safe."

"Huh?"

"A safe. I found a safe key along with the drive of his notes. I'd bet money that he put the drive with the Athena file on it in that safe at the beach."

"I'd have to say you might be right, then."

She frowned. Jonathan was in the hands of his kidnappers. If they were who she thought they were, it'd be only a matter of time before they beat the information from him.

She pressed hard on the accelerator. The sooner they got to Raleigh, the better. Who cared if she could hardly stand to be in the presence of her wingman?

23

Salt Lake City, Utah

Abigail pushed the door between their rooms almost closed and eased into bed with a sigh. She'd needed to be alone, especially after supper at one of the generic chain restaurants near the Salt Lake City airport. She should've eaten by herself. David had remained silent, his gaze probing and watchful as if he'd expected her to come clean about her outburst on the ride up. She'd do no such thing. Not with him. He didn't deserve an answer after the way he'd lectured her.

She tugged the comforter to her chin. As her body warmed the sheets, her eyes drooped closed. Nightmares of masked kidnappers beating Jonathan intermingled with the carnage she'd seen of the convoy and that of her investigation into the demise of the Mighty Men. They seemed so real, so vivid—

"Jonathan!"

Her eyes flew open, and the dreams dissolved. She released a ragged gasp. Brushing her hair out of her eyes, she sat up and stared at the clock. 10:35.

Suddenly, she didn't want to be alone. Still... *Really, God? He's the only one around to comfort me? After today?* She glanced at the doors separating her room from David's. A sliver of light slipped out from underneath. Even his company would be better than none. Had he fallen asleep with the lights on? Then she heard the turn of a book page.

She slipped on a pair of sweats to go with her nightshirt and crept into his room.

He sat on the couch, his feet on the coffee table, his right hand squeezing a foam ball, a paperback propped on his knees. His gaze flicked upward. "I thought you were sleeping."

"I had a bad dream." She remained where she was with her arms folded.

"Come over here." He patted the cushion beside him. "I won't bite."

"After today, I'm not so sure."

"I know." He sighed. "I owe you an apology. Please forgive me for tearing into you like that. I had no right. Can you forgive me?"

A sigh escaped her. "I do."

"Then come over here and sit down."

Finally, she did, which brought her into immediate proximity of whatever stuff he used on those close-cropped, tight, black curls of his. "What are you reading?"

"A Nevada Barr mystery." He laid it face down and ran his finger down the worn spine. "What were you dreaming about?"

"Jonathan. What I read regarding the convoy hit. What happened years ago." She leaned forward and rested her elbows on her knees, much like Jonathan had all those years ago after he'd lost his ten friends. "I need you to have my back as much as I need you to be my wingman."

"How so?"

"I'm scared," she confessed to the floor.

"Of what?"

"That it's not going to be him we find but his body. And I don't want to be alone for that. I don't want to be alone."

He rubbed her back. "I'll be here for you."

"Stop, will you?" She slapped his hand away. Another headache arrived, and she pinched the bridge of her nose. Finally, she sat back. "Can you promise me something?"

"What?"

"That you'll clear the air with my brother?"

He remained quiet. The dimness of the lighting turned his dark eyes liquid. Absentmindedly, he ran some of her hair between his fingers.

She brushed his hand away.

He wove her fingers between his.

Her heart sped up. "Please. I know it's easy to hold on to old grievances. I beg you to let this one go."

"If it means that much to you, I will." Seeming to catch his gesture, he released her.

"Thanks," she murmured. Then her temples throbbed again, and she winced.

"Are you okay?"

"Headache," she muttered.

"Do you have anything for it?"

"Nope."

His brow furrowed. "I've got some ibuprofen in my kit if you—"

"I don't need anything," she lied. She pushed to her feet. The less said the better at that point.

"You're sure?" He rose as well.

"Y—yeah." Not convincing, even to her ears.

"I'm not so sure of that." He caught her arm. That gaze, unnerving in the bright light of day, penetrated her defenses and hit close to that part of her soul where she'd locked away secrets of her own, those she didn't want to share with anyone.

The lie rolled off her lips. "Really, I'm fine." She forced a bright, brittle smile to her face. "I'll see you bright and early at five."

With that, she strode to her room and shut the door before he asked enough questions to unearth her fear of painkillers.

24

"Of all the best laid plans," Abigail muttered as she trundled her carry-on across the tightly-woven carpet at the Raleigh-Durham airport terminal. Weariness surged through her. "Who knew that leaving at 6:30 in the morning could lead to getting in at 10:25 at night?"

"You couldn't predict the bad weather in Chicago." David came shoulder to shoulder with her.

"Grrr!" Her steps quickened. "At least we don't have to worry with checked luggage."

"What's your plan?" With his long stride, he easily kept up.

"We get into the car. Get to the beach ASAP, albeit with stopping for coffee before we leave. Then we get the drive and figure out what's on it."

They arrived at the escalator that lowered them to the first level.

"Question," David said.

"That would be?"

"Why do you think getting the drive will help us get Jonathan back?"

"We'll have what they want. And if it has the Athena file on it like I think it does, that makes it an Army matter that CID is already working on. Then it's in the Army's jurisdiction, meaning more resources."

"Have the cops made any progress?"

"How should I know?" She conveniently ignored the fact that, during their time stuck at Midway airport in Chicago, Nick had called for a seventh time. Some people collected cats. She collected voicemails. "They haven't talked to me. And if the kidnappers were as clever as I think they were, they didn't leave behind anything that could be traced to them."

David frowned. "Are you sure they haven't called?"

She didn't answer.

They rode the escalator down to the level that allowed them to cross underneath the terminal road to the parking garage. After arriving at the elevator, she jabbed the Up button and leaned against the wall with her head hung. "This so stinks."

He slid his hand under her hair and rubbed the back of her neck. "I think we're both tired."

Rather than pull away this time, she leaned into his hand. This wasn't good. His touch put every nerve on alert. If she let her mind wander too long, she might imagine things that weren't possible.

The ding of the elevator rescued her. Once it released them to roam three floors up, she strode across the concrete. "We're down the row a few. Navy blue Honda Accord—"

"Hello, Abigail."

Dressed oh, so splendidly in a khaki suit and black shirt, Nick leaned against the back left fender of her car. One hand held a cigarette with smoke curling from the glowing tip. The other remained in his pocket, which pushed the corner of his jacket back to reveal his gun and the gold badge on his belt.

Yeah, he wanted to show her who was boss.

He glared at her. "It's about time you showed up."

"You mean to tell me you were so eager to see me that you came all the way to the airport?" Abigail put one hand on her hip.

"That's me. Your one-man greeting party." His New Jersey accent flared like the tip of his cigarette when he took a drag. He exhaled through his nostrils. It didn't take much for her to envision him charging her like a bull. "Who's your pal?"

"I'm a friend of hers. David Shepherd." Ever the wingman, David pressed closer from slightly behind her and to her right. His bulk reassured her.

She remained where she was. "Why are you here?"

"Because a good detective keeps his victim's family informed." Nick tossed the cigarette onto the concrete and stubbed it out with the toe of his loafer. "Only this good detective has tried to call the family of his vic not once, not twice, not even three times but *seven* times. You want to tell me why you haven't called me back?"

"I've been busy."

"Doing what? Visiting him?" Nick gestured toward David. "In Utah?"

"You were checking up on me?"

"Of course I was. You flew to Salt Lake City on Thursday. Returned today with the intent of getting in earlier this afternoon. So yeah, I've been waiting on you for a long time, and I'm ticked."

"So what?" Abigail popped the trunk to stow her luggage. Inside, the zippers had been pulled on both her gear bag and the suitcase containing her guns. She growled, "What have you done?"

"I searched your gear."

"With no warrant?"

"Oh, I got me a warrant." He reached into his blazer and tossed a folded sheet of paper toward her. "Read it and weep. I had probable cause since someone broke into your house." He shrugged. "I found some nice, inter-esting women's size-eight high tops that match the footprints we pulled from the soil in your backyard." In a flash, Nick grabbed her arm.

She flinched.

"You want to tell me something? Like how you conveniently left your phone in the room when you broke into your house and then lied to me?"

"Hey—" David stepped forward.

Nick put out his hand. "You stay out of it, pal. 'Fess up, Abigail."

Finally, she opted for the truth. "So I broke into the house. So what? It's my house as well as Jonathan's. I had a right to be in there."

"It's an active crime scene."

"That you wouldn't let me see." She jerked her arm loose. "Sorry, but I didn't find anything of substance in there." She lifted her chin. "Since you're so up on keeping the vic's family informed, what can you tell me? And I want everything, you understand?"

He hesitated.

"Everything, Nick."

"We found financial records in there. Things like stock, bank, and credit card statements. That's it. My boys worked through it on Thursday, yesterday, and all day today. They just finished this afternoon, which is why I came to the airport. Seems your brother went and bought himself a beach house at Holden Beach. Paid all cash for it, too."

"Where we vacationed in the summer while growing up."

Nick's lips curled in a smile.

Suddenly, Abigail realized her blunder. What was she thinking? It wouldn't take him long to figure out that Jonathan had installed a safe at the beach house—if Nick hadn't already done so. And to have the cops get their hands on that drive… She couldn't let that happen. She thrust her bag into the trunk. "Well, if that's it, we'll be going—"

Nick whipped her around and slammed her into the fender.

"Hey!"

David grabbed his arm. "Let her go."

In a flash, Nick shoved him back. "You touch me one more time, and I'll arrest you for assaulting a law officer. This is between her and me, got it?"

"No, it's—"

"Got it? Now shut your trap."

"David, it's okay." Abigail offered a weak smile.

He backed away, but he remained close.

Nick returned his fiery gaze to her. "You listen to me and listen to me good, Abby."

She stiffened as he used the nickname she hated.

"I want that drive you got. Understand? Now hand it over."

"What drive? I told you I didn't find anything." She kept her face neutral.

"Why do I think you're lying to me? Again?" Nick released her. "If I find out you've lied to me, that's it. I'll toss your butt into the clink for impeding an investigation."

"And if you touch me again like that, I'll have you arrested for assaulting a Federal law enforcement officer. Trump you, Nick Bocelli. Now leave us alone so we can be on our way. Let's go, David." She opened her door and slid into the driver's seat.

David tossed his pack into the back seat and joined her. She stared in the rearview mirror.

Nick stalked to an unmarked patrol car. He'd parked in the row behind her.

He glared at her as he lifted his phone to his ear.

A cold feeling washed over her.

Another headache, one brought on by exhaustion and her close-encounter-of-the-ex-husband kind, began building. She needed caffeine—and fast. Pinching the bridge of her nose helped.

David glanced at her. "Friend of yours?"

"Try ex-husband."

"The plot thickens." With that, he clicked his seatbelt into place.

"So it does." She sighed and put the car into Reverse. "So it does."

Raleigh, North Carolina

Frisco Montero had to admire Jonathan Ward. In the four days he'd been in their hands, Jonathan hadn't yielded a single clue, not even with a menage of starvation, sleep deprivation, and beatings known to make lesser men confess. But this particular beating? The most savage by far.

Jonathan lay on the floor, bound at the wrists and ankles by cable ties. Cal loomed over him, pool balls knotted into an athletic sock. He swung the makeshift club in a wide arc and slammed it into Jonathan's bare chest.

Over his cry, Frisco could have sworn he heard a rib crack.

"I'll...tell...you...nothing." Jonathan panted to relieve what Frisco was sure was agonizing pain.

Cal cussed and repeated his move as Roy paced around their prisoner.

Frisco turned away as Jonathan groaned again. He had to contact his handler, had to tell her that Jonathan was now in grave danger.

"I can't believe this!" Nicole stomped toward him.

He pretended to fiddle with his phone and tried to shut out Jonathan's grunts of pain. "What?"

"He won't say a word. Not a word! After everything we've done to him."

Over the hammering of his heart, Frisco said, "You could kill him."

"That would be useless." She took a sip from the coffee she held and spewed it out. "Yuck! That's it. I'm done with fast food coffee. Frisco." She speared him with her gaze.

"What?"

"Go get us some coffee."

He blinked in disbelief. "Excuse me?"

"Real coffee. Something that's not that swill we've been drinking. Like coffee from a coffee house."

"Wait. You want me to leave here, take the van, risk exposure, all so you can get some fancy coffee?"

"No, I expect you to walk on foot, boost some transportation, and then find us some real coffee." Her eyes narrowed. "Are you man enough to do that, or should I have Cal do it?"

The woman was nuts. At least it gave him the out he needed for his call. "Cal's not smart enough to avoid getting caught. All right then. But if I'm busted, this lands on you, not me. Got it?"

"Of course." She smiled to show she'd gotten her way. "I know you're the best at stealth." Abruptly, she whirled. "Cal, that's enough. String him up."

Frisco watched as Cal clipped the ties around Jonathan's ankles and wrists. Using a pair of handcuffs, he secured their prisoner's hands in front of him before dragging him over to where they'd looped a rope with a hook through a pulley hanging from a rafter of their hideout. He slid the hook over the chain of the cuffs and hauled on it.

As if he were some sort of an apparition, Jonathan rose until his toes barely touched the concrete floor. He moaned, most likely from his rib injuries.

Frisco fled into the night. He hated the warehouse where they'd hidden. The neighborhood was dangerous, and he dared not let his hand stray too far his pistol in his jacket. His head swiveled as he kept watch for anyone who could jump him.

Industrial turned to rundown residential. He peered at the first house. No transportation obvious, and a television flickered in a front room as if someone watched the late news. At the second house, a dog barked. Frisco lengthened his steps. At this rate, he'd be walking all night—if he didn't get mugged first. The third house had a car, but again, someone appeared to be home. Same thing at the fourth house.

Finally, he arrived at the driveway of a small bungalow. The lights were all out. No car in the driveway, most likely meaning that the occupants were away, hopefully out of town. A motorized scooter sat near the back of the carport with a helmet on the seat. He wasted no time in hot-wiring it. As the engine purred, he peered around him. No one seemed the wiser. He pulled on the helmet and beat feet to a better part of town.

Once the buildings changed from rundown houses to more of a university setting, he pulled over to the side of the road and removed his helmet. He wasted no time in dialing a number.

A female voice answered. "What is it?"

"Jonathan Ward is in trouble." His slight accent drifted away as he spoke to her.

A sharp intake of breath rewarded him. "You told me he was kidnapped. Is there more?"

"They're beating him. It's only a matter of time before they kill him."

"That cannot happen. You understand, yes?"

"It's a bit out of my control. I—"

"I don't care." Her own accent flared as she continued, "I know your primary duty was to stay close to him, but now, you must get him out of there."

"How?" Frisco closed his eyes. Her demand was crazy dangerous. "If I free him, I blow my cover, and we lose everything. We can't have that, now can we?"

Silence reigned for a few interminable seconds. "I always hate it when you're right. But you must, Frisco. He cannot die. He cannot!"

He winced. In the years they'd worked together, he'd never been able to tell her no. Why? *'Cause I'm a fool. That's why.* "Okay, okay. I'll see what I can do. But no guarantees."

"Do what you must. It is critical." She disconnected.

Frisco expelled a sigh. She was right. Jonathan had to live. Yet to let him live might mean he, Frisco, might have to die.

Raleigh, North Carolina

David watched Abigail out of the corner of his eye as they wound their way along the interstate and into downtown Raleigh. Once they neared Hillsborough Street, home of North Carolina State University, they crept past the Half-Moon Coffee House. The parking lot was so full that cars parked on the grass separating it from a dry cleaning business. "What's going on that's making it so crowded?"

Abigail smacked her forehead. "I forgot. It's Mother's Day weekend, and State and other colleges are probably having graduations."

"We could go somewhere else."

"No, we're already here. Besides, they have some of the best coffee around." She cranked the wheel to the right and turned onto a side street. After meandering down the road, she pulled to the side in front of a fire hydrant, which was the only open spot on the street.

"Stay here, and I'll get it. What do you want?"

"A large Kona coffee." She reached for her purse.

"My treat."

"David—"

"It's not like I'm destitute anymore. My treat. Call me if the cops show up to make you move." He shut his door and strolled down the sidewalk in the silky spring air. He paused and inhaled the sweet smell from some rose bushes of a nearby house. Only the tiniest hints of the humidity that would overtake the area rode upon the airwaves. All in all, a perfect night. Suddenly, he yearned to have Abigail walking beside him.

The thought hit him with such force that he paused. Where had it come from? That and a feeling of peace? Returning to Raleigh hadn't rattled him as he'd feared it would.

He reached the lights and noise of the coffee house on Hillsborough Street and stepped inside. People crammed into two lines. Something about it looked familiar. Was it the specials scrawled on the blackboard above the counter in colorful chalk? The NC State knickknacks everywhere? Or the hum and laughter of conversation? He closed his eyes and deeply inhaled the rich coffee scents. It hit him. He'd been to this very shop not six months before Kyra had found him.

It was late winter of 2013, March, to be exact. Late winter meant cold, and he had worn every stitch of clothing he still owned. All of it smelled. His body stank as well, enough that the patrons in the shop that day gave him a wide berth. He clasped three dollars of the meager fifteen he'd collected that day. Who cared if he needed it for food? Coffee would warm him and help prepare him for the cold night ahead.

"May I help you?" The barista, a brunette with sweet blue eyes, smiled at him.

"A…a large peppermint hot tea." His words came out as a rasp.

She filled his order. When he tried to hand over the bills, she shook her head. "Sir, it's on me."

"But—"

"It's on me." She offered a gentle smile. "Go buy yourself a hot meal."

"Sir, may I help you?" Those words snapped David back to the present.

He blinked. A redhead with green eyes now stood across the counter from him. From the impatience showing behind her smile, she must have asked the same question more than once. "I'm, uh, sorry. One large Kona coffee, and one large hot tea. Earl Gray if you have it."

Her fingers danced across a cash register. "Coming right up. Four dollars, eighty-five cents, please."

He handed over a five and got his change, then stepped back and surveyed the rest of the interior.

Business thrived that night. In a corner, what appeared to be two or three families in town for graduation had pushed a few tables together. Laughter emanated from the group. At another table near the front, a guy with headphones clamped over his ears slouched over his laptop and pecked at the keys. A couple of young women huddled together and chatted near the counter where the baristas placed their delectable brews. They took their orders and wandered outside.

"Frisco!" the barista called out.

A man a good six inches shorter than David strolled to the counter.

Something about that dark hair, the five o'clock shadow, and the heavy eyebrows seemed familiar to him. On the flight from Salt Lake City to Midway in Chicago, Abigail had read him fully into everything she'd found, including the four perpetrators Jonathan had named as part of the gunrunning ring. One of them was Frisco Montero, former Spanish army mechanic. She'd shown him their pictures, which he'd committed to memory.

Frisco took the order of four coffees and headed toward the door. He stepped into the evening air.

David shoved his way through the line. As he reached the exit, a gaggle of four college coeds blocked his path. Heedless to his need to grab the man in question, they slowed when they saw the line.

"Excuse me," David muttered. He nearly bowled them over in his desperation to stop Frisco.

He rushed outside.

Frisco bent over a motorized scooter and placed the coffees in a crate. He moved something around to secure them, then straightened.

Their gazes locked.

"Stop!" David shouted. He tried to rush toward him, but another group of families blocked his path.

Frisco cranked the scooter's motor.

David bulled through the group and earned a few dirty looks in the process.

Frisco spared him only a glance before dropping the clear visor on his helmet and pulling onto the street. He merged into traffic.

David could do nothing but commit the license plate to memory. If he'd acted quicker, they might have had a direct line to the kidnappers. Now, he collected their drinks and returned to the car to report his failure to Abigail.

She jumped as he slid into the car with their brews. "What took you so long?"

"It's as packed in there as it is out here. Are you okay?" he asked when he noticed the way she yawned.

"Yeah. I fell asleep while waiting for you. Thanks for the coffee." She put the car in drive and pulled away from the curb.

"I saw Frisco."

She jammed on the brakes. "What?"

"He was there."

"In the coffee house?"

"Right. I tried to stop him, but he recognized me."

"How could he?"

"I don't know." He shrugged. "Or maybe it was the fact that I keyed in on him. He made it outside, and I got stuck inside by a bunch of coeds." He slammed his hand into the dash. "Dang it! I was so close."

"Did you get any information?"

"He's on a moped, and I got the plate number." He rattled it off. "You know this means the kidnappers are here in Raleigh."

"I'm calling Nick. He wanted me to cooperate with him, so I am."

As they wound their way through Hillsborough Street's traffic, she made her report to Nick. He clicked through what he knew. Kidnappers in town meant that Jonathan was nearby, and after four days of being in their clutches, they'd probably beaten the location of the safe house out of him. "We need to get down to the beach ASAP."

"Ya think?" Sarcasm dripped from Abigail's words as she accelerated and slipped around some slowly plodding cars. She sped onto the Beltline that looped around Raleigh toward I-40 and the beach. "The scary thing? Something tells me that Jonathan's got a lot less time left than we think."

David tightened his seatbelt. "Then let's get down there and get that drive."

25

Raleigh, North Carolina

Four days of hiding. Four days of living like criminals on the run. Four days of interrogating Ward with beatings, starvation, and other methods. And what did they have to show for it? Nothing. Zilch. *Nada.* Nicole paced the interior of the dilapidated warehouse near downtown that they'd claimed as their hideout.

Where was Frisco? He'd agreed to her demand for coffee. Not just coffee but something better than the horrible, awful stuff from the nearest all night fast food joint.

She returned to the pool of light emanating from the construction lamps they'd set up. Thanks to some thoughtful soul who'd left the power on, at least they had light.

"Where is he?" she muttered.

"How should I know?" Irritation pushed at Cal's voice. He sat on one of their coolers, running his K-bar knife across a whetstone just like he'd done since he'd finished beating the snot out of Ward with his pool ball club.

Roy lounged on a camp chair and played with his phone.

Nicole turned her attention to her most convenient target—Ward. He still hung suspended from a hook between his cuffed wrists so that the toes of his bare feet hardly touched the crumbling concrete. His head drooped forward. She stopped and examined his face. A good layer of blond-going-to-gray stubble coated his jaw, as did dried blood from a cut they'd opened up on his left cheek during another beating. Scabbing from numerous cigarette burns covered his chest. Her gaze raked the tattoo on his right forearm. *Sola gratia.* Her lip curled. By grace alone. Really?

Roy's phone chimed. When he glanced at it, his feet hit the ground. "Darius."

Nicole kept her attention on Ward. "Tell him we need more info than the crap he's been handing over, or no ten grand."

Roy grumbled as he stepped away.

Ward's eyelids fluttered open, revealing a gaze vacant from dehydration, starvation, and probably a concussion.

"You want to tell me something, Ward? Like where you put that drive?"

He licked his lips as if priming them for a retort.

She slapped him with her left hand. The ruby commitment ring Roy had given her a couple of years before opened up a cut on his right cheek. Blood ran down his face in a scarlet line. He moaned, but he didn't say a word.

Behind her, Frisco stepped through with a carrier containing four cups.

"It's about time," she almost shouted as he joined the group.

"So shoot me," he muttered in his accent-tinged English.

"Does it really take an hour and a half to get coffee?"

"It does when I have to find, to quote you, 'Something that's not that swill we've been drinking. Like coffee from a real coffee house.' I had to walk to find some transportation to boost. Then I had to find a good place for coffee. Then wait in line for almost half an hour. Then I had to return my transportation." He dumped the carrier onto another cooler. "So where do the words 'thank you' come into play? Or do you lack those in your vocabulary?"

"Thanks," she muttered. She took her brew and walked away as her phone began chiming.

A wolf avatar popped onto the screen.

She shivered. If she didn't answer the call, he'd keep calling. She brought the phone to her ear. "Hello?"

"Nicole, Nicole, Nicole." El Lobo's deep baritone chilled her. "I understand things have gone awry. Am I correct in this?"

"I'm not sure what you mean, sir."

"Oh, I know you do. You see, I was in North Carolina for business when I happened to hear a news report about Jonathan Ward's kidnapping. And his sister has gone off the grid when she should have been on vacation seeing him. It didn't take me long at all to piece things together."

She whipped around and stared at the circle of light. Ward still dangled, his head once more drooping forward. "We had to do it. He knew too much about—"

"You are to let him go." El Lobo's voice hardened.

"How can we? He has…" Nicole crashed to a stop. She'd almost blurted out information about how Ward had stolen the drive.

An ominous pause filled the line. Then came a slight whisper of breath as he inhaled, most likely on one of the Cuban cigars he brought back from his extended family's hometown of Chihuahua. "He has what, Nicole? A jump drive? One with a file on it that I explicitly asked you to deliver to Shamal Khan?"

Nausea filled her. She crouched and hung her head. "I'm not sure—"

"Oh, I think you know exactly what I'm talking about. You see, Khan told me about your unfortunate lack of ability to carry out a simple order."

This wasn't good. Wasn't good at all. "I—I don't know what you're talking about."

"But you do. I know you do. You are to get that drive and deliver it to Khan. You must release Ward as well."

"How can we? He's the only one who knows where it is!"

"I don't care. If you kill him, you will bring the wrath of the law down on your heads. And you, my dear, will not able to withstand lengthy interrogation. If I hear any report or even a whisper that you have killed him, I will hunt you down and find you. And when I do, it will be a long, slow death for you and your comrades. *Comprende?*"

Oh, yeah. She understood, all right. Years before, when she'd been El Lobo's lover, screams had awakened her at the darkest hours of the night. She'd found him in the courtyard of his family's hacienda with a man—or what passed for a man—caught between two of his henchmen. They'd beaten the man to within an inch of death. El Lobo finished the job with a single shot to the head. "I—I do."

"Then get that drive and set Jonathan Ward free. You do that, and perhaps I will let you live." A click ended the call.

Nicole remained in her crouch. She knew what would happen if they didn't obey El Lobo. He'd keep his promise, hunt them down, and torture them before ending their lives. The same with Shamal Khan. If they didn't get that drive to him when Roy returned in a few weeks, he'd do what he'd promised a few weeks ago: overrun the compound and kill everyone there before hunting her down.

She stumbled to her feet and glowered at Ward. If he hadn't stolen that drive, none of this would have happened. A growl escaped her as she hurled her steaming coffee into his face.

He cried out.

With a flick of her wrist, she undid the rope holding him up.

Ward collapsed into a moaning heap onto the floor.

She snatched the K-bar knife from Cal's hands.

"Hey!" He jumped to his feet.

She ignored him and grabbed Ward's right arm. "You're going to tell me where that drive is. And if you don't, I'm going to cut off every single finger and toe you have until you do!"

He squirmed and tried to yank away.

"Starting with your pinkie finger." She put the blade to the joint.

Roy grabbed her wrist and jerked her backward.

Off balance, she tumbled backward.

"Baby, no." He hauled her to her feet and dragged her away.

"Let me go!" She struggled against him.

He pressed on her wrist until her fingers opened.

The knife clattered to the floor.

He grabbed her other arm.

She lashed out at him with her feet. "We need to get that drive!"

"Don't you think I know that?" He didn't loosen his grip. "Please, just...calm down. Can you do that for me?" He kicked the knife toward Cal, who scooped it up.

"Why should I?" She kept struggling.

"Because if you think with your emotions and not your head, we're sunk."

All of the fight left her. She sagged against his grip.

As if he didn't trust her, Roy maintained his hold. "Ward's not going to cave. You know he's not because he's got the same kind of training I got. He doesn't care about himself."

"We can break him."

"Sure, if we had weeks and months. We don't. I talked with Darius. Ward's sister is on the case."

"I know."

Roy cocked his head. "How?"

"El Lobo called," she said in a monotone. The sick feeling returned, and she leaned into him. "He's going to kill us if we don't get him the drive and free Ward."

"But he doesn't know what we now do. Ward has a beach house on the coast south of Wilmington. His sister and his friend, David Shepherd, are most likely heading that way." Roy smirked. "We get there first, we ambush them. Then Ward will have no choice but to give up that drive."

Hope began peeking through her doom and gloom scenario. "You think we can do this?"

He ran his hand down her face. "I know we can. So let's pack up and get out of here."

"Let's do it." She squared her shoulders and marched toward the small group.

Ward remained on the floor, his face twisted in a grimace of pain layered upon pain.

She once more knelt beside him and turned him onto his back. "Well, Ward, your shenanigans are up. Our pal, Darius, says you have a beach house, and more than that, your sister and David Shepherd are on their way down there. So guess what? We're going to meet up with them. You don't give up the drive, Cal and Frisco get to have a little party with Abigail."

From where he now stood, Cal smirked. "Don't worry, Ward. We'll take really good care of her." He cackled and held up his knife.

Ward's mouth worked, but no sound came out.

"Gang, let's break camp and get out of here," Nicole told them. "In ten minutes, we leave."

Roy walked to the camp chair and folded it up. "Boys, give Ward a little something to eat and drink. We'll tie him up when we leave."

Cal and Frisco grasped their prisoner's arms. With him between them, they half-carried him to the van. His feet dragged along the floor.

Minutes later, Nicole slid into the front passenger's seat. Roy sat behind the wheel, and Cal and Frisco occupied the only other seats on the van. Ward, now trussed up, lay in the back.

"You texting your girl?" Cal asked Frisco.

Frisco grinned. "You bet. Soon as this mess is over, I'm shacking up with her until we head back to the sandbox. Don't worry. I won't tell her about the fun we'll have with Abigail."

Nicole smirked. Now Ward had no choice about handing over that drive. And after he did? She'd figure out what to do with him.

26

For the couple of hours as they rocketed down state and US highways toward the coast, David listened to the Jars of Clay albums playing on the stereo. The lyrics challenged him about his faith, about trusting God when stepping into the unknown. Could he do what they urged? Completely trust that God had him in the palm of His hand and wouldn't let him fall as far as he had years before?

"You awake over there?" Abigail asked.

"Just listening to the music. Back when I was in SF, I'd listen to Jars a lot, even when deployed. Good stuff. They kept me going."

"Jonathan calls me a certified Jars of Clay junkie." Her smile warmed the darkness. "I have all of their albums. I try to go to their concerts when I can. And their lyrics speak to me, especially a few years ago after my parents died and everything else that happened."

"Like what?"

She didn't answer.

"Abigail?"

"You wouldn't understand."

"Oh, I don't know about that." He leaned his elbow on the door. "Try me."

217

"I'm not—" Her cell phone began ringing. She blew out a sigh. "Abigail Ward. Nick, hey."

David tuned her out and stared into the blackness pressing close against the window. They continued their winding trek through sleeping towns and small hamlets of coastal North Carolina.

He admired Abigail's profile, caressed by the soft glow of the dashboard lights. She hid something. He knew she did. What? Why wouldn't she share with him? After all they'd already been through together, didn't she trust him? Time would tell.

Abigail's voice amping up drew him out of his musings. "Look. You wanted me to cooperate, so I did."

Even above the hum of the road noise and the music, David heard Bocelli's voice squawking.

"Yeah, yeah…No, nothing else…What? You're tracking me? Nick!…Okay, okay. I'll share what we find. Satisfied?"

One more squawk, then nothing.

She shoved her phone into the slot beneath the stereo. "Talk about a distinct lack of trust."

"I think it runs both ways."

"Probably. They found the scooter—right in the owner's driveway."

"I know what I saw."

"I know. Maybe Frisco took it for a joy ride."

"I'd been to the Half-Moon before. When I was homeless the March before Kyra found me. It was so cold that night, and all I wanted, more than food, was something to keep me warm on the inside. The barista was kind enough to comp my cup of tea."

"Did it bother you to be back in Raleigh?"

He shrugged. "It's hard to say since we were barely there. What about you? How do you view Raleigh?"

"It's my safe landing place." She smiled. "Jonathan and I own the house now, and it was good to…"

"To what?"

They crossed a bridge, and the cadence of the wheels changes. "We're here. Ten more minutes, and we'll be at the beach house."

David's pulse shot up a little. Adrenaline made him focus.

The navigation device counted down the distance.

Abigail slowed as they passed an older house near the western end of the island. No light shone from any of the neighboring homes. "This is it."

"Sunset Place?"

"Yep. It doesn't look like anyone's here. Hopefully, we beat them down." She put the car into Reverse and backed into the carport. She cut off the lights, leaving them in the inky blackness of a new moon night.

David climbed from the car and listened to the whump and fizz of the waves hitting the shore. Tangy, salty air filled his nose. His buddies loved to hit the beach for some rare R&R.

The trunk clicked, and its light illuminated Abigail's face. She undid a bag in the trunk. "You need some gloves?"

"I don't carry them around in my purse."

A wisp of a smile crossed her face. "You're funny. Here. Put these on." She tossed a pair of nitrile gloves to him, then opened a case and loaded a Sig Sauer. After working the action, she slid it into a holster and stashed it at the small of her back. She caught his eye again. "You don't have a criminal record, do you?"

"Uh, no."

"Good. Have a gun." She loaded a Beretta, worked the action, and handed it to him. "My personal firearm. A round is chambered, and the safety's on."

""Wow. Two guns?"

"I have to accessorize somehow." Another brief, tight smile flitted across her features as she clipped a badge to her belt. "Guns are a girl's best friend."

"I thought diamonds were."

"Diamonds won't keep me alive in a tight situation."

He took the penlight she offered. "We're not turning on the carport light?"

Abigail grabbed another slim case. "No. I don't want to attract attention. The penlight has a red-light feature. Use it."

"Yes, ma'am."

She stuffed an earbud into her right ear.

"Please don't tell me you're listening to music."

"Police band. Just in case someone calls the cops on us. And if they do, I'm pulling out my CID badge, even if this isn't an official case." She shut the trunk. "C'mon."

He followed her to the front steps. "When you find the drive, give it to me."

She turned. "Why?"

"Because if they bust us, they're going to go after you first since you're Jonathan's sister."

"Okay." She drawled out the word as if clearly doubting his wisdom.

He surveyed the land across the street. The faint amber glow of the streetlights illuminated only low trees and scrubby vegetation covering the ground. A house sat next to the open area. "Coast is clear. I don't see any lights anywhere."

"Good. Keep an eye out."

He held the Beretta low and ready. He glanced over his shoulder. Abigail unzipped the case and extracted a set of lock picks. It took a couple of minutes, but both bolts slid back.

"We're in," she murmured. "Let's clear the rooms."

He shut the door behind them. As if they'd worked together for years, they methodically cleared each room.

Abigail's shoulders sagged as they stood in the empty master bedroom. "Maybe I was wrong."

"Why do you say that?"

"There's nothing here. No furniture, no nothing."

"I imagine that if he closed on the house right before he returned to Ghazni, he probably didn't have time to furnish the place, and he'd hardly want to do that a few days ago if all he was trying to do was survive."

"True." She heaved a sigh.

"We'll figure it out." He touched her on the arm, then stepped into the living/dining area and made his way to the kitchen. His red light picked up dishes in a drainer beside the sink and a coffeemaker. "Hey, I have signs of life."

She joined him, and he gestured to the his find. "Check it out. I hardly think the previous owners would leave behind their coffeemaker and dishware." He opened the refrigerator. "Water bottles. Another good sign."

Abigail thumped a cabinet door closed. "I found some cereal and a coffee bag. So we were right. But where would he have a safe? I didn't see anything in the closets. Wait! The owner's closet."

David followed her to the entryway and a closet with a stout deadbolt.

She knelt in front of it and used her penlight to examine the lock. "I think I can get in here. Otherwise, I'm not sure how we're going to do it."

"Crowbar?"

"If need be. I'm that desperate. Hold your light, would you?"

David did so and kept an eye out the front window.

It took a few minutes, but the bolt slid back. She opened it. "Bingo. My gut was right."

He surveyed the face of the pad and noted the keyhole. "You have a key, I hope."

"The key and the combination." She dug into her jeans pocket and produced a small, black key with a rounded end. She inserted it, briefly closed her eyes, and punched in a series of six numbers. She turned the handle.

The door popped open.

"There it is." She reached inside and extracted a silver jump drive. "Want to bet this has the Athena file on it?" She picked up another one. "I wonder if this is a copy of what I found in the safe in Raleigh."

"Could be."

She lifted the lanyards to place them around her neck.

"Whoa, wait." David caught her arm.

"What?"

"Remember what I said? Let me take them."

Her face clouded, and her grip tightened on the drives.

"Please." He tried to ignore the warm tingling that worked its way up his arms. "I'm with you. I think the kidnappers are probably on their way here. Seeing Frisco in Raleigh proves it. Can you trust me on this?"

She didn't say anything, but her fingers relaxed. She relinquished the drives to him.

He squeezed her hands. "Thanks." After a moment's hesitation, he looped both lanyards around his neck and made sure the golf shirt he wore covered the nylon cords. "Now let's get out of here."

27

Holden Beach, North Carolina

Jonathan lay on the floor of the panel van as it hurtled toward the beach. The ba-bump of its wheels and gentle rise and fall of the road told him they made their final approach to the beach. His time on earth would draw to a close soon, and he wouldn't be able to save his sister.

Lord, save her because I'm certainly out of the action now. Or at least let me live long enough to save her. That's all I ask. Please.

Frisco sat on one of two benches that provided the only other seating. His thumbs flew across the screen of his phone. His brow knotted. He shook his head slightly as if he fought an internal battle. Across from him, Cal seemed transfixed by watching or reading something on the tiny screen of his phone. Nicole and Roy argued in the front seats.

"I told you we should have taken the shorter route." Nicole turned her head.

"And get lost? I'm not from this state. I-40 was the quickest."

"Thanks to that, we got caught up in that bridge replacement." She snorted.

"And you're the one who got us lost."

"I tried, all right?" She shifted in her seat.

"Yeah, well, we should have stuck with the detour. And you'd think I was the one who had a hard time following directions." Roy slammed his hand onto the steering wheel.

"I was trying to get here faster."

"Whatever." He muttered under his breath.

Cal and Frisco exchanged long glances.

"Because you were driving like—"

"Baby, enough already. Just be quiet."

Jonathan rested his head against the metal wall and counted down the miles and the minutes remaining in his life. He shifted. The broken pieces of rib from his last beating ground against one another. He winced and worked his wrists. The cable ties around them didn't give at all. The same with his ankles. His heart sank.

"Slow down," Nicole leaned forward. "See, I told you. They're here already."

"So what?" Roy stopped and slid the van into Reverse. He backed up. A couple of sharp turns must have meant they'd parked in a nearby driveway. "Let's take care of this business once and for all."

He and Nicole hopped out.

The sliding door groaned open, which made the interior light flash on and nearly blind Jonathan.

Roy poked his head inside. "Looks like your sister's arrived, Ward. And your pal. What's his name? Oh, David Shepherd."

"Frisco and me? We gonna have fun with Abigail." Cal smirked at Jonathan. "I seen a picture of her, and she's hot. I wonder what she looks like naked." He licked his lips. "Don't you, Frisco?"

Frisco nodded, though he didn't seem as excited at the prospect as Cal did.

Jonathan tried to sit up, but he got so far as tensing to do so when the agony in his middle stopped him. He sank against their luggage with a groan. Heart pounding, he blurted, "Don't you dare hurt her."

"Naw, we won't hurt her." Cal handed Roy and Nicole a couple of pistols from a duffel. Then he slid his K-bar knife into his belt. "We'll just rip her clothes off and have our way with her."

"He's serious, you know," Roy added. "You see, we're going to get into that safe you undoubtedly have in there, and if it takes interrogating your little sister, we'll do it. Of course, you might be shark bait by that point, you and your friend. Cal, get that safe-drilling kit in case Ward doesn't cooperate at the expense of his sister and friend. Frisco, guard him. We'll call you when we've got them under control."

Frisco nodded.

Roy closed the door, once more dropping them into darkness.

Gritting his teeth, Jonathan squirmed against his bonds. He had to get free, had to save Abigail. His breath coming in quick puffs to relieve the pain from his broken ribs, he worked his wrists again. Futile. Just futile. He slumped against the van wall.

Lord, I don't want her to die here. And I don't want to die. Not now. I don't.

Frisco swiveled on the bench and faced him, elbows on knees, his thumbs flying across his phone's screen.

Jonathan tried not to think about Abigail suffering at his hands.

They'd kill David without hesitation because not even David Shepherd, the soldier's soldier, could fend off an ambush of three armed people.

Frisco stared at him for a long moment. The glow from the phone turned his face pale, like that of a ghost.

He stilled like an animal knowing it was going to be sacrificed. Maybe they'd texted him to go ahead and do the deed.

Frisco set the phone down. He reached up and cut on the interior light. Slowly, he undid the zipper to the duffel and lifted out a pair of wire cutters.

That was strange. Why use wire cutters when he had a gun and knife?

On his knees, Frisco approached him.

Jonathan cocked his head. "What are you doing?" His lips formed the question, but no words came across his suddenly dry lips.

Frisco helped him sit up and propped him against a wall. He reached down. In one deft motion, he clipped the tie binding Jonathan's ankles.

Blessed freedom. But why was he doing this? Why free him and run the risk of the wrath of Nicole falling on him?

Then Frisco took hold of his wrists and completely freed him.

Jonathan finally found his voice. "I—I—I don't understand."

Frisco met his gaze. His light brown eyes remained veiled in the dim light. Quietly, he stated, "Listen to me. I'm only going to say this once. You need to punch me. Then get out of here. Take my phone, gun, and knife."

He set those on Cal's bench and hauled Jonathan to his knees.

"Leave. Save your sister and your friend because Cal will have his way with her and kill them both. Use my phone to call for help. I changed the code to one-two-three-four. Do you understand me?"

"Uh…"

"Do it. Punch me. Hard. Now."

"I…" Shock paralyzed Jonathan.

"Don't worry about hurting me. It's…it's worth it. Your sister and friend are counting on you. I'll be fine. I'll say you cut the ties, then got the drop on me and escaped. Do it now."

The agony of what he'd endured sent a hot flash of anger through Jonathan. He drew back his fist. With his remaining strength, he slammed it into Frisco's face.

With a sharp crack, the man's nose snapped.

Frisco fell backwards.

Jonathan toppled onto him. He moaned as his ribs raged with pain. He forced himself off Frisco until he sat crumpled against the passenger's seat with his sides heaving.

Between the two benches, Frisco remained still.

Jonathan didn't wait. He grabbed the gun and phone as well as the knife and tucked them into the pockets and waistband of his jeans.

After crawling toward the side door, he turned the handle and pulled.

No give.

He pulled with all of his might.

The door inched open. Several more frantic tugs created an opening wide enough for him to slip through. He put his foot out and toppled from the van.

His right shoulder slammed onto the hard pavement. Stars sparked in his vision. Only with superhuman will did he tamp down the scream that clawed at his throat. His torso twisted as his body completed the fall. He moaned at the agony blazing up and down his side.

Slowly, he pushed himself onto all fours. With his head hung, he brought one knee to his chest, then grasped the lip of the doorway and hauled himself to his feet. He found the side and leaned against it until the pain settled to a dull roar before he opened his eyes and wobbled toward the front.

Latticework separated their hiding place from the road. He peered through one of the holes.

Three shadows darted across the street and paused under the stairs. They blended with the darkness, meaning Abigail and David wouldn't see them until too late.

Jonathan curled his fingers around the slats. Nausea roiled in his gut. He had to do something. Taking a deep breath drilled more shards of pain into his lungs.

"God, please. Just a bit more," he whispered.

He clamped his jaw against the pain and got his legs moving. If he stopped, he'd collapse and not get up. He staggered across the driveway and into the scrub across the street from his house. In the darkness, he stumbled over exposed roots. Sand spurs added pinpricks of pain in his feet, but he ignored them and pressed onward. He felt his way through low trees as bent and worn from the salt air and wind as he felt.

His legs wobbled, and he collapsed to his knees.

His breath whistled between his teeth as his vision began tunneling from the pain.

He forced his eyes open.

Panic sent one more shot of adrenaline through his fading system as he watched the front door to the house open. Two figures, one with a ponytail and one tall and built, emerged.

Abigail, no!

His plea remained locked in his throat. He tried to rise but toppled forward. No more strength, not when he needed it the most. He couldn't save them.

Not by himself.

Grasping the branches for support, he pushed himself to his knees as he fumbled for Frisco's phone. It fell to the sand beside him. His shaking fingers brushed the case. He activated the screen. A keypad appeared.

"Code…code…" he muttered. It flew to his mind. *One-two-three-four.* He punched it, brought up the phone's keypad, and dialed three more numbers. *God, let them answer.*

"Nine-One-One, how may I help you?" the Southern, feminine voice stated.

"I need your help at 3245 West Beach Boulevard in Holden Beach." Jonathan drew a sharp breath between his teeth. "Burglars have broken into my house, and they're coming after my sister and me."

"Help's on the way. Stay on the line with me, sir."

"Th—thank you." Trembling started from deep inside.

The pain worsened. He began panting in an effort to relieve it.

"Are you hurt, sir?"

"Badly." Jonathan swallowed hard.

The trembling graduated to shaking. *Hold on,* he urged himself. *Not much longer. Just hold on.* His grip tightened on branches as his world began tilting.

"Both police and paramedics have been dispatched. Stay with me."

He passed out.

Holden Beach, North Carolina

David stepped onto the front porch and surveyed the area as he shucked his gloves. Almost there. He could feel it. Problem was, the feeling of relief that came toward the end of a mission or deployment could make your guard drop. People got killed too easily during those times. He wasn't going to let that happen. Not tonight. Not on his watch. And not with Abigail. David kept his gun low but ready to fire.

The door closed with a thump. Wisps of hair tousled his cheek as she brushed by him. "I couldn't get the deadbolt locked. Oh, well. He'll just have to forgive me. You see anything?"

"Nope." He did one last scan. "Good to go."

"I'll lead." Abigail stuffed her gloves in her jeans pockets and carefully descended the steps.

Using his peripheral vision, David took advantage of what little light remained on this moonless night. Now he wished they'd turned on the carport lights.

"Coast is clear," she murmured so low that he barely heard her above the soothing rhythm of waves hitting sand.

His feet hit solid ground. "I'm not letting up—"

Abigail yelped. A thud and a grunt from her followed. "Let me go!"

"Get her to the back," a harsh female voice ordered.

David turned toward the voice. Too late, he realized his mistake. Pain exploded in his kidney. He groaned and staggered into one of the house's pilings.

"I'll take that," a man with an Australian accent said as he lifted the Beretta from his hand. It landed with a thud somewhere in the sand near the edge of the concrete.

"Get him over there." The woman again.

David finally put a name to the voice. Nicole Chardet. He pushed back—straight into the muzzle of a gun.

"I wouldn't do that, Shepherd. You see, Cal's got a gun on your girl." The Aussie twisted his arm behind him and marched him toward the rear of the carport. He jerked upward on his arm. "Down on your knees."

David sank onto the concrete to relieve the pain.

The Aussie released him. "Get your hands on your head. Cross your ankles."

David obeyed.

"Ow! Let go of me!" Abigail's shadow thrashed about in the oppressive darkness.

"Stop struggling, and maybe I will." Cal's hillbilly accent rode upon the breeze as he called her a foul name. He kept his hand enmeshed in her ponytail and shoved her to her knees. "You stay put, you hear?"

A feminine silhouette, this one with a gun in her hand, joined them. "Where is it?"

"You're talking to me?" Abigail lifted her chin.

Nicole slapped her hard enough to make her head snap.

She didn't cry out. Didn't even make a sound. Instead, she rubbed her cheek. "Ow, that hurt."

Nicole bent so they were almost nose to nose. "Where's the drive?"

"I'm not sure what you're talking about."

"Oh, I think you know darned well what I'm talking about. Your brother has a safe up there. I know he does. And I'm pretty sure you got into it. Now where is it?"

"Seriously, I don't—"

Nicole backhanded her. "Cal, search her. Strip her if you have to, but I want that drive." She turned a red light onto Abigail.

Cal loomed over her.

David's blood churned. He had to neutralize the situation, but he couldn't. Any move he made would be obvious.

Abigail tensed.

Cal shoved her between the shoulder blades.

Off balance, she toppled forward. "Hey!"

He flipped her over.

Abigail pushed against him.

He popped her across the face.

David unlaced his fingers.

Abigail flailed out and caught Cal on the face.

He grunted. He pounced and blocked David's view, but he could hear scuffling.

Abigail cried out. Her legs churned as she struggled. Fabric ripped.

David had to stop him. He uncrossed his ankles.

"Make one move to get up, Shepherd, and I'll blow your brains out." The Aussie pressed the gun barrel against his head as if to emphasize his point.

"She don't have it," Cal said a moment later.

Abigail lay curled up, one hand cupping her cheek. Cal had ripped her T-shirt from top to bottom, and she clung to what was left to hold it together.

"At least she don't have it up top." Cal ran his hand down her cheek. Once more, he grabbed her hair, making her sit up to avoid more pain. "Get up, woman. You and me? We gonna have ourselves a real good time."

Nicole turned off the light. "Get them up upstairs. Then you can have all the fun you want with her. I'll call Frisco to have him bring Ward over. We'll make the boys watch."

David had maybe thirty seconds to come up with a plan. If they got them upstairs, Abigail would be the one to suffer the most, and both of them would die.

His gaze drifted to the back staircase. The beam of Cal's red light bounced as he shoved Abigail so hard that she grabbed the railing to keep from tumbling up the stairs. "Get up there!"

"Stop shoving me, and I will." She regained her footing. "So shed some light on this situation for me, Cal. Do you blindly take orders from her?"

"Shut up!" He jabbed her.

David realized what she meant. He peered as best he could through the gloom. Then he saw it, the light switch on the piling next to the stairway.

"Get up." the Aussie lightly kicked him in the hip.

David slowly rose. In two long strides, he crossed to the stairs. He pretended to stumble.

"Keep your hands up!"

"What do you want me to do? Fall?" He grasped the railing as if catching his balance. He took a step upward and flipped the switch.

Light blazed forth.

"Get that light off!" Nicole shouted. "I can't see!"

David slammed his heel into the Aussie's stomach. He tumbled backward, air whooshing out of him.

David yanked Cal's belt, swinging him backward toward the Aussie.

The two collided.

David leapt the railing and landed in a crouch beside the staircase. Cal's gun fell from his hand.

A flash and bang blasted through the air.

Abigail cried out.

David charged the two men. He landed a punch on the Aussie's face before ramming into Cal.

They tumbled to the ground.

He drew back his fist for the final blow.

"Unh, unh, unh, I wouldn't do that." Nicole's voice taunted him. "One more move, Shepherd, and your girlfriend gets it."

She stood next to the staircase with gun pointed at Abigail, who huddled on the stairs with her right hand clamped around her left upper arm. Red oozed between her fingers and dribbled down her arm.

His heart hammered. *Abigail!*

"Get your hands up all nice and slow, got it? Now!" She jabbed the muzzle into Abigail's temple.

"Roy?" Nicole didn't bother turning her head.

"I'm fine." The Aussie hauled himself upright by clutching the Accord's trunk. He glared at David. "You and I aren't finished with this."

"Me neither," Cal grunted. In the silence that followed, he tilted his head. "Do you hear that?"

"What?" Roy asked.

"Sirens. Someone must have heard the gunshot and called the cops. We've got to get out of here!" Cal sprinted into the darkness without another word.

The faintest sounds of rescue grew louder with each passing second.

"Baby, we've got to go," Roy muttered.

Nicole glared at them. "Okay, you win, Shepherd, but you forget we still have Ward. And next time you won't walk away. I can promise you that."

With that, she dashed into the night after her comrades.

David didn't relax. He whipped around the railing and in one stride reached Abigail. "You're safe."

Shaking, she nodded.

He grimaced at the amount of blood dripping from her elbow onto her jeans. "Let me look at that."

She shook her head.

"Promise I won't poke and prod." Gently, he pried her fingers loose. Even in the dim light, he noticed how the bullet from the misfire had punctured her arm. "Can you move your fingers?"

"Y—Yeah."

He checked for an exit wound and found one. "You are one lucky woman, Abigail Ward. It seems to be a flesh wound. In and out."

"It *hurts*!" Pain thickened her voice.

"Oh, I'm sure. Where are your keys?"

"I—I don't know. I dropped them when they got us."

"I'll find them. I take it there's a First Aid kit in your car?"

"Y—Yeah. Ow!" She curled into her tuck again.

"Freeze!" The man's shout made them both jump. A police officer stood in a firing position with both hands clamped around the pistol's grip. The muzzle shook so badly that David worried he'd kill Abigail even if he fired at him.

David raised his hands and stepped away from her. "Sir, I'm one of the good guys."

The man focused on him with both the muzzle and his gaze.

"He is." Abigail's husky voice made them both turn. She'd risen. She held her gold CID badge where the officer could see it. Then she all but collapsed onto the steps.

Confusion rippled across his face. The officer's gaze switched between her and David. It landed on David. "Wait. You were the one who called it in."

He frowned. "I didn't call anyone."

"A guy called Nine-One-One. If not you, then who—"

"I did." A reed-thin voice reached them from the darkness of the driveway.

A man staggered into the golden light. His disheveled sandy blond hair became more apparent under the glow, along with the cigarette burns all over his bare chest and dried blood coating his face. He stopped, braced his hands on his knees, and hung his head.

"Jonathan!" Abigail bolted down the stairs and ran into her brother's arms. Laughing, crying, she held onto him as he collapsed.

The officer lowered his gun and faced him. "Looks like y'all have some explaining to do."

28

Southport, North Carolina

At the sound of keys jingling, Abigail opened her eyes a crack. She slouched in the passenger's seat of her Honda since David had offered to drive. Blinking in the strong midday sun made her head hurt even more than it had from the beating she'd taken at Cal's hands. Her arm was still numb, thank heavens. With her good hand, she rubbed the back of her neck. "I take it we're here?"

"Yep. And they promised us two rooms as long as we need them." A muffled click told her he'd popped the trunk. "I've also left a message with the MPs your CO assigned to guard us and Jonathan. Let's get our stuff inside so we can get some rest."

She slid from the car and lifted the trunk lid with her right hand.

She reached inside, but he stopped her. "I can get that."

"I'm hurt, not invalid." Irritation swelled from weariness.

He tightened his grip, which sent a glow of warmth up her arm. His dark eyes probed hers. "Just... let me help you for once, okay? Can you do that? Because when that Lidocaine wears off, your arm's going to start hurting like the dickens."

She huffed out a sigh. "All right. Fine."

He loaded himself up with his backpack, hers, and her two suitcases. Guilt assailed her for biting back at him. He'd saved her life. If it hadn't been for him… She shuddered at the thought of what could have happened. With a sigh, she grabbed the bag holding the items they'd picked up at the drugstore after leaving the hospital

David paused at the check-in counter. "I called earlier for two rooms. The name's David Shepherd."

The clerk smiled at them. "Of course. Yes, I have the two rooms ready that you requested. With an adjoining door." Her fingers flew across the keyboard. Then she winked. "Are you sure you need two?"

"Yes," they chorused.

"Okay, then," she drawled as she handed over the paperwork.

"I can pay for—" Abigail began.

"I've got it."

"But—"

"It's okay. I've got it."

She shrugged and promised herself she'd square up with the hotel later.

David signed where needed. His phone chimed, and he stepped away to take the call.

Abigail wandered to the elevator and rested her back against a column. Her arm began aching, a harbinger of what lay ahead as the Lidocaine wore off. She gritted her teeth. She'd handle it. She didn't need the Tylenol with codeine the doc had prescribed, and she'd conveniently left the bottle in the ER's cubicle when she'd checked out. With a small thump, she leaned her head against the column and closed her eyes.

Jonathan was safe. They'd gotten the drive back, meaning CID would call the case closed. Sal had told her to enjoy the rest of her vacation, even to extend it a few more days. Problem was, she hated hospitals. David had asked her if she wanted to stay with her brother. Did she? Yes, but her hammering pulse and damp hands told her she needed to get far away from there, at least until she was a little more rested and could face those sterile corridors, dry announcements on the intercom, and smell of antiseptic without falling into a panic attack or something.

David rolled the suitcases across the tiles toward her. "That was the captain of the MP company. They're sending over a squad right now."

Abigail opened her eyes crack.

"We've got rooms on the third floor. You look like you're going to fall asleep on your feet. Let's get you upstairs." He cocked his head as he assessed her face. "The Lidocaine is starting to wear off, isn't it?"

She nodded. Easier to let him believe that then to explain the sweaty palms and short breaths brought about by thinking about hospitals.

"We'll get settled."

"I want to take a shower," she muttered.

"I get that. At least the nurse told us of a way to do it." David grinned. "Who knew that cling wrap had such useful properties?" They stepped onto the elevator. When they reached the third floor, he said, "I'd like us to at least unlock the doors between our rooms. Call me paranoid, but I want internal access if needed."

"Couldn't agree more." She slipped inside. Oh, did that king-size bed with its soft, white duvet and myriad of pillows cast its siren spell on her. No, not until she showered and felt clean.

David joined her a moment later. "You want your suitcase on the cabinet here?"

She nodded.

"I put your backpack and other bag on the floor by the television. Where's that bag we got from the drugstore?"

"In front of the television." She grimaced and bowed her head as the burning in her arm began shifting to pain.

"Let's get that arm ready. Why don't you sit on the couch there?" With his foot, David shoved the coffee table out of the way. He bent and pulled over the chair from the worktable. Gently, he pushed up the sleeve of the T-shirt he'd bought her to replace the ruined one.

She closed her eyes. Was it her imagination, or did his fingers linger on her skin? She didn't care. His touch, coupled with the smell of the stuff he'd used on his hair the previous morning, conjured up images, ones she normally wouldn't contemplate, like maybe if she leaned into him—

"Don't fall asleep on me." His teasing interrupted her fantasy. "Hey, I'm sorry I got that T-shirt too small. I guess I'm always thinking every woman's as small as my sister."

"I like it."

"You do?" He fixed her in his gaze.

If she'd taken a painkiller, she could have blamed that sudden dizzy feeling on the meds. Now she noticed something deep within those dark chocolate depths. Desire? No, it couldn't be possible. To stave off more awkwardness, she blurted, "It'll… it'll make a nice nightshirt."

He chuckled as he secured the sleeve on her shoulder and pulled off a length of cling wrap.

Abigail drew her lips tight against the feelings raging inside her. They were too different. He had issues. She definitely did. She knew what would happen when they got Jonathan safely home to Raleigh and on the way to recovery. He'd beat feet back to Burning Tree.

He wrapped the plastic around her arm and over the bandage. Using rubber bands linked together, he secured it. "Voila. Just like the nurse suggested."

She hopped up. "Uh, thanks. I, um, think I'll get a shower before hitting the hay for a bit of rest." She winced as the pain flared to a burning.

"And you need to take your painkiller."

"I left it at the hospital." She busied herself with undoing her suitcase and pulling out her toiletries satchel.

"I got it right here." He placed a small bottle on top of the dresser.

She glared at him. "Why'd you do that? I meant to leave it there."

"You're going to need it."

"I don't do painkillers. Not for anything."

"Not even for a headache?" He cocked an eyebrow and leaned against the wall next to the bathroom, conveniently cutting off her escape route.

"Not even for that. Now let me through." She moved to the left to step around him.

He shifted and blocked her way. "Why?"

"None of your business."

"I think it's time we talked about that."

"How about if I don't want to?" She dodged to the right.

Again, he matched her. With his finger, he lifted her chin so their gazes met.

The coldness gripping her heart began melting. He was closing in on the truth. How could he understand how far she'd fallen? How much she hated hospitals because they reminded her of dark days she wanted to forget? How she never wanted to go down that long, hard road again? At the compassion she saw in those dark depths, the words fought toward the surface.

"It'll help you heal faster. I can promise you on that."

Fear chased her words away. She clamped a lid on her emotions. "That's what they said the last time."

She pushed past him and into the bathroom.

"Abigail—"

"I don't want to talk about it." She shut the door in his face and turned on the water as hot as she could stand it. Once she'd stepped under the penetrating stream, the emotion, brought about by exhaustion, pain, and something else she couldn't place, burst forth. With her forehead leaning on her arms, she cried.

Southport, North Carolina

"No one's to be allowed to even approach our doors unless they provide you with a valid ID and a valid reason. Understand?" David fixed his gaze upon the MP sergeant who stood at parade rest in the hall next to his door.

"Yes, sir, I do. Got two guys here at the fire stairs and your rooms and two guys at the elevators. We're doing four on and four off, rotating between three teams." The sergeant held up his phone. "You need me, I'm only a phone call away."

"I appreciate that. We'll be headed out around seven or so to go to the hospital. Then we'll be back for the night." David slipped into his room. He paused by the adjoining door. In Abigail's room, the shower still ran strong.

He needed to clean up as well. Once under warm water sluicing over him, uncertainty gripped him. He'd done what Abigail had recruited him to do. Now all he wanted to return to Burning Tree. Abigail didn't need him anymore. More than that, her presence introduced a whole host of unsettling feelings he didn't want to contemplate. Far better to retreat to Burning Tree.

Maybe one of the MPs could give him a ride to Raleigh first thing in the morning.

Then he remembered one thing.

He'd made a promise to Abigail.

Fool. You caved in a moment of weakness. Something touched him deep within his soul, almost as if the Holy Spirit had smacked him across the head. *God, I just want to leave. To forget this happened and return to my life in Burning Tree. Can't You let me off the hook on this one? It's easier to remain this way than to forgive.*

The answer came to him once more as if the Holy Spirit held a sign in front of him for him to read.

Forgive Jonathan. Reconcile. In person.

Not going to do it. I'm going to head home in the morning. Abigail can handle it. His mind made up, he dressed and stretched out on the couch with his mystery paperback in his hand as he squeezed his foam rubber ball. Abigail's door was cracked. Only a strip of light told him she remained awake. A hair dryer hummed. Did he detect the occasional sniffle?

Her words before she'd pushed past him echoed in his mind. "That's what they said the last time."

Did he really care? He tried to pretend he didn't, but he knew he lied.

He forced the thought from his mind by focusing his attention on the mystery's plot. Gradually, he became aware of voices in Abigail's room, that of a man conversing with her.

He lowered the book. From where he lay, he couldn't pick out words. But the man's New Jersey accent sounded vaguely familiar. Bocelli. What was he doing here?

David stepped to the door. Now he could hear everything.

"I show up at the hospital, only to find out that your CO—what's his name?"

"Lieutenant Colonel Salvador Torres." Abigail sounded like she'd listened to a telemarketer pitching his product.

"Whatever. He took not only the Athena file but my case." Bocelli's accent thickened as his voice rose.

"I had no choice."

"Yeah, right."

"Nick." Abigail sighed. "That drive was linked to a CID case. When I got the drive, it was case closed."

"But the kidnapping isn't. And those jokers are still out there. So what am I going to tell my version of a CO when he chews my tail for losing this case? Tell me that, Abby."

A drawer in the dresser thumped closed. "Honestly, why are you so bent out of shape about this? It's one less—"

"It's *my case*. It fell into my jurisdiction. And I'm going to see it through."

"But Sal—Ow! Nick, you're hurting me!"

David charged through the doorway.

Bocelli had grabbed her injured arm at the bandage and pushed her against the wall beside the bathroom's door. She thrashed out against him.

"Let her go, Bocelli." In one motion, David ripped him away from her and slammed him into the opposite wall.

"You—I'm going to arrest you!" Bocelli went for his gun.

"Don't even think about it." David pinned his arm to the the wall. "Are you an idiot? She's hurt. GSW."

The door to the hall slammed open, and the sergeant gaped at them. "Master Sergeant Shepherd? What happened?"

Bocelli thrashed against David's grip. "What happened is this jerk—"

"He didn't ask you, so shut your trap." David tightened his hands. "How did he get by?"

"He said he was a cop, that he had official business with Abigail."

"Well, his 'official business' got personal." David shoved him toward the MP. "He tried to hurt Major Ward, so escort him from the hotel. If he shows his face around here again, arrest him."

The sergeant nodded.

"You're going to pay for this, Shepherd! You too, Abby!" Nick shouted.

The sergeant yanked him out of sight.

David shut the door. For good measure, he threw the deadbolt and added the security lock.

Skin now as white as her T-shirt, Abigail huddled against the wall, her good hand over her wound, her face pinched with pain. She began sliding downward.

David wrapped his arms around her. "Easy there. I've got you."

She trembled from head to toe and huddled against him.

"I'm not even going to ask if you're hurting." He helped her to the edge of the bed. "Here. Sit down so I can look at your wound."

"It's…it's fine."

"He could have ripped the stitches." David found the bag containing the gauze and other first aid paraphernalia resting where she'd placed it when they'd arrived. With a pair of scissors, he clipped the gauze and carefully removed the bandage.

"How is it?"

David carefully examined the wounds. Though they seeped some blood, it didn't appear as if Bocelli's actions had ripped the stitches. "The tiniest of bleeding, but that's it. Let me clean around the wounds a little before I bandage them."

After washing his hands, he wet some cotton balls and gently wiped away the blood. His cheeks began warming as his fingers brushed against her skin. After securing more bandages with gauze, he ran his hand down her hair. "All done. How are you feeling?"

"Okay," she whispered. The green-flecked hazel depths of her eyes betrayed her.

"C'mon. Let's get you that Tylenol—"

"I'm not doing painkillers."

"After he grabbed you like that—"

"No!"

He tried a different tact. "You're sure?"

"I'll be fine." Again, the uncertainty in her voice told him she lied. "I just need to sleep." As if to emphasize her point, she crawled onto the king-sized bed, lay down on her uninjured side, and pulled the covers up to her chin. The duvet settled across his lap.

He remained sitting on the edge of the bed. Finally, it clicked in his mind and made sense, the way she'd high-tailed it out of the hospital earlier that day, her offhand statement when they'd arrived, her insistence that she didn't need any medication for wounds that would make even the burliest Ranger cry.

Slowly, he eased onto his knees, as if praying beside the bed, and took her hand between his. Seconds ticked by before he spoke. "You know I was both a drunk and a painkiller addict. Plain and simple, that's what I was."

She nodded.

"After I returned to Burning Tree and got clean and sober, I was so worried about taking any kind of painkiller stronger than aspirin. That lasted until last spring."

"What happened?" She raised her head from the pillow.

"March of last year, Mitch and I went mountain biking. We started goofing off and doing stupid stunts. Then I crashed. It wouldn't have been a big deal except for the fact that my leg landed on a rock, right where the bullet from The Incident had fractured my femur. Talk about hurting!" He shook his head at the memory. "Somehow, we got back to his truck, and he took me to my doc in the next town over. I'd only bruised the bone. But that didn't mean it didn't hurt like hell. It did. The doc prescribed me some heavy-duty painkillers."

"Did he know about your addiction?"

"Oh, yeah." He gently rubbed his thumbs across the top of her hand. He tried to ignore its smoothness, the way his cheeks heated. "He did. First, he said that one prescription should be enough. Second, he monitored me closely. Each day after I took a painkiller, I was supposed to journal how I felt after it wore off. Third, he saw me every other day until I finished my prescription. That's when I realized my addiction had been psychological."

"How so?" Curiosity made her sound almost childlike.

"I'd used it as a way to escape circumstances I perceived as hopeless. I did have real, legitimate pain after I returned home from The Incident, most likely for the rest of the year. But after that, the doc said my wound had healed."

"But other wounds remained."

"Right. My life fell apart around me. And with a doc who was too free with prescribing me pain meds, I became addicted. I thought I couldn't live without them because they made things seem manageable." Before he realized what he was doing, David brought her fingers to his lips and kissed them. He closed his eyes as he considered his next words with care. "When

I took that first pill last spring, I felt like I was jumping off a cliff, big time. Quite frankly, it scared me."

"Did it work?"

"What?"

"Did you heal faster?"

"I did. I took them for a week, and after that, I was pain free and back to riding bikes again, this time with a little more care."

That earned a ghost of a smile.

"Does my story make sense?"

She didn't speak for a moment. "It did. I know what you're saying. The…the time's not now."

She slid her hand from his and tightened her grip on the duvet.

"That's okay." He brushed a strand of that dark blond hair off her face and tucked it behind her ear. "I know how scary it can be." He pushed himself to his feet and turned off her light. "Sweet dreams. I'll wake you at seven. I figured we'd go get some vittles and then see your brother after that."

A soft snuffle answered him.

He stood in the gloom and simply drank in the image of that strong jaw and the lashes brushing against her cheek. Then he bent and kissed her on the forehead. The touch of his lips on her tender skin sent every nerve of his body on alert. He lingered and inhaled that gardenia scent that must have come from her soap. He closed his eyes, then whispered, "Have a good rest, Abigail."

He retreated to his room but left the doors between their room open. No way would Bocelli surprise her like he'd done before. David pushed back the covers on the bed. After shucking his T-shirt, he lay down, content this time to let images of Abigail fill his mind. As drowsiness overtook him, all intents of escaping to Burning Tree had completely slipped his mind.

29

Nicole huddled on one of the double beds in the motel room. She ran a comb through her wet hair. Her cell phone sat on the red-and-green plaid bedspread.

Please stay silent.

Thanks to Shepherd and Ward's sister, they hid at a rundown motel somewhere in the woods outside of Nowheresville, North Carolina. Somehow, Ward had gotten ahold of the wire cutters. Then he'd jumped Frisco and nailed him hard across the face. When they'd dragged Frisco's sorry butt to Urgent Care to get his nose fixed, they told the doc in a box he'd been in a bar fight. All thanks to Ward. The bastard.

She hurled the comb at the mirror. It hit with such force that a small crack appeared before the comb bounced onto the sagging dresser. She shrugged. So they'd leave a five to cover the damage.

Her phone began chiming. That all-too-familiar wolf avatar glowed from the screen as if taunting her.

The chill of fear dumped its ice onto her anger.

The ringing ceased, then resumed.

El Lobo wouldn't stop until she answered.

Finally, she lifted it to her ear. "Yes?"

"Nicole, Nicole, Nicole, what were you thinking?"

"I—I'm not sure what you mean." She jumped up and began pacing between the beds.

"Oh, I know you do. You see, it's come to my attention that you lost the drive." A low cuss word reached her. "I had no choice but to return it to where it belonged. And thanks to you, Shamal Khan has severed ties. What do you have to say for yourself?"

"I'm sorry. I tried to get it back. But Ward and—"

"You are a fool!" El Lobo barged through her protests with his fine, aristocratic voice. "I will hunt you down, and when I find you, you'll wish you were dead. You and your lover and friends. Only then will I put you out of your misery. That is what happens to people who can't do their jobs."

"Please!" Nicole slumped onto the bed. "I'm sorry. Give me another chance."

Silence answered her.

The phone slid from her paralyzed fingers. It was as if she'd been pulled into an alternate universe. Through the thin walls, the water splattered onto cheap fiberglass. Roy hummed like he always did when in the shower. From next door where Cal and Frisco stayed came the tinny sounds of the television. Neither man made a peep. Nicole had that odd detachment of an alien observer.

She shifted and winced as a spring from the old mattress bit into her rump. It brought her back to reality. Her crappy reality.

"Baby, what happened?" Roy asked. "Are you all right?"

He gently shook her.

His image came into focus. "El Lobo called. We're done. He made that much clear."

He sat on the edge of the bed next to her, his hair mussed, water running in droplets from his sideburns. He cocked an eyebrow.

"He's going to kill us, and it's not going to be pretty."

"You don't know—"

"He told me. And I know what happens to people who double-cross him like we did. He doesn't just kill them; he cuts them to pieces." She shuddered.

"Easy there." He gathered her close and held her until her shaking subsided.

"I'm sorry. I know I'm usually strong, but—"

"It's okay. Promise."

"No, it's *not* okay." She pushed him away, jumped to her feet, and began pacing. "The Army's got the drive and returned it to the server. And what do we have? We're on the run. Frisco's down for the count with a busted nose, and most likely, we're hours away from getting arrested. And when that happens, El Lobo's going to know where we are, and—"

"Listen to me." He met her on her return trip to the front of the room. He smoothed her damp hair. "While you were in the shower, I had a nice talk with Darius. Seems like he's found out more about our adversaries, specifically David Shepherd."

"I fail to see what that has to with anything. We're done."

"We're not done." A smile flickered across his face. "My theory is he has a burr under his saddle because Shepherd's with Ward's sister. He told me Shepherd's got a sister in a place called Burning Tree, Utah. She's a widow with three kids."

For the first time since they'd fled the beach, hope pushed its way through the soil of defeatism. "Are you saying we're *not* finished?"

He smirked. "We take Kyra Martin and her children. Then it's the drive for them."

"And Ward. I want him to pay for putting us on the run."

"And Ward." He held her at arm's length. "I'll go rouse the guys while you find us a route to Burning Tree. We get rid of our phones, which will also stop any calls from El Lobo. We'll get burner phones once we're safely out of the area."

As Roy stepped from the room, Nicole tapped into the Internet and located Burning Tree, Utah. It would take thirty-one hours of hard driving. That was okay. They had three drivers, maybe four if Frisco recovered enough. They could do it.

Once they had Ward back in their hands, she'd make him pay dearly for sending them on the run.

For that, she couldn't wait.

30

Raleigh, North Carolina

Voices brought Jonathan into the real world. For a few minutes, he remained still as one by one, his senses came online. He opened his eyes. Above him, a blurry circle hovered, but a few blinks brought the blades of a ceiling fan into focus. His brain finally made the connection. He lay on his bed at his house in Raleigh. A light blanket covered him. How he'd gotten there, he had no clue.

Gradually, the past few days gelled in his mind. He remembered arriving home from the hospital and making some remark about the house's disheveled condition, then popping a pill and falling into bed. Reality returned briefly as pain raged. Another pill sent him into blackness. The cycle repeated itself a few more times.

Until now.

Free of the last vestiges of the painkiller, he sat up.

Instantly, his ribs protested. A groan escaped his lips. Grasping one of the posts of the four-poster bed, he hauled himself upright and stood there for a few moments. He took in the room in a long, sweeping look. No lampshades sat on the two lamps on the nightstand or on the one on the dresser. Someone had rearranged his pictures. He ticked through his memory to see what explained the changes. Abigail had said she cleaned up his room the day before while he'd slept under the influence.

He swayed. "Lord, have mercy."

He remained standing. That was progress. Could he wear a T-shirt? Forget that. At the moment, he cringed at the idea of pulling something over his head. He settled for reaching for the button-down shirt he must have tossed over the post before crashing into bed the night before.

He glanced at the picture of Christine and him that his mentor, Judge MacKenzie, had taken at one of Raleigh's finest restaurants. A crack in the glass ran between Christine and him as if parting them. He hung his head as his new circumstances slammed into him. Would he ever look at pictures of them together without feeling that searing ache of loneliness etched into his soul?

In the other room, a man and woman bickered, their voice growing loud enough for Jonathan to recognize them.

"Nick," he muttered under his breath. Only Abigail's ex-husband could drive his sister to yelling.

"I told you he's asleep. The doctor's orders were to let him sleep to heal. And he gave him pain pills to help."

"Why do I think you're lying to me? Again?"

"Nick, he's on heavy-duty painkillers—"

"I don't care if he's smoking weed. I need to talk with him." Nick's voice hit rock concert levels.

"And Jonathan needs his rest." She matched his volume. "Why can't you get that through your thick skull?"

An expletive flew. Then Nick growled, "You know something? I'm done with this. You tell your dear brother the second he pokes his head out that bedroom door, I want to talk with him. Got it?"

"Whatever."

"Abigail!"

"Okay, okay. I will."

"Then I'll talk to you later." The front door slammed.

"What a jerk," she muttered. Her footsteps receded as she retreated to the kitchen.

Jonathan waited a long moment before stepping into the hall. He hobbled into the family room. Abigail had cleaned it up, returning to the table the dining room chair where Nicole and her gang had trussed him up. All his books now resided on their shelves in the glass-fronted cabinets. Two stacks of pictures sat on the rich wood of his coffee table, those that needed completely new frames and those requiring only glass. A few intact survivors occupied the shelves. His beloved chess set sat unharmed in its place under the picture window.

In the dining room through the rectangular archway, pieces of china and crystal littered the rug. Only a few plates had survived. Drawers hung open, and not a shelf in the hutch had anything on it. It figured that they would have completely destroyed everything that he'd loved. At least they hadn't gotten their hooks into Abigail. He had his friend to thank for that.

In the kitchen, David knelt and tossed pieces of broken pottery into a pile. Abigail leaned against the granite counter top and stared at a list. She jotted something down before chewing on the pencil's eraser.

She glanced up, and a wide smile crossed her face. "Well, look who's finally up. Welcome back to the real world."

"Good morning, y'all." Jonathan grimaced at the way his reality had skewed. "What time is it?"

"Thursday morning, 0900 hours." She crossed the kitchen and gently hugged him. "Sorry about getting into your room while you slept. I figured you wouldn't notice."

"I didn't." He glanced at David. Clad in a pair of cargo shorts and a T-shirt, his friend now swept. Shards scraped across the tile floor.

"Hey, good news. The insurance adjuster came yesterday morning. Do you remember any of that?"

Jonathan tried. He scratched his head. "I think I talked with him before I passed out in my recliner."

"Right. You said enough to give me permission to run things for you, which I did. He called late yesterday afternoon and said they'll deposit the check on Monday. That means I can go shopping." She grinned as if the idea positively excited her.

"For how much?"

She quoted him the figure, and his eyes bugged a little. "Oh, wow. Try not to spend it all on clothes."

She stuck her tongue out at him.

David, who years before would have laughed at such antics, remained still as if he watched some strange display of animal affection.

"Well, let me run my errands. You don't mind if I take the Cherokee, do you?"

"It's not like I can drive right now." Jonathan forced a smile to his face. "Run along now before I send David as your escort."

David scowled, turned his back on them, and resumed sweeping as if to get every speck of dust and flour that had escaped into the corners.

Why was he acting so standoffish? "Oh, by the way, I heard your conversation with Nick."

"The jerk." Her eyes narrowed.

"I'll call him back, if anything, to get him off your case."

"I appreciate it." She kissed him on the cheek. "I'll be back mid-afternoon or so. I'm glad you're feeling better."

"Yeah, me too." *I only wish Christine were here.* A lump filled his throat, and he shut down thoughts of her before emotion could strangle him. "Be gone with you. We'll hang here."

As the back screened door slapped shut, Jonathan stood in middle of the kitchen.

Nearby, David stilled once more. His gaze remained where Abigail had stood. He resumed his work.

Jonathan opened the refrigerator. His ribs punished him for picking up the orange juice container. "Hey, are there any cups remaining?"

"Just plastic ones." David made no move to help him.

"Thanks, bro." He pulled a NC State Wolfpack cup from the lowest shelf. He sucked in a breath at a stab of pain. Once it eased, he poured himself a glass.

David swept broken pottery into a pile.

Jonathan leaned against the counter and sipped his juice. "Thanks for helping Abigail find me."

"I did what was needed." David hauled the trash bag full of debris over to the pile.

"I sense you're angry at me."

David dumped the dustpan full of shards into the black plastic.

"If you're so angry, why are you still here?"

His knuckles whitening where he gripped the trash bag, David glared at him with such ferocity that Jonathan inwardly cringed.

David dropped the bag, snagged another one from the box on the counter, and stalked into the dining room and out of sight, crunching crystal under his feet.

Jonathan shuffled after him.

David set a plate on the table, then pulled out a chair and reached underneath.

"I'm trying to understand. That's all." Jonathan propped himself against the opening.

"How can you? You didn't suffer like I did." Those words came out like a cat's low, angry growl.

Suddenly, it clicked in Jonathan's mind. "You're talking about six years ago, aren't you?"

David tossed a silver spoon onto the table.

"How about if I make you a deal?" Jonathan pulled out the chair at the head of the table and eased onto it. "We talk. We clear the air. If you're still angry after that, I'll personally drive you to the airport, even though I shouldn't drive right now. Can you do that?"

David poked his head above the table. His glare told him to get lost, but he didn't move.

"Please, hear me out. That's all I ask," Jonathan softly added.

Finally, he sank onto a chair perpendicular to Jonathan's and folded his arms across his chest.

Jonathan had only one shot at this. He remained quiet for a moment and tried to phrase his thoughts. "When we got hit, I entered my Hell Year. Or years, depending on how you look at it. Losing ten friends and nearly losing you impacted me greatly."

"Abigail told me she was there when the choppers arrived."

"She was. Some might call it coincidence, but not me. And coming home... Man, that was one of the best things ever. I needed to bunk with you."

"Even as messed up as I was?" David studied him.

"Absolutely." Jonathan sighed and scooted his cup around in little circles. "Abigail separated from Nick later that year. Then she hurt her back in an accident that following January."

David frowned. "What caused it?"

"Ice. She'd moved down to Quantico after they separated and was on her way back from DC after seeing friends. Then—" Jonathan clamped his eyes shut against the pain of losing his parents. Six years later, their deaths still pierced his heart.. "Mom and Dad died in that crash. And not a month later, Abigail…"

"What?"

Abigail viewed her fall with shame. It wasn't his story to tell. "She needed me, and I mean more than just an emergency leave or leave of absence. That's why I retired. She lived here from May until November."

David's eyes narrowed at his reticence. He stared at his right forearm— at the tattoo that had bonded them as brothers so many years before.

Now a long scar tattered it.

When David met his gaze again, anger simmered. "Do you know how much it hurt when I called you in August to tell you I was retiring? And I got the speech about no room in the inn?" He jumped up and paced to the window. "Then when I called you again—six months later like you told me—you never called me back. Do you know what happened?"

"I'm scared to ask."

"I lived on the streets for over two years. All because you" —he whipped around and jabbed his finger at Jonathan— "my supposedly loyal friend, couldn't even find the time to return a call."

He shoved his hands into the back pockets of his shorts and once more turned his back as he stared outside.

What months was he talking about? Abigail had improved and moved out by November. By then, he'd begun working at SecureLink full time while at the same time pursuing in MBA in a one-year period.

"You called in March."

"So you remember."

"I do." Jonathan leaned forward on his elbows. With hands clasped, he squeezed his eyes closed and pressed his lips together keep his emotions from showing. His mind roved over those dark days. "You've got to understand something."

"And what's that?"

Jonathan opened his eyes and found his friend leaning with his back against the window frame. "With everything going on, I was barely holding it together late that summer. Abigail was here, and she was still in a delicate spot. I was grieving over lots of loss. And handling Mom's and Dad's estate. I truly..." He shook his head. "I worried. I knew you were having problems."

David muttered under his breath something unflattering about Jonathan.

"At the time, I just, well, I couldn't handle it. Maybe I should have thought about it more. I don't know." Jonathan sighed. "And yes, I did get your call in March. I was probably studying. Goodness knows if I wasn't studying, I was working or sleeping. And I did try to call you back the next night."

"They disconnected my phone due to non-payment."

"And I called for five nights beyond that."

David shifted from the window and stared at him. "Come again?"

"For six nights, I tried to call you back. Nothing. No voicemail, just a message saying your phone had been disconnected." He shrugged. "I figured you'd said *sayonara* and moved away. If I'd known where to find you, I would have gone looking."

David returned to the chair and dropped onto it as if the news had stunned him. He picked up a spoon and turned it over and over in his hands. "You really tried to call me back?"

"Yeah, I did," he said. "I'm sorry, bro. Truly I am. Wow... I never knew. Had I known what had happened to you, I would have come looking. No way would I have let you be homeless like that. Can you forgive me for being a jerk?"

David's knuckles whitened around the spoon, then he set it on the table so carefully that it didn't make a sound. He took a deep breath and expelled it on a sigh. "I do." His gaze flicked upward. "You know something, once I got back to Burning Tree and got clean and sober, I realized I had to take at least some responsibility for my actions. Sure, circumstances dealt me a tough blow, but, well, I had choices I made. Hearing you say that you tried to call me back... That means the world to me."

The tightness in Jonathan's throat denied speech. Instead, he nodded. For a long moment, he stared at the tattoo on his right forearm that peeked from beneath the rolled-up sleeve of his shirt. *Sola gratia.* "Thank the Lord for the grace that rules our lives. The grace that comes through forgiveness."

"By grace alone."

In contrast to their somber mood, birds twittered through the open window as they flitted around a bird feeder.

Jonathan cleared his throat to dispel the emotion that filled the air like a heady aroma. "So, I know there's a lot to clean up, but I believe that you and I are overdue for a chess match."

A slow grin finally crossed David's features. He shifted his eyes. "Do you think Abigail will notice if we don't clean up?"

"Let's not even go there." He climbed to his feet. Somehow, his injuries didn't hurt as much now. "We'll do one quick game, then clean up."

"Or I will. You're still on the injured-reserved list."

"I might could supervise."

David chuckled and led the way into the living room.

Jonathan followed and settled onto his recliner. He'd reconciled with his brother-in-Christ. And between them, once a disagreement was over, it was over.

31

Raleigh, North Carolina

Gotcha. David moved his queen in their third chess game and smirked. "Checkmate."

"Aw, c'mon." Jonathan chuckled, then groaned and clutched his middle. "Sorry. Laughing makes me hurt right now. Well, I'll be. I'm obviously a bit rusty."

"Or they knocked you in the noggin one too many times."

"Hah. It's possible. How 'bout if I claim that?" He grimaced as he pushed himself to his feet. "Well, seeing that we've wasted most of the day procrastinating, I guess we'd better get started cleaning up." He collected the salad plates that held nothing but a few crumbs from the sandwiches and chips they'd had.

David returned the chessboard to the table in front of the picture window. He straightened.

On the street, a black Dodge Charger crept past. It moved too slowly for him.

He opened the front door and lifted the lid of the mailbox, checking out the car from the corner of his eye. Dark windows concealed its occupants.

Suddenly, the engine revved. Tires chirped, and the Charger sped down the street and out of sight.

With an uneasy feeling, David pulled out the mail, then strolled to the curb where one of the MPs sat in a white Ford Focus sedan. He tapped on the window.

It hummed downward, and a young face stared at him. "Sir?"

"Did you see that car?"

"Oh, yes sir." The kid nodded. He probably wasn't old enough to drink. "I love Chargers."

"Well, love it enough to let me know if it comes back. And be sure to let your relief know about it as well."

"Wilco, sir."

David returned inside.

Abigail's throaty voice and gardenia scent floated down the hall to him, bringing a smile to his face.

"Okay, so Jonathan admitted that y'all didn't get any work done." She looped a hanging bag on the knob of one of the upper cabinet doors. "That's okay. I'll let him slide. But you, young man." Her lips twitched upward. "What's your excuse?"

"I have none." He set the mail on the counter. "But if it will make the lady feel better, I'll carry her packages inside."

"Good, 'cause there's a bunch. I managed to make it to Greensboro to that place that sells replacement china. They had Mom and Dad's pattern in enough quantity to completely replace what's broken. Too bad I couldn't do the same with the crystal." She sighed. "So, you can also load up the dishwasher. And while you do that, I'm going to get ready to go out tonight."

He cocked his head. "You're going out?"

"With you, I assume." A beguiling smile crossed her kissable lips. She demurely lowered her lashes. "Unless you have other plans."

Jonathan snorted with laughter. He groaned. "Sorry."

"Is the fact that we're going out hurting you or something?" Abigail scowled.

"No, it's my innards." He pushed up from the table. "Well, if you don't mind, I'm going to crash. Oh, and I called Nick. We're meeting at seven at his favorite hangout."

"What? The jail?"

"No, no, no. A bar. Then I'm headed to Judge MacKenzie's house. Hey, can you get me up in an hour?"

"Sure." She returned her gaze to David. "I'll be ready in a bit." She snagged her bag and headed into the living room.

David nodded. He turned his attention to unloading the Jeep, which was no small feat.

Abigail had scored. Soon, he had a dishwasher full and running. He finished the dining room so it would be ready to receive the new china and crystal, which he washed by hand.

Upstairs, the shower turned on, then off. A hair dryer ran. Footsteps made floorboards creak. A door shut.

He unloaded the dishwasher and started another load before focusing on the china hutch. He returned to the kitchen. From somewhere upstairs, Abigail asked something, and her brother answered. David continued unloading the new pottery and drinking glasses, which would go into the next round of dish washing.

Heels tapped across hardwood. "So we have reservations in less than an hour." Abigail's words reached him. "Please tell me you're going to clean up."

The slinky black dress she wore hugged her figure. Not tightly, but enough to catch his attention. Pearls glimmered against her chest and in her ears. She'd pulled her hair into an elegant twist that rested against the base of her neck. He wanted to step forward, nuzzle her, then kiss her on that beautiful skin revealed by her hairdo.

He opened his mouth, but no reply came.

She pursed lips coated in that delightful color of deep red. "Well?"

"I'll, uh, um, I'll go and clean up." He slipped past her.

As he did so, her fingers caught his. A dull shock rippled through him.

She tugged him to a stop and released him. "Thank you."

Her perfume filled his nose, again conjuring up thoughts that might get him into trouble with her brother. "For?"

"For reconciling with Jonathan. It means to the world to me."

The look she gave him buoyed his heart. He would hike through hot Afghan desert, climb K2 in Pakistan, and swim the ocean for her. Tonight presented new possibilities he hadn't even considered, and now, he couldn't wait for the evening to begin.

Raleigh, North Carolina

They dined at one of Raleigh's oldest restaurants, then had cappuccinos at a nearby coffeehouse. Now, strolling a downtown sidewalk, Abigail didn't want the evening to end. "This is why I love Raleigh in the spring."

"What? The food?"

"No, silly. The evenings like this. You know. Warm yet cool at the same time. Smells of springtime. New foliage." She sighed blissfully.

David chuckled. "I take it spring is your favorite time of the year."

"It is. What about you?" Her bare shoulder brushed the rougher fabric of his sailcloth shirt.

"Same here. There's nothing like spring in the desert." At the wistfulness in his voice, she wondered if he yearned for Burning Tree. "That's probably the only time of year where there's so many different colors. Green, of course. Purple, yellow, pure red. Even blue. It lasts for two or three weeks, a month if we're lucky. You called Raleigh your safe landing place."

"Yeah. No matter where I go, it'll always be home for me." It had been her haven during those tumultuous months six years before. "That's part of the reason why Jonathan and I didn't want to sell the house." Her mind ticked forward a bit. "Three years ago, I got passed over for major."

"Why?"

"I started filing applications at different police departments, including Raleigh."

"Even with Nick here?"

"Even with him here. They offered me a job, but after Sal came, I got promoted to major thanks to his recommendations."

"You admire him a lot."

"I do. Without him, I'd be out of the Army."

"Not such a bad thing, sometimes."

"I know, but…well, I'd like to finish out my career under his command. I owe him that much." Suddenly, the heel of her shoe caught in a crack in the pavement. She stumbled.

David's strong hands caught her under the elbows.

"Easy there." He set her on her feet.

"Thanks."

"I never imagined I'd see you in heels."

"Why?"

"Because you chase down crooks all of the time. It's impossible to run in those things."

"You have experience in that?"

He laughed. "Can't say I do, but I watched Kyra chase after Little Bit when she was smaller. Kind of awkward."

"I may like to knock heads together, but I also like my girlie things. Jewelry, scarves, high heels. Besides," —she cast a look at him— "I haven't heard you complaining."

"Nope. No complaining on this end." He kept his hand at the small of her back.

She slid closer to him as they crossed the street and arrived at the state capitol building.

A mournful tune in a minor key wafted through the cooling air like an intriguing aroma she had to follow. She cocked her head. "Do you hear that?"

"I do." He stopped.

Someone stood on the steps on the southern side of the building and played a saxophone under the glow of a lamp.

David steered her along the walkway that meandered through the carefully tended green grass of the capitol grounds. As they drew closer, Abigail noted a backpack and a duffel against a column. The saxophone's case sat open before the musician in a silent request for tips. Only a few bills littered the interior.

The saxophonist, with his sunken cheeks and tattered clothes, was homeless.

David touched her hand. "Do you mind if I speak with him alone for a few minutes?"

"Not at all. I'll wait over here." She walked over to a nearby bench beneath a light and settled on it.

He approached the saxophonist. The notes ceased, and the two of them began conversing in tones so low, she couldn't hear anything. They sat down on the steps.

The conversation between the boy and David intensified. The boy wiped his cheeks. David raised his phone to his ear, maybe to summon help for the kid. Her heart filled. When he put his hand on the boy's shoulder and bowed his head as if praying, she did the same.

Finally, the boy laid his saxophone in its case, closed it, and hefted one of the packs. David took the other, and they shuffled toward the south entrance to the grounds.

Abigail remained where she was and watched. A movement out of the corner of her eye caught her attention. She turned her head a fraction to the right. Did someone stand in the gloom near one of the ancient oaks that dotted the grounds? She couldn't be sure, and thanks to her position under a streetlight, she couldn't turn her head to confirm without her observer noticing.

"Abigail?" David called softly.

"Hey." She took a deep breath to tamp down the sudden hammering of her heart.

"I'm sorry about that." He extended his hands in a silent invitation to help her rise.

She took him up on it.

He cast a long glance toward the steps. "He's only seventeen. His parents abandoned him. Social Services put him in foster care. They mistreated him, so he ran away. He's been on the streets for a month. I had to get him some help. I…I didn't want him to wind up where I did." His fingers tightened around hers. "The rescue mission people just picked him up to take him to their shelter. I'm sorry for ruining our evening."

"David, no. You didn't do that at all. That's one of the things I like about you. I love your compassion for others."

He brought her fingers to his lips and kissed them.

Her breath hitched. She took the tiniest of steps closer to him.

He curled his arm around her waist and slid his hand behind her neck. His thumb skimmed the skin of her cheekbone. His breath whispered across her cheek.

She closed her eyes.

Something snapped behind her.

She whipped around just in time to see someone dart into the shadows.

"Abigail?"

"I'm sorry." She hated herself for the broken moment, one she most likely wouldn't get back. Okay. Change that. "I'd noticed someone watching earlier. I swear whoever it was had eyes only for us."

"Man or woman?"

"I don't know." She huffed out a frustrated sigh. "C'mon. Let's go home."

"You want this evening to end?"

That caught her up short. "Not really."

"I'm still up for taking the longest possible distance back."

Pleasant tingling worked its way up her arm. "I'm all in." With her fingers thoroughly entwined in his, they resumed their walk, this time heading southward along Fayetteville Street, one of the main streets of downtown Raleigh. They strolled to the convention center in comfortable silence, then turned around and continued north. The whole time, he didn't let go of her, a good sign in her book.

As they finally turned their steps toward home and passed the capitol again, her thoughts returned to their unseen observer and the reason why David now walked beside her. The Athena file.

"It doesn't make sense," she blurted.

"What?"

"Why there were op plans and AARs related to the Mighty Men on that drive along with the Athena file."

His hand tightened around hers. "I thought the case was closed. And aren't you on vacation?"

"I am. But I'm not very good at leaving things alone. I mean, Nabeelah started showing up in our lives when the drive did."

"And we haven't seen her since we left Burning Tree, right?"

"True." She stopped. Something wasn't right.

He took her other hand. With a teasing smile, he cocked his head. "Can't think and walk?"

She chuckled. "Sometimes. Or it's more like when I'm thinking hard, I lose situational awareness at times. One time I ran into a street sign."

He laughed.

"But seriously. I feel like there's a link between the Mighty Men and the Athena file. Not to mention, Nabeelah's name was redacted from the profile I wrote up. It's almost like someone doesn't want anyone to know she exists." Then suddenly, it snapped into place. "Wait! I think I might have figured it out."

"How so?"

Excitement coursed through her. "What do you know about the goddess Athena?"

David scratched his head. "Not much, to be honest. Jonathan told me about her once."

"In Greek mythology, she was the goddess of wisdom and military victory. She was also a warrior, but she would only fight if her homeland was under attack, and she'd fight fiercely to save it. So my conclusion is that the Athena file has to do with her. Not that we'll find out what's in it."

"Can Sal tell you anything?"

"No." A few days before—had it really been less than two weeks?— she'd approached him about what Jonathan had found in Afghanistan. "When I mentioned that Jonathan had found a drive with the Athena file on it, he acted…oddly. Like shame on me for even bringing it up. He even threatened to write me up for insubordination."

"That is strange. He seemed nice enough when he met with us a few days ago."

"I agree."

He stepped closer. The smoldering look in his eye indicated he'd lost interest in talking about business.

Her pulse skipped. *Just a little more. Please.*

He nuzzled her neck and whispered, "Let it go."

Every nerve went on alert, and she wanted to pull him into a kiss right then and there.

He offered a mysterious smile and tugged her into motion.

The house came into view. Abigail's heart thumped a little as she considered ways to avoid ending their evening early.

A woman with long, flowing black hair came toward them and stopped a mere ten feet away. Nabeelah

Abigail tried to call out to her, but her cry remained locked in the back of her throat.

Nabeelah's jaw dropped.

David beat her to it. "Little sister! I'm so happy to see you."

Abigail rushed toward her.

Nabeelah reached out, not for a hug, but to shove her into the street.

Abigail stumbled. The heel of her shoe snapped. She lost her balance and fell. Burning flashed across her shoulder, her knees, and her hands as she hit and rolled.

Headlights blinded her.

An engine roared.

Tires squealed.

She closed her eyes and braced herself for the impact of a car.

"Abigail!" David grabbed her and tumbled with her to the edge of the street. "Abigail!"

She hadn't been hit. Instead, she lay sandwiched between David and the wheel of another car. Her face was planted securely against the sailcloth of David's shirt. She squirmed. "Can't...breathe."

"Sorry about that." He sat up and propped her against the wheel. "That was close."

She grimaced and rubbed her sore shoulder. "That's...that's one way to put it."

"Hey, are you guys okay?"

Abigail looked into the unfamiliar face. "Are you—were you the driver?"

"Yes, ma'am." The man nodded toward the Toyota Camry standing in the middle of the street, its interior lights on. "I'm so sorry. When that woman pushed you, I didn't have time to brake. Thank goodness for your boyfriend's quick action."

David helped her rise. "Did you see her?"

"She ran away. But those cops chased her." He pointed at the two MPs who loped toward them. "I can stay if you need me to."

"We're good. Thanks for stopping." David put his hands under her elbows, and she limped to the white Ford Fusion parked on the street in front of the house.

She leaned against the fender. "I don't understand."

"Neither do I," David said. The MPs joined them, and he shifted his attention to one of them. "Sergeant, what did you find?"

"She's a world-class sprinter," replied the sergeant through huffs. "She jumped into a black Dodge Charger and sped off. Her plate was covered in mud."

"Of course," Abigail muttered. Her shoulder, hands, and knees began stinging.

"But she didn't cover all of it. It was a US government plate."

32

Raleigh, North Carolina

"Of all things." Abigail pulled off her heels and limped up the front sidewalk to the porch. "Why would she do something like that? And what agency is she working for?"

"I was going to ask you that," David replied. "Do you have your key?"

"Rats! They're in my purse, which I dropped somewhere in the street."

"Wait here and don't move, okay?"

"I'm not going anywhere."

He darted into the shadows.

She stared at her shoes. The left heel had broken clean off, rendering the pair ruined. She scowled. Thanks to nearly getting squashed, any romantic semblance of an evening had vanished. The sooner she got inside, upstairs, and behind a closed door, the better.

David returned, toting her purse on his shoulder like he owned it.

That brought the tiniest of smiles to her face. "You don't look the least bit uncomfortable carrying my purse."

"Why should I be?"

She didn't have an answer for that.

He fished out her keys, turned off the alarm, and undid the lock.

Once through the door, she made for the stairs.

"Hey, where are you going?"

"It's late."

"No, it's only nine. Besides, you and I have a couple of items of unfinished business." He tugged her toward the leather couch in the family room. "We need to get your scrapes cleaned up. Where does Jonathan keep a first aid kit?"

"Under the counter in his bathroom."

"Have a seat. Don't move."

She sighed and slouched on the soft cushions. Already, her body barked at her for taking such a tumble. She'd be really sore in the morning thanks to that. Wincing as she shifted, she studied her hands again. Blood oozed from the scrapes. Same thing for her knees and shoulder.

"So you can at least take orders," David teased.

She glowered at him.

He shoved away the coffee table and pulled up the ottoman from a nearby wingback chair. After setting a bowl of water on the table, he picked up a wash cloth. "I know this is going to sting, and I apologize."

"That's okay—ouch!" She drew in a sharp breath through her teeth as he cleaned the scrape on her shoulder.

"Easy there." He took her hands. Though his touch was like a caress, the pain still arced through her nervous system. The same with her knees. He applied ointment and a couple of Band-Aids to the scrape on her shoulder. Was it her imagination, or did his fingers linger on her neck before he resumed his seat?

"Does anything else hurt?" he asked as he bandaged her knees.

"No, but I'm definitely going to ache in the morning."

"That's why I want you to take some ibuprofen."

Automatically, she began shaking her head. "You know how I feel—"

"That's item of business number one."

"Huh?"

He took her right hand, applied the ointment, and gently rubbed it in with his thumbs. "I've heard enough from you and your brother to know something happened to you six years ago, right after your parents passed, that involves painkillers."

Abigail winced as if he'd slapped her. "Jonathan didn't—"

"No, he didn't tell me anything." He placed Band-Aids over the scrapes and moved to her left hand. "I may be a clueless guy at times, but even I can read between the lines."

She clamped her jaw shut. The lump rose in her throat.

He spread a line of ointment over the scrapes. "You should know I'm not someone who's going to judge you or belittle you for what happened. What grounds would I have to stand on if I did that?"

"I don't want to talk about it." She rose and fled to the kitchen. Oh, great. She'd essentially trapped herself. If she wanted to escape him now, she'd have to run out the back door, to the street, and down the sidewalk to the front door. She grabbed the teakettle and ran some water into it before placing it on the stove.

"I know it's hard." David poured the water from his bowl down the drain. "There's a certain power secrets have over us. They bind us to silence. The problem is, we can collapse under their weight. And somehow, secrets lose their bondage over us when confessed."

Oh, how right he was. Thing is, could he hold that confidence?

"This goes no farther than here?"

"No farther than here." He placed two mugs beside her.

She wasn't so sure, but she had to start somewhere. "Did Jonathan tell you about Nick and me?"

"He said you split in November 2009. You told me he ran around on you."

"Right. So I moved to Quantico. Ten minutes if that from the gate, but farther from my friend, Gabrielle, and her husband. In January 2010, I was coming back from visiting them. It was a nasty night. Cold rain turning to sleet and icing up. I hit a patch and skidded into a tree." She nodded toward the mugs. "You like tea too, I assume."

"I hate coffee and love tea. Peppermint, if you have it."

She opened the cabinet. "Fortunately, I didn't have really serious injuries, just the normal whiplash but also some muscle and ligament damage from the seatbelt. The doc on base prescribed pain medication and PT. I...I was in a really busy period of work, so I told myself I didn't have time for the two sessions a week of PT. It was easier to pop a pill."

"Didn't your doc notice when you kept asking for refills?"

"My first one got transferred to Afghanistan. The next one? He was clueless about a lot of things. He never questioned my requests for refills, never did an exam to see why I wasn't getting better, never lectured me on not doing PT." She dropped two tea bags into the mugs. "Soon, popping pills became easier than dealing with the pain from my parents' accident."

David's warm hands gently turned her so she leaned with her back to the counter. He ran his hand down her face.

"I remember your folks died in April of that year."

"They did," she whispered. She gazed around the kitchen she and Jonathan had redone. They'd both cried during the process, but it'd healed them as well. She moved to the bar table where they took their meals and slid onto a chair.

"I came to the funerals, you know."

"I remember." A smile briefly crossed her face. "I popped pills the entire time people were here. It was an easy way to deal with everyone and all of their condolences."

He rubbed her shoulders.

She leaned against him. "Then when everyone left, the serious business of grieving began. In those first three weeks, while we were on bereavement leave, we got rid of their personal belongings like clothing. But then…"

The kettle whistled.

David poured their tea, then set her mug before her and a small plate nearby. Rather than take a seat across from her, he remained by her right side, his hand resting on her uninjured left shoulder. His thumb caressed her skin.

A tear slid down her cheek. "I got back to work, but I felt very, very alone in my grief. Only the pills got me through the day. I felt like such a loser."

"Why?"

"Can't you see it?"

His motion ceased.

She sighed. Of course he couldn't. He hadn't been inside of her head during those awful days. "I'd lost my marriage because my husband ran around on me. Read: I wasn't good enough for him."

"Bocelli's a jerk."

"I know that now, but back then? I'd thought I'd lost my health because I was still in a lot of pain. I thought God hated me for everything and took my parents as punishment."

"What?" The other bar chair scraped across the tile as David pulled it over. "Abigail—"

"I know it's dumb, but that's how addled my thinking had become. I didn't think life was worth living, so in May, I called in sick, locked myself in my apartment, and popped the pills. A whole bottle's worth. Oh, I didn't do it right away. I stared at that bottle the entire day. Finally, a little after five, I did the deed."

He didn't say a word, only removed his teabag and set it on the plate.

"Now, I realize how God saved my life. I'd completely forgotten that Gabrielle and I had promised to meet in Quantico for supper. Miraculously, she got out of DC on time, got to my apartment, and found it strange when I didn't answer the door even though my car was out front. Then she heard the cats yowling. That's when she called the cops. They found me in the bathroom and got me to the hospital."

"I remember when Jonathan got that call. We were at supper ourselves."

She took an unsteady sip of tea. Her fingers clenched the mug. "When I woke up, like three or so days had passed. He hadn't changed from his ACUs and looked like hell. I don't think he slept a wink until I woke up. I was on a twenty-four-hour suicide watch, restraints and all. I felt horrible, had this nasty taste in my mouth. They wanted to lock me up on the psych ward since Jonathan was still on active duty and couldn't be with me, but he would have none of that. That's when he told me he was retiring."

David reached up and ran his fingers down her cheek. "He made the right choice."

"He came back a week later when they were ready to release me. He'd spoken with my CO and arranged for long-term leave. We only stayed a night in my apartment. He told me to pack everything I wanted to take because I wouldn't be coming back for six months. He brought me here, to this house. And that's when he read me the riot act. I was to go to PT, Bible study, and counseling. At first, he'd drive me to make sure I actually went. And I'd go to church with him." She fell silent and sipped her tea.

"You obviously recovered."

"I did. Now you know why I'm so scared to take painkillers, even ibuprofen or aspirin."

"You won't get addicted—"

"I know. I know." She hopped off her chair and braced her skinned hands against the counter. "I didn't say my fear was rational."

"A lot of them aren't." He reached into the cabinet and pulled out a freshly washed glass. He opened a couple of doors and pulled down a pill bottle. He placed it before her.

She stared at it. Her heart hammered. She began shaking her head as she backed away from it. "I—I can't."

"Abigail, please. You'll sleep better. Heal faster. I know it's like jumping off a cliff. I'll be right here for you, okay?" He ran water into the glass and handed it to her.

He pressed two pills into her hand.

Before she lost her nerve, she popped them into her mouth and chased it with a swig of water.

Her world spun.

He caught the glass before it slipped from her hand.

She took a deep breath and steadied. "You're right. It's definitely like jumping off a cliff."

"I'm proud of you." David drew her close, and she clung to him.

"For?"

"Releasing that secret. Do you feel lighter now?"

She pulled back as she thought about that one. She did. "I'd say freer is more like it."

"Good." His fingers drifted down her arm. That dark gaze of his shifted to desire.

Her nerves got the best of her. "I'll, um, well, I'm…" She edged toward the hall. "I'm going to go and change."

"Wait."

"What?"

"There's a second item of business."

"That would be?"

"Us. I haven't forgotten what started on the capitol grounds." A smile quirked his lips upwards as he took her hands and drew her toward him.

She backed against the counter. "Um, I, um, well…need to…"

"What?" David reached up and ran his hand down her hair. With small tinkles, the bobby pins holding her chignon in place fell onto the granite.

Rational thought totally failed her. "I, uh, don't know." Could she sound any more idiotic?

Her hair fell across her shoulders, and he wove his fingers through it.

"You're funny."

Her pulse thudded out of control as his fingers traced her jawline. "I try."

He tipped her chin and kissed her.

"Oh, my…" she managed when they came up for air.

He smiled and drew her close again to nuzzle her hair. He kissed her ear. "Now you can go and change, but only if you come back down."

"That, I can do." She led the way into the living room.

As she climbed the steps, David called, "How about wear something cute, like a negligee?"

"I'll pretend I didn't hear that, David Shepherd."

He laughed.

She stepped into her darkened room. She grinned, somehow feeling so much lighter now. Still giggling at his suggestion, she flipped on the light.

And screamed.

"Abigail!" Footsteps pounded up the steps.

"She…she was here!" Abigail pointed at the mirror.

Once more written in her lipstick was a message.

It's not over.

"How did she get in?" he asked.

Abigail rushed into Jonathan's study and searched the window sill. She pointed at the scrape marks. "The same way I got in and out as a teenager. This window's not connected to the alarm system since it's on the second floor."

"First in Burning Tree, and now—"

"She didn't do the one in Burning Tree."

"What?"

"Here." Abigail crossed the landing to her room and snatched her phone from the dresser. "Before we cleaned the mirrors, I took pictures of the warnings, remember?" She flicked her fingers across the screen.

He took the phone and studied both sets of writing. "You're right. But then who did it there? And why? And what is she talking about?"

"I wish I knew." Abigail shivered as she considered the warning. "I wish I knew."

33

Raleigh, North Carolina

David's feet pounded down the street in a steady cadence as his breath came out in gentle puffs, and sweat trickled down his body, which made his T-shirt stick to him. Reminders of rebirth and renewal popped up all around him. The chatter of birds. Dew that glistened like God had laced the flowers and lawns with diamonds. The heady aromas of spring.

God had renewed him as well. In helping Abigail find Jonathan, he'd rediscovered his purpose, found new meaning. God meant for him to protect, to care for others. A high purpose he'd be honored to pursue.

His steps slowed. How was it possible to feel such peace and contentment in the city that had brought him to his knees years before?

A cool breeze washed over his face, and a scent teased his nose.

Gardenias. Not from Abigail this time but from the bushes of a nearby house that were laden with tender white blossoms.

His steps stuttered, and he slowed to a walk for the remaining quarter mile. How far they'd come in eight days, from her being a nuisance who'd upset the peaceful rhythm of his life to a woman who now occupied more of his mind with each passing hour. Even now, he could feel the touch of her lips on his.

He truly cared for her. Did they have a future together?

They did—if he left Burning Tree. Could he do it? Could he leave the place he loved and return to Raleigh?

Thankfully, he didn't have to think about that right now. He could simply enjoy living in the present.

He approached the carport at the house. He peered over the gate. Two low steps led to the screened-in porch.

Abigail slouched on a sofa. She had her feet propped on the edge of the coffee table, and a book rested on her lap. For a moment, she didn't move, and he wondered if she dozed. He wouldn't blame her since he'd lain awake almost the entire night and listened to the floorboards in the room above his creak as she'd paced.

Mindful that Jonathan still might have been sleeping on the other side of the french doors, he softly called, "Abigail."

"Hey." A sleepy smile crossed her lips, and she set her book on one knee. "Did you have a good run?"

"I did."

"Sorry I didn't join you. You were right. I'm sore."

"I know you didn't sleep well either." He bent and kissed her.

She curled her hand behind his neck and prolonged it. Then she sat back with a sigh. "I could get used to that."

"Me too. Where's your brother?"

"On a telecon with his CEO. Can you believe that? It's barely past seven."

"You've had breakfast?"

"Yeah. I just finished."

"How about some tea?"

"I'd like that."

"Let me get my shower, and I'll be right out. Fifteen minutes, tops." He headed to the guest room.

Upstairs, the muffled sound of an unfamiliar voice reached him. Jonathan said something. A conversation ensued.

After showering and grabbing his mystery book, he headed outside with steaming mugs of Earl Gray. "Here you go."

Abigail yawned and stretched. "His and her tea mugs?"

"Something like that." David eased down beside her.

They drank their tea and read in comfortable silence. Chalk one up for why they fit so well together. Abigail leaned her head against his shoulder, and her hair spilled down his arm in silky wisps. It tickled his skin and conjured images of what could be. Her chest rose and fell in an even pace. Good. She needed to rest after the past week.

The french doors opened. Jonathan chuckled. "Well, look at the lovebirds."

"Hey, man." David grinned. Jonathan had ribbed them the night before when he saw them curled up together watching television.

Abigail lifted her head a moment, then laid it against his shoulder again and murmured, "You woke me up."

"Sorry." Jonathan eased onto a rattan chair. "Hey, bro. Want to run out with me to grab some coffee, er, tea?"

"Sure."

Abigail didn't move. "I can't come?"

"You need to rest."

"The bromance continues," she muttered. Then she climbed to her feet and stretched.

David followed her movements with his eyes. He caught himself since Jonathan sat not three feet from him. Rising, he mumbled, "Let me get some shoes on. Abigail, why don't you grab some shuteye while we're gone?"

She tossed him a mock salute and headed inside.

Once he returned, Jonathan opened the gate to the carport. "Do you mind walking? It's too nice of a morning to drive anywhere."

"Are you sure you feel like it?"

"Yeah, I'm doing better." A smile unvarnished by pain crossed his face. "I sat up without groaning, and breathing doesn't hurt anymore. I guess that's progress."

They stepped onto the sidewalk and strolled toward the capitol a few blocks away. Jonathan cast him a sideways glance. "I take it you two are an item now."

"You don't mind?"

"Mind? Not at all. You're good for her, you know."

"How so?"

"You're an encourager. Always have been. You're strong and steady, someone who's genuine. I think she's been cautious about dating anyone because she got so burned by Nick."

David let that one pass in silence as they made their way south and arrived at the capitol grounds. The boy he'd sent to the shelter the night before reminded him all too much of his own state five years ago. What would have happened if someone had intervened that first night? If he'd only swallowed his pride and walked—yes, he could have walked—to Jonathan's house? None of this would have happened. But, if it hadn't happened, would he have ever united with Abigail?

"Here we go." Jonathan slowed.

David had been so lost in his thoughts that he hadn't realized how they'd traveled south on Fayetteville Street for a few blocks.

Jonathan opened a door leading into a café already crowded by people in business suits, those in jeans and T-shirts, and a few law enforcement uniforms. "It's on me."

Once they had a hot tea for David and a steaming brew of the daily coffee special for Jonathan, they settled at an outdoor table.

His friend braced himself as he lowered into a chair. "Sorry. Getting up and down is still the hard part. The doc said I'd heal up a lot in the next few days. I sure hope he's right." He took a sip and gazed around him at the hubbub of people walking along the sidewalk. "I like this time of day. It's not too hot yet. Not too humid either. It's neat to observe people walking along the street. Sometimes, I'll make up stories about them, like where they're going, what their past is. This is where I truly feel at home."

"Abigail called Raleigh her safe landing place."

"I think it is for both of us. When I was working at the Ghazni compound, I'd only be halfway through my three-month tour and yearning to come home to Raleigh." Jonathan cleared his throat. "Speaking of which, I was on a telecon with the SecureLink CEO, Wyatt Edwards. Bryson Bishop, who used to work with Abigail and was my law guy at the Ghazni compound, ran the investigation on the convoy that got hit. I guess the way

Nicole discredited me got to him, and he sent everything—and I mean everything—in a FedEx package to Wyatt, for his eyes only."

"He jumped the chain of command?"

"Big time because Boss Man ignored everything."

"Boss Man?"

"Harry Bossman, the former CEO of the Ghazni compound. Wyatt told me that when he got the package, he reviewed everything. He called Boss Man into his office and got the run-around. I don't know the gory details, but the long and short of it is that he gave Boss Man two choices, either retire effective immediately, or be fired. Guess which one he took."

"Retirement."

"Bingo. That happened on Monday. I think that got to Wyatt because he realized how Boss Man tried to cover up everything, including refusing a team from the home office to investigate. He decided SecureLink needed some sort of internal accountability, kind of like Internal Affairs in a police department—and a special projects team. That's why he called me. He wants me to lead that division."

"Hey, that's great. Congratulations." David grinned and offered his hand.

Jonathan shook it. "The cool thing is, I get to pick and choose who I want. Internal or external, it doesn't matter. He said the only thing that mattered was that they're not easily influenced and have knowledge, skills, and abilities that would enable them to function like a police force or special ops team. You know. Different specialties but the ability to cross-train. I've already contacted Bryson, and he's onboard as heading the investigations unit. I need someone for my deputy to oversee special projects."

David raised an eyebrow. "You...you want me to be that man?"

"You got it." Jonathan leaned forward and took another sip of coffee. "Look. We made a good team when we were with the Mighty Men. A great team. We worked well both as comrades and as friends. You watched my back, and I watched yours. I envision you overseeing the special projects unit."

The anxiety that had nibbled at his soul exploded to the forefront. "That's…that's quite an opportunity. But are you sure I'm the right guy? After everything that happened to me?"

"I know you are. You've got the instincts and smarts needed. Look." Jonathan paused and looked him in the eye with an intensity in his own. "I know your history. I know what happened to you, but I also know you've recovered and put your life back together."

"But I don't have a college degree."

"Not necessary. Educational background doesn't matter so long as you have a secondary education or equivalent. What does matter at this point is experience. And skills. You've got natural-born talents at leadership and the ability to think through a mission in excruciating detail. You know what it takes to flesh out a team, and I'm confident that between the two of us, we could stock the Special Projects Unit with the right people."

"I'm still not—"

"Let me sweeten the deal for you. This is what I'm authorized to offer in terms of a salary." Jonathan quoted a sum.

"Wow." The figure was six times what he made as the maintenance man at the hotel in Burning Tree.

"And, I can offer a signing bonus, plus other periodic bonuses where appropriate. And get this—Wyatt gave me permission to set up shop here in Raleigh since he thinks the Special Projects and Investigation Division needs to be separate from the rest of the company. That's the best part. If you took the job, you wouldn't be too far from Abigail."

"I'm…I'm flattered. This is a lot to take in." The opportunity. The money. Abigail. The offer boggled his mind. But he'd have to leave Burning Tree—his security. He'd have to leave Kyra and his family, the only ones he'd trusted.

He'd have to live in Raleigh, the very place where he'd hit his lowest point.

Jonathan seemed to sense his worries. "Why don't you take a couple of days to think about it? I know you have to talk with Kyra and your folks too. But know this. I'm not going to lay you off, and I definitely am not going to let you wind up on the streets again. You're my brother-in-Christ, and that means I've got your back. Always." His friend gingerly pushed himself to his feet. "We'll talk later, okay?"

David managed a nod. As they began the walk back to the house, two sides battled within him. The safety and security of Burning Tree versus the opportunity of a future with SecureLink and Abigail.

He didn't know which he wanted more.

That was what terrified him.

34

Burning Tree, Utah

From her customary place in the front passenger seat of the van they'd stolen in Denver, Nicole surveyed the main road as they rumbled into town. What a piddly little place. Even at mid-morning, only a few cars meandered along the streets. It was the same on the sidewalks. At least they only had one cop car that she could see. All the better for their plans. They pulled into the parking lot of the town's only gas station, and she picked up the burner phone, then dialed a number.

"Kyra Lane Café and Restaurant," a perky female announced.

"Is Kyra Martin in?" Nicole glanced at Roy.

The faintest of smiles crossed his stubbled face.

"No, ma'am. She isn't due until five today."

"Do you know where I could find her?"

"Probably at home. Would you like to leave a message?"

"No, thanks. I'll call back later." Nicole lowered the phone and nodded. "She's where we need her to be. Too bad we couldn't get the kids too."

"That would be too much for the two of us." Roy put the van into gear. "Are you ready?"

"Ready to get the drive and my life back." She leaned over and kissed him. "And once we get it to Shamal Khan to help El Lobo, I'll be ready to skip the country and never return."

"Agreed there." He slowed and almost coasted to the stop sign at the junction with the main highway.

Nicole undid her seatbelt. "I'll walk from here. What say you do a loop through town? That should be all the time I need to do what I need to do."

"Roger that."

She hopped from the van. After glancing into her handbag to ensure her gun lay within reach, she crossed over the river and slowed at the short set of steps leading to the front yard of the Martin house. Inside, a vacuum cleaner hummed. A shadow briefly crossed in front of the rectangle of light created by the open back door.

Perfect.

Nicole sashayed up the front steps. She rang the doorbell.

Nothing.

She rang again.

The noise ceased, and the silhouette reappeared.

A petite woman approached the screen.

"Kyra Martin?" Nicole asked in her most official voice.

"That's me." Kyra didn't smile. "And you are?"

"Nicole Chatain. I'm with the VA. They sent me down from Salt Lake City because there's been some discrepancy with your brother's benefits. Is he here?"

"He's not."

"May I come in and leave some paperwork for him?"

"No." Kyra's answer came out hard and flat. Her dark eyes narrowed. "I need to see some ID."

In one smooth motion, Nicole yanked open the screened door, stepped inside, and shoved Kyra.

Off balance, the woman stumbled backward. She clawed at the staircase railing. With a cry, she tumbled into the foyer's console table before falling to the floor.

Nicole kicked the main door shut, grabbed her gun, and pointed it at Kyra's head. "This is all of the ID I need."

Kyra's eyes widened. "Who are you?"

"Your worst enemy, Kyra Martin."

284

From somewhere nearby, a dog frantically barked.

"Where's the dog?"

"He—he's in the bedroom. He hates the vacuum, and—"

"Shut up." Nicole noted a puppy whining in a crate by the kitchen's door. "Get up and go to the kitchen."

Kyra climbed to her feet, then whipped around and clawed at Nicole. She stumbled backward.

Kyra fled toward the back door.

Roy blocked her escape.

"No!" Kyra snatched a knife from the butcher block and brandished it in front of her.

Roy charged her. Before she could react, he grabbed her wrist with one hand, and with the other, he took her by the throat and rammed her into the cabinet. Her head cracked against the deep cherry wood.

The knife clattered to the floor.

Kyra moaned.

Roy released her.

She slid to the floor, and her hands shot to her throat.

He tied her wrists and ankles with cable ties.

"Nice try." Nicole jabbed her with the toe of her hiking boot.

"What…what do you want with me?" Kyra glared at them.

Nicole smirked at the blood that ran down her cheek from the cut her fall into the table had produced. "It's not you we want. Or your brother. It's his pal. Ward."

"Jonathan Ward?"

"You guessed it. Let's get out of here."

Roy slapped a piece of duct tape over Kyra's mouth and tossed her over his shoulder like a bag of feed.

Nicole closed up the house and followed. They stashed Kyra in the back and headed south into the mountains. An hour's drive took them from pavement to dirt, and one last turn brought the double-wide they'd commandeered into view.

Cal came outside, the rifle they'd retrieved from Roy's house at a relaxed ready position in front of him. He grinned as Nicole hopped from the passenger's seat. "Who'd you bring me this time?"

Roy slid open the side door, revealing Kyra lying on the floor.

She squirmed, and muted bleats seeped through the tape.

Roy tugged her to a sitting position. "Kyra Martin, Shepherd's sister." He clipped the cable tie around her ankles.

Cal stepped forward and fingered her dark curls.

Kyra cringed and tried to pull away.

His hand drifted to her cheek. "She's mighty pretty. I think I'll—"

"She's not for play," Nicole said. She sneered at Kyra. "At least not right now. Let's go." She grabbed her by the arm. "You're coming with me."

Kyra stumbled beside her.

Nicole sneezed as they entered the dusty trailer. In the dim light, Frisco slept on a ratty velour couch in colors of orange, rust, and yellow. He was still out of it, thanks to the pain meds the doc-in-the-box had given him. She swore at Ward under her breath. They needed Frisco at one hundred percent, not ten.

She yanked a blue vinyl chair from underneath the kitchen table and shoved Kyra onto it. "Sit there. Roy, get that camera set up."

Next to her, Roy placed a webcam on a shelf of a nearby bookcase.

Nicole hit a few keys, and Kyra came into sharp focus. A few more taps opened a Skype session. Kyra wriggled in the image.

Nicole ripped the tape from their hostage's mouth, causing her to yelp. She spun the laptop around. "You see this, Kyra Martin? You're going to help deliver a message for us."

"I'll not—"

Nicole slapped her hard across the face, and an angry red hand print blossomed on her cheek. "You don't have a choice. Do it or join the owners of this trailer six feet under."

She reached for her phone.

35

Early afternoon rain pattered onto the roof of the Ward house. Abigail hummed as she stirred the spaghetti sauce. Through the open screened door came scents that had always reminded her of home, those of Carolina jasmine, gardenia bushes, and azaleas. It felt good to be home, to have her brother and his best friend reconciled.

"Aw, man! You beat me again." Jonathan laughed from the living room. "Okay, bro. Enough for today."

A few seconds later, David strolled into the kitchen and set his empty drink glass on the counter.

Abigail soaked up his dark gaze like spilled wine onto a soft towel. "You didn't beat him too badly, did you?"

"Nah. He almost got me when he forked my king and rook." He slid his hand behind her neck and drew her into a kiss.

Oh, my. He could do that all afternoon, and she wouldn't mind. Nope. Not at all. She rested her hands on his chest. "Kitchen romance?"

He chuckled as he laced his fingers through her hair. "I wouldn't have it any other way. What's cooking?"

"Spaghetti sauce for tonight. The top-secret-need-to-know Ward recipe. Want a taste?" She reached into a drawer and handed him a spoon.

287

Jennifer Haynie

He dipped it into the pan. After sampling it, he grinned. "Absolutely delicious." He kissed her again.

She snuggled closer.

"Okay, you lovebirds, knock it off." Jonathan mock-punched his friend on the shoulder. "I take it we're eating in?"

"Uh, yeah." She disengaged from David's embrace. "I didn't cook all of this sauce for nothing. So when are we going to the beach?"

"She's too eager," Jonathan stage-whispered to David, who chuckled.

"I figured tomorrow. Then we could—" Jonathan's phone chimed. He glanced at the Caller ID and frowned. "Who is this? Nicole?"

Why would Nicole be calling here? This couldn't be good. Abigail shivered and took David's hand.

"I do." Her brother brushed by her and rushed into the living room. His steps thundered upward.

Abigail and David darted after him. By the time they reached his study and crowded behind his L-shaped desk against the wall, Jonathan had logged into his computer and opened Skype.

The monitor held an image of a brunette with long, dark hair draped over one shoulder. The woman smirked. "It's good to see you again, Ward."

Abigail clenched her fist.

"What do you want?" Jonathan growled.

"You know what I want. The Athena file. Plain and simple as that." She dropped her gaze as she toyed with the ends of her hair. Then she raised it, and the slate blue color radiated malice. "You put us in a hurt locker when you escaped from Frisco."

"Good."

"Maybe for you. Not so much for others. Kyra, say hello to your brother and his friends." Nicole shifted to the side, revealing David's sister—and evidence she'd been beaten.

"Kyra!" David's cry filled the study.

"Yes, Shepherd. I'm no fool." Nicole smirked. "I knew we were in a pinch. So here's the deal, Ward. You get me that file."

Jonathan shook his head. "It's not that easy. You know that. Matter of fact, it's going to be impossible to—"

288

"Impossible? Really? Kyra, did you hear that?" Nicole draped her arm around Kyra's shoulders as if they'd been sorority sisters in college. "Ward doesn't care enough about his best friend's sister to move heaven and earth to get the file. What a shame." She pressed the muzzle of a pistol against Kyra's temple. "Maybe you need a bit more motivation, Ward."

Kyra whimpered.

"Guess what? You've got a source of help standing right there. Abigail, help your brother. You've got until Tuesday to be out here in Burning Tree. Ward, it's you and a drive with the file on it for her. And come alone. No cops or Feds, got it? I'll call you back with more directions on Sunday." The screen went blank.

Abigail's gaze shifted from her brother to David.

Veins bulged in David's neck, and his face reddened. With a guttural cry, he swiped everything from the top of Jonathan's desk, including the five dollars' worth of pennies in the margarita glass. They crashed to the floor and rolled everywhere. He reared back to kick the wall.

"David, no!" She rushed to him and gripped his arms.

His muscles rippled underneath her fingers as he struggled.

"Please," she softly begged. She tightened her grip and wondered if she could physically wrestle him to the floor if she had to. She stared at her brother.

Jonathan rested his elbows on the now-clear part of his desk. His fingers clenched his hair. "I don't believe it."

"Well, believe it." That came out as a growl from David. "You heard her. We've got to get that drive." He took a menacing step toward his friend.

"You think I don't know that?" Jonathan shot to his feet. His chair rolled back and hit the credenza under the window.

Abigail inserted herself between them. "Both of you, sit!"

Jonathan eased onto his chair.

"You too, David." She turned and pointed at a wingback chair in the corner near the closet. She folded her arms. "I need to call Sal."

"We can't." David glared at her. "You heard her. No cops."

"I can't just waltz into the Pentagon or wherever to get ahold of the Athena file. It's on secure servers, and you'd better believe they've put more passwords and tripwires around it since it got swiped. And I'm no computer genius, got it?"

David hung his head.

"David, I'm sorry." Abigail knelt beside him. "It's the only way." She touched his arm. "Please understand that."

He jumped up and turned his back on her.

She rose. "Let me call Sal." She picked up the house phone and dialed her CO's number.

"Sal Torres."

"Sal, it's me. Abigail."

"Abigail, hi." Warmth filled his voice. "How's vacation?"

"Good. Or, at least it was."

"What happened?"

She glanced at David. He hadn't moved. "Nicole Chardet kidnapped David Shepherd's sister in Burning Tree, Utah."

"Come again?"

She repeated herself and added, "She wants Jonathan and the Athena file in exchange for Kyra."

"You know that's impossible."

"I know. But it has to happen. Otherwise…"

David left the room.

"I can't." Her CO remained firm.

"Sal, please."

"You know they're not going to release that file. It's on servers with so many firewalls around them that only a select few can access it."

Abigail drew in a breath. "If we don't get those plans, Kyra's going to die."

"I understand." Sal fell silent. "Let me think on this." More silence followed. Then he cleared his throat. "There may be a way to do this without compromising the file. Let me make a few calls, and I'll get back to you. And stay put because I'm headed your way."

"Thanks." Abigail set the receiver on its cradle.

"I'm not letting her take you," she told Jonathan as she ran her fingers gently over his bruised cheek. "Not after almost losing you to her and her minions."

She paced to the window. "Something's not right."

"What do you mean?"

"Some stuff Nick said."

"I'm not following."

"I don't expect you to." She darted to her room, and yanked out her computer out of her backpack, then ran downstairs.

Jonathan followed.

"When I had my run-ins with him, he said some stuff."

"Like?"

"He knew you'd accused Nicole."

"He could have talked to Boss Man."

"He never said he did." She set the laptop on the coffee table. "He said he knew about the drive. You didn't share that with anyone, right?"

"Only you and Bryson, and Bryson would never have said anything to him." Jonathan sat down beside her.

"And he knew what was on that drive. There's only one way he could have found out about those."

"Nicole," they chorused.

"How does he know Nicole?" she asked. "She was Army, right?"

Jonathan nodded.

"Get me a notepad, would you?" Abigail tapped into the Army's personnel database. Though she knew Nick's history, she pulled it up to confirm. Rutgers ROTC with a graduation date in 2000. Fort Leonard Wood for training followed by a stint at Fort Hood. Then on to Fort Sill as an MP in 2002 before he moved to Joint Base Lewis-McChord in Washington State, where he joined CID. From there, he headed to Germany, from 2005 to 2009, which was where she'd had her ill-fated run-in with him. Then he headed to the Pentagon, where he remained until he resigned his commission in 2010.

"Here." Jonathan set a yellow tablet on her lap.

She scribbled her notes of Nick's history. "What about Nicole? How long was she in?"

"I think she said something like only four years as an accountant."

She located Nicole's records. Zilch. Nicole had served at Fort Lee and then the Green Zone in Iraq for a year before transferring to Fort Bliss. Then she got out after her required four years.

Abigail scratched a big, fat zero onto her notepad. "Nicole and Nick never served together at the same place."

"Nick never went to Iraq?" Jonathan asked.

"No. He might have been to Bagram once or twice, but when he was in Germany, his territory was mainly Europe. What about Roy?"

"He was Australian SAS and came to SecureLink when Nicole did, I think in 2011. When Chip hired him, I sat in on the interview. He seemed like a stand-up guy."

"And Frisco?"

"He joined up in 2011 as well. But he was Spanish army."

"And Cal?"

"Same with him as with Roy." Jonathan picked at something on his jeans. "I remember thinking that he was your typical grunt. Not the brightest but competent for the work we needed him for. And, yeah, he served in the Army."

"What's his full first name? Calvin?"

"Yeah."

She entered that information, and his service record popped up. "He did his basic training at Fort Jackson. Then moved on to—you wouldn't believe this—Joint Base Lewis-McChord. He and Nick were there at the same time."

Jonathan leaned forward and studied the screen. "Do you think...that's a big base."

"It's our only shot right now."

"I'm sorry." David's voice made them both look up. He stood in the hall leading to the dining room and kitchen. Rain speckled his T-shirt. His jaw remained clenched. What startled her were his eyes. They smoldered with barely suppressed fury.

She set her computer aside and rose. Almost timidly, she approached him. "Are you okay?"

"I'm fine," he grunted. "Jonathan, forgive me for lashing out."

"Understandable." Jonathan angled her laptop toward him.

"We found something, David." She took his hand and led him to the couch. Once she'd seated herself between the two men, she summarized everything for him. She tightened her grip on his hand. "I think I need to have a discussion with Nick."

David jumped up. "Let's go, then. Where is he? At work?"

"I need to go alone."

"Abigail—"

"If he sees you, he's going to clam up. He sees you as his rival for my affections. Please stay here." She waved away any additional suggestions from both men. "Sal's on his way down. You two stay put and read him in while I talk with Nick."

Abigail kissed him, then headed upstairs. She had to catch and hold Nick Bocelli's attention, and that would require every weapon in her arsenal of feminine wiles. By the time she finished, he wouldn't know what had hit him.

36

Raleigh, North Carolina

Abigail strutted through the wrought iron Judas gate onto the patio of The Ball and Dart, a pub tucked into a narrow building with a bar opening onto an alleyway. Thanks to Nick's conversation with her brother the night before, she knew all about her ex-husband's plans for this evening.

And tonight, she'd brought the big guns to the battle. She'd taken extra care with her looks by brushing her hair until it shone, applying her makeup in the way Nick had liked it when they were married, and adding a trace of the perfume that he'd admitted drove him wild. Not to mention the sheath that revealed her figure and a lot of leg. And heels to boot since he'd loved her in heels. Normally, she would have scorned such preparations. Not tonight. Not when Kyra's life hung in the balance.

With her hand cocked on her hip, she lifted her chin and surveyed the local police hangout like she owned it.

Several appreciative glances rewarded her. A low wolf whistle reached her.

But no Nick.

Not that it mattered since six had barely passed.

"You're new here." A guy with a blond buzz cut gave her a slow, appreciative glance. "You want a drink?"

"Pass, thanks."

295

"You on duty or something?"

"Or something." She offered him a tight smile. "You know Nick Bocelli?"

"Honey, I *work* with Bocelli," the man drawled. His glance swiveled to the dart tournament taking place beside the bar.

"Does he come here often?"

"Every Friday night. Quitting time just passed. He'll show up"

"When?"

"Let me buy you a drink, and I'll find out." The blond guy grinned.

Oh, great. Just what she hadn't wanted—attention from someone else. She bit back her sigh. "Okay. A chardonnay."

"I'll call him." The guy summoned the bartender and ordered her wine. Then he picked up his phone from the scarred wood. "Who's asking?"

"Tell him a secret admirer." She cut her eyes at him and accepted the wine. She listened as he called her ex-husband. When he lowered his phone, she set her glass on the bar. "And?"

"He said half an hour. Which leaves me a bit of time to chat with you."

Abigail endured meaningless conversation and an invitation to dine with him later. She politely turned him down and focused on the crowd. A group of four guys laughed and tossed darts toward a board. Others had pushed a set of tables together and lounged, the two front legs of their chairs high in the air. Several women sat with them as well and laughed over mugs of beer and glasses of wine with a few margaritas and martinis thrown in for good measure. At the bar, several couples chatted over drinks and appetizers.

Nick opened the gate. He high-fived and bumped fists with some of the guys. His free hand loosened his tie.

Abigail leaned her back against the bar, her elbows resting on the dark wood in a pose that had made his mouth water in times past. In her most sultry, husky Southern accent, she said, "Hi, Nick."

He gave her a once-over. "What are you doing here?"

"Can't I see an old *friend*?" She sashayed toward him and ran a finger down his chest alongside his tie.

He glowered. "The case is closed. Or at least, according to your CO, it is."

"Right. So there's no detective-victim relationship anymore. Thanks, Bart," she added to the wine buyer. She slid her hand into Nick's. "Join me."

She led him toward a small table for two that had opened up near the entrance.

"Maybe I should go home," Nick grumbled. He called to a passing waitress for a beer from one of the local brewing companies.

"I think you want to know why I'm here." Abigail released him and took a seat on the bistro chair. As she crossed her legs, she hiked the hem of her skirt up ever so slightly.

She smiled when he stilled.

As he settled on a chair across from her, his gaze roamed downward to where her sandal dangled from her toes. "You're here to make my life miserable."

"Yet you're not getting up." She smiled a saccharine smile. "It must be my charm. Or my looks."

He scowled. "It's not your charisma, that's for sure."

She placed a hand on her chest. "You break my heart," she drawled in her honeyed Southern accent. Yep, she could play this game with the best of them. Abigail toyed with her wineglass and let the smile drop from her face. "I think you have some explaining to do."

"I'm not sure I follow. And since I'm a busy man, I'm out of here." He grabbed the beer the waitress had dropped off and made to rise.

She grabbed his arm. "I'm not done yet. Have a seat."

"Yeah? You think your little 'I'm a good-looking tiger' routine's going to work on me? You thought wrong, babe." He shook loose.

Abigail jumped to her feet. "Explain to me how you know Cal Bacon."

His face lost all expression. "I don't know any Cal Bacon."

Abigail raised her brows. "Let me get this straight. You let a complete stranger stay with you at Lewis-McChord for three months? Why, Nick, I'm surprised."

"Okay. Okay." Nick rolled his eyes. "I knew him."

"Then sit and explain it to me."

As if she'd greatly inconvenienced him, Nick almost fell onto his chair.

"We had mutual friends." A muscle twitched in his cheek. "We got to know each other at a party and started hanging out together. When his roommate moved out before Cal's enlistment ended, I let him stay with me until he mustered out three months later. Satisfied?"

"No." She rested her chin on her hands and stared at him until he squirmed. So quietly that her voice barely carried above the hubbub of the patio, she stated, "Do you realize what you've done?"

"I'm really not following." He tensed. "And since you can't seem to tell me—"

"Kyra Martin could die because of you."

"What?"

"Cal's been running with Nicole Chardet and her gang. Somehow, they got you to rat on the case. Am I correct?"

"I don't know—"

"You don't know what I'm talking about? Let me ask you a few questions that might jog your memory. How did you know there was a drive in my brother's safe? Or that there were was a file called Athena on that drive? And tell me, Nick" —she crossed her arms on the table and leaned forward— "how did you know Nicole had discredited Jonathan?"

Nick's tawny complexion turned a sickly yellow.

He didn't say a word.

"That's what I thought." She'd won the first round. "Talk to me now, or I'm taking everything I have straight to RPD's IAD. Once they start digging, they won't stop until that hole you've gotten your professional self into is six feet deep."

Nick glared at her but kept silent.

"Okay. I'm out of here." She pushed back her chair.

"Wait!" He grabbed her arm. "What's in it for me?"

"Are you so dense? Your career. You ruined it in the Army when you ran around on me with a subordinate. You want to ruin it again here with the RPD?"

Conflicting emotions ran across his face. He lowered his head, then raised it. "What do you want to know?"

"Everything." Abigail set her phone on the table and pressed the button for the digital recorder. "By the way, I'm recording this. You lie to me or try to deny you ever said anything, and I've got this to prove you lied."

"I got it, all right?" He swiped a hand over his face. "When we were getting our divorce, I made the mistake of hiring a horrible lawyer who did nothing for me but get me a raw deal. Then when I moved down here March 2010, I was feeling sorry for myself, so I decided some retail therapy was in order for me."

Abigail couldn't help it. She smirked.

"Guys do it too, okay? Except I bought a new big-screen television, a new stereo with surround sound, and some other electronic stuff. I suddenly found myself thirty grand in the hole thanks to that and lawyer bills. Yeah, I'd been paying it off slowly. Then Cal called me up about a month or so ago and made me an offer."

"Had you two been talking since you roomed together?"

"Off and on. I knew he'd gone with another firm as well as SecureLink after mustering out. He told me your brother was trying to persecute him and his friends."

"Not true."

"Whatever." Nick dismissed that with a wave of his hand. "He asked for me to keep an eye on Jonathan's house and to let him know when he showed his face. Then to run the case after they kidnapped him."

"And it never crossed your mind to question why they wanted him?"

"Not when he offered me ten grand for the job, enough to get me out of debt. Hey, money talked louder than morals, okay?" Nick sat back and crossed his arms. "Satisfied?"

Abigail ran her finger along the rim of her glass before crooking it in a gesture that she knew had always made his blood race. He fell for it again and obeyed. Only this time, she grabbed his tie and drew him closer until their faces were inches apart. To the casual observer, it might have looked like a flirtatious gesture. Not in her mind by any stretch. The tangy smell of the beer teased her nose. "Let me tell you something. Because of what you did, an innocent person could very well die."

"What?"

"You know who David Shepherd is, I presume."

He nodded. A dull red began replacing the sickly pallor. A muscle in his jaw twitched.

"Nicole and her gang have his sister as hostage, and thanks to your double-crossing everyone, she could very well die."

"I didn't know." His Adam's apple bobbed. He began shaking his head. "I didn't think it would come to this. I thought this was between them and Jonathan."

"It was until we got that drive." She released him.

He pulled back and stared at the table.

"I should take all of this to IAD right now."

"Abigail, please, no!" Nick's hand shot out and grabbed her arm.

"What do you mean, no?"

He glanced around, and she did too. Fortunately, everyone hunched over tables or at the bar as they laughed and talked. No one had turned curious glances in their direction.

He leaned forward. His words came out low and pleading. "I need this job. Honestly, I do. I like the work. I've made a life here for myself."

"Then help me out."

"What do you want?"

"Is Cal your contact?"

"No, a guy named Roy Wildman."

"Have you talked to him since we got the drive back?"

"Once. He wanted information on David."

Abigail narrowed her eyes. "Then you have his current number."

"I don't."

"What?"

"He told me they were getting rid of that phone. I'm sorry, but that's all I've got." He spread out his arms, palms up, as if to confirm his words.

Abigail lowered her head. So that was that. She switched off the recorder.

"I'm sorry."

"What?" She studied him.

Regret simmered in his eyes. "I'm sorry. I had no idea it would come to this. If I'd realized it, I would have never gone along with it."

"You should have never gone along with it in the first place." She dropped her phone into her purse and rose.

He popped to his feet. "Don't take this to IAD, Abby."

She gazed at him for a long moment. "Then give me a good reason why."

"I'll tell them you coerced me."

"And when Kyra's body shows up, you'll get booked as an accessory for murder."

He visibly wilted, something she'd never seen him do before. Softly, almost pleading, he said, "Okay. Okay. I'll help."

Every fiber in her being yearned to make him pay not only for his double-cross but also for the way he'd made her suffer six years before.

Only this time, greed—or maybe desperation—had been his motive, not maliciousness related to their acrimonious breakup.

Flashes of her own difficulty flitted through her mind. She understood the need to keep a job. She'd been spared the pain of being forced out of the Army after her suicide attempt.

She sighed. "Okay. I'll keep this away from IAD on two conditions. First, you'll fly straight from now on. Second, if you hear anything—and I mean anything—from Roy Wildman or his pals, you call me. Got it?"

He nodded. "I'll do you one better. If he calls, I'll keep him on the phone long enough to do a trace."

"Don't fail me on this." Abigail rose. She held his gaze for a moment before turning away. She stepped into the cooling night. She'd ratted out the source of the leak. So what? It didn't get her any closer to discovering where Nicole and her gang held Kyra.

She passed through the mouth of the alley. Beyond her, the street was deserted in the direction she was headed. The scraping of shoes on the pavement made her turn her head.

A figure stopped, its shape mostly blackened into a silhouette thanks to the shadows. But the shape was feminine, and the dim light glinted off the barrel of a gun she held.

Nabeelah.

Abigail stood her ground. She wouldn't let herself be intimidated. Not this time.

Then Bart the buzz-cut blond and one of his pals stepped onto the sidewalk.

Nabeelah turned and fled.

"Man, Bocelli said you were a firecracker. He wasn't kidding." Bart chuckled. "You look kind of upset. Want to join us?"

Abigail managed a smile. "I'll be fine. But…would you mind walking with me back to my street? I think someone was following me."

They nodded.

As she turned her steps toward home, Abigail knew that time and options slowly trickled away.

37

Burning Tree, Utah

Saturday night, Little Bit's heartrending sobs tore at David as he sat on the edge of her bed. He stroked her hair, but she only cried harder. He didn't how how to help her, how to ease her pain, and his ineptitude only increased his rage against those who took her mother.

"I...I...I want...Mommy!" Little Bit began hiccupping.

"I'll take this," Abigail murmured. She sat on the other side and held the little girl close.

Leaving his niece in Abigail's more capable hands, David wandered to the kitchen and found Jonathan, Sal and Marti, Abigail's sergeant, poring over maps and aerials of the area. The jump drive, which at that point was worth more than all of the gold in Fort Knox, sat in a decorative bowl on the middle. On it resided the key to getting Kyra back alive.

He joined Jonathan at the kitchen island. "Any luck?"

"None. Utah's too big a place." He sighed and shook his head. "Unless Nick comes through, we're kind of stuck."

"I could have my men comb the area for signs of them," Sal said. His dark eyes focused on David. "As much as we need, until we find them."

David shook his head. "We can't take that risk." He cast a glance at Jonathan.

His friend looked like he were about to argue.

"I want Mommy!" Little Bit's shriek made them all glance toward the hall.

"I'll help Abigail," Marti murmured.

"We can't, understand?" David emphasized his point with a rap of his knuckles against the island, then strode from the room.

Once on his deck upstairs, he collapsed onto an Adirondack chair. A stiff breeze had begun, and the scent of dampness rode upon it. Clouds drifted in the silver light of the waxing moon. From over the mesa came the lonely howl of a coyote. Another answered with a wail of its own. Then another started up. Normally, he enjoyed their music. Now, it sounded like a funeral dirge. He clamped his hands over his ears.

"God, no. Please. I can't take this anymore. Let her live. Please! If You do, I'll do whatever You want me to do. Just don't let Kyra die. I—I don't think I could live if she did."

Finally, he lowered his hands and opened his eyes. Silence reigned.

"It's hard." Abigail's husky voice came from his left. She stood at the top of the stairs, her hand on the railing. "I know what it's like. We bargain with God, tell Him we'll do anything He wants just as long as He changes our circumstances."

She sat on the arm of his chair. "The problem is, God doesn't want bargaining. He wants our trust."

"It's too hard," he rasped.

She wrapped her arms around him.

He curled his hand around her forearm and held on.

"I know. I did the same thing after my suicide attempt. I bargained with God, told Him that if He brought me back complete, I'd do anything He wanted me to do. Jonathan and I talked about that over the summer when we studied the Bible together. God spoke to me through my brother. He told me not to bargain with Him but to trust Him, that He'd provide for me and take care of me no matter what, even if it'd meant leaving the Army."

"I don't know what I'd do without Kyra."

"I know. I think…God wants us to trust Him no matter what. Jonathan told me to look at the ways He had provided for me in the past, how He'd brought me through difficulties."

God had called David nearly twenty years before, and He'd watched over him throughout his time in the Army, even through his injury and losing so many friends. When he'd been destitute on the streets, He'd sent Kyra to find him.

"I'm so scared she'll die."

Abigail's arms tightened around him. "God is with her. I promise."

"I'm not sure I can trust Him."

The barest traces of a sigh reached him. Or was it the wind? Abigail wove her fingers through his hair and smoothed it. Her lips brushed his head. "I know. I'm sorry this is so difficult."

He wanted to ask her to stay with him, to let him wrap his arms around her for the night as if she could provide the security only God could give. He shook his head as his heart struggled with what she'd said.

God, I'm not sure about this. I'm truly not sure. I'm so scared to make myself vulnerable like that, to put my trust in You.

"Come down when you're ready." Her fingers touched his cheek. Then she was gone, her footsteps receding down the wood.

Burning Tree, Utah

As she hit the bottom of the steps, Abigail's mood darkened. They remained in their predicament with no clue of where Nicole held Kyra. If they didn't find out…

No, no. I can't think that way. I cannot. Forget grabbing her cell phone from the kitchen counter. She needed to be alone, to think through all that had happened, to pray. She made her way around the house and onto the sidewalk. Her steps turned away from town and toward the desert.

Shortly beyond Kyra's house, the sidewalk ended. She shifted to the asphalt of the highway as her thoughts darted toward David.

"God, I love him," she admitted. "I do. You surprised me like I never dreamed. You are so good. You know David's heart. Comfort him."

At the sound of an engine coming toward her, she stepped off the road and onto hard soil. A pickup heading into town passed her in a cloud of exhaust.

She walked on, her heart heavy, silently praying for David and the impossible situation they faced. Around her, the breeze freshened and brought clouds to cover the moon in a thin veil. Gradually, its silvery light diminished as the breeze shifted to a steadier wind. She paused and sniffed the air. Did she detect moisture? Suddenly, Abigail realized how far she'd strayed from civilization during her prayer walk. She couldn't see the lights anymore. Only a faint, sickly glow reflected off the clouds.

She turned around and shifted to the other side of the road. Another car, this one speeding away from Burning Tree, passed her.

God, I wish You'd show us something, tell us something that could help us find Kyra. I don't know if David could take finding her body. And her kids? Kyra's death would leave the kids as orphans. *No, no that can't happen! What are we missing?* She cringed as a truck passed her.

She heard water rushing over rocks. The river must have swept close to the road at that point. How had she missed that on her way out? Of course, she'd been thinking so much that she'd been oblivious to her surroundings.

Another noise caught her attention.

A dark form sped toward her with a rush of footsteps.

She opened her mouth to shout.

Her assailant slammed into her, sending her off her feet. She plummeted toward the ground, landing hard on her back. The air whooshed from her lungs, and she rolled to the toe of the slope.

Abigail tried to suck in a breath.

Her attacker grabbed her by the collar of her leather jacket and began dragging her toward the river.

Finally, she pulled in a refreshing breath of air. She struggled. "Let me go!"

"I cannot do that." Those words came in a contralto voice of finely accented English.

A she, not a he.

Abigail struck out with her legs. She caught the woman at the ankles, and she went down with a grunt. Abigail grabbed her by the wrists. "Who are you?"

As a reply, the woman got a foot against Abigail's middle and thrust hard.

She tumbled toward the bank of the river. After rolling several times, she landed face down, her cheek at the edge where water murmured along sand. She got to her hands and knees, only to be flattened when the woman pounced on her back.

Her attacker grabbed a handful of hair and heaved her farther into the water. "It is I who ask the questions, not you."

Abigail drew a frantic breath before the woman plunged her face into the water. Her brain made the connection. Nabeelah. But…why this? Her lungs began burning. She struggled, but Nabeelah's knee between her shoulder blades kept her from rising. She fought the impulse to draw a breath.

Nabeelah released her.

Abigail coughed as she pushed herself onto her hands and knees. "What is it with you? I—"

"Shut up." Nabeelah forced her into the river a little farther.

Abigail stumbled and sat down hard with the water up to her chest. "We're on the same side."

"Are we?"

"You tell me." Abigail shifted.

"I do not believe you." Nabeelah stalked her.

"Who do you work for?"

"*I'm* the one asking questions."

"Then what do you want to know?" Abigail slid her legs around until her hiking boots found purchase on a rock. She sprang toward Nabeelah.

Nabeelah stumbled backwards and lost her footing.

Abigail put a half Nelson on her and held her face under the water. She released the pressure.

Nabeelah sucked in a breath with a noisy gasp.

"We're on the same side," Abigail said.

Nabeelah bucked and jerked her weight to the right.

Off balance, Abigail staggered. With a splash, she tumbled off her feet and into water that was now a foot deep.

Nabeelah flipped her and pressed her into face down into its chilliness.

Abigail got her hands underneath her and drove herself upward as hard as she could.

With a cry, Nabeelah fell back with a splash.

"Why do you think we're enemies?" Abigail blurted. She tried to scramble toward shore.

Nabeelah caught her by the ponytail and dragged her backward until she landed on her rear. "Because of your association with Nicodemus Bocelli." She didn't release her hold on her hair. "You have been passing along information to him about finding your brother and the drive."

"What? Why would I do that? He's my *ex-husband*, for crying out loud! We can't stand each other." Abigail grabbed Nabeelah's calves and yanked.

She sat down hard in the water. "Then why did he take the case when Sergeant Jonathan was kidnapped?"

Abigail jerked free but remained sitting where she was. "I have no idea. Honestly, I don't."

"I have not missed the way you are close. At the coffee house, and then Friday night. You were passing information you learned to him."

"I think we need to talk without trying to drown each other. C'mon." Abigail crawled toward the bank and sagged onto the mud.

Nabeelah collapsed beside her. "I could not stay silent when I saw the way that you have influenced Sergeant David."

"I love him. Why would I harm him? And why does this matter to you anyway? And why are you so obsessed with the drive? It's over. Safe and secure at the Pentagon." Abigail hunched and wrapped her arms around her knees. "Wait a minute. The Athena file. It *is* about you!"

"I am DIA," Nabeelah murmured after a few tense moments. "Do not think I forgot you, Abigail Ward. Seven years ago, the night after you interviewed me, men came and got me. They offered me a deal, as you like to say. Come work for them or get sent back to the village. Then I, Nabeelah Khan, ceased to exist on paper. That file is my profile and has everything about me on it. My true name. My aliases, passport information, where I live, safe houses. Had it fallen into Shamal Khan's hands, I would have been dead within days."

"Your uncle?"

"Who else?"

"Why would he care?"

"Revenge." A grimace twisted Nabeelah's lips. The tension radiated from her as surely as if she'd turned to uranium. "As well as the fact that I have been tasked to find an Army officer with the alias of El Lobo who is profiting from the running of guns with Shamal Khan. We suspect he is the one who stole the file."

"I had no idea."

"We have had a man on the inside for a few years. He went along with the gunrunning because we had no evidence of who El Lobo was. Only when the convoy at Ghazni compound got hit did I grow alarmed because I knew that Sergeant Jonathan would become involved."

"He did, and he suffered." Abigail winced. "But he busted the ring wide open and stole the drive."

"He did. And I got the evidence needed to link my uncle to El Lobo when I got the exchange on video. I thought Sergeant Jonathan would be safe...until my contact told me that he had stolen the drive. He knew Nicole had plans to kill him. I—I knew what I had to do." Nabeelah didn't go any further. "I warned him to leave early. Fortunately, he did. I followed at a distance and made sure he stayed safe—at least until he got kidnapped. The way you were—how do you say it—cozy with Nicodemus worried me. How do I know you have not been passing information to him?"

"Because Friday night, when you thought I was cozying up to him, I was actually getting a confession. It's here..." She fumbled for the pocket in her jacket. No phone. Not that it would have mattered since the water would have ruined it. "My cell's back at the house. I have his confession there."

"And how do I know you do not intend to deal the final blow? I have seen how you've grown close to Sergeant David. I know he cares for you." Nabeelah's eyes narrowed.

"Look, Nabeelah. I would never harm Sergeant David. Never. I knew Nick was passing information. Friday night confirmed it. We simply don't know where they're holding David's sister, Kyra."

"I don't believe you."

Well, then, don't! Abigail wanted to shout. "Please. You've got to trust me on this."

"I don't."

The woman was impossible! Abigail thrust a hand into the air. "Then why don't you get your 'inside man' to tell you?"

"He has been unable to communicate with me since they escaped from the East Coast."

"What's in it for you?"

"Getting my man to safety—and getting Nicole Chardet alive. She knows the identity of El Lobo. With her in custody, we can find him and arrest him. That will make the Athena file totally secure."

"We can work together. I can tell Sal—"

"No!" Nabeelah gripped her arm.

"What?"

"No. No one must know who I am."

"Jonathan and David know about you. And Sal's trustworthy to—"

"No, Abigail." She raked her hands through the wet strands of her hair. "The only two people I trust are Sergeant David and your brother."

"You don't trust me?"

A long moment passed. "No."

Abigail flinched. "Then let me *show* you that you can trust me."

Nabeelah stared at her. She gazed across the river, almost like she searched for something. "So be it. But I want you to remember something."

"What?"

"Sergeant David watched over me when I worked with their team. If you hurt him, break his heart, do any harm to him, I will come and find you no matter where you are. And I will kill you. Do you understand?"

"I do."

"Then perhaps maybe, when this is all over, I can trust you, yes?"

Abigail pushed herself to her feet. She held out her hand. "C'mon, I'll help you up."

Nabeelah reached out but yanked hard as she came to her feet.

With a yelp, Abigail tumbled into the water once more. She flopped around until she landed on her rear again the shallows.

She pushed herself to her feet and staggered onto dry land.

A car engine roared. Up on the road, it sped away with a chirp of tires.

"Of all the crazy things." Abigail stumbled up the embankment. The taillights of the car faded into the distance heading east.

Abigail began her trek west toward town. It began raining, but she was too wet to notice. The wind freshened and chilled. Lightning arced around her. She shivered.

So they were on the same side, Nabeelah and she, though Nabeelah clearly didn't think so. DIA was involved. Who was the traitor who'd swiped the Athena file? And who, of all people, was the inside man with Nicole's gang? She couldn't remember the details of her interview with Nabeelah so long ago, not when shivering and chattering teeth took precedence.

Thanks to the ambush by someone she'd thought to be an ally, she was no closer to finding Kyra and would most likely die of hypothermia.

Headlights bounced toward her. She shifted as close to the shoulder as she dared since the last thing she wanted was another tumble down the slope.

The vehicle slowed. A window hummed downward, and a voice from heaven called, "Abigail?"

"David?"

The door popped open. "I've been looking for you. Get in."

Abigail climbed inside.

He cut the map light on. "What on… What'd you do? Go swimming?"

"S—something l—like th—that," she mumbled through chattering teeth.

"Looks like you're going hypothermic." He switched on the heater to full blast before making a three-point turn and speeding toward town. "Do you realize you were gone for over two hours? We were worried."

"N—no. I—I'm freezing."

"We'll get you warmed up."

"Is S—Sal still there?"

David sighed. "No. We sent him and Marti to the hotel. There's nothing more to be gained unless Nick calls us." They pulled into the driveway and parked under the carport.

"I—I don't want to go in like this."

"Then I'll take you upstairs." He wasted no time in bolting to the other side of the Jeep and helping her down. "One more time through the rain. C'mon."

He hustled her upstairs to his apartment.

With each step, water squished in her hiking boots. "I'm s—sorry."

"Shhh. It's okay." David shoved open the sliding door and thumped into his bedroom. He pressed a bundle into her arms. "Here. Get changed. Then we can talk about why you were gone for so long."

She slipped into the bathroom. Sure enough, when she slid from her wet clothing, it left a puddle on the floor. The warm softness of David's sweatshirt and sweatpants felt heavenly against her skin. A whistle of the teakettle greeted her as she stepped into the living area.

"Here." He placed a blanket over her shoulders, then shoved a steaming mug of peppermint tea into her hands before sitting beside her and holding her close. "Why did you slip away like that?"

"I had to think. And pray." She buried her face in his shoulder and inhaled deeply. Thanks to the blanket, the tea, and his presence, she began warming. "I saw Nabeelah."

"What?"

In terse words through chattering teeth, she explained their encounter, conveniently leaving out the younger woman's parting threat about what would happen if Abigail broke David's heart.

He gripped her harder, the emotion of hearing that his "little sister" was indeed alive and well clearly evident.

Gradually, the rain, the shakes, and Abigail's emotions calmed.

Footsteps thundered up the stairs. Then came Jonathan's voice. "David, hey, bro! Did you—" He stopped at the open door screen. "You did. Abigail, where were you?"

"Taking a long walk," she muttered. "I have some news."

She repeated the story for him.

"She's alive? Praise God! We could use her on our side." He settled back in his chair. "I have some news of my own."

David released Abigail and leaned forward. "What?"

"Thank goodness you left your cell behind, Abigail, because Nick called. Roy contacted him. He kept him on the phone long enough to trace the call." Jonathan brandished a slip of paper. "We've got the coordinates. Now, at least, we can make tracks to rescuing Kyra."

38

Cedar City, Utah

Mitch Patterson stood in the cool darkness of his daughter's bedroom and gazed at the sweet face of his sleeping Vespa. His five-year-old snuggled under the down comforter to ward off the chilly night air seeping through the cracked window. All that was visible were the head and ears of her stuffed horse and the top of her head. Now that a couple of weeks passed since her last chemo treatment, a fine brown fuzz coated her scalp.

They'd done her room in all pinks and purples and plastered pictures of ponies everywhere. As many stuffed horses as possible were piled on the foot of her bed. She wanted to take riding lessons when she turned six. Now maybe that was possible. Balloons hovered above the bedposts, remnants of that evening's party to celebrate the good news they'd received the day before from her oncologists. All of those months of enduring side effects of the chemo had paid off. She was in remission. If things held, she'd be pronounced cured a year from now.

Let it be so, he thought.

His phone began vibrating.

He checked the number and winced. His light mood vanished. Who had so generously offered to pay for those treatments his insurance wouldn't cover? El Lobo. In exchange for his services, of course.

Mitch slipped into the hallway and made his way through the quiet, darkened house to the patio outside. "Hello?"

"Mitch, I heard you received good news on Friday."

"How did you know?"

"I have my ways. Congratulations. I hope that a year from now, you receive even better news." El Lobo puffed on his interminable cigar. "But you know that nothing is ever free, eh?"

Mitch closed his eyes. "What do you want? I told you that Shepherd left Burning Tree with his girl."

"Ah, but that's where you err. He's returned."

"How do you—Wait! You're here?"

"In Utah, yes. You see, four people who I thought were trustworthy have made an utter mess of things. They've kidnapped David Shepherd's sister."

"Kyra? What? Are you sure?"

"As sure as the rock is red where I am. You hunt, yes? From what I remember in Kandahar, you were quite a shot with a scoped rifle. They are not to be arrested by Abigail Ward, do you understand?"

Mitch leaned against the rock wall surrounding the patio and rubbed his forehead. "I can't do that. I was a soldier and shot only under orders. You know I—"

"I know how much you love your family. Then I would hate for another tragedy to befall you." The threat came out almost as a hiss. "Do you understand?"

Nausea rose inside of him. "I do."

"Then you will take care of this problem. They meet on Tuesday. I've just sent you the coordinates and pictures. Do this, and if little Vespa sickens again, she will receive the treatment she needs." Silence reigned.

His phone pinged. He pulled up the message and stared at the faces of his four targets. He squeezed his eyes shut. "I...I can't do this."

"Mitch?" His wife stood in the doorway, her robe tied around her, sleep holding her eyes half closed.

"Hey. What are you doing up? It's past midnight."

"Shouldn't I be asking you that question? You hadn't come to bed, and I was worried."

He tried a smile despite the magnitude of his orders from El Lobo. "Sorry. I was too hopped up from the party tonight to come to bed."

She approached him, eyeing his cell phone. "Who were you calling?"

He scrambled for a lie she'd believe. "Harry just called. They've got a big job coming out of Salt Lake where they need extra hands on deck."

"This late? He couldn't have called on Monday or even tomorrow?"

He shrugged. "You know Harry. He can be a bit of a workaholic, and he said this was a rush that starts Monday first thing. So I'm going to need to go up tomorrow night."

"When will you be back?"

"Tuesday night," he replied. Bile rose in his throat.

Her gaze searched his as if she sensed his lie. Then she stood on tiptoes and kissed him. "All right. Tell Harry that next time, I'd appreciate it if work could wait until Monday. Well, don't stay up too much longer."

She wandered into the house and shut the door behind her.

Mitch turned and scanned the horizon. In the distance, the light from the waxing moon painted the surrounding mountains in a silvery glow. All so peaceful. A far cry from what churned in his gut. He dialed another number.

When Harry's voicemail picked up, he said, "Hey, Harry, this is Mitch. Sorry to be calling so late, but something popped up. I'm going to be out of town on Monday and Tuesday and should be back at work on Wednesday."

39

South of Burning Tree, Utah

"This is crazy," Jonathan muttered Tuesday morning as he drove toward his fate.

All around him, the ruddy buttes and mesas stood out in bright contrast against the blue sky. For miles around, no houses existed. Or businesses. Certainly not any cops. He squinted in the bright morning light at the red rock and scrubby ranch land. The isolation was so total that he doubted even the Army would have been able to help had David allowed them to assist.

He slowed and stopped as he glanced at the directions he'd scrawled on the sheet of paper he held in his hand. The name on the tattered sign standing by the side of the road matched the one Nicole had dictated to him. Red Death Road. He turned Kyra's Forester to the right and bumped down the steep slope. It descended toward a dry creek bed at the southern toe of the mesa's slope.

The small SUV bounced along crumbling asphalt. He slowed. To his right above him was the highway, and the mesa rose to his left. It split to allow the passage of the creek and the road. A sharp turn revealed the rickety bridge the trio had discovered during their reconnaissance on Sunday.

"We go in and recon," Abigail had told them once she'd warmed up and recovered from her tussle in the river Saturday night.

Jonathan studied the map. "We can't let them see us."

"But if we don't know what we face, we can't plan."

He couldn't argue with her, not when she was right.

Now, he clattered over the rusting steel trestle, and the asphalt shifted to dirt.

In five minutes, his actions would determine whether he lived or died. Kyra too.

He gripped the steering wheel tighter.

Lord, I need Your help here. I really do. If this doesn't work, I'll be seeing You really soon.

He glanced to his left. Unlike the creek he'd crossed, this one was devoid of water from the weekend storm. Abigail and David had used it to infiltrate the enemy camp the night before.

He stopped the SUV, heart thumping against his ribcage. His fear struggled to dominate. Maybe they should have let Sal handle this.

No.

They were responsible. If anyone, *he* was responsible for getting Kyra into this mess. He'd get her out of it with David's and Abigail's help.

"God, it's You and me," he murmured. He took his foot off the brake and searched for the small bit of survey tape that David or Abigail had hung. It marked a quarter mile from the sight line of the double-wide trailer where they held Kyra. More than that, the marker lay slightly inside a disturbed area of road that showed where someone had installed a land mine.

"Nicole's going to double-cross us," Jonathan had warned as they planned their mission. "She doesn't want me to escape alive. The same with Kyra. She'll try anything she can to have no witnesses. Look for signs they've installed land mines."

During their reconnaissance, David, the ordnance expert, had carefully dug around the mine. He'd reported, "This isn't homemade. It's set to activate with a remote so that you can check in, but you can't check out. Problem is, clipping a wire might be detrimental to our health." They'd had no choice but to back away and do a work-around.

That had sealed it in Jonathan's mind. Nicole intended for no one to survive.

He slowed to fifteen miles per hour and timed the last quarter mile. One minute exactly.

He rounded the bend.

His heart nearly seized.

Nicole stood in front of a beat-up trailer. Her long, dark hair, pulled back in a ponytail, shifted slightly in the breeze. She rested her hands on her hips and lifted her chin, the very picture of a woman who knew she'd already won.

Jonathan stiffened his resolve to wipe that smirk off her face.

Her cohorts flanked her: Roy to her left, with his rifle slung over his shoulder and a tablet in his hands, and Cal to her right, with his rifle at re-laxed-ready.

As Nicole had instructed in her call late Sunday night, Jonathan lowered the windows and shut off the engine. With a flick of his wrist, he slid an index card over the speedometer that would catch Kyra's attention when she climbed inside to leave.

On it, David had blocked in bold letters the following words. *Turn around and drive at 15 mph for one minute. Then stop, blow the horn, and get out of the SUV. Hide behind the boulders on your left.* That one minute would get her around the bend and safely away from any danger yet keep her away from the land mine. Hiding would ensure that she'd be out of the line of fire.

"Kyra's good at following directions," David had said the night before as he'd prepared the card. "She'll know her life depends on it."

Jonathan earnestly prayed this was true.

"Ward, get out of the car and put your hands on your head," Nicole called. "Keep your keys in your hand."

Slowly, he climbed from the Forester and placed his hands on his head.

"Now shut the door and walk toward us. Slowly."

He kicked the door shut with his foot. "I want to see Kyra. Where is she?"

"Frisco!" Nicole called over her shoulder.

The door to the battered double-wide creaked open. Two forms made their way down the steps.

Frisco, with colorful bruises peeking from under the white tape over his nose, dragged Kyra out by the arm.

She saw Jonathan.

Frisco marched her to the small group.

"You're okay?" Jonathan asked.

"Just bound." Kyra lifted her hands, which were tied together at the wrists with a cable tie. They'd cleaned the cut on her cheek, but it remained an angry red line.

Nicole grabbed her arm. "Ward, you'd better have the jump drive."

"I do. But I'll not give it to you until she's free and driving away. That was our bargain."

"So it was. Toss your keys onto the ground in front of you."

He did so.

Nicole brandished her knife and slashed Kyra's bonds. "Now you leave, Kyra Martin. Leave and don't look back, 'cause if you do, it won't be pretty."

Kyra stared at her as she rubbed her wrists. Then she backed away and approached Jonathan. Her eyes misted. "I—I'm sorry."

He turned sideways. "I'll be fine."

Gaze not leaving the group, she stooped, picked up the keys, and walked to the Forester.

"Hey Ward, look here!."

Nicole smirked and held up a remote control. "You see this?" She pressed a button, and the green light turned red. "Now there's a little present waiting for Kyra a quarter mile from here."

Jonathan's heart caught. David had been right.

Behind him, the Forester's engine started. Gravel crunched as Kyra made a U-turn. Its sound began fading.

Slowly.

Kyra must have read the message.

He took a deep breath and fought against the panic suddenly filling him.

Sixty seconds to go.

Lord, let her go 15 miles per hour. Don't let her hit that land mine.

Now he had to stall Nicole.

Somehow.

"So nice of you to invite me to your place."

"Shut up. Where's the drive?"

"In my pocket. Are we going to play Scrabble? Sing songs around the campfire?"

She slapped him.

Jonathan winced. "Ow. You know, if you'd told me, I would have brought stuff for s'mores."

"Didn't you hear the lady? Stop your talking." Roy approached. "Now where's the drive?"

"I said, on my person. What songs do you want to sing? *Kumbaya?*"

Roy slammed his fist into Jonathan's stomach.

Pain exploded in his solar plexus. He folded onto his knees before crumpling in dramatic fashion into the dust. He didn't have to feign much since he still recovered from his previous stay with them.

Roy roughly patted him down, then yanked the drive from his shirt pocket. "Got it."

He plugged the drive into the tablet. After a few taps, he nodded. "It's the genuine article. The Athena file."

"The password screen is a match?"

"Looks like it." Roy closed the tablet and crouched in front of Jonathan. "I hear there's mountain lions here, Ward. Maybe we should cut you up. I think someone wants a rematch. Right, Frisco?"

Frisco nudged him with his foot. "Something like that. You beat me up."

"I did what I had to do," Jonathan stated after a pause. He climbed to one knee.

So close to a minute!

"But yeah, I guess if that's what you want to do, then do it. Sorry I won't be shark bait, though."

"Mountain lion bait is so much better. He's yours, Frisco." Roy set the tablet on the bumper of the van.

The four humans-turned-hyenas surrounded him. Cal even threw his head back and howled.

A horn blew.

South of Burning Tree, Utah

As the horn's sound bounced off the mesa walls, Abigail bolted toward the group. Beside her, David had done the same. He flattened Frisco, who'd whirled first.

Abigail angled toward Nicole.

The woman's hand shot toward the gun holstered at her waist.

Uh-Uh. Abigail refused to die by bullet or any other means. She took a flying leap.

They collided, and Nicole landed hard on her back. The gun flipped away to parts unknown. Before Abigail could tie her hands, Nicole's fist lashed out and caught her cheek.

She yelped and jerked back.

Nicole rolled away and came to her feet. "You think this is over? It's not, Abigail Ward. And you will pay. You all will pay!"

"It is over, Nicole." Abigail bounced upright and circled with her. "It's been over. You just didn't know it. The file on that drive? It's a fake, actually viruses that'll take down any computer."

Nicole charged.

They grappled like wrestlers.

Nicole grabbed her braid and pulled.

Abigail spun around to relieve the pressure. One kick behind the knees made her go down.

Nicole pounced onto her back.

Abigail slammed her head backward into Nicole's nose.

A cry rewarded her as the pressure between her shoulder blades released. She staggered to her feet and whirled.

Blood streaming down her face in a scarlet line, Nicole cussed. She wiped at it with the back of her hand and charged again.

They collided like linebackers. This time, Abigail gripped her ponytail.

Nicole reeled back and slapped her.

Blood oozed onto her cheek, but Abigail refused to let go. She pressed forward, pushing hard until the both slammed into the side of one of the old, rusting cars that littered the lot.

Nicole's head cracked the window. She sagged.

Abigail let her slide to the ground. She turned her over and secured her wrists with a cable tie. "You're under arrest, Nicole Chardet. And once Sal gets here, you'll be in his custody."

"No!"

"Oh, can it." Abigail hauled her to her feet and pushed her toward the trailer.

The fight still raged between the men, all except for Frisco, who weakly thrashed on the ground as if still stunned.

David and Roy fought. The Aussie threw a punch that David caught with his hand. The two men fell to the ground. The air filled with the sounds of grunts and groans and fists hammering skin. Roy kicked out, sending David onto his back.

Roy reached for the knife in his boot. He brandished it, making the blade flash.

"David! No!" Abigail shouted.

Roy hesitated.

The loud report of a rifle echoed across the small canyon. A pink mist exploded from Roy's head. The knife fell from his fingers. He collapsed onto the ground and lay still.

Abigail stared at the lip of the far mesa. A feminine figure stood there with a sniper rifle in her hand. The wind fanned her dark hair behind her like a raven banner. Nabeelah gazed at them for a long moment, then trotted from sight.

Relief surged through her, and she pushed Nicole ahead of her toward where David had hauled Cal to his feet. Jonathan stepped over to Frisco, who had pushed himself to a sitting position.

She shoved Nicole to her knees. "You stay here."

Nicole wailed as she stared at Roy's body.

Jonathan dragged Frisco to his feet and brought him to the small group.

"David?" a soft, feminine voice called. Kyra walked toward them. She broke into a run and charged into her brother's arms.

"Kyra!" David held onto her. As she wept, he stroked her hair and murmured, "It's over. It's finally over."

Jonathan's strong arms gripped Abigail, and she hugged him. "Praise God it's over."

"Well, I guess we need to call the cavalry." Jonathan said. "And tell them to bring a de-mining team. We're not going anywhere until that mine's disarmed, because the remote bought it when we started fighting."

"I'll make the call." Abigail pulled out her phone and dialed. It began ringing.

Jonathan scanned the rim of the mesa across from the one where Nabeelah had stood. "Gun!"

Shock rooted Abigail to the spot.

"What the—" was all Cal got out. Two spots of red blossomed on his chest. He collapsed.

Jonathan grabbed Frisco and dragged him away. David rolled with Kyra under the skeleton of a car. Abigail ran to get Nicole to safety, but two more shots stopped her. Nicole toppled backward.

"Abigail!" David's bulk slammed into her, and they scrambled toward the trailer.

She squirmed. "Frisco—"

"Stay put, Abigail." His grip tightened around her. "Stay put! Jonathan's got him."

She forced her breathing to slow.

"Nothing," Jonathan called from across the clearing. "The guy ran away. The coast is clear."

"You're sure?"

"I think he was after Nicole and the gang."

"Where's Frisco?" she demanded.

"I let him go."

"What?" She glared at him.

"I had to. I told him to get out along the creek bed because whoever killed Nicole and Cal would go after him."

Abigail smacked her head. "He was Nabeelah's inside man!"

"That's why I let him go." Jonathan's gaze turned toward the creek. "He saved my life. I got to return the favor. And let's leave it at that."

40

Burning Tree, Utah

"I could get used to this," Abigail murmured as she curled up on one of the chairs at the fire pit of the two-bedroom bungalow she and Jonathan had rented for the week. Behind a screen of cottonwood trees, the river murmured as it flowed over some rocks.

Peaceful in her mind.

What they all needed.

Especially after Tuesday. Three days had passed. They'd spent Tuesday afternoon, Wednesday, and Thursday being interrogated by Sal, Marti, and others as they wrapped up their investigation of the stolen file. Their conclusion? Case closed. Abigail got a commendation in her file, which would have made her glow except it didn't matter much to her now.

"You're thinking so hard I can see steam coming out of your ears," Jonathan teased as he eased onto the chair beside her. He handed her a glass of the chardonnay they'd brought from Kyra's restaurant after celebrating their success.

Abigail's eyes flicked to where David sat on one of the other chairs almost across from her. Little Bit, his niece, sprawled on his lap with a book in her hands. She read him a story about zoo animals. She slowed as she came to a difficult word. "Hipp...pot...tooo..."

"Try again," David urged as he held the flashlight shining on the pages.

"Hippo…pet…too…I can't do it, Uncle David."

"Oh, I think you can." He gripped the book. "Give it another shot."

"Hippo…pat…am…us. Hippopotamus?"

"That's it. Good job."

"I did it!" Little Bit grinned, revealing a gap where she'd lost a front tooth that afternoon.

The commendation didn't matter anymore because she knew without a doubt where her heart lay.

With David.

"Oh, wow," she muttered out loud before she realized it.

"Huh?" Jonathan grinned.

Her cheeks began heating, and it had nothing to do with the flames. The warmth increased, especially when David caught her in his dark gaze.

"Oh, wow, I just realized something," she hastily added. "I'm, um, well, I'm totally relaxed now."

Jonathan chuckled. "That's an alien feeling for you?"

"Has been lately." She cast another glance at her boyfriend.

David's smile turned intimate.

Oh, dear. Any hotter, and she'd be able to fry eggs on her face. The image made her giggle.

Gravel crunched along the river on the path that ran from the back of Kyra's restaurant to the secluded bungalow on the hotel's property. A man with sandy brown hair strolled into the golden glow of the fire. "Sorry to barge in on your party. I saw you guys in the restaurant, but you were gone before I got the chance to get up."

"Patterson." David set Little Bit down. "Sit over there, sweetie." He rose and shook the man's hand as he gave him a light bump on the shoulder with his left hand. "Good to see you. Oh, you remember Abigail, right?"

"I do. Nice to meet you again, Abigail."

She nodded.

"And this is her brother, Jonathan."

"Mitch Patterson. It's a pleasure to meet you." Mitch shook his hand. "Molly and I were up having our first date night since Vespa finished her chemo. I'd heard around town about what went down, so I convinced her to come all this way to Kyra's restaurant. Glad to hear she's safe."

"Thanks. And I'm very happy to hear about Vespa. Kyra had been asking about her."

Mitch shoved his hands into the pockets of his khakis and kicked at the pebbles surrounding the fire pit. "Well, let me head on out. It's getting late, and we need to get home to relieve the babysitter of two boys and one girl."

"Thanks for stopping by. You want to go mountain biking next weekend?"

Something like a sick smile crossed the man's face.

"Uh, sure. Let's talk next week. See ya."

He practically bolted toward the restaurant.

"Who's Mitch Patterson?" Jonathan asked.

Abigail sipped her wine and wondered why Mitch had fled so quickly without visiting any longer. Then she shrugged. Maybe Utahans were like that. To the point and no more.

"He lives down in Cedar City and works as a delivery driver. We try to get together occasionally to ride." David settled onto his chair again and gestured for his niece to join him.

She eagerly scrambled onto his lap and opened her book. "Uncle David, can we go to the zoo?"

"Maybe." He smoothed her dark curls.

A shadow caught Abigail's attention. She swiveled to her left just as David glanced in that direction.

"Oh, my…" The wine glass almost slipped from Abigail's fingers. She tightened her grip to make sure it didn't crash onto the granite.

"N—Nabeelah?" Jonathan finally put into words what everyone was thinking.

"What…is…?" David set Little Bit onto her feet.

The petite woman dressed in jeans, boots, and a leather jacket stepped from the shadows. Her hair flowed down her back in raven waves, and now, kohl lined her eyes. A man followed closely behind her.

"Frisco." A smile broke across Jonathan's face. "You made it out."

His former foe grinned. "Thanks to you."

"Little Sister!" The cry erupted from the depths of David's heart. He bolted forward and engulfed Nabeelah in a bear hug, then pulled back. "Even though I glimpsed you alive and well a few days ago, I was worried."

"I needed to see you. Both of you," Nabeelah shifted her gaze to Jonathan. "I couldn't stay away, though Frisco wanted—"

"Don't blame me for this." Frisco smiled. "Seriously, I know we probably owe you some answers."

"But we didn't want to approach you. Not when Lieutenant Colonel Torres was here," Nabeelah added. "May we?"

She gestured to the couch that formed the rest of the conversation group around the fire.

"Please." Abigail nodded.

"We're DIA. Well, you knew that, Abigail. But we both are. Frisco had been deep undercover with Nicole's group as we investigated the gunrunning ring."

"El Lobo?" Abigail asked.

Frisco nodded. "Right. We knew Nicole worked for someone, but we weren't getting any closer to finding out who was her boss. All we knew was that he traded guns and drugs with Shamal Khan."

David's gaze darkened. "The Shamal Khan who killed ten of my closest friends."

"Yes. Unfortunately, with Nicole's death, we're no closer to knowing." Nabeelah raised her hand to her face. "I feared you had died that day. And if it had not been for Sergeant Jonathan, I would not have lived."

"What happened to you?" Jonathan asked. "I know Abigail interviewed you, but when I went to find you the next morning, you were gone. No one would tell either of us what happened to you."

"The DIA recruited me." She glanced at Abigail. "How do you say it? They made an offer I couldn't refuse? Join them, or be sent back to the village."

"Or what was left of it," Abigail muttered.

"They fed me. Taught me more English and everything else needed to know to work for them."

Martial arts. How to gather data, to shoot, to kill people. Considering the precise shot she'd made only days before, Nabeelah had learned well.

"I was there when Nicole made the trade a few weeks ago," Nabeelah added.

"Bryson caught that on video." Those words came low and hoarse from Jonathan.

Tension now radiated from him.

"Sergeant Jonathan, when you began investigating, I knew you were in danger," Nabeelah continued. "Especially when you stole the drive with the Athena file on it. Frisco's job became one of protecting you. We knew Nicole planned to kill you with potassium to make it look like a heart attack. That's why I sent you those messages, to warn you off enough to leave early. Only it wasn't enough."

Frisco said, "My job then became to get you out of danger. That's why I freed you and had you punch me."

A terse nod answered.

Nabeelah's phone chirped. She rose and stepped to the edge of the patio as she spoke in a hushed tone.

Abigail faced Frisco. "I thought Jonathan said you were a former Spanish army mechanic."

Frisco smiled. "No, no. That was my cover story. Yes, my family is from Spain, but I grew up in the DC area. I enlisted and joined the Defense Intelligence Agency."

Abigail glanced at David. Questions filled his dark eyes, ones that most likely would never get answered.

Nabeelah rejoined them. "So sorry, but we must go." She approached Jonathan and knelt in front of him. "Sergeant Jonathan, thank you for saving me all those years ago. Allah was gracious enough to let me do the same with you."

"Thanks." That came out as a whisper as Jonathan remained rooted to his seat.

"And Nabeelah, thank you for protecting us. And for trusting me that we would get Nicole," Abigail said. "May I return the favor of protecting you one day."

"May you be blessed, Abigail." Nabeelah turned to David. She approached him and took his hands. "Sergeant David, thank you for teaching me what you did. Had it not been for you, they would have returned me to the village where I would have surely died."

"Will we see you again?" David asked.

"I don't know." She reached up and touched his cheek. "Allah go with you."

She stepped into the darkness with Frisco following.

"Oh, wow." Abigail sank onto the chair again.

"Uncle David, who was that?" Little Bit asked.

"A friend," he responded. His big hand absently tousled his niece's hair. "Let's get you to the restaurant so that Mommy doesn't have to come all the way down here."

It wasn't that far, not even a quarter of a mile to Kyra Lane Cafe and Restaurant, but Abigail figured David just wanted some time alone.

"Hey, Abigail, I'm going to head to bed." Jonathan rose. Even in the dimness, she didn't miss the tightness around his mouth or the furrows that had appeared on his brow. Memory hooded his eyes as well. She knew he relived that battle so many years before.

"Well, okay, then," she muttered as David took Little Bit's hand and headed toward the restaurant.

Jonathan slipped inside the bungalow. From somewhere nearby, a door shut, most likely to that of his bedroom where he could brood alone.

"I guess I'll hang out by myself," she whispered to the air as she sank onto the couch. She closed her eyes. The mood of the night had swung from mellow to tense.

Nabeelah had a history with David, one that stretched several years into the past. She'd impacted David, and he'd impacted her as well. She knew David better than Abigail did, and the realization made her jealous. But it was best that she stash that green-eyed monster far into the darkest depths of her soul because it had no grounds.

She rested her head against the soft cushions of the chair and quietly prayed. Gradually, her mind calmed. The combination of the river murmuring over rocks, the heat of the flames on her face, and the wine relaxed her. She drifted.

Soon, she became aware of someone stroking her face. Something trickled down her chin. Drool? Oh, great. She opened her eyes. David crouched in front of her.

"Sorry," she muttered as she straightened and wiped at the corner of her mouth. "I guess I fell asleep."

He shifted to sitting beside her. For a moment, they remained silent.

"I was jealous," she confessed.

"Of what?" He wrapped a lock of her hair around his finger.

"She knew you so many years before. Matter of fact, she knows you better than I."

"I want that to change," he whispered.

Her heart began hammering.

"I love you. I know it's early for us, yet I can't deny it. When you disappeared last Saturday night…" A shudder coursed through him. "I was so scared for you."

Her heart rejoiced at his admission. "I love you, too. I meant that a few days ago when I blurted it to Nabeelah, and I do now."

"Bear with me, then?"

"Absolutely." She smiled and snuggled closer to him. "I've already told Sal that I'm taking my remaining two weeks of leave when you come to the East Coast. When's your start date again?"

"July first," he replied after the barest of hesitations.

She pretended it was because he had to think about it.

"And this is to keep you until then." He kissed her.

As she wrapped her arms around him, she began making plans to see him whenever she could.

41

Burning Tree, Utah

Late the next morning, Abigail leaned against the front porch column of Kyra's house and peered down the highway that would soon convey Jonathan and her toward Salt Lake City. And away from David. The two weeks they'd be apart seemed like an eternity, as if leaving him would permanently sever their bond.

I'm being silly. Really. Two weeks is nothing unless you're a kid waiting for Christmas. A sigh escaped her, and she tuned her ear toward the inside of the house.

Through the screened door, she heard Kyra talking. Jonathan answered. She said something else, and her brother actually laughed.

That brought a smile to Abigail's face, especially considering the fact that last night, she'd heard him quietly weeping, most likely as he remembered losing ten of his friends and nearly losing his best friend. It had been good to see him smile that morning over breakfast, good to hear him laugh too.

The screened door bumped shut, and David joined her. "I was wondering what happened to you."

He rubbed her shoulders, and she purred deep in her throat like Sylvester. "Sorry. I had to have a little time to myself." She leaned into him. "I was thinking how two weeks suddenly feels like forever."

He chuckled as she turned and faced him. "I promise I'll call every day, starting tonight when you get to Salt Lake City." He ran his hands down her arms and entwined his fingers with hers. "At least now, we have technology to keep us connected."

"But that's no substitution for the real thing."

He nuzzled her and kissed her on the forehead.

"I already told Sal that I'm taking a couple of more weeks when you get to the East Coast." Her CO had teased that she'd forgotten how to relax. Well, maybe she had. Now she had David to help her relearn. "Have you told Little Bit yet?"

He hesitated, and she chalked it up to breaking the news to small children. "Kyra said it was best to wait a few days, to maybe leave when they were in school so it wouldn't be so hard."

At the back of the house, an engine started. A moment later, Jonathan's silver Toyota Camry rental car pulled to a stop. He climbed from behind the wheel. "Hey, Abigail, I hate to break up your good-bye, but we probably need to hit the road."

David cupped her face in his hands and kissed her long and slow. Oh, if she could just make that last forever. He smiled as he pulled back and ran his hand down her hair. "That was to keep you for a couple of weeks."

"For 336 hours and some change?"

"Something like that. I'll call you tonight. Be safe, okay?"

"We will be." Abigail shouldered her purse and headed to the passenger's side.

"'Bye, bro. See you soon." Jonathan leaned out the window for one last, parting handshake. "Just be sure to bring Ranger. We need an office dog."

"Ranger and I are a team," David said.

Something like fear radiated from his eyes before he hid it with an easy smile. "I love you, Abigail. See you soon."

What was that worry she'd noticed all about? Making a cross-country move? Or something else?

"I love you, too." Abigail climbed into the passenger's seat and buckled her belt. Two weeks was going to be a long time.

"It's only for a few days," Jonathan murmured.

"I know. You're right." She glanced in the rear view mirror at David.

Little Bit had run outside, and he stooped and picked her up. Both waved good-bye.

Abigail turned forward. She'd left as a woman scared for her brother and uncertain of God's provision. And now her brother sat beside her. God had more than answered her prayers by bringing David into her life. And for that, she couldn't be more thankful.

Acknowledgements

Novels are never an individual effort but instead require a team to pull them together. First off, I want to thank those fans who volunteered to be beta readers for *The Athena File*. Robin Barrows, Steve Booth, and Steve Humphrey, your help made the novel stronger. I especially want to thank Rich Bullock for supplying valuable input and wisdom where I needed it most. I also want to thank Gayle Tzumach Lemmon for her writing of *Ashley's War*. This nonfiction book about women Combat Support Teams in Afghanistan helped to put the last piece of the puzzle in place. I also want to thank Linda Yezak, whose copy edits made the novel what it is. Linda, I know how difficult things were during your work, and I thank you for your effort. Also, again, many thanks to Dafeenah Jameel for her work on a knockout cover. Dafeenah, your God-given talents never cease to amaze me. I also want to thank Steve, my husband for his encouragement. Also, many thanks to my family and close friends who put up with my burying my head in the computer to get this book from manuscript to final product. Without your support and encouragement, this would not have been possible. Finally, thank You to God for this talent.

www.ingramcontent.com/pod-product-compliance
Lightning Source LLC
Chambersburg PA
CBHW071210250626
47159CB00001B/266